The Artisan's Wife

Books by Judith Miller

The Carousel Painter

Bells of Lowell*

Daughter of the Loom • *A Fragile Design*

These Tangled Threads

Lights of Lowell*

A Tapestry of Hope • *A Love Woven True*

The Pattern of Her Heart

Postcards From Pullman

In the Company of Secrets

Whispers Along the Rails • *An Uncertain Dream*

The Broadmoor Legacy*

A Daughter's Inheritance

An Unexpected Love • *A Surrendered Heart*

Daughters of Amana

Somewhere to Belong • *More Than Words*

A Bond Never Broken

Bridal Veil Island*

To Have and To Hold • *To Love and Cherish*

To Honor and Trust

Home to Amana

A Hidden Truth • *A Simple Change* • *A Shining Light*

Refined by Love

The Brickmaker's Bride • *The Potter's Lady*

The Artisan's Wife

www.judithmccoymiller.com

*with Tracie Peterson

REFINED BY LOVE

The Artisan's Wife

JUDITH MILLER

BETHANYHOUSE
a division of Baker Publishing Group
Minneapolis, Minnesota

Published by Bethany House Publishers
11400 Hampshire Avenue South
Bloomington, Minnesota 55438
www.bethanyhouse.com

Bethany House Publishers is a division of
Baker Publishing Group, Grand Rapids, Michigan

Printed in the United States of America

Library of Congress Control Number: 2016931049

ISBN 978-0-7642-1257-4

Scripture quotations are taken from the King James Version of the Bible.

This is a work of fiction. Names, characters, incidents, and dialogues are products of the author's imagination and are not to be construed as real. Any resemblance to actual events or persons, living or dead, is entirely coincidental.

Cover design by LOOK Design Studio
Cover photography by Aimee Christenson

Author is represented by Books & Such Literary Agency

16 17 18 19 20 21 22 7 6 5 4 3 2 1

In memory of
Sharon Asmus,
precious friend, sister in Christ, amazing editor.
You are deeply missed.

Thou also, son of man, take thee a tile, and lay it before thee, and pourtray upon it the city, even Jerusalem.

Ezekiel 4:1

Chapter 1

Grafton, West Virginia
May 1876

A lump the size of a lemon lodged in Ainslee McKay's throat. Hands shaking, her thoughts whirled while she forced herself to once again read the brief note from her sister. How could Adaira do this? Sisters didn't run off without a word of warning. Especially not a twin sister. And certainly not with a man who was practically a stranger. There was no way to make sense of Adaira's impulsive decision.

Ainslee raced down the stairs with the note clutched tightly in her fist, giving no thought to her inappropriate attire. Inside the dining room, she skidded to an abrupt halt.

Grandmother Woodfield's brows arched high. "Did you forget that we fashion our hair and dress for breakfast, my dear?"

Although she wasn't a blood relative, the older woman had been like a grandmother to Ainslee and her sisters when they had arrived from Ireland. Even before Ainslee's brother Ewan and Laura Woodfield had married, she'd asked that the girls address her as Grandmother Woodfield. And they'd been delighted to accommodate her request.

Ainslee's sun-kissed light brown locks spilled from the loose ribbon that had held her flowing tresses in check during the night. After tracing her fingers through her hair, she clutched her dressing gown tightly around her neck with her free hand. "I apologize, Grandmother, but once all of you read this, I think you'll understand why I didn't take time to dress." Flapping the piece of stationery, she turned toward Ewan and his wife, Laura, who sat near his side at the dining table. "Did you receive a note from Adaira, as well?"

Ewan shook his head. "Why would she write to us when we live under the same roof?"

"That's just it. We no longer live under the same roof." Ainslee's voice cracked with emotion. "Read this." She handed the missive to her brother and watched his nonchalant expression change to one of utter disbelief.

"I canna believe Adaira would do such a thing. She can be a bit flighty, but she's not a thoughtless girl." Ewan's words were tinged with Irish brogue as he returned his attention to the note. "And yet . . ." He handed the piece of cream-colored stationery to Laura.

Ewan's wife visibly paled. "Surely we must have missed some clue along the way. Did you realize she was serious about Chester Mulvane, Ainslee? Had she spoken to you about him?"

Before Ainslee could reply, Grandmother Woodfield edged forward and tapped her index finger on the table. "Is anyone going to tell *me* what has happened?"

Ewan gulped the remains of his coffee and returned the cup to its saucer with a startling clank. "Adaira has eloped with Chester Mulvane."

The room fell silent; time stood still.

Grandmother Woodfield was the first to recover. "Eloped? With Chester Mulvane? Isn't he the young fellow from Pittsburgh who was here for dinner last week? Adaira barely knows him, and she's only twenty years of age. I can't believe she'd do anything so rash. Let me see what she wrote."

Ewan passed the note to his mother-in-law. "Aye, you're right about Chester. He was here for dinner last week—and a few other times, as well. He's a nephew of Joseph Horne and works for his uncle. I'm not sure what title they've given him, but he does a good deal of buying for the store. He's placed several large orders for china, and when he was last here, he purchased some of our most expensive specialty pieces for their store. While I value the company's business, I'm not pleased by this turn of events."

"Nor am I." Grandmother Woodfield read the scribbled note and returned it to Ewan. "In addition to shopping at Mr. Horne's department store on several occasions, I've attended a few social functions where he and his wife were present, but I don't recall meeting the Mulvanes. And I don't recall any of you telling me Chester was related to the Hornes."

Laura motioned for Catherine to refill her coffee cup. "I didn't think Chester's family history was pertinent, Mother. None of us thought he was anything more than an occasional visitor to Grafton."

"Yet he'd called on Adaira, so he likely considered himself a suitor, don't you think?"

Laura stirred a dollop of cream into her coffee. "Perhaps, but none of that really matters at this juncture. What matters is that we locate Adaira and discover whether she and Chester have truly married."

The older woman sighed. "I'm not sure if it's better to hope that they've exchanged vows or trust they came to their good senses before finding a preacher who would marry them. Either way, there's bound to be no end of gossip once word gets out."

"At the moment, gossip is the last thing that's on my mind." Ewan pushed his plate aside and turned toward Ainslee. "When did you last see your sister?"

"Late yesterday afternoon. She said she was going to dinner with Chester and then they were going to hear some speaker at the Emporium. She told me it would be late before she returned home." Ainslee frowned at her brother. "I mentioned this at dinner last night. Sometimes I wonder if anyone listens to me."

Ewan pushed away from the mahogany dining table and massaged his forehead. "I do listen, Ainslee, but sometimes I forget what I've been told. I now recall that you said she'd be returning home late." He looked at a loss for what to do next. "Did you look in her room before you came downstairs?"

"No. I'll go up and check now, if you'd like." She thought the note provided enough evidence of her sister's departure. The idea of checking her room seemed a waste of time, but she wouldn't argue. She shot an exasperated look in her brother's direction. "I don't think she's hiding under the bedcovers."

Ewan sighed. "Nor do I, but I do wonder if she took her belongings. I know you'd both been packing for your upcoming departure to Weston, though I'm not sure how she could have removed those heavy trunks from the house without someone noticing. If they're not in her room, it's a sure sign she's not planning to return anytime soon."

Ainslee nodded toward the maid who was removing Ewan's plate from the table. "Adaira knows Catherine goes into town for the weekly shopping on Monday afternoons. Chester could have come to the house then and loaded them into a wagon or even hired someone to come to the house and transport her belongings."

Tessa, Ewan and Laura's six-year-old daughter, jumped up from her chair. "I'll go upstairs and look for you, Daddy." Without waiting for his approval, the towheaded girl ran from the room and disappeared up the stairs.

Ewan folded his hands together and turned toward Laura. "I'm not sure what to do. Should I board a train for Pittsburgh and try to bring her home?"

Ainslee gave her brother an enthusiastic nod. "Yes. Adaira simply must come home or we'll lose the tile works. I can't go to Weston on my own."

"Let's take this one step at a time." Ewan's lips tightened into a thin line. "First we must decide what to do about Adaira. Then we'll discuss the new business in Weston."

Before another opinion could be offered, Tessa's footsteps clattered in the hallway. "Her trunks are gone."

Ainslee dropped onto one of the silk-upholstered dining chairs as the child's words seeped into her bones. She and Adaira were scheduled to leave for Weston on Friday and begin work at the tile works on Monday morning, yet her sister never said anything about a plan to elope with Chester Mulvane. Truth be told, Adaira had barely spoken Chester's name. Granted, she'd mentioned that Ewan had given the young man permission to call on her when he was in town, but there had been no indication that Chester was anything more than a handsome young man who could act as her escort to an occasional party or dinner. In Ainslee's opinion, he'd been no more than a passing fancy to Adaira, no different than several other young men who had occasionally called on her sister.

How could she have been so blind? Ainslee picked up the engraved piece of stationery and traced her fingers across the imprint of her sister's name. The personalized notepaper had been a gift from Grandmother Woodfield last Christmas. Ainslee's name had been inscribed in bold block print, while Adaira's had been printed in a delicate flowing script—to match their talents and personalities. At least that's what Grandmother had said when they'd opened their gifts.

Ainslee had agreed with the assessment. Though given to bouts of anxiety, she'd always been the reliable, no-nonsense twin, who excelled in practical studies—whereas Adaira was the carefree, animated member of the twosome who had been gifted with as much creative talent as their older sister, Rose.

Swooping up the note, she crumpled the paper and shoved it into the pocket of her dressing gown. "Any idea how we can locate Adaira and bring her home?" Ainslee glanced around the table, hoping someone would offer a practical solution.

Grandmother Woodfield touched her linen napkin to her lips. The older woman appeared as unruffled as a peaceful spring day. "I don't see what good it will do to rush off to Pittsburgh. While it seems logical they would go there, they may avoid the city since they likely believe it's the first place we would look for them. There's really no telling where they might be."

She leaned back in her chair and met Ewan's steady gaze. "I believe we should send a telegram to his family. Better yet, send a telegram to Mr. Horne at his store and inquire about his nephew's whereabouts. I wouldn't mention the possible elopement. Though I'd like to believe the telegraph operator can be trusted, there's no way of knowing for certain. Best we keep this to ourselves until we know exactly what's taken place."

Ainslee leaned forward. "Tell Mr. Horne ye'r coming to fetch Adaira and bring her home." A bit of Ainslee's own Irish brogue slipped through in her emotional state.

Grandmother Woodfield shook her head. "If they are married, we can hardly force her return to Grafton. Right now, I think you should continue with your plans to depart for Weston without your sister. Don't you agree?"

Ainslee gaped at the older woman. "Na, I don't agree. Not in the least." Her stomach roiled at the idea. She had never gone anywhere without Adaira. Did the family truly expect her to continue as though nothing were amiss? She clenched her jaw. "I won't go—not without Adaira."

Ewan sighed. "I don't think there is any other choice, Ainslee. You and your sister pursued this venture and argued the soundness of the idea. While I know it's uncommon for a woman to be in charge of a business, I recall a strong argument you waged when you and Adaira first came to me with the idea. You assured me you were up to the task of taking charge. You both pointed out that Rose had been given great responsibility at the pottery works and you wanted to receive the same opportunity."

Ainslee frowned. This wasn't going well. Ewan was dismissing her arguments at every turn. "But that was when I thought Adaira would be with me."

Her brother leaned back in his chair. "The contract is signed, and we can't walk away from the tile works. Beyond the moral obligation to abide by the terms of my agreement, a default on the contract would lead to financial disaster for all of us—not to mention the workers at the tile works, who are depending upon us for their jobs. They have families to support, and we agreed to maintain their employment."

Grandmother Woodfield nodded her agreement. "While Adaira possesses artistic talent, it was your intelligence and ability to keep a sharp eye on the costs and operation of the tile works that sealed our decision to purchase it. We were clear that without your agreement to oversee the day-to-day financial matters, we would not invest in the company."

She leaned back in her chair. "We can locate another artist to replace Adaira, but we know what occurs when an untrustworthy person takes charge of a business. We can't take such a risk with this venture. We must insist you fulfill your obligation, my dear."

"That's all well and good, but I agreed to go to Weston because it was Adaira's dream." Ainslee swallowed hard. This wasn't fair. She needed to convince them they were wrong. How could any of them even think they should place this burden on her shoulders? "You must remember that I didn't want to leave Grafton. I was happy with my teaching position, but Adaira convinced me by saying she would suffocate if she couldn't put her creative talent to use and become independent. She said we needed to spread our wings."

"And you shall. In fact, I believe you're going to soar like an eagle." Grandmother gave a firm nod.

"But I have no desire to soar. I'm the twin who's content just flapping her wings. It's Adaira who wanted to fly."

Ainslee hunched forward and wrapped her arms around her waist. If only she could follow her sister's lead and simply disappear.

Chapter 2

The Thursday morning class at the pottery works school was interrupted when Rose appeared in the doorway and beckoned Ainslee to follow her. Ainslee prayed Rose had brought news of Adaira or word that she could stay at the school rather than go to Weston and begin at the tile works. After a quick word with Miss Odell, the teacher who'd recently been employed as her replacement, Ainslee stepped to the rear of the room.

Shortly after purchasing the pottery, Rose had diligently worked to convince the parents and supervisors that the children who worked at McKay Pottery should receive an education. Though many of the parents longed to see their children educated, the extra wages earned by their youngsters were needed to provide for the family. In addition, the supervisors had objected to the children being away from their work stations when needed. Never one to be deterred, Rose had set up a classroom in a previously unused section of the pottery and developed a schedule that permitted the children's attendance when they weren't busy in the workshops. Having her twin sisters return home and elect to teach at the school for the last three years had been an added blessing—to both Rose and the twins—though Adaira had been less content than Ainslee.

Ainslee leaned close to her sister. "Please tell me you've come to tell me Adaira is returning home."

Rose shook her head. "Ewan received a response to his telegram and wants to speak with you."

Ainslee's heart pounded beneath her blue-striped frock. From the wary look in her sister's eyes, Ainslee was certain the news wasn't good. "She's not coming back, is she?"

Rose sighed. "Ewan didn't share the contents of the telegram with me."

"Then why are you acting so guarded?"

"Because, just like you, I'm concerned about what's happened. Adaira was so determined to gain the family's support for the tile works that I find it difficult to believe she'd run off and marry only days before the two of you were scheduled to move to Weston. This entire matter bewilders me."

"If it has that effect upon you, just imagine what it's done to me." Ainslee's lips dipped into a deep frown. "I've told Ewan that I will not go to Weston by myself. I don't have the courage to take over a business on my own."

Rose grasped Ainslee's hand and gave it a gentle squeeze. "Don't discount your ability, Ainslee. If it's courage you're lacking, you need only look to the Lord. He'll provide far more than Adaira ever could."

Relying on the Lord was an easy answer when you weren't the one whose life was about to be upended. While Ainslee was single-handedly expected to take the reins of a new business, Rose and her husband, Rylan, would remain in the pottery at Grafton, where they'd been for almost four years now. Nothing in their lives would change. And nothing in Ewan's and Laura's lives would change, either. Why, then, did they all expect her to be courageous?

Ewan waved them forward as they entered the office. "Come sit down. We have a great deal to discuss."

Rylan was already seated nearby and drew his chair close to Rose. "Good morning, Ainslee." He leaned forward and smiled. "I hear from several of your young students that they are fond of Miss Odell. I'm sure that pleases you and will make it easier for you to leave the classroom."

She met Rylan's eyes. "*If* I leave, it will please me to know the students are content." She shifted in her chair and looked at her brother. "Rose tells me you've heard from Adaira. When will she return?"

Using only his fingertips, Ewan pushed the telegram across the top of the wooden desk. The overcast skies matched the dreary mood that permeated the office. Ainslee let her attention descend to the wrinkled telegram. "*Married on Saturday. Letter to follow. Love to all, Mr. and Mrs. Chester Mulvane.*" She shoved the piece of paper back to her brother. "That's all? Nothing about her obligation to the tile works—or me?"

Ewan shook his head. "This is all I've received, but at least we now know she doesn't plan to return." He pinned Ainslee with a smile, but it didn't reach his eyes. "I know you have lots of questions for your sister. So do I. But no matter her answers, they won't change anything for us."

"Maybe not, but her marriage changes everything." Ainslee glanced at all three of them. "You all know the tile works was Adaira's dream, not mine. I don't have the ability to do this on my own."

"That's why I asked Rose and Rylan to join us. Four minds are better than one or two. I'm hoping we'll come up with some sound ideas."

Ainslee perked to attention. "Maybe Rose and Rylan should move to Weston and take over the tile works."

Ewan shook his head. "Nay, they're needed here in Grafton. Their designs are what have increased our sales and made the business profitable. Instead of solving a problem, moving them to Weston could create new challenges."

Rylan rested his elbows on Ewan's desk. "Would you be able to travel to Weston with Ainslee and stay until she's settled, Ewan? I know Laura might not want you to stay away too long, but a few weeks might help Ainslee feel more comfortable in her new surroundings."

Rose bobbed her head. "That's a wonderful idea. You could help Ainslee get settled into the boardinghouse, and your presence would likely provide a sense of stability during the transition. There may be some resistance to a woman taking charge of the business. You'll recall I faced a few problems with some of the men when we purchased the pottery."

Ainslee straightened her shoulders and jutted her chin. "I remember those early days. You and Ewan were running the business together. He was always at your side to reinforce your position to the men. And even then some of them objected to taking orders from a woman. Even if Ewan is in Weston for a few weeks, once he departs I'll face that same opposition."

"I don't think there will be any hostility toward you, Ainslee. You weren't with Adaira and me when we met with the workers prior to purchasing the company. We asked if any of them would object to women taking charge, and none of them were opposed. They only wanted assurance they would have their jobs and that their wages wouldn't be lowered." Ewan leaned forward. "Other than the seasonal manual laborers, there are only fifteen skilled workers. This isn't going to be like the pottery operation, Ainslee."

His comment didn't provide the depth of reassurance Ainslee needed. Truth be told, the only thing that would give her the strength and support she needed was the reappearance of her twin sister. No one seemed to understand her level of fear and frustration. Whether the business was small or not wasn't the issue. They expected her to move to a town where she didn't know a soul, move into a boardinghouse with complete strangers, and take over a tile-making operation. With her twin gone, Ainslee felt like half a person, something the rest of her family couldn't understand.

When she didn't respond, Ewan stood and stepped to her side. He leaned against the desk and smiled at her. "I know Laura will not object if I go to Weston with you. In fact, I'm certain she'll think it a wonderful idea. I can help you get settled in the boardinghouse Adaira and I visited when we were in Weston. Mrs. Brighton is a fine lady. She owns two boardinghouses that sit side by side, one for women and one for men. Adaira thought the rooms were quite suitable."

"I still don't want to go, Ewan." Her lips trembled, and she bit back threatening tears.

He reached for her hand. "I know this is not what you and your sister planned, but I'm hoping you'll keep your word to me, even if your sister did not. I have no choice but to abide by the terms of the contract I signed." His hand squeezed hers a little tighter. "Much depends upon what you will do, Ainslee. I believe you're strong enough to meet any challenge if you set your mind to it. Think about those unruly boys who attended your classes at the pottery school. You weren't afraid to set them on a straight path toward behaving and doing their lessons in order to achieve a better life."

"That's not the same thing as going to a new town and taking charge of a business. Besides, Adaira has always been with me when I faced any new challenge."

Ewan smiled. "I understand, but now you must stand on your own. I promise I'll do everything I can to help you, and

I'll begin searching for a new buyer right away. If I can manage to sell the business without a great loss, I'll do so."

"You will?" Ainslee straightened her shoulders and stared at her brother. Ewan's offer to place the tile works for sale buoyed her spirits like nothing else she'd heard all morning. "You'll place the business for sale and attempt to locate a buyer?"

"Aye, but I doubt it will be a quick process. You need to remember the business had been for sale for more than two years when we bought it." His brow furrowed. "I do na want you going to Weston with the idea that we'll soon be selling the business, but I'll do whatever I can to find a suitable buyer as soon as possible. In exchange, I need to know that you'll work to maintain a profit. If you don't, we'll have all the more trouble trying to find a suitable buyer."

Ainslee beamed at him. "I understand, and I'll do my best. I promise."

The revelation that she wasn't going to be banished to Weston to perform office work and supervise the business operations at the tile works for the remainder of her life was enough to give Ainslee the spark of hope she needed. With Ewan's promise tucked in the back of her mind, she would set about creating a profitable business that would appeal to a host of investors in short order. At least that would be her goal.

When they walked into the hallway outside Ewan's office, Rose pulled Ainslee aside. "I don't believe I've ever seen you change your mind so quickly, Ainslee. I do hope you're sincere in what you've promised Ewan."

Ainslee stopped short. "Why would you think otherwise? I'm not one to break my word."

Rose drew near and hugged her. "No, of course not." Her sister loosened her hold and leaned back with her lips curved in a grin. "But I do recall how much you and Adaira enjoyed playing pranks on all of us. In fact, when Ewan first told me about Adaira's disappearance, I thought it was just another bit of mischief on her part."

"If only it had been." Ainslee sighed. "I do feel much better now that Ewan has agreed to sell the tile works, but I wish I had gone along when he and Adaira traveled to Weston and toured the business and boardinghouse."

"Why didn't you?" Rose asked.

Ainslee shrugged. "The tile works was more Adaira's dream than mine, so I decided to remain behind to conduct classes at the school since the new teacher hadn't yet arrived."

"I know you worry over the tile-making process, but there are employees already trained to perform the work. Besides, from what Ewan tells me, there's not much in the way of artistic design in what the business produces. I know Adaira hoped to bring some new ideas and designs into the business, but you can set those ideas aside. If you keep a good set of books and are careful about your costs, you'll succeed." Rose glanced over her shoulder. "Ewan truly understands your position, but with the recent expansion of the pottery, he needs to be here to oversee the growth. The tile works is so much smaller that it would make no sense for him to move to Weston."

Ainslee didn't disagree with her sister's assessment, but she wondered if Rose would be so pragmatic if she had to leave suddenly and live out someone else's dream.

As they exited the building, the sun slanted through the thick trees that dotted the hillside. Unfurled leaves would soon spring to life and fill the stark branches in the coming weeks. A surge of sadness washed over her as a bird twittered overhead, searching for the perfect branch to build a new home. Soon she'd be just like that bird—looking for a new place to call home.

"I understand Ewan can't move to Weston, but I am pleased

he's willing to come along and help me get settled. Having him there for the first few weeks will be a relief. While I don't doubt my ability to complete the accounting portion of the business, I'll need his oversight until I learn the entire process."

"You might ask Ewan about the previous owner's wife. Adaira told me Mrs. Ploughman worked in the office with her husband. She may be able to give you some guidance, if you ask." Rose leaned forward and placed a fleeting kiss on Ainslee's cheek. "I'm really proud of you and I'm confident you're going to succeed. Rylan and I will do our best to come and visit for at least a day or two when we finish our special spring orders."

Receiving her older sister's encouragement eased Ainslee's fears a modicum, but she still didn't possess the confidence the manager should exude. What if the employees or customers attempted to take advantage of her vulnerable position? Could she summon the courage to put them in their place? Dealing with an occasional troublemaker at the school was one thing, but handling complaints from workers or customers would be another. The troublesome thoughts caused her insecurities to resurface as she trudged up the path toward the school.

Today she would bid her students good-bye. Ainslee had never relished the idea of giving up her teaching position. Knowing she would now depart Grafton without her sister was going to make her farewell far more difficult. She took a deep breath, forced a smile, and stepped inside the classroom.

Chapter 3

Weston, West Virginia

Ainslee remained inside the Weston depot while Ewan departed to hire a wagon and driver. In a futile attempt to remain calm, she paced the short length of the station, her unchecked thoughts tumbling about like stormy waves crashing on jagged rocks. A fleeting picture of Adaira sitting in a fancy parlor drinking tea skittered through Ainslee's mind, but she forced it aside. She missed her sister so badly that her heart ached, but thinking about Adaira or dwelling on what could have been wasn't helpful. She'd agreed to do her best, and the time had come to keep her promise.

A short time later Ewan returned, and a young man loaded their belongings into the bed of his small wagon. He walked around the side of the wagon, patted his horse on the rump, and hoisted himself onto the narrow bench.

He leaned forward to gain a better look at Ewan. "Where to?"

"First to the Weston Hotel. It won't take long for me to register. You can unload my cases, and then we'll go to Mrs. Brighton's boardinghouse, where you can unload my sister's trunks."

"Mrs. Brighton's? You might want to make sure she has a room before I unload those trunks. She runs the best boardinghouses in town and they're usually full up."

Ewan nodded. "I made arrangements the last time I was in town."

Ainslee leaned close to Ewan. "Didn't you say earlier that Mrs. Brighton reserved two rooms? You may be charged for Adaira's room as well as mine."

Ewan offered a faint smile. "I considered sending a telegram about the change of circumstances, but since we were arriving so soon, I doubted it would make much difference."

The wagon had rumbled along a rutted dirt road for only a short distance when Ainslee clutched her brother's arm. Mouth gaping, she nodded toward a towering sandstone building that rose up in front of them like a craggy mountain.

Her breath caught. "What is that?"

Ewan shifted to face her. "That is the Trans-Allegheny Lunatic Asylum. It was constructed for folks with mental disorders. Quite a place, isn't it."

"Aye." Nowadays she seldom used any form of the family's Scots-Irish tongue, but the scene bore an eerie similarity to the brooding castles scattered throughout the rolling hills of Ireland and Scotland. The towering edifice loomed like a beacon surrounded only by rolling hills and a lazy river. "Adaira told me about it. She said it was large, but I didn't expect anything so . . ."

"Foreboding?"

"Yes, yet it's beautiful, as well. There's a serenity to it, what with the hills and that river." She forced a smile. "Though not so beautiful that I'd ever want to be inside the walls. I'm sure it dwarfs every building in the town."

Ewan chuckled. "Aye, but it would overshadow buildings even in larger cities like Wheeling and Pittsburgh."

Unable to tear her gaze from the sight, Ainslee twisted around to keep it in view until the wagon once again made a sharp turn.

Ewan leaned toward her. "If it makes you feel better, I'm told it is nice and tidy inside. Mrs. Brighton said there are flower and vegetable gardens where the patients can work if they desire, and when the weather permits, the patients spend a great deal of time outdoors. There's apparently a belief that the sunshine helps alter the mood."

Ainslee turned toward her brother, her eyes focused upon a few wildflowers that had managed to poke through the cold earth. "I have never thought of such a thing, but I do feel much better when the sun is shining. How is it that Mrs. Brighton is so familiar with the practices in the asylum? Does she have a family member who's a patient?"

"If she does, she didn't share that information with me." Ewan smiled at his sister. "Several of the ladies who live in her boardinghouse work at the asylum, and most of the men in the other boardinghouse are employed there, as well."

The wagon made a final turn onto Main Avenue, one of the few streets paved with macadam. Ewan directed Ainslee's attention to several of the larger mercantiles that lined the street. "You'll have no trouble finding most anything you need in one of these stores. Adaira and I visited most of them on our last visit. Your sister particularly liked Darlington & Wood, although I thought Bailey & Tunstill better stocked—at least with items that interested me."

Ainslee wasn't interested in what the local stores had to offer. Truth be told, she planned on filling her time developing the tile works, not shopping. Ewan was pointing out and detailing every storefront as though he hoped to convince her Weston would prove a comfortable, long-term home for her. She cared little about the location of blacksmith shops, cobblers, tinsmiths, or the woolen mill. Her need for the services or products of any of the businesses in Weston would be trifling. After all, how many needs could she have in the few months she planned to be here?

When her brother gestured to another mercantile, she gave him a sidelong glance. "I doubt I'll have much time for shopping. By the time I'm done with the tile works, buyers will be fighting over it." She graced him with a smile. "And I hope you're going to uphold your agreement to find an interested purchaser."

"I said I'd do my best." He dismissed further mention of her remark and nodded toward a brick building on the other side of the street. "That's the Bailey House, one of several hotels here in Weston."

His jaw twitched, a sure sign she'd annoyed him.

For the time being, she would curtail further comments regarding the sale of the business. Irritating him wasn't going to produce the results she hoped to achieve in the future. As they continued down Main Avenue she offered only positive comments, although she was somewhat disappointed in the town. Her sister had painted a picture of a much more refined community.

The driver urged the horses onward. "You moving to Weston or just staying for a short time?"

Ewan leaned forward and raised his voice enough to be heard over the rumbling wagon. "A bit of both. I'm staying only until my sister is settled into her new position at the tile works."

"Tile works, eh? Most folks coming here go to work at the asylum." The driver shivered. "I wouldn't want to spend my days in there, but that's where my brother works. He says it's not so bad, and the pay is lots better than what I make driving a hack. And he says it's lots safer in the asylum than being down in the coal mines where he used to work."

He pulled back and brought the wagon to a halt in front of the Weston Hotel. Jumping down, he hurried to the back of the wagon. "I'll take your bags inside, and then I'll wait out here. Take all the time ya need."

"I believe I'll go in with you." Ainslee glanced at her brother. "I'm eager to see if the hotel is as nice as the ones in Pittsburgh."

Ewan tipped his head and laughed. "I can tell you they don't compare, but I stayed here on my last trip, and it is a fine establishment."

Her brother's assessment of the hotel had been correct. The Weston Hotel could more accurately be compared to a hotel in Bartlett rather than one in a large city such as Pittsburgh.

Ewan quickly checked in and made arrangements for his bags to be brought to his room, and when they returned outside, the driver was leaning against the wagon. He snapped to attention and hurried to assist Ainslee. Ewan gave a slight shake of his head. "I'll help her up. I'm guessing you know the location of Mrs. Brighton's boardinghouses?"

"There's not a hack driver in the city that don't know the location of every hotel and boardinghouse." He straightened his shoulders as if to emphasize the import of his knowledge. "Good thing you reserved your room. Word spreads fast about who serves the best food and keeps the cleanest rooms. I'm told she most always has a waiting list, but maybe that's just for the men. Not as many women have need of boardinghouses."

Ainslee inched forward on the uncomfortable seat. "I would have thought the opposite. What with the war, I'm surprised there aren't far more widows and single women working and living in boardinghouses."

"You might think so, but we've got lots of men moving here to work at the asylum, and the ladies are eager to snag a husband." His voice rumbled low in his chest. "You're a fair-looking young woman, so it probably won't take long for you to catch some fella's eye."

Ainslee stiffened at the remark. His assumption that every single woman was looking for a husband galled her. Granted, most women wanted to marry and have children of their own—and truth be told, she did, as well, but she hadn't come to Weston looking for a husband. A man was the last thing she needed in her life right now. Finding some local fellow to court her would only muddy the waters.

"What kind of job do you hope to get at the tile works? I heard Mr. Ploughman sold the place. Hope you didn't come down here for nothing. Did ya know the place had sold?"

"Aye, that we did. Our family purchased the tile works, and my sister is going to be managing the business for our family."

The driver jerked around and nearly unseated himself. "You're joshing! A lady taking charge of the tile works. Now, don't that beat all! A woman half the age of those men is gonna be telling them how to do their jobs." He shook his head. "I wish I could be a fly on the wall the first time you give one of them fellas orders." He arched his bushy brows at Ainslee. "You think you're gonna be able to deal with them?"

"My sister is more than capable of managing the tile works."

"I meant no offense. Around these parts, you seldom see a woman in charge of a business." He shot Ewan an apologetic look. "That's all I was saying."

Ewan gave a slight nod. "No offense taken." The wagon slowed and came to a halt, and he turned to Ainslee. "Here we are. I hope you're not disappointed. It doesn't look like much from the outside, but the rooms are large, and I think you'll be comfortable."

The frame house had received a recent coat of white paint, and several flower boxes filled with fresh dirt hung from the banister that lined the wide front porch. Cushioned chairs were arranged in several conversation groups on the porch, where the ladies likely gathered to visit after the evening meal. Ainslee wasn't certain she would partake on a regular basis, though. No need to become well acquainted when she didn't plan to remain in Weston for long.

Ewan grasped Ainslee's elbow and escorted her up the five steps leading to the porch. The moment they topped the final step, a woman with white hair pulled into a severe bun stepped to the door. Her blue eyes twinkled a welcome. "Mr. McKay. I'm delighted you've arrived." She narrowed her eyes and squinted at Ainslee. "You must be the twin sister I heard about from your brother."

Ewan stepped forward. "Aye, this is my sister, Ainslee." He glanced back at his sister. "Ainslee, this is Mrs. Brighton."

The older woman smiled and gave a slight nod. "Pleased to meet you, Miss McKay." Her gaze traveled toward the wagon and returned to the two of them. "Is the other Miss McKay arriving on a later train?"

Ewan stepped to her side. "Why don't we have the trunks delivered to Ainslee's room, and then I'll speak to you inside."

The woman's forehead creased for a moment, but she soon regained her composure. "Of course. If the two of you will wait in the parlor, I'll show the driver where to take Miss McKay's trunks."

There'd barely been time to look around when Ewan sat down on one of the wooden chairs with a tapestry-covered seat and pinned her with an expectant look. "What do you think? Quite nice for a boardinghouse, wouldn't you say?"

"The parlor is well-appointed and comfortable. I don't expect a boardinghouse to be as lovely as our home in Grafton. Besides, I'm not so old that I've forgotten our early years in

Ireland. Back then, I would have thought I'd died and gone to heaven if given an opportunity to live in this house."

"Aye, 'tis true. I would have been pleased for such a home back then, too, but it's been many years since you left the homeland. We've all become accustomed to a finer way of life."

What Ewan had said was true enough. For the most part, they'd lived well since coming to America. Partly because Ewan had married Laura and partly because he was a good man and worked hard to achieve his own success. And while Ainslee had enjoyed living in a lovely home and eating the fine food served each day, it had been Adaira who'd truly enjoyed the parties and beautiful gowns their new life had offered.

"If Adaira approved, I'm sure that you'll have no objection from me."

Ewan settled back in the chair. "After hearing what you told me earlier, I'm not sure whether she agreed to this boardinghouse because she thought it acceptable or because the two of you had already discussed moving into a house so she didn't think she'd be here for long."

"What's this about moving into a house?" Mrs. Brighton frowned at Ainslee.

Neither of them had heard Mrs. Brighton approach, but the landlady's comment was enough to reveal she'd overheard their discussion. Ainslee gave a slight shake of her head. "You need not concern yourself, Mrs. Brighton. I plan to stay in your boardinghouse as long as I live in Weston."

"You might not want to obligate yourself for that long. A young man might come into your future, and I don't rent to married couples." The gray-haired woman sat down on the divan beside Ainslee. "Now, when is it I'm to expect the other Miss McKay?"

Mrs. Brighton's smile wavered when Ewan explained Adaira's

recent marriage. "I didn't see any reason to telegraph you since we were arriving so soon after receiving Adaira's message. I doubted a few days would make much difference." Ewan leaned forward and rested his arms across his thighs. "I understand this change of circumstances will cause you a loss of income. Do you have any suggestion on how we can resolve this matter?"

The older woman whisked her hand as though she were brushing crumbs from a tablecloth. "There's nothing to resolve. Sounds as though Miss McKay was in love. I can't fault a young lady for following her heart, though I was looking forward to hearing more about her ideas for the tile works." She smiled at Ainslee. "Your sister was such an affable young lady, and so full of exciting ideas."

Ainslee forced a smile. "Adaira and I are twins, but you'll discover that our personalities are quite different. I'm more quiet and introspective. I'm afraid we won't have the opportunity to implement her ideas since I don't possess the same creative talents."

The landlady's brow furrowed as she looked back and forth between Ainslee and Ewan. "From what your sister told me, you folks planned to expand the tile works as soon as she learned a bit more about the operation. So has that changed, as well? I told the men in my other boardinghouse to spread the word that you folks might be looking for some new employees come summer."

"You never can be sure what will transpire with a new business venture, Mrs. Brighton. Adaira shouldn't have speculated about the future at a time when we hadn't even taken possession of the business." Ewan pushed to his feet. "I'm sure my sister is eager to see her room and get settled."

The landlady popped up from the divan and gestured to Ainslee. "Yes, of course. I didn't mean to keep you with my idle chatter. Come along, my dear, and let's see if the room suits you. We can always move things around a bit. I gave you a corner room that has two windows. One looks out on the garden. I think you'll find the view pleasant. If you enjoy gardening, you're welcome to plant some flowers or tend the ones I have planted. I never refuse help pulling weeds." The woman continued to chatter as they climbed the stairs. When they arrived at the end of the hallway, she opened the door with a flourish. "Here we are."

Ainslee quickly surveyed the room and nodded her approval, partly because the landlady's desire to please was evident and partly because the room was cozy and neat—not like living at home, of course, but certainly nicer than she had expected. A handmade quilt of pale blue and cream squares adorned the bed, and curtains boasting the same pale blue hung at the windows. A large oak wardrobe and matching chest stood along one wall, and a small writing desk with a straight-backed wooden chair had been placed in front of the window overlooking the garden.

Mrs. Brighton pointed toward the far corner. "If you'd like a comfortable chair, I can have one moved into that corner. Your sister thought it would make the room too crowded. She said she'd prefer to join the other ladies on the porch or in the parlor."

Though Ainslee would have liked an additional chair in the bedroom, she feared the request might cause her to be immediately labeled unsociable. "This will be fine for now. If I decide I would enjoy another chair in the future, I'm sure you'll agree to accommodate me."

"Of course I will, but I don't think that will occur. We have a lovely group of ladies, and I'm sure you're going to find their knowledge of the town will make your adjustment much easier. They're occasionally prone to a bit of gossip, but nothing meanspirited—mostly talk about their work. Now, the men in my other boardinghouse don't have a whole lot to say. They sit out on the porch or in the parlor and play checkers or card games. They don't appreciate the art of conversation much.

"I'll leave you to your unpacking. If you need anything, I'll be preparing supper in the kitchen. I forgot to mention I serve meals at the same time every day. Breakfast at six thirty, supper at six o'clock. I don't serve a noon meal, except on Sunday. The women who work at the asylum are furnished their noon meal there and I pack lunch pails for the others. Will you want me to pack your noonday meal, or will you eat at the café near the tile works?"

Ainslee had no idea where she'd be eating. She hadn't yet seen the tile works or the café, but eating alone in a café didn't appeal. "I would be grateful if you would pack my dinner. Is that included in the monthly rental fee?"

Ewan touched her shoulder. "No need to worry about the cost, Ainslee. I plan to pay Mrs. Brighton for six months before I depart."

"Six months?" Her voice caught, and she choked out the words. Regaining her composure, she shook her head and frowned at her brother. "I don't think six months is necessary, Ewan. Two or three months should be more than sufficient."

Confusion shone in Mrs. Brighton's eyes as she took in their conversation. "Perhaps you misunderstood my rules, Mr. McKay. The current month's rent is all that's due."

Ewan smiled and nodded before turning to Ainslee. "I'm going to walk back to the hotel and unpack. Why don't you unpack or rest until suppertime? I'll return and we can dine at the hotel."

"Supper at the hotel sounds wonderful." She followed her

brother and Mrs. Brighton to the door. Ewan's voice drifted from the stairway. She couldn't make out what he was saying, but if she knew her brother, he was arranging to pay Mrs. Brighton for six months.

She turned back and closed the bedroom door. She hoped the landlady would return a portion of the payment to Ewan, because Ainslee planned to see the tile works sold long before the expiration of six months.

Chapter 4

The following morning Ainslee donned a navy blue skirt topped with a navy and white pinstripe shirtwaist. She took one final look in the mirror before descending the stairs. It wouldn't be wise to arrive late for breakfast on her first day at the boardinghouse. Several women had already taken their places at the table and looked up when Ainslee entered the dining room.

"You must be Miss McKay." A young woman with auburn hair tapped the chair beside her. "Come sit by me." She shifted in her chair as Ainslee sat down. "We thought we would get to meet you last evening, but Mrs. Brighton said you were out to dinner with your brother. Will he be living here in Weston, too?"

Before Ainslee could answer, the woman across the table leaned forward. "Is he married?"

Another woman with light brown curls bobbed her head. "Yes, do tell us all about him. I'd venture he's good-looking. Am I right?"

Their interest in Ewan surprised her. She'd expected to be quizzed about her move to Weston and perhaps criticized for planning to manage a company that employed men, but she certainly hadn't anticipated an inquiry regarding her brother's marital status. Maybe her earlier assumptions about women and marriage had been incorrect, for it appeared these ladies were more interested in Ewan and his marital status than in why she'd taken up residence in the boardinghouse.

She removed the linen napkin from atop her plate and spread it across her lap. "I'm sorry to disappoint, but my brother is happily married and will be in Weston only long enough to assist me as I begin my position at the tile works."

Though her smile faded, the young woman sitting beside Ainslee looked at the other ladies. "Well, we're pleased to have you among us. I'm Sarah Wilson. I'll let the rest of the ladies introduce themselves to you, Miss McKay."

"Please call me Ainslee."

Sarah smiled. "All right." She looked at one of the other boarders. "Please introduce yourselves to Ainslee, and maybe tell her where you're employed. I forgot to mention that I work at Bailey & Tunstill. Mr. Bailey began hiring women to help in the mercantile during the war when there was a shortage of men. Fortunately, he's continued the practice. He says women are better suited to selling many of the products they carry in the store."

Ainslee took a sip of water. Perhaps she wouldn't encounter as much discrimination as she'd anticipated. "It's good to know that business owners in Weston realize there are women who must earn a living."

The girl with the light brown curls shook her head. "Speaking for myself, I hope I won't have to work much longer. I'm supporting myself only until I can find a man who will marry me." She sighed. "I'm Mae Fulton and I'm employed at the woolen mill."

One by one, the others gave their names and places of employment. Cecelia Mosely was the final resident to introduce herself. She appeared near Ainslee's age and had a spatter of freckles across her nose and cheeks. "What kind of position is it that you're going to have at the tile works, and why does your brother need to assist you? Can't someone working there train you?"

Mrs. Brighton bustled into the dining room with a platter of sausage patties in one hand and a heaping bowl of scrambled eggs in the other. The ladies immediately bowed their heads. Ainslee followed their lead while the older woman offered a prayer of thanks for their breakfast. The "Amen" had barely escaped her lips when she passed the bowl of eggs to Sarah. "Miss McKay's family are the new owners of the tile works, and she's going to be in charge of things—aren't ya, Miss McKay?"

Mouths gaping, all of the women turned and stared at her. Sarah nudged Ainslee's arm and broke the silence. "Is that true?" She offered the eggs to Ainslee before taking the platter of sausages from Mrs. Brighton.

Ainslee spooned a small portion of scrambled eggs onto her plate. "Yes, it's true, but the idea of a woman managing a business is not unheard of in our family. My older sister has made many decisions regarding the family's pottery in Grafton. And before my brother married, his wife helped him at the brickworks our relatives purchased from the Woodfield family. Laura had done her best to keep the business operating when her father went off to fight in the war. When Mr. Woodfield died in battle, Laura's mother decided to sell the brickworks."

The lady who'd introduced herself as Dulcye Hamilton sucked in a breath. "Sounds as though you were born with a silver spoon in your mouth, and then your brother added to it with a clever marriage." She cast a scornful look across the table. "With all that family money, I'd think ya'd be living in a finer place than this."

"Excuse me?" Mrs. Brighton's features tightened into a scowl. "Are you saying my boardinghouse isn't good enough for someone of means?"

Dulcye didn't seem intimidated by Mrs. Brighton's scowl. "One look about the table and you can see there's no one living here but working-class women." She bobbed her head toward Ainslee. "Except for her, of course."

Mae clanked her fork onto her plate. "Just where do you think she should live, Dulcye? Besides a boardinghouse or the hotels, there are not many choices. And why is it any of your business?"

"I didn't say it was my business, but if I were rich like her, I'd buy a house so I could have me some privacy." A spark of resentment flashed in Dulcye's dark eyes when she looked at Ainslee.

"That will be enough, ladies." Mrs. Brighton's brows dipped low on her forehead. "I told Miss McKay you ladies would provide her with friendship and assistance as she adjusted to living away from home. Instead, you're revealing jealousy and a lack of respect. I'm disappointed."

"It was only Dulcye who was unkind, Mrs. Brighton. We're pleased to have Miss . . . I mean, Ainslee, living here with us." Mae's lower lip unfurled into a childish pout.

Meeting these women had proved to be even more difficult than Ainslee had anticipated. Adaira would have been comfortable fending off Dulcye's attack while soothing Mae and assuring Mrs. Brighton that the boardinghouse met her every need and expectation. But Ainslee didn't possess her sister's ability to charm people—she'd always been more forthright.

"No need to be concerned, Mrs. Brighton. I'm not offended

by the remarks or questions." She glanced toward the clock in the hallway. Ewan wouldn't arrive for another ten minutes, which was time enough for her to reveal a bit about her life before arriving in America. Perhaps knowing she'd suffered her share of poverty would ease Dulcye's jealousy and provide her a glimmer of hope.

Ainslee grasped Ewan's arm as they descended the steps of the boardinghouse. He looked particularly handsome in a dark gray jacket and black-and-gray checkered vest. "You've managed to disappoint every woman who rooms with Mrs. Brighton."

"And how is that when I haven't even met them?" Ewan arched his brows as he assisted her into the buggy.

"Because you're married. They all thought an eligible bachelor had arrived and they'd be able to impress you." She settled into the leather-upholstered seat. "This is nice. Did you rent it from the livery in town?"

"Aye." He chuckled. "Did you think I might have stolen it from some unsuspecting patron at the hotel?"

"No, but I am rather surprised. The rentals at the livery in Grafton are not nearly as new—or fancy as this one." She gathered her skirt to the side as Ewan climbed in beside her. "Was your room at the hotel comfortable?"

"Aye, but not so comfortable that I don't miss being at home with Laura. Did you sleep well?"

"Not so well that I don't miss being in my own bed at home."

Ewan chuckled. "Then we've something we agree upon as we start our day. That must be a good sign. We'll tour the tile works as soon as we arrive, and then we'll go to the office and begin our work in earnest. Both Mr. and Mrs. Ploughman should be present most of the day."

"Do you have a full understanding of their books and records? I know I'm going to need a great deal of training, or I'm going to make a mess of things once you're gone."

She didn't tell him she'd awakened from a terrible dream last night. One in which she'd entered all of the wrong figures into the books and caused the business to fail. She didn't know what time it had been when she'd startled awake and recalled the horrid dream of being tied to a post while angry employees hurled tiles at her. Sleep had eluded her as she'd attempted to push the ugly picture from her mind. Even now it haunted her.

"I went over their records before making the decision to purchase, but I wouldn't say I'm well-acquainted with their recordkeeping system. That's what you'll need to learn. That's why Mrs. Ploughman is going to be present today."

Ainslee gasped. "She can't possibly teach me everything I need to know in one day." Panic seized her and she clutched her midsection. "I think I'm going to lose my breakfast."

"Do I need to stop the buggy?" Ewan's eyes shone with concern. "Please don't worry, Ainslee. If need be, I'm sure I can hire Mrs. Ploughman to return for as long as you need her assistance." He arched his brows. "Does that help?"

His promise calmed her roiling stomach. She crumpled against the seat and inhaled a deep, cleansing breath. "Yes, knowing you'll have Mrs. Ploughman assist me as long as necessary is reassuring. Will they eventually move away from Weston?"

"No. Mr. Ploughman's health has been failing, but I believe they'll remain in town."

Ainslee tucked away her brother's tentative response. Once she and Mrs. Ploughman became better acquainted, Ainslee would ask for herself. Knowing the previous owners would be available to help her once Ewan departed was important.

Should anything go awry, she wanted an immediate source of assistance.

Ewan held the reins in one hand and pointed into the distance. "Over there. That's the tile works."

Bracing her feet and using the seat handle to steady herself, Ainslee boosted herself several inches to gain a better view. From Adaira's earlier description, Ainslee had expected an unusual structure, but the concrete, mission-style building appeared out of place in a lush green valley surrounded by tree-covered mountains.

"The style is rather an odd choice, don't you think?"

Ewan grinned. "I thought the same thing when I first set eyes on it, but there are some advantages to the style. I'm not sure Mr. Ploughman was thinking about the benefits when he had the building constructed or if he was just trying to imitate the missions he'd seen in California."

"California? I don't think I've ever met anyone who has traveled that far."

"He went out there during the early days of the gold rush but said he soon returned."

"Did he find gold?"

Ewan chuckled and shook his head. "No. That's why he came back home and went back to work in the business for his father. Eventually, he took over. When the business continued to grow, they needed a new location, and that's when he bought this land. He said it took about two years to complete the building."

Learning about the Ploughmans intrigued Ainslee, and her earlier apprehension subsided as Ewan circled around the expansive building and entered the large courtyard. The massive walls boasted curved pedimented gables. On the east and west sides of the courtyard, arched corridors supported projecting eaves that covered the wide walkways where workers were protected from the elements. Two beautiful tile-covered cupolas and seven chimneys flanked one end of the building. A multitude of windows, both large and small, had been strategically incorporated to provide liberal lighting throughout the workplace.

Ewan assisted her down from the carriage. "Mr. Ploughman designed the structure so the office spaces would be situated away from the work areas, an arrangement that pleased his wife." Ewan gestured toward several large stockpiles of clay that had been piled at the far end of the courtyard area. "The clay is purchased from surrounding farms and brought here to weather—much like we weather clay for bricks and the pottery."

"I'm surprised he didn't purchase land that was rich in clay rather than choosing to purchase from local farmers."

Ewan shrugged. "Who can say what land was available for sale when he decided to expand? I'm sure he explored all the possibilities before he made his choice. He seems a wise businessman, but you can inquire when we visit with him if you like."

"Ewan! Good to see you."

Her brother turned and waved to the approaching couple before grasping Ainslee's elbow. "That's Mr. Ploughman and his wife."

The man leaned heavily on a walking stick. His shock of gray hair flew in every direction as a stiff wind caught his cap and carried it across the courtyard. Ewan broke loose and retrieved the hat as it landed against one of the far pillars that divided the arched walkway. Ainslee continued toward the older couple and Ewan met her as they drew near.

He handed the woolen, flat-billed cap to Mr. Ploughman, then returned his hold on Ainslee's elbow. "Mr. and Mrs. Ploughman, I'd like you to meet my sister, Ainslee McKay. You became acquainted with her twin sister, Adaira, during our last visit."

Mrs. Ploughman's cheeks plumped like two rosy apples when

she spread her lips in a welcoming smile. "You're as pretty as your sister, and I believe the two of you are going to make quite a team here at the tile works. I always say that two heads are better than one. That's why Herman and I have done so well with the business, isn't it, Herman?"

Mr. Ploughman nodded. "I couldn't have done it without you, Etta."

Mrs. Ploughman stared at the carriage for a moment. "Where is Adaira? Is she resting at the boardinghouse? Traveling can tire a body out, and that's a fact. I need a day or two to rest up whenever I travel—which isn't often nowadays. Not with Herman ailing the way he is."

She rattled on until her husband held up his hand. "Give him a chance to answer your questions, Etta."

"Sorry. I do have a way of keeping the chatter going. Tell me about Adaira." The older woman's lips curved in a generous smile that caused her eyes to crinkle into narrow slits.

"Adaira changed her plans and won't be moving to Weston, so Ainslee will be taking charge of the tile works by herself. I know she's eager to learn everything she can about the business from both of you."

Mrs. Ploughman placed her arm around Ainslee's shoulder. "Set your mind at ease, dearie. You can depend on Herman and me. We'll do everything we can to make sure the change is smooth." She turned her gaze toward Ewan. "Is there any other member of the family that might be coming to give Ainslee a hand with the operation?"

Ainslee's stomach somersaulted. The worry in Mrs. Ploughman's voice left no doubt—she didn't believe Ainslee could take charge on her own.

Chapter 5

Ainslee looked back and forth between her brother and the Ploughmans. Ewan's lips bore a smile, but his eyes shone with more concern than merriment when he turned to face Mrs. Ploughman. "No one else will be joining my sister, but there is no need for worry. You'll soon discover that Ainslee's a most capable young lady with a good head on her shoulders. She's quick to learn, and our family has great confidence in her ability to take charge."

"I don't doubt your family's confidence, Mr. McKay, but stepping into the position without anyone else nearby to help would be difficult, even for . . ." Mrs. Ploughman caught her bottom lip between her teeth.

"For a man? Is that what you were going to say?" Ainslee's bonnet blocked her view, and she tipped her head to the side in order to gain a better look at the older woman.

Mrs. Ploughman's cheeks turned scarlet, but she didn't back down. "Yes. Even a man would have difficulty running this place without someone to assist him. Ask my husband. He's had me helping in the office since we expanded. He realized he couldn't be in two places at once, so he took charge in the workrooms and I'm kept busy in the office."

Instead of shrinking back at the comment, Ainslee bristled. If she was going to return home, this tile works had to succeed under her leadership. One way or another, she was going to see that it became a profitable business that would appeal to a host of buyers.

"Then I suppose I shall have to find a capable workman I can trust to take a leadership role among the men. Surely, there is someone among your current workers who will prove a good choice."

Ewan's eyes shone with pride and heightened Ainslee's determination. She nodded toward the entrance to the tile works. "Why don't we begin the tour? I want to gain a better idea of the tile-making process before I begin to learn the office procedures."

Mr. Ploughman signaled for a young boy to take care of their horse and carriage. While he was instructing the boy, Mrs. Ploughman stepped to Ainslee's side. "I didn't mean any offense, my dear. I'm sure you are extremely bright and capable. When we first spoke with your brother, I expressed my concern that the business operation might prove a challenge. Needless to say, with only one of you here to manage the entire business, I worry you'll be overwhelmed and want to give up."

"I know I'm faced with a huge challenge, Mrs. Ploughman, but I do plan to succeed. Knowing you and your husband will be remaining in Weston gives me added comfort."

"You can call on us whenever you need to." As they crossed the courtyard, Mrs. Ploughman hooked arms with Ainslee. "The design of the tile works has proved one of my husband's best ideas. The courtyard provides a perfect place for the wagons to deliver clay and coal, and when tiles are ready for shipping, the empty wagons can be drawn close to the doors and loaded. Even in bad weather, the covered walkways help protect the workers."

Ainslee agreed that the courtyard and covered walkways were ideal. "I was curious why you didn't purchase land rich with clay rather than deciding to buy from local farmers. Was there no land available with clay deposits?"

The bun atop Mrs. Ploughman's head bobbled when she nodded. "Oh, yes, there was other land available, but Mr. Ploughman weighed the cost of a less expensive piece of acreage and the cost to purchase clay from other farmers against the cost of paying a higher price for the land and hiring the diggers. He also considered that there might not be men who would want to do the job when we needed them. Since the war, there's been a shortage of able-bodied men. In the end, cheaper land and purchasing the clay was a better option. Once you go over the books, you'll see we've had good success with the farmers. Their prices have remained reasonable."

When they entered the building, Mr. Ploughman's gait slowed and he leaned more heavily upon his walking stick. He glanced over his shoulder. "I'm going to show you each step in the process we use to make our paving and flooring tiles, Miss McKay. We make several sizes and shapes. You'll be able to see a sample of each in the cutting room. When a new customer comes to the office, it's important to tell them they have choices. Most of the manufacturers around here don't offer more than one or two sizes. We pride ourselves on the variety we can offer."

Sunlight cascaded through the windows and provided ample light in the mixing room. A young man with broad shoulders and bulging muscles nodded before heaving a heaping shovelful of clay into a steam-powered mixing machine.

Mr. Ploughman gestured to the man. "Harold, these are the

new owners of the tile works. Why don't you explain your job to Mr. and Miss McKay?"

Using his forearm, the young man wiped the perspiration from his brow. "Ain't much to tell." He glanced toward the man standing nearby. "Me and Robert take turns, so we each know how to do both jobs. Right now, I'm shoveling the clay into the mixer, then I add some water." He lifted a bucket and dumped water into the mixer. The machine churned the mixture until the clay slowly appeared and pushed through the opening at the other end of the machine, where it was squeezed through a screen. "Once the clay has been screened, we remove the screen and put a die on the end of the machine. The die allows the clay to come out in a continuous slab. We cut the slabs into blocks with this." He tapped a large metal arc that had been strung with thick wire. When pulled into the clay, it sliced the clay into workable-sized blocks. "The fellows in the next area prepare the slabs, and then they're sent down to dry."

Mr. Ploughman thanked the two men before continuing through an arch that led them into a room where the slabs of clay were being cut. "This is Joseph. He's foreman here in the cutting room."

The man nodded but continued with his work.

Mr. Ploughman picked up a three-inch by three-inch tile. "This is our smallest tile—it's called a Cluny quarry and that's the press used to cut them. All the square shapes are referred to as quarries, but each size has a different name." He set the Cluny quarry on the worktable and picked up another square. "This is a medium-sized square known as an English quarry, and the largest one is a German quarry." He returned the English quarry to the table and then tapped his finger on the largest square. After taking a few more steps, he gestured to a small rectangle. "These are called little bricks and this larger rectangle is known as a cut blank."

Ewan picked up one of the hexagons. "What about these hexagons—any special names for them?"

Mr. Ploughman laughed. "Nope. They're sold as medium and little hexagons." He picked up a large wooden frame. "This is a form used for the Cluny quarries. There are several forms for each size we offer for sale. Two good men can prepare fifty-five hundred Cluny quarries in a day. Of course they have to be dried, fired, and cooled after they're cut."

Ainslee picked up one of the small reddish tiles. "It would take a lot of these to cover a large floor. Do you receive many orders for these?"

Mr. Ploughman nodded. "We do. They outsell several other sizes. I quit making the large hexagons because we received too few orders for them, but the forms are still here if you decide you want to make them again."

"I'm surprised the little ones are chosen. Wouldn't it be less expensive to lay a floor with the larger tiles?" She returned the Cluny tile to the worktable.

The older man nodded. "Yes, but many folks think the smaller ones much more pleasing to the eye, and much depends on the location. If a customer is purchasing tiles for an area such as a train station, where the usage will be great or heavy equipment will be used, the larger ones are more likely to crack than the smaller ones."

Ainslee bobbed her head. "A matter of weight disbursement."

Mr. Ploughman grinned. "Your brother is right—you're a bright young lady. My wife has all the figures in the office that detail the number of tiles required to fill specific areas. Once you have those figures and your customer gives you the size of the area he wishes to tile, it's only a matter of arithmetic to figure the number of tiles needed and the cost to cover any area."

Ainslee motioned to the two young men placing the cut tiles onto racks. "What happens to the tiles after they have them on those racks?"

Using his walking stick as a pointer, Mr. Ploughman gestured to the far side of the room. "The racks are placed on that dumbwaiter and lowered into the clay pit to dry."

Ainslee stepped close to the dumbwaiter and peeked around the edge of the frame into the pit. "It's quite deep."

Joseph's grin revealed a gap between his front teeth. "Nah, it's not so deep. Only 'bout twelve feet to the bottom." He crooked his neck toward the other side of the room. "The steps are over there. Couple of the boys unload the racks from the dumbwaiter, and we hoist it back up and fill it. Want to go down and have a look?"

"Perhaps another time, when I'm more appropriately dressed for climbing stairs, but thank you for the offer."

Joseph's grin faded, and she wondered if he had hoped to embarrass her. One day soon, she might surprise them all and wear the pair of Ewan's old workpants she'd stuffed into her trunk. She bit back a smile at the thought. That would likely cause a commotion.

They continued into the loading room, where several men carefully placed the various flooring tiles into oval fireclay saggers in preparation for firing in one of the five kilns. Other men unloaded the tiles from cooled saggers and placed them on wheeled racks. In another room two men carefully packed the finished tiles into crates and barrels for shipment to their final destination. The crates and barrels were carefully marked with the type and number of tiles in each container.

Mrs. Ploughman hurried Ainslee past a brawny young man

shoveling coal into one of the kilns. With each toss of his shovel, the fire popped and danced as though eager to be released from the restraints of the kiln. By the time they returned outdoors, perspiration dotted Mrs. Ploughman's plump features.

"There's no need to take you to see the other kilns. They're all the same. Why don't we go back to the office so we can go over some of the records?" She withdrew a handkerchief from her skirt pocket and pressed it to her forehead.

Even though Ainslee would have preferred walking through the entire work area, she didn't pursue the matter. Such a request would have been insensitive, given Mrs. Ploughman's discomfort around the heat and Mr. Ploughman's difficulties walking. There would be time enough to see the location of the remaining kilns in the coming days. The two men tarried outside while the ladies headed for the office.

Ainslee sat down at the oversized desk while Mrs. Ploughman removed folders and ledgers from a cabinet. "My sister mentioned Mr. Ploughman had given some thought to creating designs for some of the tiles. I know Adaira wanted to pursue that idea, as well. How far along have you progressed with that concept?"

Dropping the armful of books and papers onto the desk, Mrs. Ploughman exhaled a *whoosh* of air and inhaled deeply. "Dear me, I don't think he's done anything more than sketch a few designs. If he's finished anything, he hasn't told me. 'Course, that doesn't mean you can't try something new once you're in charge. I know your sister had some big ideas." She plopped down in the chair beside Ainslee. "Your brother never did say what changed her plans."

"She decided marriage was more important. Her husband couldn't move to Weston—he has a position in his uncle's business in Pittsburgh." Ainslee leaned toward a pile of papers and moved them closer. She didn't want to use valuable time discussing Adaira's marriage.

The older woman's eyebrows arched high on her forehead. "Husband? You mean she's married already? Strange that she didn't mention any wedding plans while she was here. In fact, she seemed exceptionally excited about the prospect of . . ."

"Why don't we begin going over the books? I want to be certain I have a clear understanding of the methods you've used before I take charge."

Three weeks had passed since their arrival in Weston. Ewan was missed at the pottery in Grafton and would likely depart for home in the near future. There was no doubt he missed his family. And he belonged with them—not here in Weston. For the past week, he had insisted Ainslee make all decisions at the tile works, and he'd repeatedly praised her abilities. She had reveled in his adulation and hoped to prove herself worthy of his praise. She'd learned a great deal and hoped to create a thriving tile works that would interest a host of buyers.

Ewan sat across from her in the hotel dining room, where much to Mrs. Brighton's dismay, Ainslee had continued to join her brother each evening for supper. After placing their order, Ewan took a sip of water. "I've had a letter from Laura. She's asked that I return home as soon as possible."

Ainslee's stomach tightened. "Is something wrong?"

He leaned back and grinned. "Nothing except the fact she wants her husband at home with her. Oh, and she mentioned receiving a letter from one of her friends in Bartlett. Seems Aunt Margaret has been stirring up a bit of trouble among some of the ladies by spreading unkind gossip."

Ainslee blew out a sigh. "Nothing Aunt Margaret does would

surprise me after all the havoc she created among the family. No doubt one of the ladies said something Aunt Margaret disliked and our meanspirited aunt is set upon ruination of the poor lady."

The mere mention of Margaret Crothers sent chills racing up Ainslee's spine. Their Uncle Hugh's wife had made life miserable for every family member who'd left Ireland to begin a new life in America. Although Uncle Hugh had changed his harsh and tyrannical ways in his final year of life, Aunt Margaret had never turned loose of her scheming ways. She was a deceitful woman who took pleasure in causing trouble.

"I'm sorry to hear Aunt Margaret is up to her old tricks, but I'm pleased Laura and Tessa are well. I feared you might tell me one of them was ill or something had happened to Tessa. To be honest, I'm surprised Laura hasn't insisted upon your return before now."

Throughout their marriage, Ewan and Laura had revealed a devotion to each other that Ainslee hoped to one day experience. Through all their past difficulties, the couple had remained steadfast and true, always encouraging and supporting one another. She had no doubt these weeks apart had been difficult for Ewan and Laura. Although Ewan could help Ainslee broaden her skills managing the tile works, she wouldn't attempt to detain him.

"Laura's willingness and patience hasn't surprised me—she wants what's best for all of the family—but it's time for me to go home." Ewan's lips curved in a broad smile. "You've shown me that you can oversee the tile works without my help. The men have accepted you, and I don't think you'll have any problems. You have all the necessary information to place a sound bid for future business. I'm not expectin' you to need his help, but Mr. Ploughman is available should you need him. Of course, you can always write or telegraph me if you have questions, but I have every confidence in you."

His assessment strengthened Ainslee's belief that she could accomplish her goal in short order, but she'd need to find some way to overcome the loneliness. Once Ewan was gone, she would miss her family more fully, especially Adaira. The ladies at the boardinghouse seemed nice enough, but she'd spent little time with them since her arrival. Perhaps friendship with a few of them as well as long hours at the tile works would help fill the void until she returned home.

She cut a bite of lamb chop. "I am going to explore whether we should move forward with those decorative tiles Mr. Ploughman was going to produce. It might lead the company in a good financial direction that would help us sell the business." She popped the bite of lamb chop into her mouth. "Mmm, this is delicious."

"I didn't realize you were interested in exploring any possibilities beyond a possible expansion of the flooring tiles."

Her thoughts raced. "It's true I hadn't planned to try anything new, but I've been giving the idea a little more consideration the past few days. Offering something unique could increase profits and make the business more appealing."

"That may be true, but before you venture into the possibility of something new, you might want to speak with Mr. Ploughman. See if he's already assessed the demand for such tiles—and the cost to produce them." He removed the linen napkin from his lap and placed it on the table. "I'm happy to have you try new ideas, but I don't think we should acquire further debt if we're going to sell."

She nodded. "I'll keep you informed if I think there's value to the idea."

Once they'd completed their meal, Ewan removed the napkin

from his lap. "If you've finished, why don't we sit in the lobby, where it's more comfortable? There's something else we need to discuss."

Ainslee's mind raced as they navigated between several brocade-covered chairs and a leather sofa. She hadn't missed the worried look in Ewan's eyes, yet she couldn't think of anything that might have created such distress. Ewan nodded toward one of the sofas at the far end of the room.

She watched him closely as she sat down. "Is there something about the business we haven't yet gone over?"

He sat down beside her. "No, this is personal, about the family."

"Please tell me everyone is in good health."

Ewan hunched forward and pressed his fingers to his temples. Was he worried she would refuse to remain in Weston if he told her there were problems at home? No matter the circumstances in Grafton, she would do what was expected of her, but she needed to know the truth. Even if she couldn't be there to help, she could pray for them.

She lightly grasped his shoulder, longing to see his eyes. "You can tell me, Ewan. I need to know what's troubling you."

Ewan straightened and reached into his jacket pocket. "I pray this will not deepen your pain, but I'm going to be straightforward. The family received a letter from Adaira, and Laura included it when she wrote to me. You may read it, but Adaira also included this private letter for you." He withdrew the envelope from his pocket and placed it in her hand.

Ainslee's fingers trembled as she opened the letter and set eyes on her sister's familiar script.

Dearest Ainslee,

I'm certain you are angry with me, and I do not blame you, but I hope that in time you will understand why I chose to elope with Chester. First let me say that although I haven't known him for long, I love him very much. I can barely breathe when I think of being separated from him. You have not yet been in love, but one day you will understand the depth of emotion that comes with such love.

On the day I ran off with Chester, he arrived in Weston to tell me that his uncle was sending him to Paris. His uncle wants their store to become a more exclusive shopping experience for ladies, and he believes Paris will offer the most exciting fashions, as well as the latest offerings in home décor. His uncle insisted that it would take at least a year to become acquainted with and place orders for these new collections.

I know you're probably thinking I should have remained in West Virginia and come to Weston during his absence, but I simply couldn't for two reasons: The thought of being away from each other for so long was more than either of us could bear. Secondly, I would have missed the opportunity to visit Paris, to see the beauty of the city and all of the art it has to offer. Chester has even promised we will attend the Paris Opera while we are there.

You may not immediately understand or think my reasons sensible, but I pray that one day you will accept and support my decision. If I had any doubt you could manage the business on your own, I would never have left you.

The only person who doubts your ability is you. While I will miss you desperately, I know that without me, you will become much stronger. When I return from abroad, I know you will be the manager of a prosperous business. Perhaps you will even discover love during my absence.

Please don't remain angry with me. I love you with all

my heart. Above all, I beg your understanding. I will send my address in Paris once we are settled.

Your loving sister,
Adaira

"Paris!" Ainslee crumpled the letter and dropped it on the floor. "Her letter says I'll become a stronger woman without her by my side. She's convinced herself that she has done me some great favor. She likely expects me to write and thank her for leaving me in this situation."

Ewan's brows drew together. "I think you may be exaggerating, Ainslee."

She picked up the letter and pressed it flat before thrusting it at him. "See for yourself."

Once he'd read the letter, he met her gaze. "I can see that she's made an attempt to justify her actions a wee bit."

"A wee bit?"

Ainslee had longed to hear from her sister, but the words she had hoped to read hadn't been included in Adaira's letter. Rather than admitting wrongdoing on her part, she'd asked Ainslee to offer understanding. To Ainslee, the letter seemed no more than a defense of bad behavior. A letter written to ease her guilty conscience. A letter placing the burden of reconciliation at Ainslee's feet.

Ewan sighed. "I agree that the reasons your sister set forth don't change the fact that what she did was selfish and reckless. Love can sometimes cause rash behavior. Adaira's desire to marry Chester, along with her passion for art and the opportunity to visit Paris, created a situation that required an immediate decision. She likely weighed her move to Weston against marriage and Paris. I don't agree with her decision, but if you don't forgive her, you will become a bitter young woman." He lifted her chin with his index finger. "You have a sweet and gentle spirit, Ainslee. You must forgive. Don't let anger fester and change you."

She turned away and stared out the lace-curtained hotel windows.

Forgive. Easier said than done.

Chapter 6

Levi Judson brushed a shock of wavy brown hair from his forehead and strode toward the white boardinghouse he'd been advised was the best in town. His arrival in Weston the previous evening hadn't permitted enough time to seek a boardinghouse, so he'd rented a room at the Bailey House Hotel. The room had been far more stylish—and expensive—than he'd expected. While he'd enjoyed a single night's stay at the establishment, he was a simple man who had no desire to learn the proper rules of etiquette or live among the wealthy. Besides, he'd come to Weston for something far more important than a fancy hotel room.

The hotel clerk who'd recommended Mrs. Brighton's boardinghouse for men had added that the rooms were usually full, so he offered a silent prayer when he knocked. Moments later, a plump lady holding a dusting rag pulled open the heavy walnut door.

Her gaze settled on the three cases sitting beside his left leg. "From the look of things, you're needing a room."

"Yes, ma'am. My name is Levi Judson, and your establishment was recommended to me as the best in town."

"That's nice to hear, but there's a couple things I need to tell ya. Number one, I'm the housekeeper, not the owner, and number two, this boardinghouse is for ladies only. Mrs. Brighton's the owner for both boardinghouses." She stepped onto the wide front porch and flapped her dusting rag toward the adjacent white house. "That is the men's boardinghouse. You'll find Mrs. Brighton over there, but I don't think we've got any empty rooms."

With a snap of her wrist, she gave the rag a quick shake. Dust particles shimmered in the sunlight and floated onto the flower bed alongside the porch. "Won't hurt to stop and ask. I'm never sure when the men move in and out."

Levi tucked his smaller bag beneath his arm before picking up his other two cases. "Pleasure to meet you, Mrs. . . ." She hadn't told him her name.

"Hanson. And it's Miss, not Mrs."

The woman's clipped reply and stern look sent Levi scurrying for the front steps. He'd obviously touched on a sore point with the housekeeper. "Thank you for your help, Miss Hanson."

For a fleeting moment he considered cutting across the yard to the men's boardinghouse but decided the shortcut might further annoy Miss Hanson. A negative word from the woman could hurt his chances of renting a room from Mrs. Brighton.

The sun beat down warmly on the early-spring morning, and he squinted his eyes as he climbed the steps to the men's boardinghouse. Instead of flower boxes, spittoons had been strategically placed near the chairs on the front porch. He settled his cases on the porch, but before he could knock, a wiry woman with deep-set eyes opened the door.

"Good morning. I'm Mrs. Brighton. May I be of assistance?"

He glanced toward the ladies' boardinghouse. Had Miss Hanson somehow signaled Mrs. Brighton to expect a caller?

He pushed the thought aside and smiled at the woman. "I'm Levi Judson. I arrived in Weston yesterday and am in need of a room. The hotel clerk said you have the best boardinghouses in town." He pointed his thumb to the house next door. "I made the mistake of stopping at the ladies' boardinghouse, and Miss Hanson said she didn't think there were any rooms open in the men's. I'm hoping she's wrong."

Mrs. Brighton brushed her hands down the skirt of her apron before opening the door a little wider. "Come in, Mr. Judson. One of the men left this morning, so I do have a room. It's the smallest in the house, but it's situated at the end of the hallway, so there's less noise. You don't hear the boarders coming and going as much, so what you lose in size, you gain in peacefulness. If quiet is important to you and you don't mind being a bit cramped, I can show you the room."

Levi exhaled a sigh of relief. The Lord had answered his prayer. "Size won't be a problem for me, ma'am."

She waved him into the foyer. "Maybe you should take a look before you make a final decision. You can leave your cases at the foot of the stairs. No sense carrying them up until you're sure you want the room." After ascending one of the steps, she glanced over her shoulder. "And until I'm certain you'll be an acceptable boarder."

He didn't know what made a person an acceptable boarder, but he hoped he'd meet her requirements. A carpet runner in a floral pattern was centered on the stairs and through the upper hallway. Levi grinned as he followed behind Mrs. Brighton in his heavy work shoes. The flowery design was sure an odd choice for a men's boardinghouse, and so were the bucolic pictures in fancy frames that lined the walls.

Removing a metal ring of keys from her pocket, Mrs. Brighton opened the last door on the right side of the hall. She pushed open the door and stepped inside before waving him forward. "As I told you, it's not large. This was once my family home, and this room was the nursery and later a playroom used by my sister and me."

That explained the frilly décor in the house, but at least there wasn't a rocking chair and cradle in the bedroom. He was pleased to see a patchwork quilt on the bed and plain curtains at the windows. A chest was wedged along one side of the bed and a washstand on the other.

Mrs. Brighton's lips curved in an apologetic smile. "If you have need of a wardrobe for hanging clothes, you'll have to share with Mr. Wilson, who's in the room next door, or you can hang them on the hooks along the wall. This is the best I can offer for now, but if one of the other men move out, you would have first choice to change rooms."

"The room is fine. I'll take it." He smiled good-naturedly. "If you decide I'd be an acceptable boarder, that is."

"Come downstairs. I have a few questions, but I won't take much of your time." She led the way into the parlor. He was pleased to see that the room was furnished with substantial armchairs and an oversized couch covered in dark leather. Several large bookcases flanked the fireplace and though the window coverings were patterned, the deep blue color suited the room. Had the furnishings once been used in her father's library? Before Levi could consider the matter for long, Mrs. Brighton bid him to sit down while she retrieved a paper from a desk across the room.

Paper in hand, she sat down opposite him. The massive chair swallowed her thin frame, and she wriggled into a more comfortable position. She extended the paper. "These are my rules. If you can abide by them, I'll need you to sign at the bottom of the page and pay the current month's rent today. At the end of the month you can pay either weekly or monthly depending upon how you receive your pay."

Levi traced his finger down the page. Rent must be paid on the day it is due. If not, boarder agrees to vacate room immediately. Mealtimes were set forth along with a warning that one was expected to be on time, and one day's notice should be given if one would not be present for a meal. No drinking alcohol inside the house. No smoking or chewing tobacco inside the house. No female visitors allowed in any room other than the parlor, and they must leave the premises by nine o'clock.

"I'll have no problem abiding by your rules, Mrs. Brighton."

She rose from the chair. "If you'll step over to the desk, you can sign the agreement, pay your rent, and get settled in your room. You've already met Miss Hanson. She helps me with the housekeeping and cooking. I spend time in both of the boardinghouses, but mostly I'm with the young ladies, since that's where my room is located."

Levi carefully signed and blotted his signature. The boardinghouse owner hadn't asked where he planned to work or why he'd come to Weston, a fact he appreciated since he hadn't yet located a job. Of course, he expected it didn't much matter. He'd already agreed to vacate the room if his rent wasn't paid on time.

"Will you want a lunch pail for your noonday meal? Most of the men carry their lunches to work, and I don't serve a noonday meal in either of the houses except on Sundays."

Levi hesitated, then gave a quick nod. "Yes. That would be most welcome." He didn't know where he would be at noon tomorrow, but if he met with any success later today, perhaps he'd be working at the McKay Tile Works.

Mrs. Brighton followed him to the hallway. "Just remember. No ladies in your room. Seems that rule is the most difficult for some of the men to remember, and it's also the reason I've had to send them packing."

"No need for concern, Mrs. Brighton. I'll not forget." The last thing on Levi's mind was a woman. Far more pressing matters consumed his thoughts.

After depositing the cases in his room, he tucked the brass key into his pocket and returned downstairs. He could unpack this evening. Right now, a visit to McKay Tile Works was more important.

The location of the tile works would make it possible for him to walk each day, though the trek would likely prove daunting in frigid or rainy weather. Still, he couldn't afford to spend money on a horse. Even if he had the funds to purchase one, there would be the weekly expense of feeding and boarding the animal. Besides, he'd have to walk to and from the livery each day, which wouldn't save him much time or shoe leather. Although walking to the tile works would be possible, the asylum was at least four miles from the boardinghouses. Did the men and women employed at the asylum walk each day? Surely not. He pushed the matter from his mind and bounded down the front steps.

The midmorning sun beat warmly on Levi's back, and beads of perspiration soon dotted his forehead and upper lip. His woolen suit jacket was far too heavy for the summer heat, but he didn't want to wear his old work clothes—bad enough he had only heavy work shoes. He needed to make a good impression.

Once he'd begun the short descent to the tile works, a breeze stirred through the copious oaks, pines, and spruces that saturated the hillside. He admired the tile work's mission-style structure, though, much like the asylum, it appeared strangely out of place deep in these hills. Smoke rose from the kilns and beckoned him onward. When he neared the office door, he breathed out a prayer that the Lord would be with him when he met with Mr. McKay. He needed to live near his brother and safeguard his care. He'd made a promise to Noah and to God. A vow he intended to keep.

A brass bell hanging over the front door clanged an announcement of his entrance into the office of McKay Tile Works. An attractive young lady sitting at a desk in the far corner next to a bank of windows waved him forward. He strode forward while attempting to hide his surprise.

"May I help you?" Golden shades of sunlight danced through her light brown hair when she lifted her head and met his gaze. Her blue eyes shone with an intelligent curiosity that caught him unaware.

"I-I-I'm Levi Judson. I'm looking for work and hoped I might speak to Mr. McKay. Do you know if he has any openings? I have experience working for Mr. Kresie at the Philadelphia Tile Works, and he wrote a letter recommending me." Levi nodded toward the men working in the courtyard. "This place is a lot different than where I worked before."

The woman returned his smile. "Probably far more different than you realize."

Her answer pleased him. Perhaps they had developed some new techniques and would be interested in his ideas. The thought caused his pulse to quicken. Levi reached into his suit jacket and retrieved the letter Mr. Kresie had given him. "I'm new in town and need to find work as soon as possible. I've had experience working most any position in a tile works. I was a supervisor and managed the business when Mr. Kresie was out of town." He didn't want to sound like a braggart, but he hoped that stating his qualifications might gain him access to the owner. "I wasn't sure if I needed to make an appointment to see Mr. McKay, but I decided to take my chances that he'd be here."

"The only member of the McKay family who works here is me, Mr. Judson." She extended her hand toward the letter.

"I see." But he truly didn't see—not at all. He glanced over his shoulder and into the hallway. Surely there must be someone nearby who was going to talk with him. He forced a smile and continued to clutch the letter. "I suppose I need to speak to the manager or foreman, then. What is his name?"

"*Her* name is Miss Ainslee McKay, and you are speaking to her. If you want a job, you'll need to turn loose of that letter, Mr. Judson." Her impatient tone caused him to take a step forward and offer her the missive. She gestured toward a chair near her desk. "Do sit down."

Heat raced up the back of his neck and perspiration trickled down the sides of his face. He removed his handkerchief from his pocket and mopped his face. "Quite warm in here, don't you think?"

"On the contrary, I thought it a wee bit cooler than usual. Perhaps your warmth has to do with something other than the weather." She grinned, obviously enjoying his embarrassment. "Before I read your letter, why don't you tell me why you left your previous employment?"

He traced his index finger beneath his collar and longed for a breeze to blow through one of the windows. "I was at the Philadelphia Tile Works for five years and performed most every job from shoveling clay to loading and unloading saggers and firing the kilns. They produce fine paving and roof tiles, though nothing of a decorative style. As I said earlier, I managed the business when Mr. Kresie was out of town or ill, and had been a foreman in all of the shops. When Mr. Kresie learned I was moving to Weston, he told me he was friends with the owner of a tile works here. He wrote to Mr. Ploughman and asked him to give me a job, but . . ."

"But Mr. Ploughman wrote back and said he'd sold the place to the McKay family."

Levi nodded. "Yes. Mr. Kresie figured it would be better if I carried the letter with me. That way, if I didn't get a job with you, I could use the letter at other places I might look for work."

"You still haven't mentioned why you left your position with Mr. Kresie. Do you have family in the area?"

"I do. A brother." He scooted back in the chair and folded his arms across his chest.

"I only ask because I don't want employees who are here one day and gone the next. I need dependable workers who will be here on time every day."

He gestured toward the letter he'd given her. "If you'll take a look at that recommendation, I think you'll see that I have been a faithful and reliable employee. If you have any doubts about my character, I'd encourage you to write or telegraph Mr. Kresie."

Instead of quizzing him, why didn't she just read the letter? Maybe that was one of the differences between men and women running a business. Women liked to discuss things, while men didn't waste time talking. Then again, maybe it was her way of sizing him up. There was no way to be sure since he'd never before had to ask a woman for a job.

"Unless I discover something unforeseen in Mr. Kresie's letter, I don't think there will be any reason to contact him."

Levi's attention remained fixed on Miss McKay as she unfolded the letter and scanned the contents. Hopefully, the portion of Mr. Kresie's letter that referred to Levi as a true artisan would result in a job offer. Otherwise, he'd need to look for work elsewhere. Jobs were usually available in the nearby coal mines, but going underground to eke out a living would be his last resort.

When she'd finished reading the letter, Levi leaned forward. "What do you think, Miss McKay? Do you have a job for me?"

"Had you come here last week, I wouldn't have hired you no matter how glowing your letter of recommendation. But things have changed. We've received a large order from a new customer, and I could use another tile cutter."

"I'll be pleased to—"

She lifted her hand to stay him. "Let me finish before you accept, Mr. Judson."

Embarrassment seized him. "I'm sorry. Go on."

"As I was saying, I'll need another tile cutter, but you would be required to fill other positions where needed. We are a small operation. With the exception of burners, our workers are able and willing to perform most any job within the tile works. If I need men to load barrels for shipping or to dig clay rather than to cut tiles, I can depend on them." She tapped her finger on the letter. "Mr. Kresie says you're a skilled burner. Most likely I'll need you in that position as much as cutting. Would that suit you?"

Levi nodded. "I'll work wherever I'm needed."

Burners received higher pay than cutters, but he'd wait and see what she proposed when it came to wages. Either way, he'd accept the job. Low wages would be better than no wages. She inched forward in the deep leather chair and rested her arms atop the broad desk. The massive furniture dwarfed her slender frame. Odd that she didn't replace it with pieces that would prove a better fit. Perhaps a local carpenter had been commissioned to create a desk that would accommodate her small stature.

"Working hours are seven in the morning until six in the evening with a half hour for the noonday meal. I'm told the thick walls keep the temperature in the building bearable throughout the summer. That has proved true thus far, but if it should change, we'll begin work at five thirty, take off a couple hours in the heat of the afternoon, and then return. Of course, burners will need to be here to tend the kilns if we're already firing. Will that cause you any problem?"

"No. As long as the foreman lets me know when and where I'm needed, I'll be here to do my job."

Even though he wanted time to visit with his brother, Miss McKay had already mentioned that there was another burner. Most burners didn't like to leave another man in charge of their kilns, so Levi doubted he'd be asked to tend the fires very often. Besides, he'd have Sundays to visit with Noah.

"Wages are paid at the end of the workday on Saturday. When you're at the kilns, you'll be paid ten cents more an hour than when you're cutting. If you prove to be a good burner, I'll raise it to twelve cents more. I pay my cutters two dollars a day. If you have any questions about what you're paid, you can examine the books to make sure I have your hours correct. If that's agreeable, you can begin work tomorrow."

"Thank you, Miss McKay. You won't be sorry you hired me."

"I'm sure I won't. You can report here in the office, and I'll give you a tour of the tile works and introduce you to the other workers." When she stood, he pushed to his feet. "Are you living at your brother's home?"

"W-w-what? My brother?" Confusion momentarily washed over him.

"You said your brother lived in Weston, and I wondered if you were staying at his home."

"No. I have a room at Mrs. Brighton's boardinghouse. It's a little over a mile from here, on Fleming Street."

She smiled. "Yes. I'm familiar with the location."

She must think him a dolt. No doubt she knew the locale of every business and residence in the town. Before he could make a bigger fool of himself, he waved and hurried out the door.

Chapter 7

Ainslee leaned back in her chair. From the wide bank of windows, she watched Levi Judson dash across the courtyard and begin his ascent up the path that would take him back to the boardinghouse. He moved as though he feared she'd run after him and rescind her offer of employment, but he need not worry on that account. He was exactly what she needed—a worker who had experience in all aspects of the business. If Mr. Judson's account of his abilities was true, he'd be able to assist and help manage the business whenever and wherever she might need help. While the other workers were skilled in their own positions and could fill in on others when necessary, none of them had the overall experience Mr. Judson seemingly possessed. She watched until he was out of sight. Curious that he'd revealed such discomfort when she'd mentioned his brother.

However, perhaps he was like her—a person who preferred privacy. If so, she certainly couldn't fault him. There was little doubt the good-looking young man would be the topic of conversation at the dinner table tonight. According to Mrs. Brighton, a new man in town never escaped the ladies' notice—

especially if he was living next door. If the weather cooperated and Mr. Judson stepped outside after dinner, the ladies would be aflutter. They'd take to their chairs and fan themselves while directing coy looks across the short expanse that divided the two porches. They'd giggle and whisper among themselves until one or two of the men would arrive and escort them across the small divide.

They wouldn't expect Ainslee to join them. She'd made it clear to all of them that she wasn't interested in pursuing a man. At first they'd expressed disbelief that she wasn't seeking a possible suitor. Soon, however, they happily accepted her decision—likely because she was one less woman with whom they would need to compete.

She reached into the desk drawer and withdrew a sheet of stationery. She'd promised to keep Ewan informed. The new order she'd received at the tile works had been unsolicited, a complete surprise—just like Levi Judson. Taking pen in hand, she smiled. She was certain this was the beginning of an answer to her prayer. Coupled with Mr. Judson's arrival, the large unexpected order could mean nothing else. More orders and skilled employees would gain them higher profits, and higher profits would cause businessmen to take note. Surely it wouldn't be long until she boarded the train for a permanent return to Grafton.

After detailing the recent order and setting forth Mr. Judson's abilities, Ainslee asked if Ewan had placed for-sale advertisements in any broadsides. She then closed the letter with a more personal paragraph. "*I'm getting on with the other ladies quite well.*" She stared at the sentence. She should have left out the word *quite*. It was true she was getting on with them well enough, but *quite* made it sound as though she was truly enjoying their company. She could scratch through the word, but that might create a bit of uneasiness as well as a flood of discussion at the McKay dinner table. Her only other option was to rewrite the entire letter. No. She'd leave it as written.

I visited the small church located not far from the boarding-house. All of the boarders who attend church go there. I'm told they have picnics and other socials during the summer months. Mrs. Coates, the preacher's wife, invited me to Sunday dinner at their house so they could "get to know me better," but I declined, as I wasn't feeling well.

Ainslee sighed. Though she could have accepted the invitation, she hadn't felt particularly well that day. Maybe writing a personal note hadn't been such a good idea. Each sentence stretched the truth a bit. Better to write nothing more than continue with her half-truths. She dipped her pen into the ink pot.

Please write and tell me how things are going at the pottery, especially at the school. Tell Tessa to draw me a picture, and give her a kiss for me. I miss you all a great deal and look forward to the day when I'll return home.

Any further word from Adaira?

Ainslee's heart pinched as she penned the question. She had hoped Adaira might write one final letter before she departed for Paris, but she and Chester had likely already sailed.

On several occasions, Ainslee had taken up her pen to write her sister, but she'd crumpled and tossed each one. Her attempts had been stilted and formal, and without Adaira's address, she'd given up trying. Yet the ache for her sister and what had been gnawed at her. Things between them would never be the same. Adaira now had a husband, who would always be her first consideration. That was as it should be, but that didn't ease the void in Ainslee's heart. And it didn't change the fact that Adaira was the one who had broken her promises and damaged their bond. Forgiveness would be easier if her sister's letter had contained a genuine apology. At least that's what Ainslee told herself.

Ewan's admonition to forgive continued to haunt her. He was right, of course. She would eventually forgive, but she doubted whether the wound would totally heal.

The bell in the tower clanged and pulled her from her thoughts. Workers spilled out of the doors into the shaded courtyard to eat their noonday meal. Ainslee silently scolded herself. Instead of dreaming about what could have been, she needed to attend to the task at hand. Instead of writing Adaira, she needed to contact prospective and current customers and grow the tile works into a prospering business. Instead of holding on to her anger, she needed to look to God for deliverance.

Ainslee arrived at the boardinghouse with only enough time to wash up for supper. When she returned downstairs, Mrs. Brighton was standing at the end of the table and waved Ainslee toward her chair. Before Ainslee's feet were under the dinner table, the older woman had finished saying grace and bustled into the kitchen.

"Have you heard?" Sarah leaned across the table and nearly tipped over her water glass.

"Heard what?" Ainslee unfolded her napkin and arranged it across her skirt. "I just arrived home. Is there something I need to know?"

"There's a new boarder at the men's boardinghouse. Of course, I know you don't care since you're not interested in marriage, but he's awfully nice-looking."

Ainslee arched her brows. "You've met him?"

Sarah shook her head. "No, but Mrs. Brighton said he's a nice-appearing and a well-spoken young man. Those are her very words, aren't they, Mae?"

A wisp of Mae's light brown hair fell across her forehead when she bobbed her head. "Yes. Exactly. Well-spoken and nice-appearing. Isn't that truly exciting?" Mae didn't wait for a response. "You should join us on the front porch this evening, Ainslee. Even if you aren't looking for a husband, you could still meet him. That's the hospitable thing to do, isn't it?" Mae glanced around the table, but her question was met with groans and several glares.

Ainslee swallowed a chuckle. "Thank you for your invitation, Mae, but I believe I'll go upstairs and read this evening. No need for me to take up space on the porch."

She considered telling them she'd hired Mr. Judson earlier in the day, but Cecelia immediately suggested that they take turns guessing why the new man had come to Weston, where he worked, and who would be the fortunate lady to win him as a suitor. Ainslee couldn't believe her ears. Surely the other ladies would think the idea outlandish.

Instead Sarah scooted forward on her chair. "I'll go first!" Her eyes glistened with excitement.

The other ladies sat at full attention as Sarah gave her answer to each question. When she finished, they all applauded. All except Ainslee, who choked on a bite of pickled beets when Sarah guessed that the new boarder was likely a doctor who'd come to work at the asylum. Mae pounded her on her back while Cecelia thrust a glass of water toward her.

As soon as Ainslee's cough had subsided, the guessing game continued, with each guess becoming more outlandish than the last. Except for Mae, they all guessed he'd arrived in Weston to work at the asylum. Mae guessed he was a journalist who'd come to purchase the town's newspaper, even though it wasn't listed for sale. Not surprisingly, each woman chose herself to be the future love interest of the new man in town.

After supper Ainslee remained at the table while the other ladies hurried off to primp before going outdoors. She reached across the table and was filling her teacup when Mrs. Brighton stepped back into the room. "I thought everyone had gone upstairs. Are you not finished with your supper just yet?"

"I've finished. The meal was delicious, but I thought I'd enjoy one last cup of tea before going upstairs to read. The other ladies have gone to their rooms to make certain they look their best before going outside."

Mrs. Brighton chuckled. "They're wanting to impress the new boarder. I figured the minute they knew a single young fellow was in town, they'd be on the front porch, hoping for an invite to meet him. You have no interest in meeting him?"

Ainslee took a sip of her tea before glancing toward the other room. "The truth is, I've already met him—and hired him—but I didn't say anything at supper. I knew it would cause a stir. The ladies would have asked far more questions than I could have answered. I'd rather they gain their information from him. It didn't seem proper to talk about him since he's now my employee. I wouldn't want him to think I was spreading tales before he arrived at work tomorrow."

The creases in Mrs. Brighton's forehead faded, and recognition shone in her eyes. "I think Mr. Judson will appreciate your decision, but the ladies may take you to task for not telling."

Ainslee shrugged. "I think they'll be more disappointed when they discover he's a tile worker rather than a doctor or journalist." Ainslee downed the last of her tea. "Earlier you referred to Mr. Judson as a single man. Did he tell you he wasn't married?"

The older woman hesitated. "No. I just guessed he was single, since he's rooming at a boardinghouse. Did he tell you different?"

"No. We didn't discuss his marital status. I asked only because the ladies are counting on the fact that he's eligible. They'll be sorely disappointed if they find out otherwise."

Mrs. Brighton just smiled. "If he's married, their lives will be no different than when they got out of bed this morning, now, will they? I'm not going to worry myself with what those ladies will think if the new boarder happens to have a wife."

"What? He's married?" Mae rounded the doorway into the dining room, her features knotted together like a crumpled piece of paper. She peered back and forth between Ainslee and Mrs. Brighton.

The older woman continued to scrape the dirty dishes. "I don't know if he's married or not. He didn't say. But since he arrived without a wife, I guessed him to be a single man. The two of us were having a private conversation, and the question came up as to whether he'd said he was single. There's no need to get all stirred up, Mae." She picked up one of the napkins and waved it toward the front door. "You can ask him for yourself if he's got a wife."

Mae straightened her shoulders. "I plan to do just that."

Mrs. Brighton moved around the table and added the dirty utensils to her stack. "Mae won't have the courage to ask, but Sarah will find out before the evening is over. You can be sure of that."

Ainslee smiled as a twinge of curiosity nudged her. Earlier she'd been curious about his brother, and now she wondered if he was married. To her surprise, she found herself hoping Sarah would find out.

No more than an hour had passed when a knock sounded at her bedroom door. The knock was quickly followed by Mae's distressed voice. "*Psssst.* Ainslee! Answer the door. I know you can't be asleep yet. Sarah and I want to talk to you."

Ainslee sighed. After placing her book on the small bedside table, she crossed the room and opened the door. Sarah and Mae stood shoulder to shoulder, arms crossed, chins jutted, and eyes smoldering.

Sarah pushed past her and stepped into the room. "Why didn't you tell us you knew Mr. Judson? You let us go over there and make fools of ourselves." She marched across the room, turned around, and waved at Mae. "Get in here, Mae, and close the door behind you."

Mae did as she was bid and then leaned against the door.

"I don't *know* him. He applied for a job at the tile works and I hired him. How did that cause any of you to make fools of yourselves?"

Sarah wagged her finger in Ainslee's direction. "We all went over there with high hopes, thinking Mr. Judson would be an eligible suitor for one of us. While we were going around the table guessing his profession and the reason he'd come to Weston, you knew he was a tile worker and that he'd come from Philadelphia."

"And that he's engaged to be married to a woman who lives in Philadelphia." Mae flung the remark in Ainslee's direction.

"Engaged? How do you think I would know that? We never ask such questions when we're hiring employees." Why were they so angry with her? She had no control over Mr. Judson's marital status. "I'm sure Mr. Judson will tell you that the subject of his marital eligibility was never discussed." Ainslee squared her shoulders. "Beyond that, I have nothing more to say about Mr. Judson."

Though she was certain they weren't pleased with her answer, Mae and Sarah left the room without further inquiry, and Ainslee returned to her reading—or at least she tried. Though she stared at the printed pages, she couldn't concentrate. Instead, her thoughts were of Levi Judson and the questions she'd asked him earlier in the day. While he'd told her he had a brother in Weston, he had never given her a reason for why he quit his job and moved here. Odd that he wouldn't live with his brother. And odd that a man would quit a job where he was highly valued and move to a town where he had no promise of work. Especially a man who was betrothed to a woman in another city.

There must be more to Levi Judson than she'd imagined.

Chapter 8

Levi hurried downstairs and sat down at the breakfast table with the other men who lived in the boardinghouse. The minute he arrived, Fred Masters pretended to swoon. "Oh, Levi, do tell us about life in the big city." Fred spoke in a high-pitched tone and fluttered his lashes. The rest of the men guffawed and joined in with jibes of their own.

Levi joined in the laughter. Meeting their jokes with anger would only prolong the teasing. Besides, at supper last night the men had warned him what to expect so he wouldn't be caught off guard. He'd thought they were exaggerating, but the deluge of ladies seeking his attention was even more intense than the men had predicted. Two of the ladies had edged close, one on either side, and they'd been unwilling to relinquish their spots until Fred told them Levi was engaged to a young lady in Philadelphia.

That comment had been enough to send them running off. The one who'd introduced herself as Mae was in tears. And Sarah, the other one, had accused him of toying with her affections. He didn't know how she could charge him with such a thing. She was the one who'd fluttered her lashes and leaned close and cooed questions in his ear. All the while, he'd backed away from her and avoided answering her bold inquiries.

Levi had been stunned by Fred's remark to the visiting ladies. Later, Fred laughed and said it was the only way to deter the women. Levi wasn't sure if Fred had been trying to protect him or gain some of the attention for himself, but he was thankful for the reprieve. He hadn't corrected Fred's announcement, and he had no plans to do so. He didn't know what the future held for him.

Levi had suffered the pain of being pushed aside when the woman he loved had discovered his brother, Noah, suffered from insanity. Though she'd said it was her family who objected to their marriage, Levi was certain she was relieved to be released from their engagement. Even though Noah had periods of lucidity, her parents harbored the fear that Noah's mental disorder might be hereditary and they couldn't risk their daughter giving birth to an imperfect child.

Levi had argued there was no guarantee of perfection with any child, but Ann's family had remained steadfast. Even when Levi explained that Noah had been quite normal until he'd suffered a high fever as a child, they'd remained steadfast in their decision. He couldn't completely fault them, for he hadn't met their expectations as a suitable match for their daughter in any way. Yet he'd been surprised when Ann had so readily agreed with her parents.

Fred nudged his arm. "You better get moving if you're going to walk to work."

Most of the men worked at the asylum, and they had an arrangement with a liveryman in town who sent a hack each morning to deliver them to work and pick them up in the evening for a reasonable rate. But Levi planned to walk the mile to work when the weather permitted.

Before he departed the room, Levi tapped Fred's shoulder.

"Don't be telling any more whoppers about me to the ladies—or anyone else."

Fred chuckled. "I won't. But if you meant what you said about not wanting the ladies hounding ya, you'd be smart to let them keep on believing you got a woman back home."

Bill Wilcox raked his fingers through thinning hair. "Besides, we don't need no more competition. An old geezer like me can't compete with you pretty boys."

"Pretty boys?" Levi laughed and shook his head. "This is the first time I've ever been called a pretty boy, but you don't need to worry about me, Bill. I'm not looking for a woman to complicate my life."

Bill forked another sausage onto his plate. "That's good to hear. Believe me, your secret's safe with us." He glanced around the table. "Ain't it, fellas?" When they didn't immediately respond, Bill repeated the question until the men finally nodded and mumbled their agreement. "That's more like it." Bill's lips curved in a satisfied grin.

A twinge of guilt edged up Levi's spine. He was leading folks astray with half-truths and silence. He hadn't planned on being secretive or misleading folks about himself, but Fred had done it for him. And any attempt to set things aright would serve no purpose. Likely it would make things worse. When the ladies learned the truth, they'd be angry with Fred, and then Fred, in turn, would become angry with him. The consequences of straightening things out were far too daunting.

Levi tugged his cap low on his forehead and bounded down the porch steps. The sound of chattering ladies drifted toward him from the boardinghouse next door. He offered a silent prayer of thanks that the tile works was located in the opposite direction. Facing any of those ladies this morning would only add a dash of embarrassment to his nagging guilt.

The birds were chirping morning songs, and a warm breeze carried the scent of wildflowers that bloomed along the roadway and up the steep hillside. He needed to push aside his worries of last evening before he arrived at work. Today was important. He needed to make a good impression. While he wanted the foreman and Miss McKay to view him as a skilled worker and a good choice, he didn't want to appear brash or boastful. He'd worked with men who thought they were the biggest toad in the puddle, and he knew there could be a fine line between revealing one's skills and appearing arrogant. Yesterday he'd done his best to impress Miss McKay—but only enough to secure employment. He hadn't overstated his abilities, yet he'd departed her office unsure about what she thought of him or his skills.

Working for Miss McKay was going to be much different than working for Mr. Kresie. Granted, the work would be similar, but Mr. Kresie had been a mentor and friend. That wouldn't be the case with Miss McKay. From his recent contact with her, it appeared she wasn't interested in forming friendships with her workers, and she didn't have the experience to be a mentor. Truth be told, she was the one in need of a mentor. And while he'd be willing to help her, she didn't seem particularly interested in any assistance.

He wanted the opportunity to prove that his new ideas could be successful. If he couldn't convince Miss McKay, it would probably be years before he'd have a similar opportunity. He'd wrestled with leaving Philadelphia just when Mr. Kresie had been willing to look at the new techniques as a possibility for expansion. In the end, his brother's needs had won out. While the doctors hadn't been completely negative about his brother's ability to leave the asylum one day, they'd given Levi only a thread of hope.

He doubted whether another tile works would open in Weston,

so the best hope for producing his new designs lay with Miss McKay. If she was going to be convinced, it would take more than a winning smile and smooth words. He'd need the Lord's help.

At the sound of an approaching horse and buggy, Levi stepped to the side of the road. He knew few people in Weston, so there was no need to turn and look. The sleek, black horse trotted by at a steady pace, causing plumes of dust to rise from beneath the wheels of the buggy. If the owner of the rig was going to his job at the tile works, he was going to arrive at least half an hour before the start of the workday. Then again, maybe it was a supervisor or foreman. Mr. Kresie had insisted that his foremen be at work fifteen minutes before the first bell to ensure the workers were punctual. Maybe Miss McKay didn't tolerate tardiness, either.

Soon after the rig passed him, voices drifted down from the hillside, and Levi caught sight of several men as they navigated their way down toward the path. The steepness of the hill made it impossible to traverse in a straight course, so they moved in a zigzag pattern, dodging tree limbs and loose rocks with surprising agility.

One of the fellows grabbed hold of a sapling. "You the new fella?" His feet skittered and the sapling bent low bearing his weight.

"I am." Loose rocks tumbled toward him, and Levi jumped back. He waited until the men completed their descent and then introduced himself.

"Pleased to meet ya, Levi. I'm John Burgess." He gestured to the other two men. "This here's Martin Kohl and that lad with the red hair is Lawrence Gault."

Martin shook his hand. "Pleased to meet ya." Lawrence nodded. "I hear tell you were hired as a cutter and burner. That right?"

"That's right." He was surprised the men knew of his arrival. Miss McKay had said she'd take him on a tour of the place and introduce him this morning. Instead, she'd already told the workers she'd hired a new employee.

Levi waved toward the hillside. "That's quite a skill you've developed. I think I'd break an arm or leg if I attempted to come down that hill like the three of you. Have you ever taken a tumble?"

"Of course." Martin glanced at his friends. "We all did back when we first started coming that way, but after a few months of practice, we got it down. Once in a while one of us still slips, but during those early days we suffered a lot of scrapes and bruises."

Martin raked a hank of dark hair from his forehead. "It saves us a lot of time since we all live a good ways from Weston. 'Course, we can't come that way when it rains or snows—way too slick once it gets wet and muddy."

Martin and Lawrence started along the path leading down to the tile works, and John dropped back to walk alongside Levi. "You come here from Grafton, like Miss McKay?"

When a squirrel scampered across the path in front of them, Martin let out a loud sigh. "Wouldn't you know it? I always see squirrels and rabbits when I don't have my gun."

Lawrence gave Martin a playful slap on the shoulder. "Quit your complaining. It's too warm to hunt squirrels."

Levi chuckled at their playful banter. "No, I'm not from Grafton. I lived in Philadelphia before coming here."

"So how'd she come to give you a job? Was there some kind of notice in the newspaper? None of us even knew she was looking to hire anyone else."

Levi couldn't tell if John and the other men were troubled by his arrival, but he likely needed to be careful. He didn't know how much Miss McKay had told them, and he didn't want to say anything that might contradict her.

"I don't know if she advertised in a newspaper. If so, I didn't see it. Mr. Kresie, the man I worked for in Philadelphia, is the one who told me there was a tile works in Weston, but I didn't know if there were any jobs until I got to town yesterday."

John shifted his lunch pail to his other hand. "So did that Mr. Kresie shut down his place in Philadelphia?"

There was no doubt that this conversation was going to lead into questions about why he'd moved to Weston. Since his arrival, he'd been careful to keep Noah's whereabouts a secret. He wasn't ready to tell anyone his brother had been admitted to the asylum. While he wasn't ashamed of Noah or his illness, it seemed folks always treated him differently when they found out about his brother.

The time would come when he'd tell the men at the house, but not yet. They worked at the asylum, and he hoped to glean a little insight before they learned he had a relative admitted there. He'd visit Noah next Sunday during visiting hours. By then, he'd be willing to tell others his reason for coming to Weston.

Lawrence dropped back beside Levi. "What'd you think of this place when you saw it? Really something, ain't it? Mr. Ploughman sure had him some fancy ideas. Looks kind of out of place out here in the valley surrounded by these hills, but the design works real good. Don't it, fellas?"

Martin looked over his shoulder. "Yeah, it works good, but I don't think this here building is as strange as a woman being in charge of a tile works. You ever heard of a woman being in charge of a place like this, Levi?"

"Can't say that I have, but I guess it doesn't matter if it's a man or woman in charge as long as you've got a job and you're treated decent." Levi kept his attention fixed on Martin. "Have things changed since Mr. Ploughman sold the business to the McKays?"

"Nah, nothing's changed. She's running things just like he did. We're doing the same work for the same pay. Right now most of the contracts are ones Mr. Ploughman had before the McKays bought him out. I'm not so sure she's going to be able to bring in many new customers. Think about it. How many men want to sit down and discuss business with a woman? If she can't bring in new customers, then this place will go under pretty quick."

Levi hiked a shoulder. "She told me she hired me because she just got a new contract. According to her calculations, she needed another cutter and burner to keep up with the old orders and the new one."

John snorted. "How's she think she's gonna make any money if she hires more help as soon as she gets a new contract? She could've waited and had some of the men work extra hours until she knew she'd really need more help."

Lawrence shook his head. "I'm a big believer in the good Lord sending what you need when you need it. I think Miss McKay needed another cutter and the Lord sent Levi into her office."

Martin gave Lawrence a shove on the shoulder. "When'd you become such a believer in the Almighty taking care of everything?"

Lawrence's forehead creased. "I've always thought that was true, but it's hard to remember that when things aren't going the way I think they should."

Martin waved aside Lawrence's explanation and remained at Levi's side as they neared the entrance to the courtyard. "Where you living, Levi?"

"I rented a room at Mrs. Brighton's boardinghouse—the one for men."

Martin chuckled. "I didn't think she'd put you in the one with the women. I hear tell she's got some strict rules. She's made more than one fella leave her place for smoking in his room and another for drinking in the parlor."

The early-morning sun cast long shadows across the courtyard. Several men were already shoveling clay from the huge mounds that had weathered at the far end of the yard.

The three men started off toward the doors along the side of the building, but John stopped and turned. "Was it Miss McKay who sent you to rent a room from Mrs. Brighton?"

Levi shook his head. "No. A clerk at the hotel where I stayed on my first night in town recommended her. He said she had the best places in town. Why do you ask?"

"'Cause Miss McKay rents from her, too."

Levi gaped at him. After he'd gathered his wits about him, he pointed toward the office. "*That* Miss McKay? She lives in the women's boardinghouse? You must be mistaken. Why would a lady from a rich family live in a nice but very average boardinghouse?"

"Don't know. Maybe 'cause she ain't had time enough to find a place to buy, or maybe 'cause she wasn't sure she'd be happy in Weston. I got no idea how women think. That's why I'm still single. Guess you could ask her. I hear tell the men and women visit with each other out on those front porches each evening."

The bell in the tower pealed, and John ran after Martin and Lawrence, leaving Levi to consider what he'd said. What was it Miss McKay had said when he told her he was living at Mrs. Brighton's boardinghouse?

He kicked a pebble across the courtyard and continued toward the office with his thoughts racing. He clicked his middle finger against his thumb. He'd mentioned the house was on Fleming Street and then felt like a fool when she said she knew where it was. Yet why hadn't she told him she lived next door?

He stopped short before he entered the office. Had Miss McKay been on the front porch last night when Fred told the ladies he was engaged? To think she'd been listening to the ladies discuss him as a possible suitor caused his stomach to churn. Worse yet, what if she'd heard he was engaged to a young lady in Philadelphia? Then again, why would she care if he was engaged?

Chapter 9

Ainslee looked up from her ledger as Levi Judson entered the office. "Good morning, Mr. Judson." She blotted the page before closing the ledger. "I trust you had a pleasant evening at your new residence."

Though he appeared somewhat taken aback by her comment, he merely nodded. "Good morning, Miss McKay."

Ainslee pushed to her feet, rounded the desk, and gestured for him to follow her. "We won't spend a great deal of time on the tour since you're already familiar with the tile-making process. I told the other employees that I'd hired a new man and that you'd begin today."

"Yes, I know." He followed her into the courtyard.

She stopped and turned. "And how did you know, Mr. Judson? None of my employees live at the boardinghouse."

"I met three of the workers when I was on my way here this morning. They were scrabbling down the hillside along the main road."

She continued on toward the heaping piles of clay. "Oh, yes. Martin, John, and Lawrence. Am I right?"

He nodded. "Their surefootedness impressed me."

"Their work skills are impressive, too. I think you'll discover all of the men well-trained and good at their jobs. Most of them have been here for many years, and all of them were hired by Mr. Ploughman."

She stopped and introduced Levi to the diggers. "A few of the unskilled men like the diggers come in and work only as needed. Most of them are farmers or have other jobs, as well. We purchase our clay from area farmers and let it weather here."

"What if they're working for someone else, or their crops need to be planted and you need them here to shovel clay?" Levi asked. "It could throw off your whole production schedule."

"Mr. Ploughman provided me with a long list of names I could call upon if the regulars aren't available. If I couldn't locate anyone to do the job, I'd pull men from other jobs to help. A cutter or burner might not want to spend the morning as a digger, but . . ."

"You're paying them to do the work you assign them."

Her eyes widened in surprise, but she quickly regained her composure lest he see through her bravado. "Exactly."

They returned to the covered walkway and entered the building, where the thick-walled construction provided a cooler temperature. A wide hallway led them into the mixing room, where Ainslee introduced Levi to Harold and Robert, the two men who operated the huge clay mixer.

Ainslee stopped beside the machine. "Are you familiar with this type of mixer, Mr. Judson?"

Levi nodded. "I've worked a similar mixer."

She gave him a half smile. "Good. Then I know who I can send to help with the mixing if Robert or Harold should be absent in the future."

Levi tipped his head to the men. "I look forward to getting to know both of you better."

The men grunted in return. Ainslee had expected them to behave in a more welcoming manner, but she didn't know either of the men very well. Perhaps they didn't take to strangers.

Ainslee waved him onward. They'd walked a short distance from the mixing room when she pointed to stairs leading to the lower level. "This is where the dumbwaiter delivers the slabs of clay to dry." She glanced back toward the mixing room. "I thought Robert and Harold would be pleased when they learned you had experience mixing and could take over if they were absent."

Levi shrugged. "I'm not surprised. Rather than considering it a good thing to have someone who can help with their work, they may view me as someone who could cause them to lose their job."

"Surely not. That's just silly." Ainslee gave him a sidelong glance. "They've worked here for years and should know I wouldn't replace either of them, but Robert hasn't been well. He's missed a number of days since I took over, and it slows the process when Harold is alone in there."

Ainslee's thoughts churned as they walked to the cutting room. Had bringing another employee into the workplace caused the workers to feel threatened? One of the reasons she'd told them she had hired Levi was so they wouldn't be caught unaware. Maybe she should make rounds later in the day and offer each of the men reassurance. On the other hand, maybe that would only make matters worse. She'd wait and see how the other workers reacted.

Next they made a stop in the cutting room, where Ainslee introduced Levi to the foreman. Joseph was a slow-moving, meticulous man, considerably older than Levi, who preferred perfection over speed. Even though Ainslee didn't know much about Levi's work habits, she thought the two men would work well together. She'd been surprised when Joseph looked at Levi with a hint of suspicion in his eyes and doubt in his voice. "How much experience have you had cutting?"

Ainslee stood to the side and watched the exchange between the two men. Joseph continued to ask about Levi's qualifications but nothing more. There had been neither words of welcome nor signs of elation that would indicate Joseph was pleased he would have someone to share the workload in the cutting room. He'd been as cold and distant as the other men, especially when she said that Levi would return and work in the cutting room once he'd seen the rest of the operation.

Maybe Levi was right: Maybe the men did view his arrival as a threat to their jobs. Maybe she should have told them about the new order before introducing Levi. A sigh escaped her lips. She didn't have enough knowledge to operate the business, much less know how to handle a group of unhappy men.

With her head bowed low against the wind, she hurried to the opposite end of the courtyard. Once inside, she turned toward him. "The kilns are in this section. Having them a distance away keeps the rest of the building cooler in the summer."

Levi told her the kilns weren't as large as some he'd seen in various operations but that he'd have no problem if asked to fire and tend them.

When they returned outdoors, Levi pulled his cap onto his head and touched the brim. "Thank you for showing me around. You have a nice operation, Miss McKay. I believe I'm going to enjoy working here."

"I've had no complaints about the working conditions, though I doubt you'll find it as enjoyable as evenings on the front porch of the men's boardinghouse." The moment those final words slipped out of her mouth, she wanted to snatch them back. Why hadn't she left well enough alone?

"You seem particularly interested in my free time last night, Miss McKay." His brown eyes twinkled with mischief as they continued toward the office. "I would have enjoyed it much more if you would have joined the other ladies who paid a visit. I understand you rent a room from Mrs. Brighton, as well."

Her breath caught. One of the other women must have mentioned her name last night. She struggled to maintain her decorum. What had been said? She forced her lips into a tight smile. "Was it Mae or Sarah?"

His brows dipped. "I'm sorry to disappoint, but your name wasn't mentioned last night. At least not while I was outside."

A rush of heat climbed up Ainslee's neck and quickly spread across her cheeks. *Wonderful!* Now he was going to think her a self-centered woman who thought she would be the topic of every discussion.

They came to a halt outside the office door. "I'm not disappointed, Mr. Judson. Quite the contrary. I don't enjoy being the focus of attention. I was curious how you'd learned of my living arrangements and wrongfully concluded Sarah or Mae had told you." She arched her brows and waited.

And waited.

When she could bear the silence no longer, Ainslee folded her arms in front of her and tapped her foot. "Well? Are you going to tell me how you learned where I live?"

"Sorry." He rubbed his palm along his jawline. "I didn't mean to annoy you, Miss McKay. It was one of the men I met on my way to work this morning. I believe it was John." He furrowed his brow. "He didn't act like he was divulging a secret."

"Of course not. Most all the employees know where I live. I was merely curious about who told you."

"Once I found out, I was curious why you hadn't told me yourself."

She hesitated. They'd both been careful what they told each other. She had inquired why he'd come to Weston, yet he hadn't yet told her—at least not to her satisfaction. There was more to the reason why he'd arrived here. She had a feeling that his secret was much deeper than the reason why she'd hesitated to mention where she lived. Of course, she'd been secretive about her desire to leave the tile works and Weston behind her. Divulging that piece of information could prove fatal to the company.

He mimicked her earlier stance and folded his arms across his chest and tapped his foot. "Well, are you going to tell me why you kept it secret?"

"I didn't tell you because when I was a young girl, my brother warned my sisters and me against telling strangers where we live. Besides, revealing personal information flies in the face of proper social etiquette."

He flinched as though she'd slapped him. "Now that I know, I promise I won't take advantage, Miss McKay." He tipped his hat. "Should I return to the cutting room and begin work?"

"Yes, and why don't you tell Joseph I've secured a large order? He'll spread the word among the men. That will likely ease some of the tension I sensed when I was introducing you to the other workers."

Instead of looking at her, he made a half-turn toward the cutting room. "Whatever you think is best. I did mention the new order to Martin and his friends. They seem to think you should have offered the men extra hours instead of hiring me."

She sighed. Was nothing she did correct? "I'll return and speak to Joseph later this morning. He may not have heard and perhaps he'll think my decision was sound."

With no more than a curt nod, he strode away. She hadn't intended to offend him with her earlier remark about proper etiquette, but it appeared Mr. Judson was unhappy.

After a final glance over her shoulder, she pulled open the office door. Why was she worried about Mr. Judson's reaction? She didn't need his approval or acceptance. He was no different than any of the other workers. Or was he?

Since his arrival in Weston, Levi had been to the asylum to visit his brother, Noah, as often as time would permit. Oddly, he'd not run into any of his housemates during his visits. He didn't inquire but presumed that those who worked on Sundays were assigned to other units of the asylum. Things at the tile works had fallen into a comfortable routine, and the men seemed amiable. Miss McKay, too, appeared to be embracing her role of leadership.

During Levi's visits to the asylum, Noah had appeared well cared for, although he'd exhibited bouts of restlessness, pacing back and forth in front of the bedroom window. While some of the male patients enjoyed working outdoors in the gardens, others, including Noah, resisted the idea. Even as a child, Noah had disliked being dirty, and that hadn't changed.

Levi's concerns that the endless hours of pacing would cause his brother's condition to worsen had resulted in many late-night prayers. Last night while he'd sat on the side of his bed asking God what he could do for Noah, an idea had come to mind. He'd need to gain permission from the asylum staff, but he hoped his suggestion would be met with enthusiasm.

He bounded down the steps and took his seat at the table with several other men who were eagerly awaiting breakfast. The boarders who worked at the asylum were always first to arrive downstairs since they departed earlier than the other tenants.

Henry nodded to him. "You're earlier than usual, Levi. Going into work early this morning?"

"No. I wanted to get down here and talk to you before you left the house."

"Why's that?" Henry's bushy brows knit together. He glanced toward the kitchen. "I wish Miss Hanson would bring the coffee in. I can barely keep my eyes open."

The other men mumbled their agreement, obviously none of them particularly interested in Levi's reason for joining them.

He waited only a moment longer, then cleared his throat. "I haven't mentioned this to any of you before, but I have a brother who is a patient at the asylum."

Miss Hanson stepped into the dining room with the corner of her apron snug around the handle of the large tin coffee boiler. She stopped short and gaped at Levi.

Henry hoisted his cup and waved it in her direction. "You gonna pour us some coffee or spend the mornin' staring at Levi?"

She startled to attention and scurried to Henry's side, but her gaze soon returned to Levi. "Did I hear you say you have a brother at the asylum?"

Levi nodded but said no more until she'd finished pouring coffee and returned to the kitchen. No doubt Miss Hanson would tell Mrs. Brighton, and soon the word would spread. While some folks didn't seem to find his brother's medical condition disturbing, others did. Levi preferred being the one who decided when to tell others, but that didn't usually happen. A few always seemed to enjoy carrying the news; this time would likely be no different.

Henry downed a gulp of coffee and leaned forward. "How

come you've been so secretive about your brother? We could have let you know if he was having any problems. What's his name? What wing is he in?"

"His name is Noah Judson, and he's in the west wing. He's in a room that overlooks the courtyard." Levi ignored the question about why he'd been secretive. "I know a lot of the patients spend their time working in the small vegetable gardens or over in the dairy, but my brother has no interest in that type of activity. He spends a lot of his time pacing back and forth, and I don't think it's good for him."

"You're probably right about that, but we don't force the patients to do anything. You think he might want to help with some of the farming? Those small vegetable and flower gardens are mostly for the women and a few of the men we can't take over to the farm. Maybe we could find something over there. Is he good with horses? We could use some men in the horse barn."

Levi shook his head. "No. He doesn't like working outdoors and he has a fear of large animals."

Miss Hanson reappeared with bowls of scrambled eggs and fried potatoes and a plate of biscuits. After placing the food on the table, she gestured toward the kitchen. "I'll be back with the sausages and gravy."

"And more coffee." One of the other men pointed to his empty cup.

She nodded. "And more coffee."

Henry picked up the plate of biscuits, helped himself, and then passed them to the man seated beside him. "That kind of limits things, Levi. So what did you have in mind?"

"Last night I had an idea that some of the men might enjoy drawing or painting pictures. Noah once had an interest in art, and I brought some supplies from home. If anyone wants to join Noah, I'd be willing to help." Levi heaped a spoonful of potatoes onto his plate. "I couldn't be there during the week, but maybe on Sunday afternoons I could hold a class and someone else could help them during the week."

"I don't know about holding a class. Most of the patients don't sit and listen for long." He took a bite of biscuit. "You know how to paint pictures?"

"I've painted some pictures, mostly landscapes. I know enough to get the men started. If they have an interest in art, maybe I can help with some other projects, too."

One of the men at the end of the table shook his head. "Never would have thought a fella from the tile works would know how to draw pictures."

Maybe one day Miss McKay would become interested in his ideas, and then the men at the boardinghouse would see how art could be used in making tiles. But this wasn't the time to talk about his ambitions. Instead, he needed to try and gain approval to hold a few art classes at the asylum. At a minimum, he wanted permission to take art supplies to his brother.

Levi turned his attention back to Henry. "Who should I talk to about my idea? Do I need to go to the administration building or talk to one of the doctors?"

Henry pushed the last bite of his biscuit through the remaining gravy on his plate. "I'll ask one of the doctors assigned to that wing who would know your brother. That's probably the best place to start. If the doc says you'd need to get permission from higher up, I'll see who you should talk to in administration. Will that help?"

Levi grinned. "You bet. I appreciate it. Otherwise, I'd have to wait until Sunday, and there's no one in the administration building then."

One of the men snorted. "Not many doctors around on Sundays, either. They depend on us to run things so they can enjoy time at home." He nodded toward the clock. "We better get out the door or the driver will be complaining."

The men who worked at the asylum took the cue, and soon their chairs scraped across the wooden floor. When he rounded the table, Henry gave Levi a light slap on the shoulder. "I'll do my best to have some answers for you this evening."

Levi nodded and lifted the napkin from his lap. He'd like to believe talking to Miss McKay about new designs would go as easily as this morning's discussion with Henry, but he doubted that would happen. Besides, he needed to wait until he'd been at the tile works a while longer. The men hadn't been particularly welcoming, but they'd become more friendly of late. He didn't want to do anything that might change their mood. As for Miss McKay, it was difficult to know exactly what she thought about him or the tile works. From what he'd observed thus far, she was excited to gain new orders, but that was the extent of her enthusiasm for the business. She performed her work, but clearly she didn't feel passionate about it. He prayed that would soon change.

Chapter 10

Levi entered the wrought-iron gate of the asylum and walked down the center footpath leading to the administration building. Created from hand-cut blue sandstone in the Gothic style, the structure possessed a formidable beauty. A fountain was to the left of the walkway near the entrance of the main building, and the long spire above the central clock tower rose so high it appeared to touch the clouds that hung over the valley.

The four-story asylum was touted as one of the finest available for patients suffering from mental disorders, but Levi soon learned the patients had been placed in the asylum by their family members for a variety of reasons. The men at the boardinghouse who worked at the asylum claimed there were patients who'd been diagnosed with everything from laziness and grief to cerebral softening and snake bites. With so many patients still capable of performing daily tasks, Levi hoped a few of them would be interested in an art class.

Though it had taken longer to arrange a meeting than he would have preferred, Levi had finally met with a committee that consisted of several doctors and an assistant administrator.

After a brief discussion, Levi was granted permission to oversee art lessons for male patients on Sunday afternoons. There were fewer employees at the asylum on Sundays, so the committee likely would have approved any conventional activity that didn't require assistance from the asylum aides. Levi didn't care why he'd received their approval; he was simply thankful for the opportunity to see if the idea might help Noah and possibly some of the other men.

At the fountain, he took the pathway that veered left and led to the west wing. His excitement mounted when he entered the room designated for activities and spotted Noah and four other men awaiting his arrival. The administrator had explained that all those enrolled in the class had been approved by their doctors as being calm and willing to follow instructions. Even so, Levi had hoped a staff member might be present for at least a portion of the first lesson, but there was no one in sight.

He greeted his brother and then introduced himself to the other men. They all appeared eager and gathered close while he withdrew watercolors, brushes, charcoals, and thick sheets of paper from a canvas case.

"Why don't we move the table and chairs a little closer to the windows so there will be more light?" The men did as Levi asked and then sat down. "Does anyone want to draw rather than paint?"

One of the men nodded and another raised his hand into the air. A third shrugged his shoulders and met Levi's gaze. "I ain't never drawed or painted no pictures, so I don't know what I should use."

Levi suggested he begin with pencils. Noah and one other man selected watercolors. During their time together, Levi assisted and made suggestions when asked, but he wanted to see what each of the men would draw without his prompting. By the end of the two-hour class time, none of the men had a desire to return to their rooms, but Levi didn't want to break any rules that might cause the classes to be cancelled. He'd praised their work before placing the drawings in a small cabinet that had been allocated for their use. Except for Noah's painting, only one of the other patients had revealed any artistic talent. But who could say after only two hours? With instruction and time, the abilities of the other men could advance, but that wasn't his primary goal. His brother had appeared calm and happy during their time together, and that brought Levi the satisfaction he desired.

A surge of happiness swelled in Levi's chest as he walked down the long walkway leading out of the asylum. Once outside the wrought-iron gate, he turned and lifted the hasp to settle it back into place.

"Mr. Judson?"

Levi swung around and was met by Miss McKay's inquiring blue eyes. Her gaze shifted to the asylum and then back. "I didn't know the asylum grounds were open to the public." The brim of her hat shaded her face when she took a step toward the gate. "If it weren't for the asylum, I would think I'd arrived at a lovely park."

"If it weren't for the asylum, those lovely grounds would still be a rolling hillside of uncultivated land."

"I suppose you're right. Do you come here often?"

Had someone told her about Noah, or was this simply coincidence? "I do. Every Sunday afternoon and occasionally in the evening."

"Truly? Have you ever been inside the building? I find it strangely beautiful, yet I wonder about the misery contained inside those walls."

"I've been inside and it isn't as miserable as you seem to

believe." He tipped his cap. "Nice to see you, Miss McKay. I won't disturb your walk. I'm returning to the boardinghouse."

She hurried to match his stride. "I was returning home as well. It's such a lovely day, I walked farther than I'd planned."

He shifted the canvas bag to his other hand. "You walked all the way here from the boardinghouse?"

"No. Some of the ladies arranged for a carriage to take them for a ride. I joined them but left the carriage and decided to walk once we were close to town. I had hoped they would pass on their way back to the boardinghouse, but so far there's been no sign of them."

"Unless you walk at a faster pace, you may miss your supper, Miss McKay."

"I could say the same about you, unless there's food in that bag you're carrying."

He shook his head. "There's no food in my bag, but I won't be going without supper. I'm walking only as far as the livery, where I've already arranged for a hack to take me home."

"Excellent. I'll join you and pay half the cost." She grinned, obviously pleased her problem had been solved. "If that isn't food in your bag, what is it?" When he didn't immediately answer, she realized her mistake. "I'm sorry—that was rude of me."

"Art supplies."

"Art supplies? For drawing and such? Do you go to the asylum grounds to gather ideas for your drawings?"

He sighed. Never before had he heard Miss McKay talk so much. And why did her conversation have to be filled with questions?

"Yes, I have supplies for drawing and painting in the bag, but I don't go to the asylum for ideas. I go there to visit my brother, who is a patient." He stared straight ahead but heard her gasp.

"Noah, my brother, is a talented artist. The asylum has given me permission to take charge of art classes on Sunday afternoons."

Her eyes opened so wide they resembled Mrs. Brighton's dinner plates. "With the patients? You go in and spend time with patients you don't know? Have any of them ever attempted to harm you?"

"Today was the first lesson, but I've been in the asylum many times before, and no one has ever done anything that caused me fear. I believe the more violent patients are in another part of the asylum. The men I'm with are more like my brother, sad and depressed, unable to feel happiness in their lives. I hope they'll find pleasure in painting. I'd like to think art will do more for them, but I don't know what heals a person who is plagued by problems that affect the mind. Even the doctors seem uncertain."

"I admire you for trying to help. It's easy to slip into depression when you feel as though you've lost control of your circumstances." Ainslee touched her fingers to her waist. "You feel a hollow place of despair deep inside."

Miss McKay was a puzzle. At work she exhibited an assured presence, yet he'd heard the dejection and sadness in her voice. She'd pulled at his heartstrings, and he wanted to help her—to somehow fit the pieces of her puzzle together and see a glimmer of happiness in her eyes.

"You sound like someone who has fought that battle of despair, yet I'm sure that can't be true. I see a young woman who is in charge of her future—a young lady moving through life without fear. There are few women who would ever consider taking charge of a tile works." He grinned. "Perhaps a millinery or dress shop, but not a tile works."

"I never had a desire to be in charge of anything other than a classroom of children. Owning the tile works was never my dream."

She accepted his arm as they crossed the street and waited outside the livery while he went inside to see about the carriage. He returned quickly. "There will be a short wait. The carriage driver didn't think I'd be here this early, and he took another fare." He gestured to a wooden bench. "I think this is the best I can offer."

"The bench is fine." A light breeze tugged at her bonnet as she pulled her skirts aside and sat down. She patted the space beside her. "There's plenty of room for both of us. No need to stand."

He was careful to sit as far from her as the short bench would permit. Even though she'd invited him to sit beside her, he didn't want to appear forward. "Tell me more about the dream of owning the tile works. If you didn't want to own it, who did? Your brother?"

Several of the men at the tile works had mentioned meeting Ewan McKay. Most had hoped he would be the one to take charge and manage the business.

"No. It was my twin sister Adaira's dream."

Levi remained silent and attentive as he listened to Ainslee tell of Adaira's desire to use her artistic talents at the tile works, but how she'd eloped and was likely now in Paris.

"I can see how frightening it must have been for you to keep your commitment and come here by yourself." He wanted to encourage her, for she seemed to be doing a good job managing the company. "Even though you were plunged into deep water, you didn't sink. You should be happy. I'm sure your family is proud of you."

She sighed heavily. "What would make my brother truly proud is if I would agree to make the business my life's work, but this isn't what I want."

"So you want to leave? What about the tile works?"

She gasped and placed her hand over her lips. "I'm talking too much. Please disregard what you've heard."

He nodded his agreement, but he couldn't forget what she'd said. And oddly, he found himself caring about helping to ensure Miss McKay's happiness.

Ainslee leaned forward and glanced down the street. Where was the carriage? Her thoughts raced. She needed to say something that would remove her earlier comments from Mr. Judson's mind. Why had she said so much to him? Never before had she so willingly confided in a stranger. Yet he hadn't felt like a stranger. Talking with him seemed more like visiting with an old friend—like chatting with Adaira. She silently scolded herself. He wasn't Adaira, and there was no way to know if he'd keep his word.

He followed her gaze down the street before turning back toward her. "I don't think the carriage will be here for a while longer. I can see the concern in your eyes, but there's no need for you to worry. I give you my word that anything you say to me will remain between us. I hope you will do the same."

"Yes, of course. I won't repeat a word you've told me." She had much more to lose if he betrayed her. If he told the men at the tile works she was unhappy and wanted to leave Weston, any number of problems could arise.

He leaned back and rested his shoulders against the rough gray planks of the livery. "I understand feeling obligated to leave your home when you want to stay put, but I'm not going to let it keep me from my dreams, and you shouldn't either."

She weighed his words. So he hadn't wanted to leave Philadelphia. When he'd come looking for work, she'd asked him why he left his job in Philadelphia. Now she understood. He'd come here because of his brother. He hadn't been forced, but a sense of duty and love caused him to move here. Her respect for him grew tenfold.

"And how would you suggest I keep my dream alive when I'm here and the school where I taught is in Grafton?"

"If it's teaching you love, why not do something that brings you that same satisfaction right here in Weston?"

What was he thinking? "How could I ever teach when I need to be at the tile works every day?"

He rubbed his forehead. "Maybe you could teach some sort of classes to women in the asylum. I could go with you and meet with the doctors. Maybe they could suggest some way your teaching skills could help. What do you think?"

She swallowed hard. "I-I-I'm not sure I could teach adults. I've taught only children. Some of the boys were older, but they hadn't had much schooling. I don't imagine ladies in the asylum want to take classes in arithmetic or spelling."

"Maybe not, but they might be interested in geography and learning more about places they've never been, or reading books they've never had an opportunity to enjoy." He pushed his cap back on his head. "It was just an idea, not something you have to do. I hope I'll be able to help not only my brother, but also some of the other men who take the classes."

"And do you think that takes away the pain of leaving your work and fiancée in Philadelphia?" She hadn't planned to ask about his intended bride, but curiosity won out.

She wasn't sure if she'd angered or surprised him. His lips tightened, and he stared at his shoes for what seemed an eternity before he finally lifted his head. "I won't say that making simple floor tiles gives me pleasure, but I'm holding on to my dream that one day I'll still be able to create the beautiful tiles I've designed. I don't have to live in Philadelphia to make my tiles any more than you must live in Grafton to teach. I'm sure the Lord will open a door for each of us when the time is right."

She edged forward on the bench. "Have you ever considered the possibility of owning your own tile works? If you were an owner, you could produce whatever you wanted."

Levi chuckled and shook his head. "I don't think I'm going to be the answer you're seeking in order to escape the tile works, Miss McKay. There's no way I could afford to buy a tile works—or any other business for that matter." He nodded toward the asylum. "Most of what I've earned has been used trying to find help for my brother, but I've made peace with my situation. Isn't that what the Apostle Paul did? I hope you'll be able to do that, too."

His words pierced her. Was that what she needed to do? Make peace with her situation? Ewan said she needed to release her anger and forgive Adaira. She'd done her best and believed she'd forgiven her sister, but did she need to do even more? Levi made it sound as though she needed to go beyond forgiveness, accept what had happened, and seek happiness and fulfillment in order to find true peace. Was that even possible? If so, she would need God's help.

The hack appeared down the street and soon rolled to a stop near the bench. After Levi assisted her into the carriage, she settled against the worn leather cushion. Thoughts tumbled through her mind all the way to the boardinghouse. Just as they arrived she was struck with an idea. She couldn't change her situation, but maybe she could change things for Levi.

Chapter 11

On Monday morning, Ainslee arrived at the tile works with an enthusiasm she hadn't experienced since her days teaching at the pottery school. Levi had been correct. She needed to embrace her new life. While she still didn't plan to permanently remain in Weston, she was now determined to stretch her knowledge and become more involved in the tile works.

After completing a portion of her bookkeeping entries, Ainslee strode across the courtyard. Several men were busy beneath the covered walkway, packing crates and barrels. Amazement shone in the workers' eyes when they caught sight of her. They nodded in recognition, but their initial surprise was soon replaced with looks of apprehension. Since she seldom left the office, her unexpected appearance was likely the cause of their concern. She smiled and offered them a cheery greeting, but it didn't lessen their uneasiness. They stole wary looks at one another, and she felt the tension rise as she passed by and entered the building.

She chided herself for having kept to the office all the time. If she'd demonstrated more of a presence since her arrival, the men wouldn't now be worried to see her appear in the workrooms. As Ainslee continued along the interior walkway, she decided regular morning visits to each of the work areas would be in order. Today she was intent upon a visit to the cutting room, where she could talk to Levi.

When she stepped inside the mixing room, Ainslee greeted the men operating the mixers. Perhaps if she told them of her recent decision to make daily visits, they would pass along her pronouncement during their lunch break. She stopped beside Robert and told him of her plan. He frowned, and Ainslee caught her lower lip between her teeth to stifle a laugh. His wrinkled features were a match for the neighbor's pet bulldog in Grafton.

"Has something happened that makes you think we're not doing our jobs?" Robert turned away and poured water into the mixer.

Ainslee sighed. Why did he immediately want to link her presence with something negative? "Quite the contrary, Robert. I think you men are performing well. We're meeting our orders on time, and there have been no complaints from customers."

Robert gave a firm nod. "That's good to hear." The lines in his brow once again formed. "Seems you'd have plenty to do in the office. Mrs. Ploughman said she had trouble keeping up with all the timecards, contracts, and such."

Robert looked at Harold in obvious expectation, but Harold merely shrugged. "Maybe Miss McKay can work numbers quicker than Mrs. Ploughman."

Ainslee chuckled. "I doubt my abilities are greater than those of Mrs. Ploughman. However, I want to visit the work areas more often so I can expand my knowledge of the products we offer for sale. My brother has learned a great deal regarding the production of both bricks and pottery because he not only worked in the office but also visited with the workmen and became aware of what would help them produce a better product. I hope to do the same."

Robert blew out a long breath. "We been making the same tiles for years, but I guess if you want to see if you can improve things, that's up to you. This is your business, but I don't see how changing things is going to help."

This wasn't going at all as she'd planned. She should have expected some of the men would resist having a woman in the workrooms—especially the ones who'd been there for years. While they'd come to accept her presence in the office, her visits to the work areas would be another matter.

She needed to assure them she wasn't there to change things or spy on them. "I don't plan to change anything regarding our current tile production, Robert. Even if we added something new, the flooring tiles would remain our most important product."

He didn't appear completely convinced, but she didn't plan to back down. She crossed to the far side of the room and stood a short distance from where Levi was operating the cutting machine. He had inserted the blades that would cut the clay into the small tiles known as Cluny quarries.

Levi looked up as he lifted the cutting arm. "Good morning." The same concern she'd seen in the eyes of the other workers appeared in Levi's eyes. "Is there a problem?"

She smiled and shook her head. "It seems my appearance in the work areas is causing a great deal of alarm."

He chuckled. "We're all accustomed to seeing you only in the office. This is the first time I've seen you in the cutting room since I began work here."

"I took a tour when I first arrived. Until today, that and the day I introduced you were my only times inside this portion of the building." She squared her shoulders. "I've taken your advice and plan to learn more about the tile-making process. I thought I'd begin by learning to cut tiles."

He frowned and shook his head. "Using any of the equipment isn't for a lady. It would be far too dangerous. You don't need to use the tools in order to learn about making tiles. Observation is all that's necessary."

She shook her head. "Watching you doesn't let me experience how difficult it is for the blades to cut through the clay or feel the weight or strength needed to use the equipment. I think I can learn a great deal if I try to use the cutter and forms."

"That may be true, but I don't see how that's going to help you understand more about the business. I think you'd learn much more by observing and asking questions. I know you are my employer, but I won't supervise your use of the machine."

She didn't argue, but if he thought she wasn't going to try using the cutting tool, he didn't know her very well.

"Did you have some question I can answer about my work in the cutting room?"

"I know how many tiles can be cut in a day and the various sizes. I also know you exceed the quota. I have to be acquainted with that information for the contracts. I've seen the forms and other equipment." She hesitated a moment. "Maybe you should tell me about the ideas you have for making decorative tiles."

He'd mentioned the fact that he had some new ideas; perhaps now was the time for her to hear about them. When the McKays had first taken over, she'd mentioned the idea of decorative tiles to Ewan—mostly because she thought it might make the tile works more sought after by potential buyers. Since her primary desire had been to sell the tile works, he'd dismissed the idea, stating costs and risk as his defense. She hadn't argued, but if Levi could prove Ewan's assessment wrong, perhaps her brother could be convinced.

He gave her a sidelong glance as he picked up a slab of clay. "If you think there is an opportunity to try some of my new methods for decorative tiles here, I would be pleased to share them with you, but we'd need time so that I could show you the process that interests me the most." The excitement in his voice mounted. "I have some drawings at the boardinghouse if you'd like to see them."

"Wonderful. If I find your ideas promising, we can speak to my brother when he visits next. I can't promise he'll be open to the idea, but I know he'll at least listen."

When the bell clanged to signal the lunch break, Ainslee gestured to the door. "I don't want to keep you from your lunch. We can discuss this more when I can look at your drawings."

His enthusiastic grin was contagious. "I could also explain the process for some of the decorative tiles already being produced in a few other tile works. I think we could create some unique designs, and I have ideas for glazes that aren't being used anywhere else."

She returned his grin with a smile of her own. "I look forward to hearing about them. I think expanding our products could prove beneficial."

He stooped down and picked up his lunch pail. He turned for the door, then hesitated and glanced over his shoulder. "It's time for lunch. Are you going to eat?"

She moved a short distance from the equipment. "Yes, but I'm going to look around a bit more."

Careful to wait until she was certain Levi had joined the other men in the courtyard, Ainslee turned to the sharp-bladed piece of equipment. A thick piece of wood held twelve sharp blades spaced at equal distance. When plunged into the clay, it would cut the large rectangles referred to as cut blanks. A groan escaped her lips as she hoisted a slab of the heavy clay onto the cutting bed. Levi had cut these same rectangles only a few minutes ago, and she'd carefully observed how he'd completed the procedure.

Certain she could maneuver the blades, she stepped to the side and released the latch with her left hand. The blades descended with a mighty thrust and sliced through the clay with precision.

A primal scream echoed throughout the cavernous building. A searing pain shot through the side of her right hand as blood gushed from the wound and spilled onto the floor and across the clay. Within moments, Levi, Harold, and Robert were rushing into the cutting room. She stared into Levi's horrified eyes for only a moment before her body betrayed her and she slumped to the floor.

Voices murmured around her, and Ainslee willed her eyes to open. Blurred figures hovered over her. A stinging ache pulsed along the side of her hand. She tried to lift her arm, but failed.

"Ainslee, can you hear me? It's Levi and Dr. Thorenson. You injured your hand and the doctor has stitched it."

Her futile attempt to use the cutting blades now zigzagged through her hazy thoughts. Visions of her blood dripping across the tiles caused her to shiver.

"Are you cold? Do you need a blanket?" Levi leaned closer, and his features gradually came into focus. "Is there a great deal of pain?"

"I'm not cold, but my hand hurts." She turned her head and opened her eyes wide. "Where am I?"

"At the asylum. Both of the doctors in Weston were away from their offices, and there was no time to waste, so I brought you here. Dr. Thorenson was kind enough to care for you."

"Thank you, but I think I should go back to the boarding-house." Her thoughts still remained jumbled, but they had become clear enough for her to realize she didn't want to spend the night in the asylum.

Dr. Thorenson pulled a chair close to the bed. "You aren't in any danger here, Miss McKay. This is a room in the administrative section of the asylum that is used when a staff member is injured or ill. The patients have no access to this portion of the building. There is a doctor on duty all night, and I think it would be wise for you to remain. You lost a great deal of blood."

Shifting on the asylum bed, she looked at Levi. "You said I only needed stitches. That isn't serious. I'm fine. See?" She followed her question with an attempt to sit up, but dizziness overtook her and she fell back against the pillow.

"The doctor's right, Ainslee. You need to stay here, at least until tomorrow." Concern tinged his voice.

Had he called her Ainslee rather than Miss McKay? She remained a little fuzzy, but she was sure she'd heard him correctly. The thought warmed her heart. He may have a fiancée in Philadelphia, but there was nothing to prohibit them from becoming dear friends. "If you think it's absolutely necessary, I'll stay, but I believe I'd do well at home."

Relief shone in his eyes. "I think it's best you remain in the asylum. Thank you for not arguing any further. Since you are here, maybe you could speak with Dr. Thorenson about a project for the ladies in the women's wing." Levi turned to look at the doctor. "Miss McKay was a teacher before she took over management of the tile works, and she misses her previous work. I suggested she might find a way to put her skills to use here at the asylum."

Dr. Thorenson cupped his chin between his thumb and index finger. "What a wonderful idea. Your art classes have proved helpful to the men, and I believe some of the women would enjoy that same opportunity."

Ainslee held up her bandaged hand, but a shooting pain caused her to immediately lower her arm. "No, you misunderstood Mr. Judson. I can't teach art. While I might be able to sketch a tree or flower, my skill is teaching fundamental education."

Dr. Thorenson nodded. "Ah, like English, geography, arithmetic, and such. Have you ever worked with adult students, Miss McKay?" When she attempted to push herself higher in the bed, pain assailed her and she winced. The doctor wagged his finger. "You are in pain. I'm going to give you something to help you sleep. We will talk more in the morning, when you aren't in as much pain."

Ainslee forced a weak smile. Something to relieve the pain and help her sleep was exactly what she needed. The doctor left the room with a promise he'd return with the medicine in short order.

Levi moved close to her bedside. "I suppose I should go. I'll likely be in trouble with both Miss Hanson and Mrs. Brighton since I've missed supper without giving proper notice."

"I didn't realize it was so late." She looked toward the window and glimpsed the evening shadows that now shaded the asylum grounds.

Muddled remembrances of the accident suddenly flashed through her mind. She'd decided to take matters into her own hands and look at the result. Tears gathered in her eyes and she turned her head—she didn't deserve pity from anyone, especially Levi. He'd told her it could be dangerous and using the equipment wouldn't provide her with necessary knowledge to manage the business. He'd been right.

She swallowed the lump in her throat and forced a smile.

"Please tell Mrs. Brighton and Miss Hanson that I take full responsibility for your tardy arrival, and that I would count it a personal favor if they would forgive you and warm your supper."

Levi chuckled. "They may forgive me, but I don't think I'll find my plate in the warming oven." He patted his stomach. "Missing one meal won't hurt me. Besides, helping you was far more important than suffering the possible wrath of Mrs. Brighton or Miss Hanson."

"Thank you." His kindness touched her. Not once had he scolded or berated her for her foolish behavior.

The doctor returned with her medicine. She wrinkled her nose as she swallowed the bitter concoction. "I know it doesn't taste good, but you'll be grateful for the relief it will bring you." He turned to Levi. "I'm glad you haven't left for home just yet. Shall I arrange for a carriage to return Miss McKay to the boardinghouse tomorrow?"

Levi shook his head. "I can come by with a carriage after work."

The medicine was beginning to take effect, but Ainslee's thoughts were still clear enough to offer a protest against remaining at the asylum all day. "I'd rather leave earlier." The pleasure in Levi's eyes was immediately replaced by a look of disappointment. "If it won't disrupt your work too much, perhaps you could arrange to come by during your lunch break. Tell Robert that I've asked for your help. I should be well enough to return to the office, shouldn't I, Doctor?"

The doctor looked skeptical. "I would think so, but it might be good to go home and rest the remainder of the day. We can decide tomorrow."

Ainslee's eyelids drooped, and she struggled to force them open. In the distance she heard someone tell her to sleep. She obliged.

Chapter 12

Ainslee slowly opened her eyes and blinked against the sunlight streaming through the window across the room. She lifted her right hand to shield her eyes from the sun. A dull ache reminded her of yesterday's events, and she cringed as she recalled her foolishness.

An asylum attendant wearing a crisp shirtwaist entered the room with a purposeful step. She balanced a breakfast tray in one hand and a piece of paper in the other. Her hair was twisted into a snug knot at the nape of her neck and was giving way to gray. Her lips formed a tight line, and deep creases etched the soft, fleshy skin around her eyes.

She gave a cursory nod before setting the tray on a bedside table. "Good morning, Miss McKay. I have your breakfast and medical notes from Dr. Thorenson. He'll be in to visit with you later this morning."

"Thank you." Ainslee stretched her neck to see if the pin on the woman's bodice would reveal her name, but it bore only the name of the institution. "Have you worked here long?"

The attendant placed the notes on the foot of Ainslee's bed. "Since the asylum opened. Is there anything else you need?"

"No." Ainslee shook her head and refrained from further questions. The woman seemed as friendly as a poisonous snake, and she might be every bit as dangerous. A peek under the silver dome revealed scrambled eggs, sausage, a large biscuit, fried potatoes, and a bowl of oatmeal. A small pot of coffee sat off to one side of the tray, along with a linen napkin and silverware. She wondered if this was the daily fare for the patients. If so, they must have hearty appetites, for she doubted whether she could eat half of what she'd been served. She picked up the paper from the foot of her bed and settled into a chair that the attendant had placed near the bedside table. If she balanced them properly, she could possibly eat and read at the same time.

Attempts at using a fork with her left hand proved to be a brutal awakening. If she could barely manage to get food to her mouth, how was she going to complete her duties at the tile works?

Eating only a small portion exhausted her. She pushed away the tray and looked at the note from Dr. Thorenson. Beneath the medical notes, he'd written instructions that she should rest and return to him or another doctor of her choosing for continued treatment of her wound. Dropping the paper onto the bed, she walked to the door, hoping to catch a glimpse of the doctor, but he was nowhere in sight. If he would remove the large bandage that had rendered her right hand immobile, she might be able to function at work.

She paced the length of the room for what seemed an eternity. At the sound of heavy footfalls on the tile floor, she rushed toward the door. She prayed it would be the doctor and not the cranky attendant who'd delivered her food.

"Good morning, Miss McKay. How are you feeling this morning? I trust you enjoyed your breakfast." Dr. Thorenson lifted the dome and shook his head. "You didn't eat much. Is your stomach upset? Sometimes medicine can cause indigestion. How's the hand?"

Ainslee didn't know which question to answer first, so she decided to begin with her hand. After all, that was the most important in his list of questions. "My hand aches a little, but I'm sure it's much better. I thought if you could remove all of this bandaging, I could perform my work with greater ease. I do a great deal of writing, and this bulky dressing is in the way."

"I understand the problem created by the dressing, but if the hand is to heal properly, you need to keep it bandaged for a week and then we will see how it is doing. Your injury was more than a mere cut. The blade cut deep, and I worry there may be damage to the fibers and nerves in your hand. Only time will tell."

Ainslee stared at the bandage. One swift, reckless decision could cause her to suffer a lifetime of regret. "Are you saying I could lose partial use of my hand?"

"I am. As I said, much depends upon whether the nerves were severed. You are quite fortunate that you didn't lose several fingers or your entire hand. I think you have much to be thankful for, Miss McKay." A somberness darkened his eyes. "I trust you will refrain from further attempts to use any equipment at the tile works—or anywhere else, for that matter."

"You may set your mind at rest, Doctor. I've learned my lesson. I'll follow your orders."

"I hope that means you'll follow all of my orders and stay home for at least the rest of today. I think you're going to find that your hand is going to cause you greater pain than you expect. Frankly, there may be some residual pain for the rest of your life."

Ainslee flinched. Dr. Thorenson certainly hadn't worried about sweetening his medical opinion, but she did appreciate his honesty. "You'll learn that I can be quite determined when necessary, so I'll do whatever I need to do in order to achieve a good recovery."

The doctor sat down in a chair near the window. "It pleases me to hear you say that, but sometimes even our best efforts aren't enough. Deep wounds can remain for a lifetime; the real achievement is learning to live a full life even when scars remain."

The doctor's tone was subdued, and Ainslee wasn't certain if he was referring to the cut on her hand or to a deeper wound he carried inside. Silence hung over the room until the sound of footsteps in the hallway captured the doctor's attention. He looked up and greeted the attendant who'd delivered Ainslee's breakfast.

The woman bid the doctor good morning, then looked at Ainslee while gesturing toward the breakfast tray. "You done with your breakfast? I need to get it back over to the women's wing." Without waiting for an answer, the attendant crossed the room and picked up the tray.

The doctor shifted in his chair and craned his neck toward the older woman. "Miss Mardel, have you met Miss McKay? Her family owns the tile works here in town."

Miss Mardel grunted and gave a nod. "I brought her tray to her earlier this morning."

The woman's curt response appeared to have little effect on the doctor. "Miss McKay was a teacher before coming to Weston, and she's expressed interest in providing some form of extra classes for the women. Perhaps something similar to the classes Noah Judson's brother oversees in the men's wing."

"Art classes?" Miss Mardel placed the tray on the foot of the bed.

Ainslee shook her head. "No. I don't paint or draw. I was

thinking something more general. Geography or arithmetic, something of that nature."

The older woman curled her lip. "Don't think you'd get much interest from the ladies with that kind of offer, but some of the patients who still have some brains rattling around inside their heads think we should have a library." Miss Mardel chuckled. "Imagine that—they think we should feed 'em three meals a day, furnish 'em clean linens, wash their clothes, provide 'em with medical treatment, and they expect a library, too. I say they should be thankful they're living in a day when they got this fine asylum instead of a cage in a jail."

Ainslee shivered at the callous remarks. Granted, the asylum was a beautiful facility, but the patients weren't free to come and go at will. Surely having books to read wasn't such a major request. "Maybe I could help start a library for the ladies."

The older woman snorted. "Exactly how you planning to do that? You need lots of books to fill a library."

The doctor frowned. "I believe Miss McKay knows that libraries require books, Miss Mardel."

The older woman stiffened at the doctor's retort, and her cheeks flamed bright red. Until she turned, Ainslee wasn't certain whether Miss Mardel had been seized by embarrassment or anger, but one look at her eyes told the story. She was furious—not at Dr. Thorenson, but at Ainslee.

"I wasn't questioning her knowledge of libraries, only how she would obtain enough books to fill a library." Miss Mardel spoke through clenched teeth and held her arms tight to her sides.

Truth be told, when Ainslee blurted out her offer, she hadn't given the slightest thought as to where she'd locate enough books to fill a library or how she'd manage such a feat. She'd made her offer as a defense to the patients' request—an attempt to prove that their wish for a library wasn't foolish. She hadn't planned to make an enemy of Miss Mardel, especially since she worked in the women's wing.

Her stomach churned, but Ainslee forced a broad smile. "I didn't take any offense at your remark, Miss Mardel. Your question about where I would locate books is sound. I can't set out a specific plan for gathering books at this moment, but I believe there are people in the community who would be willing to donate some of their books and we might even consider a fundraiser of some sort. Perhaps I could look to you for advice and assistance."

Miss Mardel directed a triumphant look at the doctor. Her shoulders relaxed as she turned toward Ainslee. "I believe I could spare a little time to help. Some of the patients' families might even be willing to donate books."

The knot in Ainslee's stomach eased. "I would be delighted to have your help, Miss Mardel. I'm sure the asylum administration will need to approve any project, but if they do, please know that I'll look forward to your assistance."

Miss Mardel beamed as she picked up the breakfast tray from the foot of the bed. "I work during the days, so I could be present for any meetings you schedule with the administration."

"That's good to know. Thank you, again, Miss Mardel. It's been a pleasure to meet you."

With her smile still intact, the older woman departed the room.

The doctor grinned at Ainslee. "You handled that with expert aplomb. I apologize, for I fear it was my remark that caused Miss Mardel's defensive behavior."

"I'm not sure I managed matters well at all. I have no idea if I'll be able to succeed with such a large project. Setting up a library wasn't at all what I had in mind when I volunteered to provide classes to some of the ladies."

"You need not make the library your only focus. The ladies who would be included in your group are alert and capable. Most are suffering from various sorts of depression or grief. Having a project to occupy their minds will be helpful. They may find greater joy in helping form a library rather than simply being furnished with books to read."

Excitement seized her as she listened to the doctor. "That's true. They could help write letters to various businesses and see if they would donate money or books for the cause. If I set my mind to it, I'm sure I can come up with many business establishments and friends who will help." She glanced at her bandaged hand. "Until my bandage is removed, I'm afraid I'll have to rely upon the ladies to complete the letter writing. How many do you think could assist me?"

"I believe there are at least thirty women who possess the mental stability to assist you, but I'm not certain how many read and write. We need to gather that information from the patients' records, but I think you could count on around thirty who would possess the ability and desire to be included in the project. And don't forget Miss Mardel. I'm sure she'll help. In addition, she'll likely stop every visitor who comes into the women's wing and request a book or donation." He chuckled. "With that stern look of hers, I believe most folks will be quick to comply."

"I think you're right on that account." She placed the fingers of her left hand atop the bandage. "You mentioned further visits for the care of my hand. You've caused me to wonder if the injury is serious enough that I should contact my brother and seek his opinion regarding any additional treatment."

"As I said, your injury is more serious than a simple cut, but I believe the treatment you receive here in Weston will be as good as any you would receive anywhere else. However, another doctor's opinion is never a bad thing. Whether you seek the advice of your family members is your decision, but you'll need to disclose what happened at some point. Unless you intend to wear gloves the rest of your life, you won't be able to hide the scar from them." The doctor stood. "I have several patients I need to see. I'll talk to the administrator about your ideas for obtaining books and a possible library. I can send word with Levi when he comes to give his art lesson."

"Thank you."

She gave little attention to his comments regarding the library. Right now her thoughts remained engrossed on her foolish behavior and the need to tell her family. If she sent a telegram to Ewan, he'd likely be on the next train; he might even take over the tile works and insist she return home. A week or two ago, she would have jumped at that idea, but now it didn't appeal. She wanted to hear more about Levi's ideas, she wanted to see if she could assist the hospitalized women in some small way, and she wanted the tile works to succeed.

What had caused her change of heart? Was it the accident or something else?

The clock in the asylum bell tower struck twelve as Levi approached Ainslee's room. He'd arrived early, partly to surprise her, partly because he was worried, and partly because he knew if he waited until the regular lunch break, some of the men would make jokes about him going to fetch the boss. He'd let Robert or Harold explain where he'd gone should the other workers inquire about his whereabouts.

Mrs. Brighton had been far too worried about Ainslee to chide him about his tardy return home last night. She'd learned of the accident when one of the men from the tile works stopped on his way home. When Levi arrived, she'd quickly produced a warm plate of food and plied him with questions. She'd been aghast to learn that he'd taken Ainslee to the asylum, and even more upset to learn he'd left her there for the night.

He'd done his best to assure Mrs. Brighton that Ainslee was in good hands and would come to no harm, but the boardinghouse owner had remained unconvinced. After listening to her for far too long, Levi had begun to question his decision. Perhaps he should have brought Ainslee home and placed her under Mrs. Brighton's care. When he'd finally gone to bed, he'd been unable to sleep. All night he'd tossed and turned, worried she might come to some harm—and it would be his fault.

Ainslee looked up when he entered and smiled at him. "You're early."

He sighed with relief at the sight of her. She was fine—at least as fine as one could be with a deep cut to her hand. "Did you sleep well? Were you well cared for?"

"Why do you sound so worried? You're the one who convinced me I should stay overnight and assured me I would be fine." She tipped her head to the side and pinned him with a questioning look.

"Yes, but that was before Mrs. Brighton chided me for not bringing you home and allowing her to attend to you. Have you decided whether you want to go to the tile works or to the boardinghouse? She's eager for you to return. I think she plans to coddle you."

"I'm afraid she's going to be sorely disappointed. I'll remain at home for the rest of the day, but I'm returning to work tomorrow."

Levi glanced at the door. "Did the doctor agree?"

"He didn't disagree. My biggest problem will be writing. I'm not sure how I'm going to log the employee work hours or complete the bookkeeping duties when I can't even hold a pen. I suppose I'll need to hire someone to assist with my duties." She sighed. "I won't even be able to write letters to suppliers, submit bids, or respond to inquiries from customers."

"I'd be willing to help you on my lunch break and after work, if you'd like." Levi wasn't sure how much time would be needed, but he wanted to do whatever he could to help—and to make certain she didn't do anything to slow the healing process or further injure her hand, especially since he felt guilty over his role in her accident.

Yes, Levi thought, there was something compelling about Miss McKay. She revealed both determination and curiosity, yet she possessed a vulnerability that he couldn't resist. Volunteering to help might mean extra work, but if it meant being in her presence, it would be worth every minute.

Chapter 13

Ainslee settled beside Levi at the large desk in the tile works office. When she'd accepted his offer to assist her with the paper work, she hadn't expected to need his help for quite so long. Although she'd accepted the fact that she might have a scar on her hand, she hadn't been as quick to accept the amount of time involved with the healing process. She believed her healing was taking far too long, yet Dr. Thorenson had declared she was making excellent progress. They obviously had differing views of progress. She was eager to once again dress without assistance, eat meals without someone cutting her food, and make entries in the work ledgers on her own.

Levi hadn't complained about the many hours he'd been required to spend with her each day, and his handwriting had proved excellent. Though she'd dictated the correspondence and figures, his entries in the ledgers were neat. At the end of each session, he was careful to verify all of the records and calculations for errors. He'd even penned business correspondence with a faultless script. She couldn't have hoped for better support with her duties.

They focused upon the business during most of their time

together, but a friendship had blossomed through the past few weeks of close contact. Each of them had shared more about their personal lives, yet Levi never mentioned the woman he'd left behind. On a couple of occasions, she'd considered asking him, but courage failed her. She didn't want him to think that she was prying, yet she thought it odd he'd disclosed so much about his brother and deceased parents but never mentioned his betrothed. She'd lain awake at night and wondered why it disturbed her that he didn't mention the woman. Was it because she'd been so open and honest when she revealed that she'd never had a suitor, or when she'd bared her soul about Adaira? Or was it because she was jealous? During her wandering nighttime thoughts, she told herself she still wanted to leave Weston, but the thought of departing had become more confusing. There were still things she wanted to accomplish.

Creating a library at the asylum remained a priority, and she wanted to help Levi with his idea to produce mosaic tiles. Those were things she couldn't do if they sold the tile works and she returned to Grafton. But when she weighed those motives against her increasing affection for Levi, she realized he was the chief reason she wanted to remain in Weston. She'd attempted to guard her feelings, but she'd become increasingly fond of him.

"Did you hear me?" Levi lightly touched her hand. "Do we need to complete the payroll this evening since your brother arrives tomorrow?"

Ainslee jerked to attention. "What? Oh, yes, the payroll. I hadn't considered doing it tonight, but that's a good idea. It will give us more time with Ewan. I want him to have ample time to review our ideas about the mosaic tiles."

Levi's jaw tightened. "I'm excited to show him, but I wonder if we should have waited to have him come."

Had she misunderstood what Levi wanted? Even though she'd avoided telling the family about her injury, she'd sent a telegram to Ewan and asked that he visit. She was willing to face Ewan's expected anger over her foolish behavior with the cutting machine because she wanted Levi to have an opportunity to pursue his dream. Now he thought they should have waited?

"Why would it be better to wait? The more time we put off discussions with him, the longer you must wait to begin producing the mosaics."

He wrung his hands together. "You're angry. I can hear it in your voice. Surely you can understand my fears about presenting the project to him. If he says no, my dream will disappear. Can you understand how that feels?"

Her stomach clenched at his question. "Yes, Levi. I realize what it's like to have someone else make a decision that erases your dreams." Recognition shone in his eyes as she answered him. "I recall that you advised me to accept my circumstances when I told you about Adaira and my dreams to continue teaching. Didn't you tell me you were devoted to caring for your brother and that willingness had helped you make peace with your situation?" She met his eyes. "Did that acceptance mean you were willing to give up your dream of living in Philadelphia, but you still held on to your dream of creating the tiles?"

He frowned, and a deafening silence hung between them for several moments. "When I spoke to you, what I said was true. And it still is. I remain dedicated to living here in Weston so I can make certain my brother receives proper care. I'm willing to give up my dream of ever seeing my mosaics created, but I will still be sad if your brother refuses my ideas. If you were suddenly presented with an opportunity to teach while continuing to manage the tile works, would you not do everything in your power to take advantage of that opportunity?"

She nodded her head.

"And if it didn't come to fulfillment, would you be sad?"

Once again, she nodded her head.

"Yet that doesn't mean you haven't made peace with your situation and accepted your circumstances, does it?"

"I suppose not." She smiled. "I very much want Ewan to accept the idea, and I'm going to do everything I can to convince him. I don't want your dream to disappear. At least not this one."

He arched his brows. "What do you mean? How many dreams do you think I have?"

She hadn't planned to mention his pending marriage, but he'd given her the perfect opportunity. "Isn't your marriage a dream? I'm told you're engaged to a young lady in Philadelphia. Do you plan to give up that dream for your brother's well-being, or will she come to Weston after you marry?"

Her questions were personal and abrupt, but she needed to hear about his intended future with another woman. Her increasing fondness for him would surely dissipate when he affirmed his marriage plans.

Instead of the solemn countenance she'd expected, Levi chuckled and his eyes glistened with merriment. What was wrong with him? Did he not consider marriage to be a matter of import?

Ainslee stared at him. "I don't believe the affections of a young woman are a laughing matter."

"You're absolutely correct. A woman's affections should never be taken lightly, and I would never do such a thing. I laughed because there is no young woman waiting for me in Philadelphia or anywhere else."

Ainslee reared back in her chair. "That can't be true. On your first night in Weston, the girls came home from the men's boardinghouse and told me of your engagement. There's no reason to hide the truth from me. A pending marriage will not influence Ewan's decision about the tile project."

"I'm telling you the truth," he insisted. "Fred was the one who told them the engagement story. I suppose I should have spoken up and told the truth right then, but when they advanced onto the front porch like a swarm of buzzing bees, I lost my courage and remained silent."

Ainslee giggled at his response. "I doubt they'd be pleased to hear themselves referred to as a swarm of bees, but I do know they were sorely disappointed to hear of your pending marriage."

She didn't add that she had felt a sense of relief upon hearing the news—pleased that he could be a friend and nothing more—that he wouldn't become a reason for her to feel tied to Weston. So much had changed in such a short time.

"And you? How do you feel after learning I have no marriage plans?"

She gently tapped the fingers of her left hand atop the wooden desk. "I must admit that I'm somewhat concerned that you didn't set the matter aright with the ladies." A momentary pang of guilt stabbed her. Hadn't she hidden the fact that she hoped to sell the tile works? Was that so different from what he'd done? She pushed the thought aside and met his steady gaze. "While I understand your reason, permitting a falsehood to stand as truth isn't an honorable quality and can create doubt when discovered."

"Doubt?" Levi pushed away from the desk. "If what happened has given you reason to mistrust me, I apologize. I consider myself an honest man, but I can see how you might believe otherwise after hearing what I did." He sighed. "I can only tell you that everything I've told you about my work and myself is true." Sorrow clung to his words like a wild vine gripping a tree. "I hope you will believe me."

"Thank you for your apology, Levi. My brother will need to rely upon my opinion about you and your abilities. I wouldn't want to provide him with information that might jeopardize the future of his investment in the tile works."

"I understand, but I hope you know that I would never do anything to place your family's business at risk. It is my hope that what I offer will help the tile works grow, but you must weigh this out and decide if you want to cancel the meeting with your brother."

"Cancelling the meeting hadn't entered my thoughts." Ewan would be arriving tomorrow afternoon, and she wanted him to see and evaluate the possibilities of creating the mosaic tiles. Still, her brother would expect her to be completely forthright when she presented any business proposal. What would give Levi the best chance at winning Ewan's favor?

"What if *you* told Ewan about your mosaics?" She waited for Levi's response.

He inhaled a deep breath and blew it out. "If you think it's best, I'm willing to speak with him."

She smiled and nodded as warmth pooled in her stomach. He was honest, caring, and not betrothed.

Ewan would value Levi's honesty. She knew she certainly did.

The following afternoon, Ainslee arrived at the train station only minutes before Ewan's train pulled in. When she'd dressed for the day, she'd attempted to find some way to hide her bandage, but wearing a cloak in the middle of summer would have been more conspicuous than the bulky cloth that still surrounded her hand.

Instead of waiting on the platform, she remained inside the station with her right arm close to her side. With any luck, the folds of her dress would cover the bandage until after their initial greeting. In retrospect, she realized it would have been better to write and warn Ewan rather than surprise him with her hand looking like a misshapen truncheon. From her position, she could see him looking for her on the platform, but forced herself to remain in place.

After a final look, Ewan strode toward the baggage cart and grabbed his case before heading toward the door. Removing his hat as he entered the station door, his gaze fell on her and he hurried forward and gathered her in an embrace.

The moment he released her, she turned sideways to hide her arm. "Before you say anything, I need to tell you that I have a slight injury to my hand. Please don't be alarmed."

Only then did she turn enough to permit him a view of her arm. He gaped at the bandage, grasped her elbow, and then led her to one of the empty benches. "Did you injure yourself this morning? You should be in bed. How did this happen?" His eyes shone with concern as he looked around the station. "Did you come alone?"

"I'm alone, but you need not be concerned. The injury happened several weeks ago. In fact, the bandage will soon be permanently removed. I'm practically healed."

He leaned back against the hard wood with a thud. "I can't believe this. Tell me what happened and why you didn't let us know."

For the next fifteen minutes, she detailed the events leading up to the accident and her subsequent care at the asylum. "Dr. Thorenson has proved most capable, and when he replaced my bandage earlier in the week, the wound looked good. There will be a scar, but I've learned my lesson."

Ewan withdrew his handkerchief and mopped his perspiring forehead. "I canna believe you would be so foolish." The Irish brogue betrayed how upset he was.

Several people turned in their direction and Ainslee scooted closer. "You don't have to talk so loud. I knew you'd be angry, but all's well that ends well. Don't you agree?"

"Do na try to dismiss what you've done with a smile and an old saying." He tucked his handkerchief back into his pocket and shook his head. "Maybe I did make a mistake leaving you here by yourself."

"No, Ewan. Just because I injured my hand doesn't mean that I can't manage the tile works. All has been going well, and I'm eager for you to meet with an employee about mosaic tiles he's designed. I think they could breathe new life into the business."

He sighed and nodded toward the front door. "Let me get registered at the hotel, and then we'll talk further."

Their ride from the station to the hotel was short, so Ainslee directed the conversation to matters of the family rather than the business. When they arrived at the hotel, she waited in the carriage. Ewan planned to be inside only long enough to register and leave his bags with the clerk, and she needed a few minutes alone to gather her thoughts and regain her composure.

Ainslee wanted Ewan in the proper mood to meet Levi. Right now, he would likely remain fixated upon her fateful decision to operate the cutting machine, but she planned to turn his attention toward other aspects of the business, such as several new contracts, and letters she'd received from customers praising the reliability of the business as well as the fine quality of their tiles. Then she would introduce him to Levi.

As he approached the carriage, Ewan gave the driver orders to take them to the tile works before he stepped inside the conveyance. His gaze remained fixed upon her hand until he was seated. "I'm sorry I was so ill-humored with you at the train station. When you told me how you'd been injured, my fear turned to anger. I still would like to know why you didn't let us know as soon as the accident happened."

"There were several reasons. I was ashamed that I'd been so foolish. Also, I feared you'd arrive in Weston, send me home, and take over the business."

Confusion appeared in his eyes and he leaned forward on the carriage seat. "Your answer makes no sense to me. I thought the sale of the tile works and a return to Grafton was exactly what you wanted."

"That is what I wanted when I first arrived, but I've had a change of heart. At least I think I have." She drew in a deep breath. "Before you take any further steps toward selling the business, I'd like you to talk to Levi."

"Levi?"

"Levi Judson. He has an excellent idea I'd like to implement."

Ewan's brows knit together. "I'm not sure what that means. Are ya telling me you want to remain in Weston and manage the business? I thought you were intent on me selling the place."

Her heart pounded a new beat. Maybe Ewan had already secured a buyer. If so, that would change everything. "You haven't signed a contract to sell, have you?"

"No, but I've had some talks with a fellow who is a good prospect. He's sent me papers to verify he has the money to purchase the place. All that remains is a visit to view the business and go over the books. He's coming to meet me here in Weston in a couple days."

"You need to send a telegram. Tell him not to come—at least not now. The business is doing well. The ledgers will show you that we've been making a profit—not huge, but enough that we can at least try something new. Once you've gone over the books, I'd like you to meet with Levi."

Ewan expelled a long breath. "I'm not willing to delay the arrival of Mr. Heskett just yet. I don't doubt what you've told me about the profitability of the company. I can review the books later. First let me hear what Mr. Judson has to say, and then I'll decide if I want to contact Mr. Heskett."

"Even though you think you may have an interested buyer, please don't be hasty. I think you'll see that there is a great deal of merit to his tile designs. They're different from any other decorative tiles you've ever seen."

Her brother gave her a sidelong glance. "I must say that you've gained my interest with all this talk of Mr. Judson. I'm curious to meet him, for I'm beginning to think there's more than tiles that have captured your interest, sister."

Ainslee objected, but Ewan's lips curved in a sly smile as he winked at her. Perhaps her brother knew her better than she knew herself.

Chapter 14

An unusual hush in the cutting room caused Levi to turn. Ainslee and a man he assumed was her brother stood in the arched doorway. The afternoon sun beamed over their shoulders and cast long shadows across the dirt floor.

Levi's mouth turned suddenly dry. Had he misunderstood? He was certain Ainslee had planned to go over the ledgers with Ewan before the three of them met. Was it worry he detected in Ainslee's eyes? Had something gone amiss? Had withholding word of her injury caused more difficulty than she'd anticipated? A thousand questions raced through his mind and rendered him speechless. Unsurprisingly, Robert had already moved from the adjacent mixing room and was quick to rise to the occasion and fill the void.

"Good afternoon, Mr. McKay. A pleasure to see you in Weston. Come to see how well your sister is doing managing your workers?" Robert let his gaze rest on Ainslee's bandaged hand.

"Nay. I've come because she requested my presence. I do not worry about her ability to manage the business or the men who work here. She's a McKay. I know she will do well at anything she attempts."

Robert chuckled. "She didn't do too good trying to use that cuttin' machine."

Ewan frowned and took a step forward. "Nay, but she had the courage to try. Sometimes our most important lessons are learned when we must suffer pain and failure." He clapped Robert on the shoulder. "While you may think she knows little about such matters, I can tell you that all of my sisters know a great deal about suffering. We came here from a country plagued with famine and woe, yet they have proved themselves to be made of stern stuff. I'd rank their abilities above most of the men I know."

Robert's cheeks flamed. "I didn't mean no disrespect, Mr. McKay."

"I'm sure you didn't." Ewan turned and extended his hand toward Levi. "You must be Levi Judson."

Levi nodded and stepped forward to shake Ewan's hand. "I'm pleased to meet you, Mr. McKay."

"I believe my sister has arranged for us to meet and discuss a new project, Levi."

Ewan's grasp was firm and his smile warm enough that Levi relaxed a little. He looked at Ainslee for affirmation. Although she smiled, he detected a worried look in her eyes and his concerns heightened anew.

Neither Robert nor Harold made any attempt to return to their work in the mixing room. Instead, they remained focused on Ewan. With their mouths gaping, both had edged a bit closer, their curiosity obviously piqued by the conversation.

Ewan glanced at them and gestured toward the large mixer in the adjacent room. "Don't let us keep you from your work. I'm sure Miss McKay doesn't want you to fall behind." He turned back toward Levi. "Let's go to the office and discuss these ideas of yours."

Levi longed for a moment alone with Ainslee to find out why

they were meeting so early, but it didn't appear that would happen. He stepped alongside Ewan as they crossed the courtyard. "I trust you had a good trip from Grafton."

"Aye, but I must say I was surprised to see that bandage on my sister's hand. She tells me your quick action getting her to the doctor prevented the injury from becoming any worse. Please accept my thanks."

"Any of the workers would have done the same. I happened to be the first one to realize what had happened. Miss McKay has done her best to be a good patient and follow the doctor's orders."

Ewan craned his neck for a glimpse of his sister. "Is that true, Ainslee? Have you followed doctor's orders? How have you managed to keep the ledgers current?"

"Levi volunteered to help me. When he has free time during the day, he comes to the office, and we've also worked in the evening at the boardinghouse when needed. Mrs. Brighton has given us use of the dining room table after supper." She grasped her brother's arm. "If you would have done as I asked and reviewed the ledgers first, you would already know they are in fine order."

Her brother pulled open the office door and gestured for Ainslee and Levi to enter. "Given the time constraints and other matters we've discussed, I think it's best to address Levi's project first." He motioned for Ainslee to be seated at the desk before he sat down in a chair opposite her. "Ainslee has told me about your tiles. Do you have some of them that I could see? Or at least some of the drawings you've made?"

"I have several sample tiles here in the office, but my drawings are in my room at the boardinghouse." Levi stepped across the room and lifted a cloth bag from the shelves that lined the west wall. "I believe these will give you a good idea of the finished product. Before coming to Weston, I worked at the Philadelphia Tile Works. The owner, Mr. Kresie, let me make these while I was working for him."

Ewan studied the tiles for a short time. "They are beautiful. Well made. Different than anything I've seen before." He leaned back in his chair. "Why didn't Mr. Kresie make these at his tile works?"

Levi returned to the straight-backed wooden chair and sat down. "I completed developing the process only a short time before my move to Weston. He didn't have the skill or knowledge to make these without me. Besides, he isn't an artist. Except for a few, all of the designs are mine, and so is the technique for creating them."

Ewan traced his fingers over the carefully crafted mosaic of a woman hanging clothes on a rope strung between two trees. "Who else has created the designs?"

Levi hesitated a moment. "My brother. He is an excellent artist."

Ewan scooted forward on his chair. "Does he wish to join you in this venture?"

Levi gave Ainslee a sideways glance and shook his head. "No. At least not in the near future. You see, my brother is a patient at the asylum. He suffers with problems of the mind. The doctors don't think he will ever again be completely normal, but only God knows what the future holds for him."

Ainslee leaned forward and rested her bandaged hand on the desk. "Levi gives art lessons at the asylum every Sunday afternoon. Some of the artwork is very good. And I'm helping establish a library there, as well."

Ewan's head snapped up at the remark. "You're going inside the asylum and mingling with women who suffer from brain disease?" He shook his head. "I'm not sure that's safe."

"It is quite safe. I'm not around any dangerous patients. I met with a committee of doctors and asylum staff before I began my visits."

Ewan shook his head. "I don't think Laura would approve."

"Once she has talked to me or visited the asylum, I think Laura will agree that it is an excellent cause. Most of the ladies in my group are depressed and grieving. Some from the loss of their husbands or children, and some simply due to unhappiness. Being with them has permitted me to discuss literature and poetry, which I greatly enjoy. And we've begun to gather ideas to form a library. Of course, we'll need funds to purchase books, but I'm hoping we'll receive donations, as well. I'm also going to write to Laura and Grandmother Woodfield to see if they would like to contribute some books from their libraries."

"I think we need to return to our discussion of these mosaic tiles. Why don't you tell me a little about the process, Levi?"

Levi picked up one of the mosaic pieces. "Once I have a drawing or painting, I re-create it in a simplistic drawing that will work for a mosaic. I enlarge the image and place it on top of a sizeable slab of clay. The image is then traced onto the clay to make an impression. Once that's done, I remove the paper image and the outline is deepened. This process requires cutting deep into the clay. Then plaster is poured over the clay impression. Once hardened, the plaster mold is removed from the clay." He traced his finger around the individual pieces that had been pieced back together to form the mosaic. "Smaller pieces of clay are placed in the sections of the mold and tamped into place. The individual pieces are then removed and fired."

Ewan shook his head. "I think it would be difficult to remove all of the pieces, fire them, and then be able to place them back in order to form the mosaic. Even if I looked at the drawing while attempting to re-create the picture with these small pieces, it would be impossible for me. It's like a child's puzzle, only much more complicated."

Levi chuckled. "After my first attempt, I learned that each piece must be numbered on both the drawing and the pieces of clay before they are fired. Then, if I'm confused, I can look at the drawing and see the number of the piece that is needed. After they are fired, the pieces are glazed with various colors and fired again."

"This is so much more than flooring or paving tiles. This is art." Ewan leaned back and looked at Levi. "I think your work is beautiful and it interests me, but I'm not so sure that money can be made with these mosaics. The cost of the materials is not so great, but there is much more time needed to create them." He hesitated. "I'm not sure something like this would ever be profitable. Who would buy them?"

Levi hunched forward, rested his arms across his knees, and met Ewan's quizzical look. They were at the crucial moment in their conversation—his one opportunity to convince Ewan to move forward with this idea. Levi said a silent prayer.

"These mosaics are as sturdy as any flooring or paving tiles," Levi explained. "They can be used around fireplaces or to decorate walls. They're strong enough to be interspersed among regular tiles to embellish the floors of mansions and public buildings. There is no limit to where they can be used. Once they are seen, I believe you will receive more orders than you can imagine."

Ewan stroked his jaw. "You may be right, and I am usually a man willing to take a chance on new ideas. 'Twould be good to explore the possibilities and see if interest is as strong as you believe."

"Oh, thank you, Ewan, that's wonderful news. I know you won't be sorry." Ainslee beamed at her brother. For a moment, it appeared she was going to jump up from the desk and rush to his side.

"Wait a wee minute, Ainslee. You interrupted me before I finished." Her brother's eyebrows knit together. "I was going to say that it would be good to explore the idea, if I didn't already have a meeting scheduled to discuss the sale of the business with a promising buyer."

Levi's chest tightened in an unyielding grip that made it difficult to breathe. Why had Ewan allowed him to get his hopes up? It would have been better to know from the onset that the McKays had located a buyer and planned to sell the tile works. The sale seemed to be news to Ainslee, as well, for her joyful appearance was replaced by a look of gloom.

"But you said you would contact Mr. Heskett if you thought Levi's proposal was sound. Didn't you say that you wanted to meet with him before going over the ledgers so you'd have as much time as possible to cancel the meeting with Mr. Heskett?" She frowned at her brother. "I believe these mosaic tiles will bring both orders and renown to the tile works. How can you simply dismiss something so unique?"

"Please remember that you are the one who insisted I place ads to sell the business." Ewan tapped his finger to the side of his head. "If my memory has not betrayed me, you wanted the tile works sold as quickly as possible." His features softened. "I can see that you've had a change of heart, but you waited to tell me until I arrived in Weston—just like you waited to tell me about your injury. 'Tis your own doing that put us in this murky mess, so do na direct your anger at me."

Ewan's Irish brogue had become more pronounced as he continued to state his case to Ainslee. At first, Levi had been certain Ainslee didn't know about the impending sale, but it seemed he'd been wrong. Why hadn't she told him their family was attempting to sell the business? Not only did he need to convince Ewan that production of the mosaics would prove to be a good business venture, but he also needed to persuade him to keep the tile works—and he wasn't sure he was up to the task.

Levi remained silent as the exchange went on between brother and sister, but his disappointment in Ainslee increased with each passing moment. Though she continued to wage a stalwart battle with her brother, he wasn't sure he could believe her. Did she truly want to keep the tile works, or was she privately telling her brother she wanted to sell the business? He didn't know what to believe.

"Say something, Levi!" Ainslee's sharp command pulled him from his private thoughts.

"I'm sorry, but I don't know what you want me to say." A heaviness pervaded his body, and he longed to return to the peaceful solitude of his room at the boardinghouse. "I've told your brother I think it would be a wise business decision to produce the tiles, but if you and your family have decided to sell the business, there's nothing more to discuss."

"No decision has been made. At least not yet." Ewan drew his fingers across the tile. "Right now I'm not certain what to do." He turned toward Ainslee. "Much of the reason for selling the business was because you wanted to return home as soon as possible. Now you tell me you want to remain here and create a library at the asylum and begin making these new tiles. If Levi's project fails, will you once again want to sell the tile works?"

Ainslee shook her head with vigor. "No. I give you my word that I'll remain here and manage the tile works even if we don't find buyers for the mosaic tiles." She grinned at Levi. "But I don't think that will happen."

"Let me pray about this tonight, and I'll give you my answer in the morning. If I'm going to cancel my meeting with Mr.

Heskett, I need to send a telegram first thing tomorrow." He pushed up from his chair. "Why don't both of you join me for supper at the hotel? Afterward, we can return and go over the books. If I decide to meet with Mr. Heskett, I want to have a full understanding of the finances."

Levi inwardly shuddered. The idea of a formal dinner at the hotel didn't appeal. He had little appetite for food or polite small talk. He had hoped for a few minutes alone with Ainslee to ask why she hadn't told him the business was for sale. Since that wasn't likely to happen today, he wanted to complete his work and return home.

"Thank you for the invitation, Mr. McKay, but there's a rule at the boardinghouse about missing meals without giving Mrs. Brighton or Miss Hanson notice. Due to your arrival, I'm sure they'll overlook your sister's absence at supper, but I don't think they'll be as willing to excuse me." He gestured toward the cutting room. "I have some work I want to complete before day's end. It's been some time since you've visited, so I'm sure your sister would enjoy catching up with you." Levi pushed to his feet and picked up his tiles. "Thank you for your time. I look forward to your decision."

Ewan's chair scraped on the wooden floor as he shifted around. "I want you to join us, Levi. Ainslee tells me you have created some new glazes for other decorative tiles as well as the mosaics. I'd like to hear about those tiles as well as the glazes. I'll speak to Mrs. Brighton. I don't think she'll make a fuss."

Levi sighed. Had there been no mention of selling the business, he would have been delighted to talk for hours about his designs for low-relief and brocade tiles. He longed to discuss the glazes and enamels he'd developed while working long into the night at the Philadelphia Tile Works, but not when such talk could once again lead to disappointment.

He shook his head. "I thank you, Mr. McKay, but until you've made a decision to keep the business, I don't think it serves any purpose. You mentioned you were going to pray about what you should do. I believe I'm going to spend my time praying the Lord will reveal what is best for all of us."

Ainslee stood and drew close to his side. "This is your opportunity to convince Ewan to keep the tile works and produce the mosaics, Levi. You should join us for supper." When he shook his head, she sighed. "You're making a mistake."

He leaned close to her ear. "Ainslee, spending time in prayer is never a mistake."

Chapter 15

When midmorning approached, Ainslee stood, strode across the room, and peered out the office window. Dark, heavy clouds sat on the distant horizon. They appeared to be resting before moving westward to empty their fullness onto the valley below. She had hoped to see Ewan arrive before now, but with the threat of heavy rains, perhaps he'd decided to wait at the hotel until the storm passed.

Her thoughts remained fixed upon Ewan's decision, and she'd accomplished little since her arrival. Instead of worrying, she should complete her work or spend her time in prayer. What was that verse that Grandmother Woodfield sometimes quoted from the book of Matthew?

When she recalled the verse, she recited it aloud: "'Take therefore no thought for the morrow: for the morrow shall take thought for the things of itself.'" She needed to take that verse to heart. Worrying wasn't going to accomplish anything, and there was work that needed her attention.

The skies were still overcast when Ewan strode into the office an hour later. "Sorry I'm late. Time got away from me."

"I was remembering the verse Grandmother Woodfield used to recite when one of us would fret about one thing or another."

Ewan chuckled and nodded. "I well remember. She still points those who worry to Matthew 6:34."

"Thank you. I hadn't been able to remember the chapter and verse." She pushed aside the ledger. "I will say that I am curious about what took you so long."

He crossed the room and stood beside the desk. "Maybe we should get Levi in here before I go into detail. Then I will have to tell it only one time." Ainslee started to push up from the desk, but Ewan gestured for her to remain seated. "I'll get him."

Ainslee remained at her desk, her thoughts skittering to and fro. Ewan seemed in a good mood, but he might have flashed that charming smile of his to hide the fact that he still planned to meet with Mr. Heskett. But she hoped his good mood might be due to the fact that he wasn't going to destroy Levi's dream.

She tapped the fingers of her left hand atop the desk as she stared at the bandage on her other hand. The doctor had given her hope that she'd be free of the thick wrapping once he examined her tomorrow. Though she would miss having Levi help her each evening, she longed to be free of the bandage. The doctor had mentioned the possibility of nerve damage, but she wouldn't let herself dwell on that possibility. She was murmuring Matthew 6:34 when Levi and Ewan opened the door.

"Talking to yourself?" Ewan grinned as he entered the room.

Ainslee returned his smile. "Myself and God. I'm still reciting Grandmother Woodfield's favorite verse."

She turned her attention toward Levi. With disheveled hair and sad eyes, he appeared as downcast as a stray dog on a rainy day. Ewan gestured toward the two chairs on the other side of her desk.

"I'm not going to keep you waiting any longer. I've already apologized to Levi for my late arrival." He glanced at Ainslee. "I told you both that I planned to spend time in prayer last night."

"I did a great deal of praying, too." Ainslee looked at Levi. "I'm sure Levi did, as well."

"I did." Raindrops spattered on the windows as Levi turned in his chair. "Did your prayers help you with a decision, Mr. McKay?"

"Aye. As I prayed, I recalled something that allowed me to make my decision. I'm sure the Lord brought the remembrance to mind."

Levi leaned toward Ewan. "What did you recall?"

"Josiah Harrington, a wealthy businessman in Wheeling who is a friend of the family and was also a good customer when I was operating the brickworks, is partially financing and overseeing the construction of a museum in that city. He attended the Centennial Exposition in Philadelphia when it opened in early May and was inspired by what he'd seen. After visiting with any number of influential people, he came to a decision that he should construct a museum where area residents could view paintings, sculptures, and historic artifacts. He has commitments from many of his wealthy friends to assist with the finances, so the project is taking shape."

Ainslee stared at her brother, wishing he'd reveal whether he'd made a decision. While construction of a museum was interesting, she didn't know what it had to do with anything they'd been discussing.

She gestured for her brother to continue. "And? I'm not sure how this was an answer to prayer."

"I believe Levi's mosaics could be interspersed with regular tiles and provide the flooring throughout the museum. The museum would provide a showplace for your work and the publicity would bring in more work than we could likely manage without additional workers."

"We? Does that mean you've decided to keep the tile works?" Levi spoke so softly that Ainslee had to lean forward in order to hear him.

"Aye! Although it was late, I managed to convince the clerk at the hotel to give me the name of the telegraph operator. I went to his home and asked him to return to the telegraph office and send a message."

Ainslee's mouth gaped open. "And did he agree?"

Ewan laughed. "For a few extra coins. I would have paid whatever he asked since I wanted to be sure that the telegram reached Josiah as soon as possible. I waited this morning in the hopes I'd receive a response before I came here." He beamed at Levi. "And I did. Josiah's excited by the idea and is coming here to see samples of your work. He plans to arrive next Wednesday."

"But how does that resolve anything, Ewan?" Thunder rumbled overhead, and a flash of lightning ignited the sky outside the office windows. Ainslee rolled her chair a little farther from the windows. "Mr. Heskett is arriving before then."

"I also had the telegraph operator send him a message last night—and cancelled our meeting."

Ainslee sighed. "I'm confused. What if Mr. Harrington sees the mosaics but decides they aren't what he wants in the museum and doesn't place an order? Will you then try to reschedule a meeting with Mr. Heskett?"

Ewan shook his head. "Nay. You've given me your word that if I agreed to keep the tile works, you would stay here and manage it to the best of your ability. If Josiah doesn't want the mosaics, we'll produce enough so that we can advertise them for sale and we'll see what happens. I believe the Lord is going to open doors for these tiles to be sold."

"I don't want to sound proud, but once these tiles are seen, I fully believe there will be a demand for them." Levi's downcast appearance had been replaced by one of excitement and confidence. "If Mr. Harrington doesn't select them for the museum floors, we'll need to develop another plan so they can be seen by large groups of people. I think that's the key to success. Because they are unique, the tiles can't be fully appreciated unless they are seen."

"You are probably right, Levi, but let's try to remember that verse in Matthew. We'll do what we can today and let tomorrow take care of itself. Agreed?" Ewan glanced back and forth between Ainslee and Levi.

They both nodded and offered their enthusiastic agreement. Ewan rubbed his hands together. "Since we are unified in our plan, I think the next step must be to offer Josiah a plan for the tiles. Do you think the tiles should be tied together by some sort of theme or basic concept?"

"Yes, a theme that would keep the visitors interested as they walked through the museum. I would want it to be something exciting, yet simple enough that even young visitors would soon see what was being presented."

Ainslee tapped her foot beneath the desk, her thoughts whirring in time with her tapping foot. "What about depictions of important events in this country's history, such as the arrival of Christopher Columbus and his three ships, the Pilgrims at Plymouth Rock, the settling of Jamestown, the Revolutionary War? Or if you didn't want to do that, you could portray various occupations—everything from farming to coal mining to glassblowing or shoemaking. You could also consider simple drawings of various scenes in the Bible, such as Adam and Eve in the garden or Moses holding the Ten Commandments. Could any of those ideas be simplified enough for your mosaics?"

The storm passed as they continued to talk, and bright afternoon sun radiated through the office windows. Countless raindrops glistened in the sunlight and seemed to wink their approval as they discussed their plans. Much depended upon Levi, since he was the one with the true artistic talent and requisite knowledge to create the tiles. While they talked, he nodded and jotted notes on a piece of paper.

After Ewan and Ainslee had given him numerous ideas, Levi leaned back in his chair. "All of these ideas are good and I can make sketches that would work, but do you know how large the museum will be? Have you seen any plans for the building?"

"Nay, I've no idea about the size or type of construction he's planned. Those are questions we'll need to have him answer when he comes to Weston."

Ainslee didn't miss her brother's reference to "we" when he answered Levi. Did he think her unable to proceed with the negotiations without him? "Are you planning to remain until Mr. Harrington arrives next week, Ewan?"

"That was my plan." He hesitated. "Unless the two of you prefer to meet with him alone."

Levi folded the piece of paper and tucked it into his shirt pocket. "I would like for you to be here, Mr. McKay. You have years of business experience. I'm an artist and tile maker, so I'll be pleased to discuss the designs and tile-making process with him if you and your sister will handle the business portion of our talks."

Ewan turned his hands palm side up. "And what would you like me to do, Ainslee? I trust your ability to negotiate with Mr. Harrington, but since I know him, I thought I could help win him over if needed. However, if you prefer to handle this on your own, I'm willing."

Her brother must have detected the reservation in her voice

when she'd asked if he was planning to stay. Now that she'd received assurance of his belief in her abilities, she wanted him to stay. "I think it's best if you attend the meeting with Mr. Harrington. I'm certain he'll expect you to be present, and he may not be as willing to do business with a woman." She offered him a half smile. "Not all men are as forward thinking as you."

"I'm glad you've agreed to have me stay because I planned to send a telegram to Laura and ask her to bring Tessa to Weston for a short visit."

Ainslee perked to attention. She'd been longing to see the rest of the family. "That would be wonderful. What about Grandmother Woodfield? Do you think she might come as well?"

"Nay. Her pleurisy is much better so she has returned to Woodfield Manor for the summer. She still enjoys time in Bartlett and doesn't want the house to sit empty all year."

"I'm pleased for that news. I know she misses her friends—and her house in Bartlett." Ainslee thought of the huge library in Woodfield Manor. "I may write her a letter and ask her if she'll go through her library and see if she wants to donate some of her books to the asylum."

Ewan nodded. "She'll probably light a fire under her ladies' group and convince them to donate some of their books, as well."

"That would be wonderful." Ainslee would have clapped her hands if one of them hadn't been bandaged. "Perhaps one of you could help me write a letter this evening."

Levi nodded and pushed up from his chair. "I think I should get back to cutting tiles. I've been gone for quite some time."

Ewan stayed him with a shake of his head. "I think you need to prepare drawings we can present to Josiah. The next six days will go by quickly and you want the sketches you present to impress him. Is there no one else who knows how to operate the cutting machine?"

Levi turned toward Ainslee. "Not your sister." When their laughter had subsided, Levi hiked a shoulder. "There is no one else who has been properly trained to operate the cutter. I could teach one of the men, but they are all needed to perform their own duties. Perhaps we could see if one of the diggers is available, but they usually go to work in the mines during off-season."

Ewan massaged his forehead. "I've performed almost every job in a brickyard and can even do a few of the jobs in the pottery. Why don't you teach me, and I'll do the cutting while you work on the drawings? I have nothing else to occupy my time until Mr. Harrington arrives."

Ainslee leaned forward and looked at her brother. "If you want to learn, I think it would be fine for Levi to train you. However, if we're definitely going to produce the mosaics, doesn't it make more sense to train someone who can remain at the job? I'm certain there are men who pack the tiles who would be pleased to be trained in cutting."

"You're right." Ewan touched his index finger to the side of his head. "You're thinking ahead and considering the possibilities. That's the sign of a good manager." He got to his feet and laid his hand on Levi's shoulder. "Until my sister finds the proper fellow, why don't you begin by teaching me and then you can set to work on your drawings?"

Levi tapped the pocket where he had placed his notes. "I know you said we'd need to wait and talk to Mr. Harrington about the size of the museum, but we didn't make a decision about the theme. If you want me to begin the drawings, we'll need to decide."

Ainslee pushed away from the desk. "Maybe it would be

best to create a drawing that represents each of the ideas we presented. If he sees several ideas, it may make it easier for Mr. Harrington to choose."

"Or make it even more difficult." Ewan chuckled. "Still, if it isn't too hard, I think Ainslee's idea is a good one. Do you think you can have the drawings ready for him by the time he arrives?"

Levi nodded. "I'll do my best. I know there is much to prepare before the meeting, but I promised to escort Ainslee to the doctor tomorrow and I also planned to look in on my brother while we were at the asylum. Since you're here, I didn't know if you planned to go with her."

Ewan shook his head. "I don't want to interfere with any plans the two of you have made. Just show me to the cutting machine, give me a lesson, and I'll see if I can manage the contraption any better than my sister did. I'm sure I can keep busy cutting while the two of you are at the asylum tomorrow."

Ainslee exchanged a fleeting smile with Levi. Having the doctor remove her bandage was vital to her work, but time alone with Levi was even more important, particularly for her heart.

Chapter 16

Once settled in the buggy, Levi flicked the reins and glanced at Ainslee. "Are you excited to see the doctor today?"

Ainslee bobbed her head. "Yes. I don't want to have my arm wrapped in this bandage when Laura and Tessa arrive. 'Twas bad enough that Ewan had to see it."

"Your brother's slight brogue is beginning to rub off on you." He grinned. "I like it."

"Do ya now? Well, if it's a lass with an Irish lilt that pleases ya, then I'll be doing me best to regain a brogue." She grinned at him. "Have ye had yer fill of an Irish lass, Mr. Judson?"

"Never." The rhythm and inflection of her words caused his heart to sing. "I could listen to you all day. I don't care if you speak with an Irish brogue or in a foreign tongue that I can't understand. I just want to hear your voice and be alone with you for a while." He placed his free hand atop hers.

Her cheeks flamed red and she bowed her head, so he withdrew his hand. He hadn't meant to embarrass her. His comments and actions had been far too intimate, and his words had spilled out without warning. Her hand had been so near that it begged to be touched, but that was no excuse for his bold behavior. Anyone who looked into the buggy as they passed by could have seen his hand covering hers, and he didn't want her to be the subject of gossip.

Before Ewan's arrival, the two of them had been together each evening while they maintained the ledgers and payroll. Since then, he'd had no time alone with Ainslee. Though it had been only two days, it seemed an eternity.

"I've been longing for time alone with you, as well." Her lips curved in an endearing smile that caused radiating warmth throughout his body. "I know helping me with the ledgers and all of my other office tasks has left you with little time to yourself, but I do miss seeing you each evening."

"I'm glad you've missed my visits, but I'm sure it's been a pleasure having your brother at your side each evening."

Ainslee chuckled. "Having Ewan at my side is different. While I appreciate his advice and assistance, he sometimes forgets I'm the manager of the tile works and he reverts to acting as though I'm still a schoolgirl."

Levi grinned and gave a slight nod. He could understand Ewan's dilemma. On the one hand he'd insisted his sister honor her obligation to manage the tile works. On the other hand, she would always be a little sister in need of his protection. Did most siblings experience that same protectiveness toward younger or more helpless brothers and sisters? Levi had possessed the distinct urge to safeguard Noah for as long as he could remember.

"Don't be too hard on your brother. I can see in his eyes how proud he is of all you've accomplished. When he questions your decisions or gives you advice, I think it is to make certain you'll avoid any pitfalls in the future rather than questioning the decisions you've already made."

She leaned closer to him. "You always know how to make me feel better. I understand that it isn't Ewan's intent to be critical, but sometimes I need a reminder."

The warmth of her shoulder against his arm felt like a ray of sunshine on a cloudy day. He wished they could remain in the buggy like this for the remainder of the day, but the asylum soon came into view, and Ainslee straightened her shoulder. His arm now felt strange without the slight weight of her shoulder against him, and he longed for the warmth of her touch.

Ainslee tugged at her gloves. "Why don't you escort me inside and then go and visit Noah? I want you to have as much time as possible with him while we're here."

Levi pushed aside thoughts of continuing onward and spending the entire day riding through the countryside with her by his side as he pulled back on the reins, set the brake, and jumped down from the buggy. After tying the horse to the iron hitching post, he hurried forward and extended his hands to help Ainslee down. Together they walked to the front entrance of the asylum and up the steps. Levi pulled open the heavy oak door and followed her down the hallway to Dr. Thorenson's office.

He knocked and stepped aside for Ainslee to enter. A sour-appearing nurse opened the door and looked at them as though they were another aggravation that had just been added to her day. "Which one of you is the patient?"

Levi nearly laughed aloud. How could the nurse not have seen the bandage on Ainslee's hand? "Miss McKay is the patient. Dr. Thorenson is expecting her."

The nurse grunted. "There's nothing in his notes that indicate any new patients being admitted today. Beyond her hand, what's the problem? Grief? Hysteria? Alcohol?"

Ainslee stifled a laugh. "Do I appear to be a woman suffering from the abuse of alcohol or any other mental disease? I am here to have Dr. Thorenson examine my hand. Would you please tell him Miss McKay is here for her appointment?"

The nurse appeared ruffled by her mistake and hurried from the room with a quick apology and promise to locate Dr. Thorenson. Immediately after the woman closed the door, they both burst into laughter.

When Levi finally caught his breath, he pushed several strands of hair from his forehead. "I know being admitted into the asylum isn't a laughing matter, but when she added the possibility that you might have a problem with alcohol, it was all I could do to keep a straight face. The poor woman is likely mortified."

"If nothing else, it erased that sour look from her face. By the time she escaped the room, she looked as though she'd been twisted in a strong wind."

Levi began to laugh once again but stopped when the door opened and Dr. Thorenson appeared. "Sounds as though you two are in good spirits." When the doctor mentioned spirits, Ainslee burst into laughter. "I don't know what I said that caused such laughter, but it's good to see you are both enjoying yourselves." He gestured toward Ainslee's hand. "I hope you'll be as jovial once we remove the bandage. Why don't you come into the examination room and I'll have a look."

The doctor stepped to the side to allow her entrance into the attached room. "Come on, Levi. I'm sure Ainslee thinks you should be present for the unveiling." He glanced at her. "Don't you, Ainslee?"

"I'm happy for him to come along, but he was going to go and spend some time with Noah while we're here. And since I can't go into the men's ward . . ." She let the sentence hang in the air.

The doctor hesitated for only a moment. "While Levi goes to visit Noah, perhaps you could take time to meet with a couple of the patients. It won't take long, but they, along with several others, have indicated a desire to meet you and learn more about the possibility of a library."

Levi nodded his agreement when Ainslee looked in his direction. The doctor's suggestion would provide ample time to visit Noah, and Levi could still be present with Ainslee when the doctor checked her hand. He was pleased to hear that some of the patients had taken an interest in her project. She'd expressed a bit of concern when the nurses who directly worked with the ladies hadn't included any of the patients in the earlier committee meeting.

The doctor waved Levi forward. Once inside the room, Levi took a chair on the other side of the room. Ainslee sat on the edge of the wooden examination table and extended her hand to the doctor. When Dr. Thorenson reached forward and loosened the outer wrapping, Ainslee lifted her chin and looked at Levi, her eyes revealing unspoken fear.

She'd been acting so unconcerned, but now he realized she'd been dreading today's appointment. He forced a broad smile. "She's been an excellent patient, Dr. Thorenson. I haven't caught her attempting to use that hand at all." He chuckled, hoping to lighten the mood. "Of course, with that huge bandage, you made it nearly impossible."

The doctor glanced over his shoulder. "That was my intention, Levi. I know a strong-willed woman when I see one."

Ainslee straightened her shoulders and exhaled an exasperated sigh. "I'm not strong-willed, merely determined."

"Ah, I see. I'm glad you straightened me out, Miss McKay." The doctor slowly lifted the last of the bandage away from the wound and gave an affirmative nod. "I'd say you have healed well. The scar will diminish over time."

Levi pushed to his feet, eager to see. "It looks excellent. How does it feel? Can you move your fingers without pain? Is there any numbness?"

The doctor turned toward Levi and grinned. "I think I'm the one who's supposed to ask those questions." Before Levi could apologize, Dr. Thorenson gestured for Ainslee to move her fingers. "Repeat the motions I make with my hand, and tell me when you have any pain." The doctor made a fist and slowly extended each finger, one by one, and then his thumb.

Until she extended her thumb, Ainslee had mimicked the motions without hesitation. "Ouch." She winced and immediately turned her thumb inward. "Why does my thumb hurt when all of my other fingers feel fine?"

"I expected you'd have the most trouble with your thumb. That's why I waited until last to extend it. The cut you received was closer to the nerves near the thumb. I am hopeful that in time you'll no longer have pain, but there's no guarantee. However, since your hand has healed so well, you won't need the bandage any longer." He reached out and helped her down from the table. "Why don't you go in and have a seat at my desk?"

Levi was confused by the doctor's request, but he followed the two of them back into the adjacent room. Ainslee looked at him and shrugged her shoulders. Obviously, she didn't know what to expect either. Dr. Thorenson withdrew a piece of paper from one of the desk drawers and placed it in front of Ainslee. He nodded to his pen and ink pot.

"Please write your name on the paper so we can see how much impact the injury has had on your script." He pushed the ink pot a bit closer, pulled a chair close to the desk, and gestured for her to begin.

Ainslee penned her name and, beneath, she wrote:

Thank you for restoring my ability to write, Dr. Thorenson.

Levi's heart soared when he viewed Ainslee's handwriting. He didn't realize that he, too, had been fearful she might not regain the full use of her hand. And though he'd warned her not to use the cutter, he still felt a modicum of responsibility that he'd left her in the cutting room without supervision.

The doctor smiled. "You are most welcome, Miss McKay. I only wish it was as easy to restore my patients here in the asylum to wholeness."

The doctor's kind words caused a thickness in Levi's throat, and he swallowed hard to keep his emotions at bay. "I know how hard you try, Doctor. Unfortunately, there are no simple cures for what ails the patients in this asylum." Levi forced a smile. "Since all is well here and you've completed the examination, I'll go over and visit with Noah."

"I'll have one of the orderlies come for you when Miss McKay has finished her meeting."

Ainslee lifted the pen in a triumphant wave. "Be sure you tell Noah about our new project and the drawings you've planned."

"I will." Levi hurried out the front doors and circled around the building. Returning outside and circling to the side of the asylum was much faster than trying to follow the meandering hallways inside the building.

Noah was in the large activity room, standing near one of the windows. The easel Levi had provided him was set up near the window, and Noah was looking out the window while painting on the canvas. Levi approached from behind his brother and viewed the painting Noah had begun several weeks earlier—a landscape of the view from his window. Noah had captured the curved walkways bordered with blooming flowers, the manicured hedges and shrubs, the small gardens planted by patients, and the towering trees that had been protected during construction of the asylum. But today his brush was filled with black paint and he was covering the picture with thin, dark lines.

"Noah, what are you doing?"

With paintbrush held high, his brother spun around on his heel. "I'm finishing the picture. You told me I should look out the window and paint what I see. I need the black lines or it isn't complete."

Noah stepped around the easel. When he tapped on the window, Levi was struck with understanding. Noah was including the thick wires that crisscrossed the windows to provide a barrier against patients either making an escape or attempting to jump to their death. The fact that Noah thought the picture incomplete without the ugly wires caused Levi to cringe inwardly. While he understood the necessity of protection, he'd given no thought to what it must be like to view the world through those dreadful black wires.

"Why don't you put your painting aside for a while and let's talk. I have some exciting news about my work that I want to share with you." Levi motioned toward a small wooden table in the middle of the room. As if unable to decide, Noah's gaze flitted between the painting and the table until Levi gently removed the brush from his brother's hand. "Once I leave, you can finish the painting."

Hearing that he could finish painting later appeared to calm Noah, and he walked alongside Levi to the table. Once seated, Noah placed his elbows on the table and rested his chin in his cupped hands. He looked like a young child awaiting further instructions.

Levi pulled his chair closer. "I'm going to be drawing a lot of sketches during the next week, Noah."

His brother's glassy-eyed look disappeared, and he listened intently while Levi told him about some of the designs for the tiles. "I want to present a variety of choices to Mr. Harrington and then he can decide what he likes the best. What do you think of our ideas, Noah?"

"I like them." He bobbed his head up and down. "I think flowers and birds and maybe animals would be good, too—especially the ones here in this state." He grinned at Levi. "Do you like my ideas?"

Levi placed his arm around his brother's shoulder. "Those are excellent ideas. Thank you, Noah."

His brother beamed at the praise. They continued to talk until the orderly appeared at the door and signaled.

Levi nodded and touched Noah's arm. "I need to go back to work now, but I'll be back on Sunday to see you." The two of them stood, and Levi gestured toward the painting. "I liked it better without the lines."

Noah offered a half smile. "I liked my life without those lines, too."

Levi fought back tears. At that moment, his brother was as sane as any person he knew. Yet his lucidity would likely be short-lived. It always was.

Ainslee followed Dr. Thorenson down one of the meandering hallways to the east wing of the asylum. A set of large double doors with small wire-covered windows loomed in the distance. He came to a halt and gestured toward a small office to his left. "You can wait here while I fetch the patients. Taking you inside the unit might create problems for a few of the ladies who become quite fearful when strangers enter their living area. Believe me, when a new patient arrives in the dormitory, it can create havoc for several days." He removed a ring of keys from his waist and selected one. "We keep the dormitories locked.

When outside of the dormitories, they're under the supervision of the orderlies and nurses."

Ainslee nodded. She wouldn't want the responsibility for the well-being of all these patients. "I'll be glad to wait in here. I don't want to do anything that might cause any of the ladies difficulty." Once seated in the small room, Ainslee expelled a long breath, thankful for Dr. Thorenson's knowledge.

Moments later, the doctor returned with two ladies. One who appeared to be near Laura's age and the other somewhat older, though she carried herself like a much younger woman. The doctor gestured toward the younger woman. "Miss McKay, I'd like to introduce you to Mrs. Nettie Brinker and Mrs. Zana Tromley. Both would like to help you with the library." The doctor smiled at the two patients. "Isn't that so, ladies?"

They both nodded. Mrs. Brinker's lips quivered in a brief smile. "I'm pleased to meet you, Miss McKay. I'm one of the patients who asked for a library. I like to read, but I don't have any books."

Mrs. Brinker lightly nudged Mrs. Tromley, who straightened her shoulders and looked Ainslee in the eyes. "Pleased to make your acquaintance, Miss McKay. I can read and write. Maybe not as good as Nettie, but I'm a hard worker and I'd like to help however I can. The good Lord knows we need something to keep our minds occupied, especially in the winter when we can't work in the vegetable and flower gardens."

Dr. Thorenson tapped the back of a wooden chair. "Sit down, ladies. I'm sure Miss McKay would like to talk to you at greater length."

Ainslee bobbed her head. "I'm delighted to meet both of you. Having assistance will be a great help since I work six days a week. However, I'm dedicated to this idea, and I think we're going to be successful."

Both ladies had followed the doctor's invitation to sit, but it was Mrs. Tromley who leaned forward. "Have you made any plans of how we're going to do that? The doctor said you'd put us to work helping, but where and when? What's the first step?"

The woman's questions surprised Ainslee. She wasn't sure what she'd expected, but it hadn't been two ladies with bright eyes and a list of questions. These patients were ready to begin work. Unfortunately, Ainslee wasn't prepared for such a meeting.

She didn't want to brush aside their offer, so she quickly explained her lack of preparation. "If I'd known we were going to meet, I would have written out a form letter that I want to send to possible donors. I need to gather a list of names and addresses of those who might be willing to send books or contribute financial assistance." Ainslee paused. "I'll write out the letter today and have it, as well as stationery and ink, delivered to the doctor so you can begin."

A slight frown wrinkled Mrs. Brinker's forehead. "If we don't have the names of possible donors, what salutation shall we use in the letters?"

Dr. Thorenson waved in Ainslee's direction. "Instead of using personal names, why not open the letter with a general greeting? Perhaps 'Dear Friends of the Trans-Allegheny Lunatic Asylum.'"

Zana shook her head and Nettie shivered.

Ainslee suggested, "What about simply beginning with 'Dear Friends and Family Members'? I'm going to be writing to some of my friends as well as several family members and I believe the same will be true for other workers and patients." She looked around. "What do you think, ladies?"

They nodded their heads in agreement. Nettie folded her hands in her lap. "Is there anything else we can do?"

Ainslee hesitated a moment. "Could one of you ask the

other patients if they want letters sent to their friends or family members?"

Nettie nodded. "I can do that. I'll keep a list for you."

"Thank you, Mrs. Brinker. That would be a great help."

She pushed up from her chair. "Call me Nettie, please. I'm not fond of the Brinker name."

"And you can call me Zana. Makes me feel younger." The older woman chuckled and stood. "Guess you better go unlock that door for us, Doc."

Minutes later, the doctor returned to the small room to escort Ainslee back to his office. "What do you think of Zana and Nettie?"

"I think they both seem to be as rational as anybody I know. I'm not sure why they're in here." When he didn't immediately respond, she decided to question him further. "Can you help me understand why two lovely women with obvious intelligence and more than meager education are living in this institution?"

"I can't discuss any of the patients with you, Ainslee. It wouldn't be proper. However, you should know that a doctor's referral isn't a requirement for admission to this or any other institution." As they neared the door to his office, he offered a slight smile. "I'm sure you're pleased that you'll now be able to set pen to paper whenever you have need." He glanced down the hallway as he spoke. "Ah, there's Levi now. I'll leave you to his care and get back to my work."

Clearly, Dr. Thorenson wanted to avoid any further questions about his patients.

Chapter 17

The wind whipped at Ainslee's cloak as she hurried up the front steps of the asylum and down the hallway to Dr. Thorenson's office. Nettie had sent word a batch of letters was ready to be sent to possible donors. While she was there, she hoped to set up a better method of communication. Nettie's message had taken three days to reach Ainslee's ears. Nettie had told Dr. Thorenson, who passed the information to Levi during a visit to Noah. In turn, Levi had passed the message to Ainslee this morning. Perhaps Dr. Thorenson could suggest a more efficient system.

Dr. Thorenson appeared in his office doorway as she rounded the corner. "Ah, Miss McKay, it's good to see you. I trust this is not a medical visit." His gaze shot toward her hand.

"Absolutely not. I've done nothing to reinjure myself." She quickly explained she'd just received his message the letters were ready this morning. "Are they in your office?"

He shook his head. "Why don't you walk with me to the ladies' wing? I need to see a patient over there." He turned and closed his office door before stepping alongside her. "In the future, I'll have one of the orderlies who lives in Mrs. Brighton's boardinghouse deliver the message to you instead of waiting until Levi comes to visit Noah."

She smiled. It was as though he'd known what she'd been thinking only a short time ago. "Thank you. I think that would be most helpful." She glanced up at him as they continued toward the ladies' dormitory. For some time, she'd wondered why Dr. Thorenson had come to the Weston asylum. "I hope you won't think me prying, but I'm curious why you chose to use your doctoring skills in the asylum. I'm sure you must have had other choices."

The doctor nodded. "Doctors can set up a private practice in most any town. I could have opened an office right here in Weston, if I'd wanted to, but that wasn't why I studied medicine. For a short time, I did consider a teaching position at the University of Pennsylvania School of Medicine. I thought I might be able to discover more about the causes of mental deficiencies in some folks and not others. After giving the idea of teaching more consideration, I decided I would learn more and be of greater benefit if I took a position in an asylum." He hesitated a moment. "I've never regretted my decision, although I don't know much more about the causes than I did when I first arrived here."

"So have you become discouraged?"

He shook his head. "In medicine, we never know when some small discovery will lead us to the answers we seek. Perhaps someday there will be more answers than questions. I'm thankful this asylum has opened to provide better conditions for the patients than being tossed into a jail cell." His voice quavered, and Ainslee looked up at him. Sadness creased his features and seemed to darken the hollows around his eyes. He met her gaze and forced a feeble smile. "Both my mother and sister suffered tragic deaths in one of those horrible places while I was studying at the university in Edinburgh. I believe they would still be alive if my father had kept them at home, but he said he couldn't manage them when they had spells. They died within a year, both from pneumonia—at least that's what he told me."

Regret filled Ainslee's heart, and she silently chided herself for asking one question too many. Her inquiry had obviously opened an old wound for the doctor. "I'm so sorry, Dr. Thorenson."

The doctor straightened his shoulders and shook his head. "No need to be sorry, Ainslee. You did nothing wrong." He inhaled a deep breath. "Here we are." He gestured to the small office where she'd waited before. "I'll have Nettie bring you the letters."

Moments later, Nettie appeared with a sheaf of papers in her hand and a smile on her face. "Some of the ladies asked to have us send letters to their relatives and friends, so I put them on the list. Of course, there's no telling whether some of them even remember who their relatives are, but most of the ladies gave us at least one name."

Ainslee's eyes widened at the thick stack of paper. "How many letters have you written?"

Nettie's cheeks burned bright pink. "There are twenty letters. The rest of this is a story I wrote. I brought it along to see if you'd read it. Dr. Thorenson told me you were a schoolteacher before you came here, so I'd value your opinion. I like to read books a lot, but when my husband burned all my books, I took up writing stories."

Ainslee shuddered. How could anyone be so cruel? "How clever of you. I'm glad you were able to find another way to occupy your mind."

"I was happy enough until he found out about my writing." Sadness etched tiny lines around Nettie's lips, and her gaze drifted toward the window. "I wrote on every scrap of paper I could find. I was smack-dab in the middle of my story, but I couldn't find any more paper. The story wouldn't quit rambling around in my head, so I kept searching the house trying to find something to write on. I was near desperate to finish, so I tore some pieces of old paper from the wall and wrote on the back. I tried to explain, but he wouldn't listen." She ruffled the edges of the paper as she spoke. "He said I was crazy. Maybe I am, but I don't think so. I was lonely living in that hardscrabble place he called a farm. He wouldn't take me anywhere, not even to church. He even took my Bible away from me."

She appeared to return to the present and looked at Ainslee. "It's not so bad being in this place. It's sure better than living on that farm. There are other ladies as sane as me, and we get to visit with each other." She looked up and grinned. "And they give me paper and ink so I can write my stories."

Ainslee considered asking about some of those other ladies but decided her questions might create discomfort for Nettie. Still, she wondered how many patients were in this place for little or no reason. She stared at the handwritten pages.

"I know you're busy what with your tile works and trying to get the library started. I shouldn't have asked." Nettie started to rise.

Ainslee extended her hand to stay the woman. She'd mistaken Ainslee's hesitation as a refusal. "Please, stay a moment longer. I would be delighted to read your story."

"Thank you, Miss McKay." She leaned forward and touched Ainslee's arm. "I want you to tell me the truth. If it's just the silly ramblings of a crazy woman, you can say so. I don't expect anything more." She touched her hand to her bodice. "But no matter what you tell me, I'll keep writing my stories."

Ainslee nodded. Even if the story didn't prove well written, she wouldn't be cruel in her assessment. She would help Nettie any way she could.

Ainslee peered through the depot window, eager for the arrival of Laura and Tessa on the afternoon train. Her anticipation of their visit had mounted throughout the day, and she'd finally convinced Ewan they should arrive at the station a little early.

Ewan waved to her. "Come sit down, lass. Looking out the window won't make the train get here any faster."

Ainslee returned to his side and folded her gloved hands in her lap. Before the accident, the gesture had seemed insignificant. Now she valued the ability to fold her hands together or grasp a pen. During those long weeks of recovery, she had learned how much one part of the body depended upon another—and how difficult it was to manage without the help of others.

Ewan touched her shoulder. "Pleased I am that you've gained the use of your hand again. I understand that you have a scar, but when I think of how much damage could have been done, my heart aches. I hope you won't do anything so foolish again."

"You need not worry. I plan to keep a safe distance between me and the cutting machine." She turned toward him. "This has been a difficult time for me. I'm not accustomed to relying upon others, and I didn't realize how difficult it would be to take care of myself with that cumbersome bandage on my hand. The girls at the boardinghouse were wonderful. They helped me dress and styled my hair." Her eyes took on a faraway stare. "I don't know what I would have done without them—or Levi. The books would be in total disarray if he hadn't entered the figures each day. I never before gave thought to how much we need each part of our body."

Ewan nodded. "Aye. Our bodies are much like the church. Each person who becomes a part of the body of Christ is needed to do their part so that the church can meet the needs of others and serve the Lord. And speaking of the church, are you still favorin' the small church near the boardinghouse?"

She nodded. "I like it very much. The members are like a large family."

A whistle shrieked in the distance, and Ewan lightly nudged her arm. "Ya see? It took only a few words about the Lord and his church to bring the train down the tracks." He chuckled and grasped her elbow. "Let's get out to the platform. I'm sure Tessa will be disappointed if we're not outside waiting for her."

Minutes later, six-year-old Tessa descended the steps of the train, immediately followed by her mother. Tessa rushed toward them and wrapped her arms as far around Ainslee as her wide skirt would permit. Her blue eyes sparkled with delight as she accepted Ainslee's kiss to her cheek and then bounded into her father's arms. She was a beauty of a child who had somehow escaped her birthmother's rather frumpy appearance and mousy personality. Though Kathleen Roark was a sweet woman, no one would have labeled her attractive. Perhaps living with her sister and brother-in-law, Aunt Margaret and Uncle Hugh, had been the cause of Kathleen's meek and retiring disposition. It was, after all, difficult for any member of the family to defy Aunt Margaret's edicts. Though Kathleen had no control over her physical attributes, a fitted gown and proper hairstyle would have helped. Yet Aunt Margaret was not one to spend Uncle Hugh's money to enhance the appearance of anyone other than herself.

Ainslee often wondered if Kathleen's low opinion of herself was what had caused her to give in to the desires of Terrance O'Grady and bear his child. For sure, Ewan, Laura, and the rest of the family had been thankful Kathleen had given birth to Tessa and also had permitted them to adopt her. All except Aunt Margaret, who still avowed she'd been excluded from many social circles because of Kathleen's illicit affair. Never once had Aunt Margaret viewed her own callous behavior as the primary reason she'd become an outcast. And though Tessa was now six years old, the chasm within the family created by Tessa's birth and adoption still remained. Ainslee prayed that one day the family wounds would heal: both regarding Tessa's adoption and Margaret's deceitful takeover of the brickworks.

"Ainslee!" Laura pulled her into a hug. "You look wonderful. I'm so eager for a long visit with you."

Tessa hopped from foot to foot. "And I want to go to the stores and see what kind of candy they have. Mama said we could go and shop while we're here, didn't you?"

"I did, but I didn't mean we would go the minute we stepped off the train. First we need to go to the hotel and get settled, and by then it will be time for supper. We may need to save our shopping for tomorrow."

"Aye, or even the next day." Ewan playfully tapped his daughter beneath the chin. "Once your bags arrive at the hotel, I'm going to return to the tile works. I have work to complete and Ainslee can give you all the exciting details." He gestured toward the door of the train station. "The carriage is outside and I'll see to having your trunks delivered."

Laura extended her arms. "Am I going to receive a kiss before you rush off for the baggage?"

Ewan slapped his hand to his forehead. "I'm sorry, my love. There are a thousand details dancing about in my head, but that's no excuse for letting my wife arrive without a proper welcome." He pulled Laura into a warm embrace, then lowered his head to kiss her lips.

"Ewww." Tessa grasped the tip of her nose between her thumb and forefinger and looked at Ainslee. "They like to kiss too much."

Ainslee grinned. "I know it's difficult to believe, but one day you won't think kissing is terrible."

The little girl's mouth gaped open. "Do you like to kiss boys, Ainslee?"

Ewan and Laura both turned to face Ainslee. When she didn't immediately respond, Ewan hiked an eyebrow. "Well, do you like to kiss boys, little sister?"

"I don't know. I've never kissed a boy, but when the right *man* comes along, I'm sure I'll enjoy kissing him very much." There! She hoped that would put a stop to questions about kissing and boys.

"Excellent answer, Ainslee." Laura chuckled as they walked to the carriage.

During the short ride from the depot to the hotel, Tessa peppered Ainslee with questions. When they passed one of the mercantiles, she was quick to mention the store likely had a nice display of candy inside.

"Your mother said no shopping today, but if your sweet tooth is getting the best of you, I'm sure there's a piece of cake or a slice of pie to be had in the hotel dining room," Ewan said.

"Ewan!" Laura frowned at her husband. "She'll ruin her supper if she eats pie or cake at this time of day."

"Nay. She'll clean her plate 'til it shines like Grandmother Woodfield's silver, won't ya, Tessa?"

The little girl's blond curls bounced when she bobbed her head. "I promise."

The carriage came to a halt, Ewan helped them down, and as they walked up to their rooms, Laura once again chided him for his lenient ways with their daughter.

"You and Ainslee will be wantin' a cup of tea and a chat," he said as he opened the room door. "The cake will keep Tessa busy—and quiet. You'll thank me later."

After Ewan departed, the three of them returned downstairs to the dining room, where Tessa was served a thick slice of vanilla cake with cream filling and a glass of milk before the waiter delivered a pot of tea and plate of delicate cookies.

From Ewan's telegram, Laura knew something exciting was afoot at the tile works, but she was eager for all the details. Her excitement over the mosaics pleased Ainslee. "I can't wait for you to see them and meet Levi. He's extremely artistic and kind." Ainslee removed her gloves and placed them on her lap before reaching for a cookie.

"What's that?" Tessa wrinkled her nose and squinted her eyes as she pointed to Ainslee's scar.

Laura clasped a hand to her bodice. "Ainslee! What happened?" She reached for Ainslee's hand and gently traced her finger across the scar.

The accident wasn't what she'd hoped to discuss right now, but Laura's questions deserved an answer. She withheld the gruesome details and focused upon Dr. Thorenson and his excellent care. Instead of bringing the topic to a rapid close, mention of the asylum opened the door to even more inquiries.

When she'd finally satisfied their questions, Ainslee refilled her teacup. "I'm helping with a project in the ladies' wing of the asylum, so I was pleased when Ewan said you were coming for a visit. I was going to write to you and Grandmother Woodfield, but it will be much easier to explain my idea in person. I'm hoping you'll both help."

Laura wrapped her arms tight around her waist and leaned away—as if she longed to distance herself from talk of the asylum. "I don't know if I'm called to help in such a place. I'm sorry, but I don't think I could. Besides, we'll be here only a few days."

Ainslee inched forward on her chair and quickly spoke of

the library she'd been planning for the ladies. "What I need is books. I thought some of the ladies at home might donate books or have a charity event to raise money to help purchase books for the library."

Laura's shoulders relaxed and she nodded her head. "A library for the ladies is an excellent goal, and I'm sure Mother and I can rally support, but do promise me you'll be careful going inside that place."

"I will, but there's nothing to fear." For several minutes, Ainslee attempted to ease Laura's concerns, but she met with little success. Rather than belabor the subject, she thanked Laura for her willingness to help furnish books and seek help from friends in Grafton and Bartlett. "Once you've collected books, they can be crated and shipped by train. I'll reimburse you for the costs."

Laura's smile was warm yet guarded. "I believe we'll be able to raise enough money to pay the shipping charges. If not, you can be certain we'll get the books sent to you. I think your project is noble, and I think you're brave to take on such a task." Laura shifted in her chair. "I've been wondering about you and Adaira. Have the two of you been corresponding?"

"I recently answered the letter Adaira sent me. She apologized for leaving me in the lurch." Ainslee laughed. "Well, those weren't her exact words." She shook her head. "I tried on numerous occasions to write and offer my forgiveness, but each time I ended up tossing a half-finished letter. My responses always sounded stilted and insincere."

"And were they?" Laura sipped the remains of her tea.

"Yes. I'm afraid so. But when I was finally able to complete my letter to her, it was written with genuine forgiveness. Once I decided to accept my new position as a challenge rather than a duty, my resentment began to fade. Of course, the possibility of producing the new tiles has bolstered my enthusiasm, and the prospect of doing something to cheer the ladies at the asylum has given me particular joy." Ainslee smiled hesitantly. "I've discovered forgiveness is freeing."

Laura leaned closer. "And does Levi Judson play any part in this newfound enthusiasm and joy you've discovered?"

Ainslee could feel the heat crawling up her neck and spreading across her cheeks. "Perhaps a little. I've never met anyone quite like him."

Laura smiled. "There's nothing like a new beau to help us leave the past behind. I do believe you are smitten, my dear. I'm especially pleased for you."

There was no use denying Laura's assessment. In truth, Ainslee was more than smitten—she was in love. She merely hadn't admitted it to herself before this moment.

Levi attended church with Ainslee and her family on Sunday morning and then joined them for dinner at the hotel. Soon after they'd completed the meal, he thanked them and excused himself. He was certain all but Ainslee thought he was going home or to the tile works to complete further sketches, but he'd promised Noah he would return on Sunday for his regular visit. He'd not completed as many of the drawings as he'd hoped, but Noah remained his priority.

After entering the heavy iron outer gate, he strode down the path leading to the men's wing. The fog that draped the mountains in sheer gossamer on most mornings had disappeared hours ago, and several small clusters of men sat outdoors, seemingly enjoying the warm weather. One or two were busy hoeing a vegetable plot, likely unaware they were working on a day of rest. Orderlies had joined some of the patients in a game of croquet, while others wandered around the grassy fenced area in the side courtyard.

Levi spotted his brother sitting on the grass near a small group of men. Sketchpad in hand, Noah looked up and jumped to his feet when Levi approached. He waved the drawing pad overhead, and when Levi drew close, his brother shoved the book at him. "I've been drawing instead of painting." Noah beamed at Levi.

"If you would rather sketch, that's fine." The comment from his brother surprised Levi. Given a preference, Noah had always preferred a paintbrush over charcoal pencils. "Let me see what you're drawing."

Noah presented the sketchbook to Levi once he'd settled on the ground. "I want to know what you think of my sketches. You can be honest with me. I'm feeling myself today. I've been feeling good ever since your last visit when you told me about the tiles you're going to make for that museum."

"Hopefully make. We don't have the contract yet. If Mr. Harrington is a man who makes quick decisions, we should know on Wednesday, but if he likes to give matters a lot of thought, we may not know for some time."

Levi's breath caught when he turned to the first page and viewed the delicate drawing of a Catawba rhododendron. Page after page revealed sketches of flowers, trees, and birds. A sugar maple, a fire pink, an ox-eyed daisy, a proud cardinal with its beak turned toward heaven, a downy woodpecker, and a short-eared owl, all sketched with beauty and precision, all representative of West Virginia.

"They're beautiful, Noah. Truly beautiful. You should paint these. The colors would be magnificent."

His brother frowned and reached for the sketchbook. "I didn't sketch these so I could paint them. I drew them for you—to show to Mr. Harrington." He clutched the book close to his chest. "I thought you wanted to portray a few of the flowers and birds of West Virginia on some of your ceramic tiles."

"I do. Your idea . . ."

"You don't need to lie in order to protect me, Levi. I'm not going to fly into a rage. I'm perfectly sane right now." Anger knotted Noah's face. "Sane enough to know that if you truly liked my idea, you would have known these sketches were for you."

The heated response pulsed in Levi's ears. He didn't want to say or do anything that would cause Noah to recede into his protective shell, yet Levi was never certain what words or deeds would have an ill effect upon his brother. Neither Levi nor the many doctors who had treated Noah were ever certain what or how much he understood. Truth be told, there were times when Levi found his brother's phases of normalcy even more overwhelming than his extended periods of irrationality.

"Please listen to what I have to say, Noah. You are my brother, and I love you. I would never say or do anything to deliberately hurt you. When I visited a few days ago and told you I liked your idea about using birds and flowers, it was the truth. Because of your suggestion, I sketched a hummingbird and mountain laurel, as part of my collection for Mr. Harrington. Your drawings are beautiful, but I would never assume they were meant for me to use in my set of drawings."

Noah's features softened. "Can I look at your sketches? Could you bring them before your meeting?" He didn't wait for an answer. "I know my drawings are too detailed to be used as templates, but I could simplify them for you. Are you presenting detailed sketches or line drawings to Mr. Harrington?"

"I'm going to present both to him. I start by making a more detailed sketch, although not as beautiful as these." Levi smiled and tapped the sketchbook in his brother's arms. "Then I create line drawings that will more closely reflect what would be used as a template. I think it will give him a better idea of the product he'll receive. I'm glad I have some of the tiles I made in Philadelphia as well as my original drawings so that he can see the changes that occur. I wouldn't want him to agree to the project and then disapprove or be disappointed with my work." He blew out a long breath. "That wouldn't reflect well upon me or the McKay Tile Works."

Noah traced his fingers over the cardboard cover of the sketchbook. "You never answered my questions. Will you have time to come back before your meeting?"

Levi wrapped his arm around his brother's shoulder. "I will make time to be here. Nothing is more important to me than you, Noah. You know that, don't you?"

Noah tipped his head to the side. "I know. You're a good brother."

The bell in the central clock tower bonged four times, and Levi pushed to his feet. "Do you want me to take your sketches with me, Noah?"

His brother shook his head. "No, but I'm glad you like them." He stood and walked alongside Levi to the edge of the grassy courtyard. "You promise you'll be back before your meeting?"

Levi squeezed his brother's shoulder. "I promise, Noah."

A cloak of disappointment wrapped around Levi as he trudged toward the gate. Perhaps he'd misunderstood Noah. Or maybe Noah no longer wished to turn over the drawings because Levi hadn't initially realized they were for him. He shuddered at the thought of causing Noah any pain. Those drawings were flawless, and each one would have made a beautiful tile. He pushed the thought from his mind and turned to offer his brother a final wave before he disappeared out of sight.

Chapter 18

Levi momentarily turned his gaze toward the white clouds drifting overhead in a pale blue sky. The sun warmed his back as he entered the gates of the asylum. He'd need to hurry or he wouldn't be back to the tile works when Ewan and Mr. Harrington returned from the train depot. He'd hoped to make his promised visit to Noah this morning, but there had been so many details that required his attention, and he'd been unable to depart until after the noonday break.

With a folder of sketches tucked beneath his arm, Levi raced up the steps leading into the west wing, yanked off his cap, and entered the wide doors. Taking long strides, he continued down the hallway and glanced into the dayroom as he neared the door. Catching sight of Noah pacing at the far end of the room, Levi came to an abrupt halt.

Hoping to gain Noah's attention, he waved the folder overhead, but to no avail. When he drew close, he touched his brother's arm. "I'm sorry I'm late, Noah."

Levi's shoulders slumped when he was met by Noah's glassy-eyed stare. He had prayed his brother would remain lucid forever—that these drawings would keep his mind keen and provide a way out of the tragic maze that seemed to beset Noah at every turn. For a moment, he considered an immediate return to the tile works. Noah likely wouldn't even remember whether he'd kept his word, yet he had promised his brother he'd bring his sketches.

With a gentle grasp of Noah's elbow, Levi led him to a far table. "Let's sit down and I'll show you my drawings." Noah plodded alongside him, and when Levi gestured for him to sit down, he dropped into the chair. "Do you remember I was drawing sketches for ceramic tiles, Noah? Mr. Harrington is coming from Wheeling to see if he wants to use them in a new museum." He leaned around his brother in an attempt to gain eye contact, but Noah stared out the window, his gaze fixed upon the horizon.

Levi sighed and opened his sketchbook. Before he departed, he'd at least spread the pictures on the table. He'd promised to let Noah see them, and he would keep his promise. Once he'd arranged the pictures, he tapped the table.

Noah turned away from the window and looked toward the drumming sound. For several moments he appeared transfixed, but slowly he reached forward and picked up one of the sketches. One by one, he examined the detailed sketches and then the line drawings.

When he finally returned the final line drawing to the table, he looked at Levi. The glassy-eyed stare had been replaced with a look of clarity. "They're wonderful, Levi. Mr. Harrington will be impressed. I'm sure you'll get the contract."

"Thank you, Noah. If it's God's plan for me, I'm sure the drawings will be well-received and we can begin work on the tiles."

"Do you have time to come to my room before you leave?" Noah pushed away from the table. "I won't keep you long."

The visit had already taken more time than Levi had planned. Noah's examination of the pictures had been painstakingly slow. And though he wouldn't deny Noah's request, Levi feared he would be late for the meeting. Not the way he had hoped to begin his relationship with Mr. Harrington. The two brothers walked side by side down the hallway and made a left turn down another hallway until they arrived at Noah's room.

Noah hurried to the heavy wooden dresser and withdrew his sketchbook from the bottom drawer. "Take a look at these and see if you can use them."

Levi gasped at the sheaf of drawings his brother had produced. Not only were the detailed sketches he'd seen on Sunday accompanied by line drawings, but Noah had completed ten other detailed drawings as well as the line-drawings. The immense amount of work he'd completed in so short a time seemed near impossible.

"How did you get all of this done, Noah? I haven't accomplished near as much as you, and I've been working long hours."

An orderly stepped inside the door and chuckled. "He's been sitting up day and night working on those. Even with very little sleep, making those pictures for you kept Noah feeling better than I've ever seen him."

Noah raised his shoulders in a small shrug. "While I was working on these, I felt like I had a reason to keep my head clear." His lips tipped in a lopsided frown. "It's been good. I hope you will take these, and maybe Mr. Harrington will want you to use one or two of them."

Levi's heart thudded in his chest. His brother had never before mentioned he had some type of control over his clarity of thought. Was that possible? From the time he suffered that high fever as a child, no one had ever understood why Noah could act and appear normal in one instance and insane in another.

And it had been those periods of insanity that had made it impossible for him to live in the outside world. Though he'd never hurt anyone, people feared him when he lost control of his movements and his speech became unintelligible. His glassy-eyed stare created discomfort among all who knew him—all except Levi.

There wasn't time to explore the possibility right now, but his mind raced with the thought that perhaps the only thing Noah needed in order to return to a state of normalcy was a job that would instill a sense of purpose. The doctors would likely refute such an idea, but if they were awarded a contract, perhaps there would be some way Noah could help with the project while remaining at the asylum. One day, he might be well enough to come to the tile shop and see where Levi worked. Noah touched his arm and pulled him from his fanciful thoughts.

"Do you want to take all of my drawings with you?"

The anticipation in Noah's voice tugged deep within, and Levi nodded. "Yes, Noah, all of them. I think Mr. Harrington will be exceedingly impressed with them. I need to go now, but I'll try to return tomorrow and tell you what's happened. Try to stay in this world with me, will you?"

A slight smile tipped Noah's lips. "I'll do my best. Maybe I'll start on some new sketches."

"You do that." Levi embraced his brother in a tight hold and then gathered up Noah's drawings as well as his own sketchbook. "Remember to stay with me."

A short time later, Ainslee turned toward Levi. "Mr. Harrington is here." After taking a final glimpse at the display they'd prepared, she moved to Levi's side. Together they stepped forward to meet Mr. Harrington. She wanted to grasp Levi's hand for support, but she dare not do such a thing. She swallowed a giggle as she pictured her brother's reaction to such behavior during a business meeting.

Though she had pictured Mr. Harrington as a tall, slender man with a thin mustache, thick dark hair, sharp features, and a stern countenance, he was the exact opposite. His generous paunch preceded him into the room by at least half a foot, and his broad smile and cheerful demeanor reminded her of a jovial grandfather.

The moment introductions had been made, Mr. Harrington nodded toward the table. "Before we talk, I'm eager to see the display you've created." With his short legs and generous belly, he appeared to waddle rather than walk across the room.

Levi followed and circled to the rear of the table. "As you can see, these are the few mosaics I had the opportunity to make before moving to Weston."

"Um-hum." Mr. Harrington picked up one of the tiles and carefully examined both front and back. He traced his fingers over the grooves and then moved on to each of the remaining tiles. "Your work is beautiful, Mr. Judson. I've never seen anything like these." He looked up from the tile he held between his thick fingers. "You believe these will prove durable?"

"They're as durable as any tile. Each of the pieces undergoes the same firing process and because most of the pieces are small, the impact isn't great. I would suggest the tiles be surrounded by Cluny quarries, but that would be your choice—something we could discuss in detail if you decide you want to use the mosaics."

"And all these drawings. Tell me about your ideas." Mr. Harrington rested his hand on his paunch.

The four of them sat down near the display. "When we discussed what might interest you, we arrived at a number of ideas.

As you can see, I've done some drawings that depict scenes from the Bible, scenes from fairy tales, various occupations, scenes that depict the settlement of this country, the Revolutionary War, and the birds, flora, and fauna that represent West Virginia." Levi gestured toward each group as he mentioned the drawings.

"Since I see there are far more of the West Virginia drawings, I'm guessing that's what you favor?" Mr. Harrington arched his brows and leaned back in the chair.

Ainslee's gaze fastened on the businessman's chair. If he leaned back much farther, the chair, along with Mr. Harrington, would collapse in a heap. She leaned forward and breathed a sigh of relief when the older man followed suit.

Levi glanced toward the pictures that represented West Virginia, and then returned his attention to Mr. Harrington. "I like the West Virginia sketches, but there are more of them because my brother drew some of them. It wasn't my intention to sway you in any particular direction, but to give you choices—if you decide to use the mosaics."

The older man's plump face wrinkled into deep folds when his lips curved into a broad smile. "There's no doubt I want to use the mosaics, Mr. Judson. They are superb. But I do have an idea." He turned his chair toward the table and surveyed the display. "I hope you will concur with what I suggest."

Levi's head bobbed in fervent agreement.

"Don't agree too quickly. You may not like my proposal. Mr. McKay will tell you that agreeing before you know all the facts can lead to disaster." Mr. Harrington let his focus settle on Ewan. "Isn't that right, Ewan?"

"Aye, 'tis not a good practice." Ewan winked at Levi. "So what is your proposal, Josiah?"

"The museum is going to have many rooms, with each room

dedicated to specific displays. I think it would be good if each room was tiled with a specific motif rather than using the same one throughout the museum. The entry room will be the largest, and it will be used for a permanent display of West Virginia exhibits, where I'd like to use the tiles you've drawn to represent our fine state. I'd also like to use representative tiles in the larger foyer where guests will enter the building. I believe you could also do some sketches of our wildlife. Nothing like a cougar or black bear to capture a child's imagination."

"I like your proposal, Mr. Harrington. Using a variety of themes will ensure each tile is unique, and I would do my best to adapt to the type of permanent display you plan for each room. The fairy-tale tiles would be excellent if you're planning a children's exhibit area, and the occupational tiles would lend themselves to an exhibit that portrays the variety of trades or the expansion of the country."

Mr. Harrington chuckled. "I like your enthusiasm as well as your ideas, Levi, but I believe we need to address some of the other details."

Levi dipped his head. "I will accept your ideas concerning the colors of glazes, and I would submit the line drawings to you before we proceed with each room."

The older man shook his head. "Those aren't the details we need to discuss. I trust your artistic abilities. I don't have the imagination to know what color glaze is needed to create a beautiful tile, but I do need to know how long it will take to make the tiles and the approximate cost. I have a small group of men working with me, and we'll need facts and figures in order to assess the total cost of the museum."

"How far are you in your process, Mr. Harrington?" Ainslee asked. "From what you've said, I'm assuming you have architectural plans that have been approved, but have you broken ground? And what of financing? Do we need to keep a particular budget in mind when we offer a bid? If you don't yet have a financial plan, we could make two or three bids in which the cost would diminish depending upon the number of mosaics interspersed with the Cluny tiles."

Mr. Harrington's dark eyes emanated warmth. "You speak with the insight of a seasoned business veteran, Miss McKay. I'm impressed. We have a flexible budget because I'm willing to pour as many of my own assets into the project as necessary. I don't have a wife or children, so this museum will be my legacy, so to speak. However, I won't be hoodwinked. I've been in business long enough to know unreasonable bids when I see them."

Ainslee wasn't certain whether she should be offended by his final remark, but she wanted to be clear with him. "The McKays are honorable people, Mr. Harrington. We wouldn't ever attempt to cheat you. Our bids will reflect a cost that permits us to meet expenses and make a reasonable profit."

"Forgive my brusque tone, Miss McKay. I'm accustomed to dealing with men. I know I will receive honesty from the McKay family, but I feel it's best to be forthright at the outset of our talks. I suggest the three of you review our plans for the building before I depart and make note of the dimensions of each room. I'm guessing Mr. Judson will need to do a bit of figuring since some of the rooms are an odd shape." He turned toward Levi. "Determine how many mosaics would be needed to display them to full advantage in each room, and the cost. Once I have received that bid, we can move forward from there. Is that agreeable, Miss McKay?"

Ainslee met Mr. Harrington's gaze. "Not quite."

Ewan edged forward in his chair. "Ainslee, I . . ."

Her lips tipped into a slight frown. "As I was saying, Mr.

Harrington, I believe there is one issue we need to clarify before we review the architectural plans."

He appeared amused. "What's that, Miss McKay?"

"I would like a brief written agreement that you will use a minimum of ten mosaics per room. This request is made so that we are assured it is time well spent for Mr. Judson to move forward creating the tiles. While we believe they could ultimately be sold to someone else, we wouldn't begin to produce them at this time without your agreement to use them first in the museum."

His eyes twinkled. "Your negotiation skills are admirable, young lady. As I said, I greatly admire these tiles, and I want them in my museum. Write up your agreement, and I'll sign it before I leave Weston."

At that moment, it took all the power Ainslee could muster to remain in her chair and appear calm. She wanted to leap into Levi's arms and permit her joy to overflow, but that wasn't what was expected of a businesswoman—or man. So instead of jumping up from her chair and dancing around the room, she gave a polite nod and agreed to present Mr. Harrington with the agreement before nightfall.

"Since we haven't yet broken ground, we'll soon be accepting bids for construction of the building, but that will be a slower process. I have high expectations, so I want to be certain each company hired to work on this project will perform excellent work." The older man pushed to his feet. "I'd like all of you to join me for supper at the hotel this evening." He glanced at Ewan. "Bring your wife and young daughter along, too. When we get back to the hotel, I can furnish you with the architectural plans so that all of you can go over them in the morning. Unless something arises that requires me to remain longer, I'll depart on the one o'clock train tomorrow."

Ewan accepted for all of them and then prepared to leave with Mr. Harrington. The two of them had walked outside, but Ewan soon returned. "Mr. Harrington asked if we have any objection to a news article regarding the decision to use the mosaics in the museum. He thought it would let folks know the project is moving forward and give us a bit of publicity as well. Is that acceptable to the two of you?"

Ainslee glanced at Levi, who hiked his shoulders and deferred to her. "Having our name mentioned would be good for business, but this project is going to keep us busy for quite some time." She hesitated only a moment. "Of course, if it brings us more orders, we can always hire more workers. Tell Mr. Harrington we'd be pleased to have an announcement in the papers."

The moment the two men were out of sight, Levi lifted Ainslee off her feet and twirled her in a wide circle. She whooped a shout of delight. What a wondrous day this had been.

The excitement of the day hadn't subsided by the time Ainslee walked upstairs to her bedroom. After an hour of tossing and turning in her bed, she lit the oil lamp and picked up Nettie Brinker's story. She hoped reading would help her fall asleep, but she became engrossed in the story and it wasn't until the grandfather clock in the hallway chimed three times that she forced herself to put aside the remaining pages. She needed to get a few hours of sleep before morning arrived.

After breakfast, Ainslee tucked the story into her small satchel. If time permitted, she'd complete it at work. She'd been awed by Nettie's talent. Granted, there were small errors in her spelling and grammar, but the story and the characters had proved compelling. As she departed for the tile works, Ainslee's mind whirred. The story was too good to remain packed away in a musty box of papers in the asylum. She startled and turned when Levi called her name.

He ran to her side, panting for air. "Why didn't you wait for me? I thought we were going to meet Ewan this morning. It will be our last chance before he returns home this afternoon."

She attempted to pull her thoughts back to the present. "I forgot. My mind was on something else." She hesitated a moment. "Why don't you go to the hotel and meet with him? I have another matter I'd like to attend to this morning."

His forehead formed tight creases. "More important than meeting with Ewan?"

"There's nothing the two of you can't decide without me."

"Really?" Levi's eyes were inquisitive, but he grinned. "What's so important that you're willing to miss a meeting with Ewan and me?"

She glanced at her satchel. "I'll tell you later. Right now, you better hurry or Ewan will think we've both gone missing."

Before she spoke to anyone about her idea, she wanted to complete Nettie's story. Ainslee turned and hurried off, eager to read the final pages.

"I thought you'd never get here." Ainslee popped up from her chair like a tightly wound spring. "Wait until you hear what I've been doing this morning."

Levi removed his cap and coat, surprised by her comment. He'd expected her to ask about the meeting with Ewan rather than tell him about her own endeavors. He sat down opposite her and touched a finger to the side of his head. "I'm all ears."

Ainslee pushed a sheaf of papers across the desk toward him.

"What's this? Not additions to the contract, I hope."

She chuckled. "No. This has nothing to do with contracts or the tiles. This is a story written by Nettie Brinker, one of the ladies who volunteered to help with the library project. When I went to the asylum to pick up the letters Nettie and Zana had written to prospective donors, Nettie asked me if I would read a story she'd written. Dr. Thorenson had told her I was a schoolteacher." Ainslee hesitated a moment. "I couldn't sleep last night so I started reading what she'd given me. I had to force myself to put it down at three o'clock this morning." She sighed. "I believe she's exceedingly talented. I want to help her."

So that was why Ainslee had elected to miss the meeting with Ewan. She'd wanted to finish reading Mrs. Brinker's story. He leaned back in the chair. "I think it would be wonderful for you to help. I'm certain the staff would approve both reading and writing classes at the asylum."

"That's not what I meant when I said I wanted to help. While I'd be pleased to offer classes in the future, I want to do something more with this story. If Nettie agrees, I'd like her to make a few changes and then I want to submit it to *Godey's Lady's Book*." Ainslee's eyes glistened with excitement.

Levi cleared his throat. While he longed to share in Ainslee's excitement, he wasn't certain what she was talking about. His reading didn't include the book she'd mentioned. "I don't know anything about books written for ladies, but if you think they might take a look at her story and make it into a book, I'm sure she'd be pleased."

Ainslee shook her head. "*Godey's* is a periodical distributed each month. They print short stories, recipes, household hints, and also include the latest fashions for women. The magazine is highly regarded, and some of the finest writers in the country have published with them."

He didn't want to discourage her. After all, she certainly knew far more about literature than he. Still, if they published such notable folks, why would they be interested in a story written by a patient living in an asylum? "You truly believe they would read her story?"

"The magazine says it accepts submissions." She leaned forward. "You don't think I should send it?"

"Quite the opposite. I think it's a wonderful idea so long as Nettie agrees and she won't be overly disappointed if they don't print it." Of course, Levi wasn't certain how anyone would know in advance how they would feel in such a circumstance. "Maybe you should ask Dr. Thorenson for his opinion, as well."

Ainslee nodded. "That's a good idea. Now, tell me about your meeting with Ewan. I would like to know what I am talking about when we see him off at the station."

Chapter 19

As time had permitted throughout the early summer months, Ainslee had diligently worked to prepare the library at the asylum. Now she surveyed the room in the asylum one final time. Bookshelves constructed by local carpenters lined the walls of the room, and an attractive seating arrangement and several reading tables had been strategically placed to create a calm mood and provide good lighting for the patients who would utilize the facility. Laura and her mother had both rallied around the cause. Grandmother Woodfield had spread the word and drummed up donations in Bartlett, while Laura did the same in Grafton. Together, they'd made an impressive team and raised enough money to furnish the library and pay the carpenters for the bookshelves.

Much to Ainslee's delight, Nettie had been thrilled when Ainslee suggested submitting her story to *Godey's Lady's Book*. While Dr. Thorenson initially had expressed reservations about the idea, he soon became convinced Nettie could deal with a letter of rejection. After all, she'd seemingly accepted her husband's rejection without dire consequences.

Ainslee prayed her actions would prove positive and help

Nettie progress toward life outside the institution. They'd agreed the submission would bear Nettie's name, but all correspondence would be addressed to the tile works rather than the asylum. And while Nettie had given every assurance she didn't expect a positive response from the magazine, Ainslee hadn't missed her look of expectation each time they met.

Today Laura would be arriving at Weston with a delivery of books to help fill the shelves. Her desire to accompany the shipment had come as a delightful yet unexpected surprise. There would be little time for visiting upon her arrival, since Ainslee would need to shelve the books and assist with arrangements for the tea and ribbon-cutting ceremony, but Laura planned to remain in Weston for several days, and Ainslee would have time to enjoy Laura's company after the library opening. During her visit, Ainslee hoped to convince her to visit the asylum. While her sister-in-law had expressed a fear of the patients, Ainslee hoped to prove how many of them were harmless.

Dr. Thorenson tapped on the library door. Although it stood ajar, he remained in the hallway. Ainslee crossed the room and greeted him.

"Am I allowed to come in, or are you making everyone wait until the books have been shelved before you permit entry?" With a grin, he attempted to peek around her and look into the room.

She opened the door wide and waved him forward. "You are more than welcome. I want to surprise the ladies, but any members of the staff are welcome to see what's been accomplished."

His mouth gaped and his eyes opened wide when he stepped inside and inspected the room. "I can't believe it. This is wonderful, Miss McKay."

His compliment created a rush of heat that raced up her neck and across her cheeks. "Thank you. When the patients come into this library, I hope they will be able to set aside their grief and worries for a time. Beyond what we learn from books, they can also provide a wonderful escape from the difficulties that surround us."

"You're preaching to the converted, Miss McKay. I'm already a firm supporter of your program here at the asylum, and I certainly think your library is going to prove a great asset for our patients." He leaned against one of the library tables. "Once the staff sees how well you've appointed this room, they may begin clamoring to work in this wing of the asylum."

"My brother's wife will arrive today with a shipment of books. She didn't tell me how many books had been donated or purchased so I'm eager to see how many of these shelves I'll be able to fill before we finally open the doors to the patients."

"Perhaps Mrs. McKay will attend the ribbon-cutting ceremony with you. I believe it would be a fine gesture to include her since she has played a large role in securing books and donations for the furnishings, don't you?" Before Ainslee could reply, he continued, his excitement mounting. "I believe we should present her with a certificate during the ceremony."

"I don't know all of her plans just . . ."

"Yes! A certificate of appreciation would be perfect. I'll see that one is prepared. We have an excellent calligrapher working in the office." He pushed away from the table, his eyes alight with excitement. "You don't need to concern yourself. I'll see to the preparation and make certain there's a proper presentation from the administrator." An orderly appeared at the door and gestured to the doctor. He nodded and crossed the room. "I need to see to a patient, but you keep up the good work, Miss McKay, and I'll see to the certificate. We'll have a grand ceremony right here in the library."

Ainslee stared after him, surprised by the doctor's last-minute decision but determined to complete as much as possible before Laura's arrival. There wasn't time to dwell on anything other than shelving books.

The clock in the bell tower sounded, and Ainslee startled to attention. If she didn't leave now, she'd be late meeting Laura's train. As promised, the wagon Levi had arranged for at the livery was waiting outside the asylum when she arrived at the front gate.

The driver jumped to the ground to assist her. "I was beginning to think maybe Mr. Judson gave me the wrong time." Using his thumb, he gestured toward the asylum. "I sure didn't want to go in there lookin'. I might never get back out."

Ainslee frowned at him. "Why would you say such a thing? Nobody is going to keep you in the asylum merely because you step inside the gates. That's plain silly." She tipped her head sideways. "Unless you need treatment." She hesitated a moment and arched her brows. "Do you?"

He shook his head with such vigor that his cap slipped sideways. "Nah! Ain't nothin' wrong in my head."

"Then there's no reason to be worried about going into the asylum. The patients are treated well. This new asylum is much better than being locked in a jail cell with twenty or thirty other people suffering from mental deficiencies, don't you think?"

He jumped back up on the seat, unlocked the brake, and slapped the reins across the horses' backsides. "I don't want to think about what would be better. I don't want to think about them folks at all. I know more than half the people in this town make their living working there, but I'd rather go without than work in a place like that." He shuddered. "Gives me the shivers just thinking 'bout it."

"So I noticed." Ainslee momentarily considered an attempt to dissuade his thoughts but decided against the idea. Instead, she'd use her powers of persuasion on Laura. She wanted her sister-in-law to see what her hard work in Grafton had helped to create.

Once they arrived at the depot, the driver helped her down and followed her inside. "Mr. Judson said there'd be a lot of heavy crates for me to load into the wagon and deliver back to the asylum. I hope you got arrangements for someone else to take 'em in there. I told Mr. Judson I wouldn't go inside."

Ainslee sighed. "I expect you to unload the crates at the front gate. Arrangements can be made for them to be delivered inside without your help."

"You ain't gonna have none of them crazy folks out there when I'm around, are ya?"

Ainslee clenched her teeth and willed herself to remain calm. "The men who will assist with the delivery are employed at the asylum. Some may even be your friends or neighbors." She turned toward the clanging and hissing of the approaching train. "The train has arrived. Please follow me." She swallowed the angry lecture she longed to give him, squared her shoulders, and strode toward the platform.

Moments later, Laura stepped down from the train and rushed forward. She opened her arms and pulled Ainslee into a warm embrace. "It's so good to see you again." She took a backward step. "You look lovely."

Ainslee giggled and pushed an errant strand of hair behind her ear. "I believe lovely is a bit of a stretch. I've been working at the asylum all morning and didn't have time to go home and freshen up before coming to meet the train. Preparing for the library opening has been more time-consuming than I had imagined, but it has taken shape and looks wonderful. I can't wait to shelve the books you've brought for us." She glanced over her shoulder toward the wagon driver. "I have a driver waiting to load the crates into his wagon and deliver the books to the asylum. How many crates are there?"

Laura hesitated. "Perhaps it would be easier if we go with him. That way I can be certain we retrieve all of them. Some of the books are packed in crates, but some are in barrels. There are even three large trunks, which I'll need to ship back to the owners when I return to Weston. They arrived from Wheeling and I didn't have time to unload and repack them into crates. It seems Mr. Harrington was able to elicit good support for your cause."

"Truly? How wonderful of him. He donated money to assist with the purchase of furnishings for the library, as well. He's proving to be quite a benefactor." She waved for the driver to follow them.

He hurried forward and loaded the crates onto baggage carts. "I coulda figured out these was the ones. They got the McKay name on all of 'em."

Laura nodded and smiled. "There are three trunks, as well, and they haven't been properly identified." She wove through the baggage area with a determined step. "Ah, here they are." She traced her gloved hand across the three canvas-covered, flat-top trunks. "I believe that's everything, except my personal trunk, which will need to go to the hotel. Let's make certain it doesn't get unloaded at the asylum."

"No need to worry, Laura. We'll take a carriage to the asylum, and I'll supervise the unloading there." She stepped to the side of the driver. "You might want to load Mrs. McKay's trunk onto the wagon first since it won't need to be unloaded until we go to the hotel."

"I don't need ya to tell me how to load a wagon, Miss McKay." The driver groaned. "My aching back. I woulda charged Mr. Judson more if I'd known there would be so much to load into the wagon. Them crates and barrels is mighty heavy, and I'm thinking the trunks are even worse. Books are lots heavier than dresses and hats."

Ainslee offered the driver a tight smile. "Consider your labor a contribution to a good cause."

He glowered at her as he lifted the trunk onto a wheeled cart, but Ainslee pretended not to notice. Any further comment would only make matters worse, so she hurried Laura toward the doors leading into the depot. "No need for us to wait on the platform. You can sit down inside and I'll arrange for a carriage to take us to the asylum."

Laura hastened her step. "You won't be going into the asylum, will you? If so, I'll have the driver take me on to the hotel and then have him return for you. I know you said it is perfectly safe, but—"

Ainslee shook her head. "No, I won't go in today, but I'll return tomorrow so I can log and shelve the books you've brought."

Tomorrow would be filled with tasks in the library, and Ainslee was determined to have Laura by her side. She walked outside, signaled to a carriage driver, and silently prayed God would provide her with the needed words and direction to convince Laura there was nothing to fear.

After overseeing the unloading of the books, Ainslee stopped at the hotel and waited until Laura's trunk was delivered to her room before returning to the tile works. Her full attention had been devoted to the library over the past days and the workers' time records needed to be entered in the ledger before the pay envelopes could be prepared. If she planned to go to the library first thing in the morning, she would need to complete her duties at the tile works before joining Laura for supper at the hotel.

As she entered the office, Levi looked up and grinned. "Did Laura arrive safely?"

"She did." Ainslee brushed the loose strands of hair from her face. "I'm pleased to see you, but why are you in here instead of working on the mosaics?" Perhaps he'd decided to make changes to some of his drawings. She drew closer and peered across the desk. The payroll ledger lay open on the desk in front of him, as well as a stack of time sheets. She gasped. "You don't need to do this. I told you I'd return and get the pay envelopes prepared."

"You have so much to do before the opening. I know how important the library is to you—and to me. I'm proud of what you're doing, and this is one small way I can help. I can work on sketches later, but this needs to be completed and I want you to have time with Laura."

"I will. *We* will. I told her we would join her for supper at the hotel this evening." She sat down at the opposite side of the desk and picked up a stack of mail. Her heart pounded a new beat when she caught sight of an envelope bearing Nettie's name. "Did you see this?"

Levi shook his head. "I didn't go through the mail. What is it?"

Her hand trembled when she picked up the envelope. "It's a letter to Nettie." The words caught in her throat. "From *Godey's Lady's Book*." She hesitated. "Oh, Levi. I think it must be good news." She clutched the thin envelope to her chest. "If they don't intend to publish submissions, I believe they're returned to the author."

"Then they must have liked her story. Are you going to open it?"

Ainslee placed the envelope in front of her and stared at Nettie's name. "I didn't ask what I should do when a response arrived. If it's good news, I want Nettie to know first, but if it's bad news . . ." She looked at Levi. "What do you think I should do?"

"I think you should let me complete the payroll, and you should return to the asylum so that Nettie can open her letter. If Dr. Thorenson is in his office, ask him to accompany you—just in case it's a rejection and Nettie should become distressed by the news."

Little wonder she'd come to care so much for Levi. He seemed always to provide the help and advice she needed. "You're sure you won't mind doing the payroll?"

He rested his arms on the desk and turned his open palms toward her. "I'm yours to command. I would be pleased to complete the payroll, assist you in shelving books at the library, or order you supper later this evening."

She giggled, enjoying his amusing tone and willing spirit. "Then I believe I will accept your offer to finish the payroll and order my supper later this evening. As for shelving books, I may put those strong arms of yours to use tomorrow morning."

He stood, waved his hand in a sweeping gesture, and bowed. "As you wish, my lady."

Ainslee turned and smiled as she neared the office door. "Good sir, if you can think of some way to help me convince Laura she'll be missing a wonderful experience if she doesn't attend the ceremony tomorrow, I'd consider knighting you."

Levi chuckled. "I wouldn't want to miss the opportunity to have you tap my shoulders with a sword. I'll do my best to offer a solution upon your return." He offered a deep bow.

Ainslee couldn't contain her laughter. "I'll count on that since I don't want to order a beheading."

Levi gasped and held his hands to his head. "Please don't consider such a thing, my lady. I promise I'll have an answer for you."

She opened the door and offered a final wave to Levi before departing. The good-natured role playing with him had been just what she needed.

Ainslee's shoes clicked on the Minton tiles that lined the hallway leading to Dr. Thorenson's office. She'd barely lifted her hand to knock, when the door opened and the doctor appeared.

"Miss McKay, I thought you'd left." His gaze wandered toward the hallway leading to the library. "There wasn't anyone in the library when I passed by a short time ago."

"I did leave, but when I returned to the tile works, I went through the mail." She waved the envelope under his nose. "Look what arrived. It's from *Godey's*."

He leaned back slightly and focused on the envelope. "So it is."

Her voice vibrated with excitement. Truth be told, Ainslee would have jumped up and down if such behavior hadn't been so unladylike. "Can we go and get Nettie? I can hardly wait to see what the letter says."

Dr. Thorenson smiled and gave a slight nod. "Yes, but you need to be prepared if the news isn't good. While Nettie isn't one who shows much emotion, I'm sure she'll be quite disappointed. You may need to stay for a time and offer her encouragement."

Though she had promised to join Laura for supper, Ainslee was willing to take her chances. She couldn't bear to wait any longer to know the contents of the letter. "If the news isn't good, I'll do my best, but I feel certain they've accepted the story."

He didn't say anything, but from the look in Dr. Thorenson's eyes, it was obvious he wasn't so positive. "Then, let's be on our way. The ladies should be in the dormitory preparing for supper."

By the time they arrived at the doorway to the dormitory, Ainslee could barely breathe. She startled when the doctor lightly grasped her elbow and nodded toward the room where she'd met Nettie before. "I still don't think you should go into the dormitory. It will create too much excitement for the other patients and some may be difficult to calm." A slight smile played on his lips. "Unintentional or not, the nurses and orderlies will be unhappy with me if I do anything to cause an upheaval before supper."

Ainslee clutched the letter in her hand as she awaited Nettie's arrival in the private room. When she heard the click of the dormitory door, she straightened to attention and leaned forward. She jumped to her feet the minute Nettie appeared.

"Did Dr. Thorenson tell you?" Before Nettie could answer, Ainslee thrust the envelope toward her. "You received a letter from *Godey's*."

Nettie's mouth dropped open as she glanced toward the doctor. "No. He merely said you needed to speak to me. I thought it was about the library."

When she didn't reach for the envelope, Ainslee waved it back and forth. "Here. Please open this. I've been on pins and needles ever since I laid eyes on it."

Nettie's hand quivered as she grasped the missive and opened the seal. Both Ainslee and the doctor peered at her. Moments later, she dropped to one of the chairs. "They want to publish my story." Eyes wide, she looked up at Ainslee. "The letter says they'll send a draft by separate mail if I sign the enclosed contract and agree to publication." She clasped the letter to her chest. "Can you believe it? The letter says they have a readership of more than one hundred and fifty thousand." She sighed. "If only a few of them read my story and like it, won't that be grand?"

Dr. Thorenson sat down beside her and nodded toward the

missive. "Before you sign, perhaps we should have someone with knowledge of such contracts take a look at what they've sent. I wouldn't want them to take advantage."

Nettie looked at him as though he were the one who should be a patient in the asylum. "I would sign this even if they didn't offer a cent. To have one of my stories in such a fine magazine is an honor, Dr. Thorenson. It was never my intention to make money from my writing."

He nodded. "That may be, Nettie, but the money you can make by writing may be a ticket to a new life for you. If you're declared to be sane and can support yourself, wouldn't you much prefer to live on your own?"

She nodded. "Yes, yet it will take more than the sale of one story before I can consider such a future." Her lips curved in a generous smile. "But it's a beginning. I'll save my money, and perhaps one day I'll leave my past behind."

Nettie turned toward Ainslee. "If I sign the contract, will you mail it for me right away?"

"I'll make sure it gets in tomorrow's mail."

A short time later, signed contract in hand, Ainslee returned to the tile works, where Levi greeted her with a smile. "I'm guessing it was good news since you look like you're about to bust a button."

She giggled and bobbed her head. "They sent a short contract and they're going to pay her for the story. She's so happy, I doubt she'll get a minute of sleep tonight."

Levi pushed back from the desk. "I think you might match her on that account. I don't think you could be happier if it had happened to you."

Ainslee considered his words and knew he was right. Her joy for Nettie surpassed the pleasure she'd experienced with any of her own successes. The excitement of being able to help

Nettie with her story was truly exciting, but realizing it could possibly lead to a new and independent life for the woman was truly gratifying.

She withdrew an envelope from her desk drawer and carefully penned the address of *Godey's Lady's Book*. After tucking the contract inside and sealing the envelope, she looked up and met Levi's gaze. "Do you need me to complete the payroll?"

He shook his head. "It's all done, but I do want to talk to you about a possible solution to Laura's attendance at the opening ceremony."

"So you *were* afraid I'd have you beheaded."

He laughed. "Beheading was foremost in my mind the entire time you were away."

When he said nothing more, she leaned forward. "Are you going to tell me?"

An impish gleam shone in his eyes. "We both need to get back to our rooms and change for supper. When we arrive at the hotel, just follow my lead."

Ainslee wanted to quiz him further, but she remained silent. She'd asked for his help. Now she needed to trust him.

Levi lightly grasped Ainslee's elbow as they walked into the hotel dining room. "I'm going to speak to Laura about some artwork, so I'll need you to follow along and support me."

"Yes, of course." Ainslee wasn't certain she'd be able to lend much support since she didn't know what artwork he might want to discuss, but she'd do her best.

Laura was waiting in the lobby and greeted them with a glowing smile. "I'm so pleased you could both join me for supper. I have a table reserved for us."

Over the next hour, they dined and chatted about the library, the mosaics, Tessa, and life in Grafton. When they'd nearly completed their dinner, Ainslee could hold her excitement no longer. She touched Laura's hand. "I simply must share that Nettie Brinker, an acquaintance of mine, received a contract to have a story she's written published with *Godey's*."

Laura gasped. "Truly? What an honor. They've published so many extraordinary authors. Your friend will likely become famous. I don't believe I've heard you mention her before. Does she live at the boardinghouse?"

Ainslee touched the corner of her linen napkin to her lips. "No. She's a patient at the asylum."

Laura leaned forward. "The napkin muffled your answer. It sounded as though you said she's a patient at the asylum."

"You heard correctly. Nettie is as sane as you and me, but her husband was unhappy with her. He said she spent too much of her time reading and writing rather than performing her household duties."

Laura frowned. "And you believe her? I think the woman has to be delusional. No husband would have his wife placed in an asylum because she reads books or writes in a journal."

Ainslee didn't want to argue with her sister-in-law. This wasn't the time or place, but she had hoped revealing Nettie's exciting news would convince Laura the asylum wasn't such a frightening place. She glanced at Levi. He winked before turning his attention to Laura.

"Ainslee has told me that you have an excellent eye for art, Mrs. McKay."

Laura blushed and let her gaze linger on her plate for a moment. "I like to think I can appreciate good art, but I'm not an expert. I certainly enjoy visiting museums and learning all I can, so I've come to perhaps a greater knowledge than some of my peers."

Levi enthusiastically nodded and offered a broad smile. "Excellent. You're exactly the person I need." He glanced around the room as if preparing to divulge some conspiratorial message. "If I asked you to judge several pieces of artwork, would you be willing to choose the one you believe is the best piece?"

"Of course, but art is subjective. Even the experts sometimes disagree." Laura took a sip of her coffee.

"I understand, but we won't be asking any of those so-called experts to give an opinion. If you're free tomorrow morning, I'll call for you here at the hotel at nine o'clock. Will that be satisfactory?"

She nodded. "Certainly. I look forward to it. Will I be judging a variety of works, or only the work of one artist?"

Levi wagged his finger back and forth. "I'm not going to give you any more details, but promise me you'll keep your word."

She tipped her head to the side. "Of course. I always keep my word."

A short time later, they bid Laura good-night in the hotel lobby. Moments later, Ainslee nudged Levi's arm. "How is that going to help, and what artwork are you talking about? I'm confused."

Levi escorted her out the front doors and helped her into the waiting carriage. "That's why I asked you to follow my lead. Fortunately, Laura agreed to the plan without too many questions, so there was no need for you to encourage her."

"I'm thankful I could remain silent during the conversation. I had hoped hearing about Nettie's contract would help ease her worries, but she's unwilling to believe there are patients in the institution who are as sane as you and me."

"Once inside, she's going to discover her fears are unfounded."

Ainslee nudged his arm. "I wasn't even aware there was artwork to be judged."

As the carriage continued down the rutted dirt road to the boardinghouses, Levi detailed the rest of his idea. "I don't know if it will work, but we're going to have to rely upon the fact that she gave her word." He grinned. "Just make certain you're in the library with those paintings and the other ladies when we arrive tomorrow morning."

Ainslee leaned close, enjoying the warmth of Levi nearness. How thankful she was that God had sent such a wonderful man into her life. A dependable man who willingly helped her through every difficulty that came her way. She sighed contentedly and basked in the pleasure of Levi's presence.

Chapter 20

Ainslee awakened the following morning with a sense of expectation bubbling deep within. Mrs. Brighton chastised her for eating only one biscuit for breakfast, but Ainslee's excitement was far too great to eat a large meal.

She rushed out the door to the awaiting buggy amidst the good wishes of the boardinghouse ladies and soon was hard at work logging books. Initially, she'd simply enter the titles and name of the author in the ledger. There wasn't time to organize the books. She'd truly count it a blessing if she could get all of them logged and in the bookcases. There would be ample time for organization in the coming months.

Several of the female patients arrived a short time later and began shelving the books. Ainslee directed them to the books that had already been logged into the ledger. "There isn't time to shelve them by category or author. We can see to that later."

She looked up when Dr. Thorenson entered the library and glanced around the room. "I thought your sister-in-law might be here with you. I was hoping for an introduction."

Ainslee shook her head. "She should be here a little after

nine o'clock. If you'd like to return then, I'm sure she'd be pleased to meet you."

The doctor's eyes shone with disappointment. "I'll do my best to return then. Speaking of your sister-in-law, I'm pleased to tell you that the certificate is almost completed. I hope she'll be pleased with our efforts to thank her."

"I'm sure she will." Ainslee briefly considered telling the doctor Laura might not be present, but then she remembered Laura had promised to come and judge the artwork. Her sister-in-law wasn't one to break her word. Besides, once Laura met a few of the ladies, she'd overcome her fears.

Ainslee returned to the ledger and when the clock tower bonged to announce the nine o'clock hour, she startled. The time was passing far too quickly. Levi would be at the hotel meeting Laura.

Ainslee answered questions for several of the ladies, and then continued logging books. A short time later, she clicked open the timepiece pinned to her shirtwaist. Nine twenty. They should be here soon. She pushed away from the table and stepped to the door. Her breath caught when she spotted Levi and Laura walking down the hallway.

Quickly, she stepped back inside and closed the doors. "Ladies! Could I have your attention for a moment?" The women ceased their work and turned toward her. "We're going to have a couple of guests stop in the library for a brief visit. If time permits, I'll introduce each of you, but please continue with your work. We want to have as many books shelved as possible." She waved to Nettie. "Would you please take over the logging duties, Nettie?"

The words had barely escaped her lips when Laura and Levi entered. A deep-set frown creased Laura's forehead, and her lips formed a taut line. She rushed to Ainslee's side. "You should have warned me he was going to bring me here."

"I didn't know until after we parted last night, but I'm pleased you kept your word. As you can see, this is a perfectly safe place. Let me introduce you to the ladies who are donating their time to shelve books." Ainslee led Laura across the room. One by one, she introduced her to the ladies, ending with Nettie. "And this is Nettie Brinker, the lady I told you about last evening." Ainslee turned her gaze toward Nettie. "I hope you don't mind, but I shared your good news about *Godey's* with my sister-in-law."

Nettie's smile broadened. "Of course, I don't mind. It's a pleasure to meet you, Mrs. McKay. Ainslee has been a genuine source of encouragement to many of us, especially to me. If it weren't for her efforts, my story would still be tucked away among my few belongings."

Laura's features softened as she spoke to Nettie. "I'm pleased to meet you. Congratulations on your success. Being published in *Godey's* is quite an accomplishment. You must continue with your writing. I'm sure Ainslee will assist you in any way she can." Laura looked toward Ainslee. "If you'll excuse me, I'm supposed to review some artwork."

Nettie picked up her pen and nodded. "I looked at the paintings earlier this morning. They're well done. I think you'll enjoy seeing them."

Laura stepped away from the table and drew close to Ainslee's side. "She seems lovely. It's good you can have her near you and away from all of the other patients."

Ainslee grinned. After introducing her to Nettie, she had expected Laura would guess the other ladies were patients, but her sister-in-law hadn't yet deduced the truth. "They are all very nice ladies." Ainslee gestured toward the far side of the room where Levi stood beside a group of paintings resting against the wall.

He stepped toward them as they approached. "We would

like for you to decide which ones would best suit this room. The rest will be hung in the outer hallways."

Laura seemed to forget her surroundings as she slowly examined each of the paintings. Ainslee maintained a careful watch on the ladies, worried some of them might say or do something that would reveal they were patients. She'd held her breath when Laura had carried paintings to different locations in the room.

"I believe these two are the best choice. I think all of them would be lovely in here, but the bookshelves have left the room with little wall space. The wall color will bring out the shading in the two I've chosen." She appeared far more relaxed than when she'd first entered the room. "Would you like me to stay and help you shelve books? Now that I'm here, I might as well make myself useful."

Ainslee nodded toward a far window. "I would love to have your help, but I need to first tell you that all of these ladies are patients here in the asylum. They've been working with me since I first began planning the library. As you can see, they are harmless."

Laura's eyes widened, and she glanced around the room. She leaned close to Ainslee. "All of them? Not just Nettie?"

The question hissed in Ainslee's ear. "Yes, all of them. Most suffer from depression, some are grieving, and others, like Nettie, are here simply because their husbands no longer wished to be married to them and made up allegations about their behavior."

Laura shook her head. "Women need to be warned so that they will be most careful in their choice of a husband. Don't you agree?"

"Indeed." Before Ainslee could say anything further, Dr. Thorenson entered the room.

His lips curved in a broad smile as he drew near. "I heard

that our esteemed visitor was in the library, and I thought I'd come and meet you. I am delighted that you're going to be here for the dedication ceremony. I'm Dr. Thorenson, and I've had the pleasure of lending a small amount of assistance to Ainslee while she's worked on this project."

Ainslee traced the fingers of her left hand along the scar. "He's also the doctor who so capably cared for me when I injured myself."

Laura placed her arm around Ainslee's shoulder. "We owe you a debt of gratitude, Doctor. Without your help, I'm sure she wouldn't have had such a wonderful recovery."

"Though I wish our initial encounter hadn't been due to such painful circumstances, it was my good fortune to meet Miss McKay. Her passion for this library is a godsend." Dr. Thorenson glanced around the room. "Our dedication ceremony is going to be quite an event. Has Ainslee told you that you're to be seated beside her at the head table?"

"Me?" Laura looked at Ainslee. Her sister-in-law was just as surprised as she was. "No, she didn't mention the head table, but I'd be honored."

Ainslee exhaled a long breath and uttered a silent prayer of thanks. None of this would have come together so perfectly had it not been for Levi's help and God's grace.

Several hours later, the bell tower sounded and a nurse appeared in the doorway of the library. "Time for the noonday meal, ladies. Please form a line." She turned toward Laura and Ainslee. "Dr. Thorenson asked that you join him in the staff room, where he's arranged for your meal."

Laura stiffened and Ainslee offered her sister-in-law an encouraging smile. Although Laura had been working in the library for several hours, it appeared as if the idea of moving to another location in the asylum had reignited her anxiety.

"Thank you. Please tell Dr. Thorenson we'll join him shortly." Ainslee leaned forward. "There's nothing to fear. The staff room is in the administration area. Patients are seldom in that portion of the asylum."

Laura's eyes widened. "Seldom?"

Ainslee hadn't wanted to say *never*. After all, patients were occasionally in the administrative wing. "When patients are admitted, they need to come through the main offices so that the proper papers can be completed and the doctor can perform a physical examination. I've been here frequently and haven't yet seen a patient there. At least no one who appeared to be a patient. As you discovered in the library, it's sometimes difficult to know who is a patient and who is a visitor."

They remained at the library table until the patients filed out of the room. When Ainslee stood and gestured toward the door, Laura remained seated. "I ate a large breakfast at the hotel dining room and I'm not the least bit hungry. Why don't you lock the door as you leave and I'll remain here?"

Ainslee sighed. "I don't have a key to the door, so I'll have to leave it unlocked. If that's what you prefer, I'll be gone for less than an hour."

The remark had been carefully crafted to omit any mention of safety, for Ainslee didn't want to instill the idea that harm would come to Laura if she remained in the library. However, the only way Laura was going to overcome her fears completely would be to see more of the facility and how it operated.

Laura pushed to her feet. "On second thought, perhaps I should have something to eat. If I'm going to help you log and shelve the remainder of these books, I'll be famished by the time we finish."

"I think you're right. You'll find the food quite good. I've enjoyed meals in the staff room on a couple of occasions." She looped her arm through Laura's, glad for a little time alone together. All morning, she'd wanted to question Laura about her decision to visit the asylum. Beyond that, she worried Laura might be angry with Levi. If so, Ainslee hoped to clear the air. "I hope you're not angry with Levi."

Laura shook her head. "No. Once I learned that I was to be seated by you at the head table during the ceremony, I understood why you were pressing me to attend. By insisting I keep my word and judge the artwork, Levi was doing what he thought was best for both of us. I now realize you were both correct." They turned left down a hallway. "Although I can't say that I'm completely comfortable here, being with the female patients has dispelled many of my concerns."

"I'm glad to hear that. I understand you likely will never visit the asylum after you return to Grafton, but if you could spread the word to others that neither the patients nor the facility is a place to be feared, it might help banish some of the myths. People still equate this facility with those overcrowded jail cells used to house the insane in times past. I hope we'll never see a return to those conditions, for a place like this is much more humane."

"True, but what will happen when these new asylums become overcrowded?" Laura asked. "Without enough facilities, might we see a return to the horror of the past? The only remedy will be to build additional facilities, but that becomes an issue of money."

Dr. Thorenson stood near the door leading into the staff room. "Did I overhear you ladies discussing financial matters?" He gestured for them to enter the room.

As the aroma of baked chicken drifted toward them, Ainslee's stomach rumbled. "My sister-in-law expressed concern that these new asylums may become overcrowded and the patients poorly cared for if there isn't adequate funding to construct enough facilities."

The doctor led them to a long cloth-covered table on which platters and bowls of food had been arranged. "The meal is self-service. We'll begin at the other end, where you'll find the plates and silverware." He gestured for Ainslee to take the lead.

When they'd filled their plates and were seated at one of the dining tables, the doctor filled their glasses with water. "May I pray before our meal?"

He looked back and forth between the two ladies. Both of them nodded their agreement.

After he'd finished the brief prayer, he turned his attention to Laura. "It does my heart good to know there are at least a few people beyond those who work in the asylums who realize we will soon be confronted by the same overcrowding problems we've experienced in the past. Unlike the jails where patients were previously confined, we do provide both mental and physical care for our patients. Unfortunately, we're already housing more patients than this facility was constructed to accommodate. We do have a group of doctors advocating to the state legislature for additional funds to build more asylums, but it's doubtful the idea will progress beyond a few minor discussions."

The doctor unfolded his napkin. "Tell me, Mrs. McKay, what do you think of our asylum? This is your first visit, and I'm always eager to hear what new visitors have to say."

"To be honest, it took every ounce of courage I could muster to enter. Had Mr. Judson not elicited a promise from me beforehand, I wouldn't have stepped inside the front doors." Laura cut into a piece of chicken. "Now, however, I'm glad that I didn't refuse. I can see that you're doing good work, and the ladies working in the library have helped me see there's nothing to fear."

The doctor smiled. "Fear can be a good thing or a bad thing. God gave us the instinct of fear to protect ourselves, but occasionally our fears can be illogical. Some of my patients have developed unfounded fears that have caused them to become completely incapacitated. Attempting to treat them is most difficult."

Laura wiped the corners of her mouth with her linen napkin. "Then I owe Mr. Judson a great deal of thanks for helping me overcome my fears before I ended up as one of your patients, Dr. Thorenson."

The doctor smiled and shook his head. "I don't think there's any chance you'd ever be in need of my professional help, Mrs. McKay, but I'm glad this visit has helped you set aside your anxiety."

A sense of relief washed over Ainslee. During the past few hours, all of her worry had been swept away.

A feeling of accomplishment swelled in Ainslee's heart as she entered the asylum the following day. She and Laura, along with Nettie and several of the patients who'd received special permission, had returned after supper to complete logging as many books as possible. When the hour had grown late, they'd accepted the task couldn't be completed before morning. With no other choice, they'd discontinued logging and shelved the remaining books along one side of the library. Although it hadn't given Ainslee pleasure to leave the task incomplete, all of them had been weary when they'd finally departed the library.

This morning, her feelings of discontent had vanished. There would be time to complete any unfinished tasks over the coming weeks. Today was a day to celebrate what had been accomplished rather than dwell upon what remained to be done.

Dr. Thorenson greeted her when she stepped through the front entrance. "This is an exciting day, Miss McKay." He peered over her shoulder toward the front steps. "I expected to see your sister-in-law. She is coming, isn't she?"

"Yes, but we worked until late last night. I insisted she need not return this morning since we won't be logging any books today." They stepped inside the library, and she gestured to the bookcases along the north wall. "We shelved all of the unlogged books in those bookcases. The ladies can help me complete our list in the future." She glanced toward the hallway. "I wasn't certain when your staff would begin to set up the room. The ladies and I didn't want to be in the way."

"You could never be in the way, Miss McKay, but I appreciate your thoughtfulness." He rubbed the bridge of his nose. "Since you're here, I wonder if you would consider overseeing the arrangement of the room. When I asked the asylum staff for a volunteer to take charge of the ceremony, Miss Mardel offered."

"That's so sweet of her." Ainslee said, thinking about Miss Mardel's quick change of heart toward the library after Ainslee had hurt her hand.

"Yes, and she had a committee of ladies helping her to plan it. But this morning I received a note that she is ill." He sighed. "I dislike asking you. This should be a day for you to enjoy, yet I don't know who else to ask."

Though she hadn't planned to remain at the library all morning, Ainslee couldn't permit Miss Mardel's absence to ruin the day. A cancellation would disappoint far too many invited guests as well as the patients who had helped Ainslee log so many of the books.

"I'll do my best."

Dr. Thorenson beamed at her. "I knew I could count on you." He rushed toward the doors. "I'll send some of the committee ladies to help right away."

Though she wasn't certain what Miss Mardel had planned, Ainslee made a quick assessment of the room and decided the head table should be placed at the far end of the room. That way, smaller tables could be scattered throughout the remainder of the room and guests could come and go at their leisure. A head table was irregular at a tea, but the doctor had insisted upon the idea since he wanted to present Laura with an award and the administrator wanted to make a few introductory statements. She hoped those attending would enjoy the added festivities. However, she feared most guests attending the tea would likely expect a tour of the new library and light refreshments rather than lengthy speeches.

Appearing somewhat frazzled, the committee members arrived a short time later. Ainslee took a seat at the desk and bid the ladies sit down. She offered a bright smile that she hoped would alleviate the ladies' unease. "One by one, please tell me what duty you've been assigned and if you've accomplished your task."

Ainslee jotted down notes as each lady reported. When the final woman had given her account, Ainslee stood and stepped to the front of the desk. "Even without Miss Mardel's oversight, I believe we're going to host a tea that won't soon be forgotten."

With the ease of a seasoned hostess, she told each of the ladies when she needed them to return and what items they should bring with them.

The head cook stood. "I can handle the kitchen duties without being instructed, Miss McKay. The menu was planned weeks ago. You signal when it's time for my staff to serve the tea." She gestured toward the hallway. "Right now, I gotta get back to the kitchen and see to lunch for the patients."

Ainslee nodded. "For now, I believe you all can return to your work duties. I'll see if I can arrange for some of the aides who work in the men's wing to help set up tables."

"I'll stop and tell their supervisor on my way back to the kitchen," the cook said as she departed. "He'll see that a few of them get over here in no time."

Ainslee called out her thanks, picked up her list, and dropped into one of the chairs.

Ainslee glanced at the clock and then hurried to the foyer to meet Levi and Laura. She had sent a note to Levi earlier in the day explaining her absence from work and asking that they arrive a half hour early. Laura appeared in a stylish suit of striped camel's-hair in variegated shades of brown and trimmed with a band of caroubier red braid, and Levi had donned his white shirt, black woolen sack coat, and matching trousers.

Ainslee tucked an errant strand of hair behind her ear and swiped her hand down the front of her skirt. "I should have allowed time to return to the boardinghouse and change into something more appropriate, but . . ."

Levi drew near her side. "You look perfect no matter what you're wearing."

Heat seared her cheeks. "Thank you, but I don't think that's entirely true." She ducked her head. "Come with me. I want you two to see the library before anyone else."

Laura gasped when she pushed open the doors. "It's beautiful, Ainslee. You've transformed it into a stylish tea room, but guests can still see what a wonderful library you've created."

"I'm glad you like it, Laura, but it took many people to create this library—and the tea room."

Over the past six hours, many of the asylum workers had come to her aid. Some helping arrange tables and chairs, some spreading linens on the tables, some assembling the beautiful floral arrangements that bedecked each table, some draping sheer pale blue fabric on the head table, and some preparing the serving table.

Dr. Thorenson and the other staff members soon trickled into the library, all of them astounded by the transformation. A short time later, invited guests arrived and Dr. Thorenson escorted Laura to the front table.

He then returned to Ainslee's side. "You'll be seated next to the administrator at the front table. May I escort you?"

"No." She shook her head, but when the doctor appeared shocked by her refusal, she hastened to explain. "I prefer to sit with Levi at one of the small tables, where I can help serve, if needed."

The doctor lightly grasped her elbow. "There are others who can serve. Your place is at the head table."

She turned to Levi, hoping he would take up her cause. Instead, he agreed with the doctor. "You've put much time and effort into this library, Ainslee. You should go with the doctor."

With a sigh, she took the doctor's arm and was seated alongside the administrator. Moments later, he pushed to his feet and a hush fell over the room. Ainslee blushed as he lauded her for her tremendous accomplishment. "Though it is very little compared to your efforts, Miss McKay, we are commemorating this room as the Ainslee McKay Library."

Her breath caught as she attempted to hold back her tears. "I am deeply honored, but please know that many others contributed to the successful completion of this project."

The administrator nodded. "Indeed, that's true, but without your leadership it would never have happened."

Her heart swelled with joy—not because of the honor, but because she'd been able to accomplish something that she hoped would help the patients on their path to recovery.

The administrator then called upon Dr. Thorenson, who surprised Laura with a certificate of appreciation. "Mrs. McKay, along with many of her friends and relatives, donated a good portion of the books that line the shelves of this library. We could not let her contribution go without recognition."

Though she appeared somewhat embarrassed by the recognition, Laura graciously accepted the certificate on behalf of the people who had generously given books to the library. She then gestured toward the serving table and smiled. "I do believe we'll be drinking cold tea if we prolong the festivities any longer."

Applause filled the room as the guests made their way to the serving table. Levi stepped close to Ainslee's side. "I'm very proud of you."

His praise sent a thrill of pleasure pulsing through her veins.

Chapter 21

Dirt flew from beneath her black leather shoes as Ainslee rushed across the courtyard toward the clay shop. Waving an envelope overhead and panting for breath, she glanced around the cutting room until she spotted Levi. "Come to the office!"

Taking long strides, Levi closed the distance between them. The moment he reached her side, she matched his gait. He looked down at her. "The contract from Mr. Harrington?"

"I'm sure it must be. I didn't open it. I want us to read it together."

He chuckled and lightly grasped her arm. "I know you're excited, but you can slow down a little. Whatever's in that envelope isn't going to change by the time we get to the office."

"I know, but ever since his telegram arrived, saying we'd be receiving a final contract, I've hardly been able to sleep." Ainslee tucked her head against an unexpected breeze that swirled through the courtyard. "The use of these tiles in the museum is going to bring us new business, and I believe it will also bring you the recognition you deserve as an artisan." She grinned. "As well as a raise in wages."

After their meeting with Mr. Harrington, Ewan had promised Levi that if the mosaics became profitable for the tile works, he would substantially increase the young man's pay.

Levi pulled open the door. "Let's not worry about my wages until we see where all of this leads us. The contract may only stipulate the minimum amount he agreed to."

Ainslee crossed the room at breakneck speed, dropped to her chair, and ripped open the envelope without taking time to use a letter opener. Levi pulled a chair to her side. A letter accompanied the contract and she pushed it toward Levi. "You read the letter while I scan the contents of the contract."

Within moments, she let out a whoop that startled Levi. He lost his hold on the letter and it sailed to the floor. Leaning over the arm of the chair, he quickly retrieved the missive. "Was that a shout of delight or disappointment?"

"A shout of delight! Mr. Harrington has elected to use the figures submitted in our number one bid."

Levi blew out a loud whoosh. "We're going to be extremely busy. We'll need more men. I've begun training Robert and Joseph whenever they have a bit of spare time, but we'll need men dedicated to working on nothing but the mosaics, and I'll need time to train them."

Ainslee immediately agreed. "And we'll need additional materials, as well." They'd submitted a proposal containing four different bids to Mr. Harrington. The number-one bid called for the highest number of mosaics per room, while each additional bid contained a diminishing number. Had he rejected all of their bids and decided to honor only their base agreement, Levi might have been able to perform the clay work on his own. But even that would have depended upon how much time he would have before the project required installation of the tiles.

"What does the letter say?" She craned her neck toward the letter she'd handed to Levi.

"Before I dropped it, I'd read only the first few lines that stated he was pleased to offer us a contract for additional mosaic tiles." He quickly examined the remaining paragraphs. "He says that the newspapers in Wheeling and Pittsburgh published articles about the tiles several weeks ago, and they are accepting bids for construction of the building." He traced his finger along the final paragraph. "There's no set date for the completion of the museum, but he asks that we move forward with production so that there will be no delay when the tiles are needed."

Ainslee returned her attention to the contract and passed along each page to Levi for his review. While pointing to the second-to-last page, she stopped and tapped Levi's arm. "There's a paragraph here that says none of the designs used in this project may be reproduced for any other customer. Is that agreeable to you?"

Levi rubbed the back of his neck and leaned back in the chair. "As long as he's talking about an exact replica, but I won't agree if he means that I can never portray a cobbler or Plymouth Rock or the Ten Commandments in any of my tiles. We need to clarify exactly what he means by the 'designs used in this project.' I'm willing to give him my word that I won't use any of his specific designs for another customer, but I don't want to destroy the molds or the enlarged drawings used when we cut the clay. If there should be any breaks, we want both the molds and the drawings so we can reproduce the pieces for him. Once we explain the need to keep the designs, I think he'll understand."

"He would have the right to sue if we breached the contract in any way, so I'm sure he won't insist upon destruction of those items. I do think I need to rewrite this paragraph so that it's clear to all of us and then I can send it back to him." She waited patiently while Levi continued to read the remainder of the contract.

When he'd finished reading the final page, he rested his elbow on the desk. "I would like to make one more request of Mr. Harrington. If he refuses, I would still want to move forward with the contract, but it would give me great pleasure if he'd place a plaque in the center room that would indicate the tiles were produced at the McKay Tile Works, and perhaps Noah's name could be listed as designer of the tiles in the entry hall."

"I doubt there will be any objection to such a request. However, I want your name listed as a designer, as well. I admire your love and dedication to Noah, but I believe he would want you to be acknowledged, as well."

"I asked because I think Noah needs the affirmation, but if you think it's best to list both of us, I won't argue."

She nodded and smiled. "Agreed. I'll prepare the changes and send it off to Mr. Harrington this afternoon."

Levi pushed up from his chair. "Thank you."

He leaned his body across the desk, kissed her cheek, and rushed from the room before she could speak. She stared after him, her fingers resting on the spot he'd kissed and her heart pounding a new beat.

Ainslee sifted through the mail that lay stacked on her desk. Her heart quickened at the sight of Adaira's handwriting. Levi's deep dedication to his brother had struck a chord deep within and reminded her of the closeness she and Adaira had shared throughout the years. They'd been so attuned to one another, they usually knew what the other was thinking. Usually.

The fact that it wasn't always true had become painfully clear when Adaira ran off to marry. To this day, it caused her to wonder how the closeness they'd once shared could have been so easily altered by Chester Mulvane. Perhaps that's what happened when one fell in love, for her own thoughts now centered on Levi rather than Adaira. The few letters that had passed between them in recent months had closed the chasm, but Ainslee didn't feel the same connection they'd once shared. Possibly the distance had prevented the return of those deep feelings. Maybe that was yet another reason why Levi insisted upon living near his brother.

She slid the letter opener beneath the seal and removed the cream-colored stationery from the envelope. She'd nearly finished reading when the office door opened and she looked up.

"Aunt Margaret!" A burst of fear shot through her like an explosion of cannon fire. Why on earth was Aunt Margaret in Weston? Had something terrible happened to the family? Her thoughts raced. Ewan had mentioned Grandmother Woodfield had returned to Bartlett. Was she ill? Had Margaret arrived to tell her Grandmother Woodfield had died?

The older woman closed the distance between them, her gaze flitting around the room like a bird searching for a nest. "Good morning, Ainslee. My, but you've grown into quite the young woman since I last set eyes on you." Without invitation, she dropped into one of the chairs and absently pressed the folds of her traveling dress. "When I learned you were in charge of this operation, I wasn't surprised. You were always much brighter than Adaira. She might have had a touch of artistic talent, but you—you were the smart one."

Unspoken questions jumbled in her mind as Ainslee continued to stare across the desk. "Has something happened to one of my family members?"

Margaret folded her gloved hands in her lap. "Dear me, I don't believe so. The last I heard, they were all perfectly fit. Laura's mother has returned to Bartlett, but we seldom see one another. As for your brother and his family, I've had no contact with them since they left Bartlett. An unfortunate happenstance."

Margaret's final three words jolted Ainslee. "An unfortunate happenstance caused by you and your unseemly behavior."

"You're absolutely correct."

Her aunt's agreement left Ainslee momentarily speechless. Mouth agape, Ainslee stared at this woman who had never before admitted to any of the wrongdoing she'd inflicted upon various members of the family, especially the McKays.

"Do close your mouth, my dear. I wouldn't want you to swallow a fly. Such a bothersome event when that occurs, don't you think?"

Ainslee offered a tight smile. "Yes, although I've never experienced such an unfortunate occurrence." Margaret's silly comment helped Ainslee regain her composure. "Please tell me—what brings you to Weston? I feel certain you're here for something more than to pay me a visit."

Margaret fidgeted with the decorative piping that edged the flounce on her dress. "You know you were always a favorite with me, Ainslee. From the time you were a young girl with your hair in braids, I knew you were going to make your mark in this world." She squinted her eyes and gave a slight shake of her head. "I never held out much hope for Adaira. She was too flighty and selfish."

Ainslee wasn't sure when or where Margaret had drawn her conclusions about Adaira—or her, for that matter. From the time she and Adaira had arrived in West Virginia from Ireland, Margaret had taken every opportunity either to put them to work cleaning her house or to shoo them from her sight. And now she sat across the desk showering her with praise. As usual, Aunt Margaret was up to something.

"Thank you for your compliments, but you still haven't told me why you're here. Why don't we set aside the pleasantries and get to the facts? I don't want to appear rude, but I have a great deal of work to accomplish today."

Margaret winced. "You have become quite the businesswoman, haven't you?" She unfastened her reticule and withdrew a piece of newsprint. "I'm certain you've seen this." After unfolding the piece, she slid it across the desk to Ainslee.

The clipping appeared to be the news release Mr. Harrington had sent to the newspapers. Ainslee scanned the article, then looked up at Margaret. "I hadn't seen the article, but Mr. Harrington informed me it would be in several newspapers."

"Then I'm pleased I brought it with me. You may keep it if you like." Margaret's lips curved in a magnanimous smile.

When Margaret didn't continue, Ainslee tapped her fingers on the desk. "I doubt you came here merely to deliver this news clipping."

"I know you've said you're busy, but this visit is proving difficult for me. I do hope you'll bear with me. I don't want to do or say anything that might jeopardize my proposal. Actually, an agreement, of sorts."

Proposal? Agreement? The words sent a prickling chill racing down Ainslee's arms. Margaret Crothers was her deceased Uncle Hugh's widow and had proved herself to be more cunning than most men—even Uncle Hugh. Though Uncle Hugh had changed his ways shortly before his death and had promised Ewan the brickyard in Bartlett, he'd had too little time to change his will and testament. Even though Margaret had known of the agreement, she refused to acknowledge or fulfill Hugh's promise. All of the previous proposals and agreements between the two families had resulted in the McKays suffering heartache and financial disaster at the hands of the Crotherses. And now Aunt Margaret had come here with another business proposition. She must be daft.

Ainslee frowned at the woman. "I can't imagine any proposal you might have that would be of benefit or interest to the McKays."

"I know I wronged your brother when I forced him out of the brickworks, but I was a frightened widow, fearful that I'd be left with no means of support after Hugh died. Even though I knew the papers had been prepared for Hugh to sign the brickworks over to Ewan, I believed the business should be mine."

Ainslee sighed. Rather than fear, she believed Margaret had been motivated by greed. "You know Ewan is an honorable man. He would never have taken advantage of you. If you'd wanted for anything, he would have helped you. Yet, after all his years of hard work for you and Uncle Hugh, you were willing to leave the McKays with nothing."

"You're right, and I'm willing to humble myself and beg his forgiveness, because I truly do need his help—and yours." Margaret withdrew a handkerchief from her pocket and twisted it between her fingers. "I am sure neither the McKays nor the Woodfields want to see the brickworks fail."

None of this was making any sense, and revisiting the past wasn't going to change anything. "While the brickworks still holds a place in Laura's heart, and Ewan's as well, the McKays and Woodfields no longer have any control over what happens there." She wished Margaret would get to the crux of why she'd unexpectedly appeared. "Please tell me why you're here."

"I asked you to be patient, but since you're in a hurry, I'll oblige." Her eyes were clouded with woe. "The truth of the matter is that Andrew Culligan has ruined the reputation of the brickworks, and if we don't get a contract soon, which I know we won't, we'll be out of business. I've already had to let most of the men go, and Mr. Culligan has disappeared." She hesitated a moment. "Do you remember Mr. Culligan?"

"I never knew him, but I recall his name. He's the one you brought into the brickworks after Uncle Hugh died. As I recall, you forced Ewan to teach him the contracting and how to manage the ledgers. Once Mr. Culligan was proficient in that portion of the business, you cut Ewan out. That's about how it happened, isn't it?"

Margaret bowed her head. "Yes, that's how it happened. And now I'm here to ask you to help me win a bid from Mr. Harrington."

Her words bit Ainslee's ears like a cold winter frost.

Chapter 22

The office door opened and Levi pinned Ainslee with a surprised look. "What's this about a bid and Mr. Harrington?" He shifted toward Margaret. "I don't believe we've met."

"This is Margaret Crothers, Levi. She is the widow of my Uncle Hugh." Ainslee hurried to explain Hugh wasn't truly her uncle, but a more distant relative.

"So that makes you completely unrelated to the McKays?" Levi stepped beside Margaret's chair.

Margaret's brow creased in a slight frown. "We've always considered ourselves related, even though there's no true bloodline. Isn't that true, Ainslee?"

Ainslee wanted to disagree, but Margaret's pleading eyes stopped her. The woman looked like a stray cat seeking a home. "Until Ewan married Laura, all of us lived with Uncle Hugh and Aunt Margaret." She'd discussed bits and pieces of her life in Bartlett and Grafton with Levi but had never gone into great detail about Margaret and her harsh ways.

Margaret turned her attention to Levi. "Am I correct in assuming you are the Levi Judson mentioned in the newspaper clipping I brought to Ainslee?"

"I suppose I am, though I haven't seen the article. I heard you mention Mr. Harrington when I was coming in the door. What was that about? Do you know him?"

Margaret shook her head. "We've never met, although I'm most hopeful the C&M Brickworks will be granted a contract to supply bricks for the new museum he's constructing. I've told Ainslee it will help the business tremendously if we could win that bid."

"So why is it you're having trouble with your business, Mrs. Crothers? I thought the brickworks was a thriving business when Ewan left Bartlett and moved to Grafton." Levi turned toward Ainslee rather than waiting for Margaret's response. "Is that not right?"

Ainslee nodded. "Yes, it was doing well."

Margaret's lips tightened into a knot and she scooted back in her chair like a trapped animal. "I've explained my circumstances to Ainslee, so I doubt there's any need to repeat all of my problems. Suffice it to say, the brickworks has suffered great losses due to the misdeeds of my manager, Mr. Culligan."

"And how did you think we could help you with your bid?" Levi dropped into a chair beside Margaret.

"*We?* Are you a partner in the tile works? I thought it was owned by the McKays and Mrs. Woodfield." The haughty tone Margaret had used in years past momentarily returned. "I came here to ask for Ainslee's help."

"I am not a partner, Mrs. Crothers, but I have a personal stake in our association with Mr. Harrington and this project. I don't want anything to occur that might jeopardize our relationship with him." He rested his arm on the desk. "And I'm certain Ainslee feels the same."

"I do." Ainslee returned her attention to Margaret. "Rather than coming to talk to me, I believe your first step is to make amends with Ewan and seek his help. He's the one who can help remedy the problems at the brickworks. I don't think you'll be in a position to place a bid until you've overcome those difficulties. And if you're producing inferior bricks, be assured that none of us would recommend you to Mr. Harrington."

Margaret looked miserable. "I suppose I may as well tell you everything." She stared blankly across the room while she detailed how she'd trusted Mr. Culligan and given him free rein with the company. "At first, the company stayed about the same, but after a couple years, we started to lose contracts and I received some complaints about the quality of the bricks. I talked to Mr. Culligan, but he insisted the bricks were being made just as they'd always been. Since our income remained the same, it didn't occur to me that he was using inferior products."

Levi rubbed the back of his neck. "Did you check with any of the foremen or examine the books? You should have been able to uncover any problems by taking time to look for yourself."

"I trusted him. Besides, I didn't know anything about the ledgers. Ewan had trained Mr. Culligan, but I'm not bright like Ainslee. Even if I'd looked at those books, they wouldn't have told me anything."

Ainslee could hardly believe someone had been able to fool her aunt. "But what about the workers, Aunt Margaret? They would have known changes were being made and the bricks they were making were second-rate. Surely one of the relatives said something to you."

Margaret curled her lip in disgust. "There's none of them working in the yard anymore. They were unhappy with their wages, and with Hugh gone, the lot of 'em quit. Ungrateful to the end they were, with not an ounce of loyalty to me." As her anger mounted, a bit of the brogue she'd fought so hard to overcome returned. "They're all working in the mines, even though I warned them of the danger. Wouldn't surprise me if they all died an early death beneath the ground."

"And what of the foremen who worked there when Ewan was in charge? Have they all left?"

"Aye. One by one, they quit and went to other brickyards, but I didn't have any way of knowing. I didn't go down to the yard, so I didn't know who was working and who wasn't, except for the relatives, who took pleasure in telling me they'd been hired in the mines for twice the wage they'd made in the brickyard." Margaret straightened her shoulders. "None of this matters now. What's done is done. What does matter is keeping the place up and running. I don't think Laura or Ewan would want to see it go under. With your recommendation and a promise of quality bricks, I think Mr. Harrington would accept our bid."

Levi leaned forward and rested his forearms across his thighs. "Mrs. Crothers, you've already told us that your best workers have quit, you had a manager who was willing to produce poor quality bricks and has likely filled the ledger books with incorrect records, and you can't do any of the duties yourself. How can you possibly ask Ainslee to speak on your behalf?"

A tear formed and then slowly rolled down Margaret's wrinkled cheek. Her shoulders slumped and she folded her arms across her waist. "I'll beg if I need to." A crimson blush colored the furrows that lined her face.

Never had Ainslee seen Margaret shed a tear. Not even when Uncle Hugh died. Yet here she sat, with swollen eyes begging for help. Who was this woman? Where was the meanspirited woman who had castigated her own sister, Kathleen, when she'd become pregnant and then had reviled Ewan and Laura for adopting the child? Her actions today didn't reflect the coldhearted tactics she'd used to dishearten and discourage any member of the family she could. Margaret had been the cause of untold misery—yet deep inside, Ainslee felt a need to help her.

"Begging is not what's needed, Aunt Margaret. I can't recommend you to Mr. Harrington, but here's what I'll do." Ainslee set forth a plan while Margaret and Levi listened. When she had finished, she spread her hands flat on the desk. "I have nothing more to offer, so I leave the decision to you. Before you answer, I think it would be best to wait and pray on the matter. You can give me your answer tomorrow."

Margaret tipped her head to the side. "Pray? It's been some time since I've given much thought to God."

"Then perhaps it's time you did, Aunt Margaret. I'm sure He's given much thought to you."

Two days later, with Levi's assurance that he could manage both his duties and the ledgers and after telegraphing Ewan to expect her arrival, Ainslee and Margaret boarded a train to Grafton. Her heart fluttered each time she recalled Levi's sweet declaration that he would miss her.

The train hadn't been out of the station for long when Margaret snapped open her reticule and withdrew a handkerchief. "I don't know if this is a good plan, after all." She twisted the linen square into a knot. "Did you tell Ewan I'd be with you?"

"No." Ainslee shook her head. "Had I told him, it would have raised too many questions in his mind. He would have worried until we arrived. It's better if we surprise him."

"I hope his heart is strong. Otherwise, he may fall over in a heap when I step off this train beside you." She unclipped her fan and snapped it open. "It's certainly warm, isn't it?"

Ainslee scooted farther away, hoping to avoid the breeze.

"Quite the contrary, I thought it rather cool. You're worried. Sometimes being overanxious has that effect upon me. Why don't you close your eyes and pray? Prayer settles the nerves, don't you think?"

Margaret gave her a sidelong glance. "You would be a better judge than me, but I suppose it won't hurt."

Once Margaret had closed her eyes, Ainslee followed suit. She'd spent a great deal of the night in prayer and intended to continue until they arrived in Grafton. Though she'd attempted to allay Margaret's fears, her aunt's worries were well founded. Ewan had been mistreated by both Hugh and Margaret, and she doubted he'd forgotten even one of the many wrongs that had come his way. In truth, her unexpected appearance with the matriarch of the Crothers family might very well create more problems for Ainslee than for Margaret.

Ainslee's attempts at sleep proved futile. By the time the train hissed and clanged its way into the Grafton station, she was exhausted. Her heart pounded like a kettledrum when she caught sight of Ewan on the platform, but she pasted a smile onto her lips as she stepped into the aisle.

"Come along, Aunt Margaret." The woman stared straight ahead and remained as still as a stone. Ainslee leaned down and touched her arm. "We're delaying the passengers who want to board the train. Do come on."

Margaret adjusted the ties of her cape, heaved a sigh, and scooted to the edge of the wooden seat. Her arms buckled as she attempted to push to standing. "I don't know if I can manage. This is a mistake."

Ainslee reached forward and gently assisted the older woman to her feet. "Coming to see Ewan may be a mistake, but we're here and he's waiting. We must disembark the train." Ainslee turned sideways in the narrow aisle and maintained a hold on

Margaret's arm. Otherwise, she feared the woman would drop into an unoccupied seat before they could exit.

When Ainslee stepped onto the platform, Ewan was already taking long strides toward her. Along with the help of the conductor, she assisted Margaret down the final step. Margaret straightened her shoulders, and when she looked up, Ewan stopped short. He squinted and his mouth dropped open.

Margaret hastily attempted to take a backward step, but Ainslee tugged her forward. "No turning back now. If you're going to do something to save the brickworks, you must do this." She tipped her head closer to the woman's ear. "And I suggest you maintain a careful tone and a repentant spirit. Much will depend upon this meeting."

Ewan stepped toward them with a measured gait. He nodded at Margaret and then cocked an eyebrow at his sister. "Odd it is that the two of you would be on the same train." He glanced at Margaret. "Changing trains here in Grafton?"

"Aunt Margaret traveled to Weston for a visit with me. I suggested we come to Grafton for a meeting with you." Ainslee flashed a smile at Ewan and prayed it would soften his now-hardened features. "I think it might be best if Margaret gets settled in the hotel, and then we can have a talk once we're rested." She glanced at the elderly lady. "Perhaps tomorrow?"

There was no doubt she was testing her brother's good nature, but she had little choice. The tightness around Ewan's lips relaxed a modicum and the tension eased in Ainslee's shoulders.

"If I decide to meet with you, I'll send word to the hotel, Margaret." There was little warmth to Ewan's voice. "If you're staying at the depot hotel, the baggage handler will deliver your trunks to the lobby, and the hotel clerk will see that your belongings are sent up to your room." Ewan signaled to the baggage handler.

The man stepped closer. "How can I help?"

"Mrs. Crothers will be taking a room at the hotel." Ewan turned to Margaret. "Why don't you point out your belongings, Margaret? Ainslee and I will go with you and make certain you get registered before we depart for home."

After indicating which baggage was hers, Margaret hesitated. "What about supper? Is there a restaurant in the hotel?" Her lower lip protruded a bit. "I do dislike sitting at a table by myself."

"When I travel, I find that being alone provides time for personal reflection." Ewan's tone was not unkind, but Margaret flinched at the remark. If he noticed her reaction, he didn't let on. "The restaurant serves plain food, but it's tasty. Much better than the meager fare we scratched out in Ireland."

Ainslee didn't miss the disappointment in Margaret's eyes. She'd obviously been angling for a dinner invitation. Ewan had made it clear there would be none.

Once Margaret had received a key to her room, she grasped Ainslee's arm. "You'll send word about when and where we'll meet?"

Ewan stepped between the two women. "If we're to meet, I'll send word of the time." He gestured toward the hotel dining room. "I think the restaurant would be the best place."

Margaret opened her mouth as if to object, but Ainslee pinned her with a warning look. If Margaret wanted to meet with Ewan, she needed to hold her tongue and do whatever he requested. There was little doubt Margaret had hoped to prompt an invitation to the McKay home. Ainslee thought Margaret might hope to meet Tessa. Neither of those things would occur. Ewan had taken a defensive stance, and he would do everything in his power to protect his family from Margaret's meddling and her sharp tongue.

Margaret jiggled the key to her room. "If I can't entice either of you to join me for supper this evening, I'll bid you both good day." She turned, but rather than look into Ewan's brooding eyes, she settled her gaze on the carpeted staircase. "I hope to hear from you first thing in the morning."

"Whether it be an aye or a nay, you'll receive word tomorrow." Ewan lightly grasped Ainslee's elbow and directed her toward the door.

Once they had neared the hotel door, he lowered his head close to her. "You've a powerful mite of explaining to do, lass. I'm trying to control my temper, but you're putting me to quite a test." He nodded toward the street. "The carriage is waiting."

"There really is a good explanation, Ewan."

"I'm guessin' that having Margaret along is why yer telegram said to come to the station alone?" The latent Irish brogue came out as tempers ran high.

Ainslee stepped alongside the carriage. "I feared ya might bring Tessa, and I didna want Margaret to see her without yer consent."

"Aye, and 'tis a good thing I didna bring her, even though she begged and thought me an unkind father. What if I would have ignored yer request, Ainslee? Did ya give any thought to that possibility?"

"Ya know how much I love Tessa and that I wouldna asked you to come alone if there wasn't an important reason." She stepped up into the carriage. When he'd settled beside her, she leaned close to him. "Do ya want me to tell ya why Margaret is with me?"

"Nay. I think I'd like you to wait until after you've enjoyed a short time with Tessa. I want Laura with us when you give your reasons. Besides, I'm not thinkin' I'll want to hear this story of yours twice in one day."

Ainslee had expected Ewan's stony reaction toward Margaret, but she hadn't expected him to remain so distant once they were alone.

She prayed her decision to help Margaret wouldn't fracture her relationship with Ewan and Laura. The wound between Adaira and her had only begun to heal. Her heart could not bear the thought of another chasm within her family.

Chapter 23

While Ainslee had longed to spend time with Tessa, their visit had been marred by the looming discussion that lay before her. Her ability to concentrate had been nonexistent, and Tessa had become increasingly bothered when Ainslee asked the same questions several times. Conversation during supper had been as stilted as Ewan's earlier meeting with Aunt Margaret. Though Laura made every attempt at convivial dinner conversation, the effort proved futile. Margaret wasn't a guest at the table, but her presence loomed large in the room.

When they finally gathered in the sitting room after Tessa had gone to her room, Laura retrieved her knitting. Her lips curved in a warm smile. "Ewan has told me of Margaret's arrival in Grafton. As I'm sure you know, we are uncomfortable having her nearby, but I'm certain there is a good reason you've brought her to our doorstep."

Ainslee winced, yet she also felt a need to defend herself. "I didn't bring Margaret to your home, nor was it my intention to do so. I brought her to Grafton to discuss a matter with Ewan—and you, if you so choose, Laura. Since the day we moved from Bartlett, Margaret has known we were living in Grafton. If she had wanted to find the McKay home, it wouldn't have been difficult."

"Aye, but she's too sneaky for that. She had others do her spying for her. Remember how she used Beatrice to get every scrap of news about our family?" Ewan's eyes flashed with anger.

"I remember all of it, and I'm not saying Margaret's a saint, but she came to the office at the tile factory and was filled with remorse for her actions. Do I know if she's genuinely repentant? Nay. There isn't any way for me to be sure, but this I do know: Without your help, the C&M Brickyard is going to go out of business."

Ewan's eyes opened wide, and he sat straight in his chair. "How can that be? The brickyard should be making a great deal of money for Margaret."

Ainslee nodded. "It should, but it seems Aunt Margaret trusted the wrong man. Andrew Culligan has bested her. Not only has he ruined the reputation of the company by producing inferior bricks, but he also was pocketing the profits made while selling those low-grade bricks. Naturally, he didn't tell Margaret about the complaints the company received, and soon orders quit coming in."

Ewan raked his fingers through his hair. "I told her she shouldn't trust a stranger to keep the books, but she was so intent upon forcing me out of the brickyard that she didn't heed my warnings. I wish I would have forced her to change the company name before I left Bartlett."

Laura gently shook her head. "Nothing can be gained by lamenting the past. What's important is how we act in the present." She cleared her throat. "I'm still unclear why Margaret would come to see you, Ainslee. How did she think you could help her solve the problems with Mr. Culligan and the brickyard?"

"There's nothing to be done about Mr. Culligan. He's disappeared. She has no idea where he's gone, but she hopes to bid on the brick contract for the museum in Wheeling and wants me to put in a good word with Mr. Harrington."

Ewan slapped his knee. "Sure and it all becomes clear now." He wagged his finger at Ainslee. "You cannot do this." He hesitated an instant. "Tell me you haven't promised to help her, that you haven't contacted Mr. Harrington."

Ainslee met her brother's intense stare. "The only thing I've done is tell her that it's your help she needs, not mine." She then detailed her suggestion that Margaret seek Ewan's help with the brickyard. "I didn't know what else to tell her. I believe she's sorry for what she did to you, and she needs to restore the reputation of the company."

Ewan's eyes blazed with conviction. "She needs to restore the quality of the bricks. The bricks will restore the reputation of the company, but only if she can gain another contract. Given what you've told me, I do na think that will happen anytime soon, especially not soon enough to bid on Mr. Harrington's museum."

"Even with your help? I thought if you told Mr. Harrington you'd take responsibility for the product, he might consider the bid to be sound."

"Ainslee! Surely you didn't expect Ewan to give his word that Margaret would furnish quality bricks when she has no idea how to produce them. Even if she knew what to do, you told us that most of the skilled workers have left for other jobs. Ewan can't perform the impossible."

Ainslee shrugged. "It was only a thought. Maybe if you meet with Margaret, the three of you could develop a plan."

Laura shuddered and shook her head. "I don't think I want to be present for a meeting with Margaret." She looked at Ewan. "I have no objection if you want to meet and discuss the brickyard with her, but I truly do not see how there's any easy answer. She may have to reap what she's sown, though it will break my heart to have that brickyard lay idle. My father worked so hard to make it prosperous, and you did the same, Ewan. What has happened is tragic for both the Woodfields and the McKays."

"Aye, that it is." Ewan's brow creased into narrow folds. "I'm wonderin' how it is that your mother has not written to tell us this piece of news. With so many men quitting, she's sure to have heard some talk among her friends."

"Mother's friends don't discuss brickyards and lost jobs among the working class, Ewan. They may talk about ways to feed the poor, but anything beyond charitable work wouldn't be mentioned at their gatherings. While Mother has always been forward-thinking, most of her friends are not. And I'm sure they wouldn't mention Margaret or the brickyard to Mother. They'd fear it would be a painful subject for her."

"Aye, I'm sure they would not want to discuss any matter that would cause her distress."

Ainslee had hoped Laura and Ewan would agree to speak with Margaret, but instead they seemed more interested in discussing what Grandmother Woodfield might know about the brickyard. She waited for a short lull in the conversation before she interrupted. "While I understand your concerns about Grandmother Woodfield, I wonder if we should decide if you will agree to meet with Margaret." If Ainslee didn't redirect the conversation, she feared Laura and Ewan were going to decline Margaret's request.

"I do na have any answers for her, but since she's come here, hat in hand, I suppose it's the right thing to do." Ewan turned to his wife. "I want you to go with me, Laura. If Margaret is offering apologies, she owes one to you as well as to me. It is clear she wants my help, but I want to see if she's truly repentant for her misdeeds. I can use your help making that judgment. Besides, the brickyard belonged to your family for many years, and I'll value your opinion before I make any decisions."

"I don't know, Ewan. If we open a door to Margaret, we may never again be able to close it. We must consider Tessa in all of this, too—and Kathleen. What will she think?"

Ainslee leaned forward. "But Tessa knows she's adopted. You've told her Kathleen lives in New York and that she has other relatives she may want to meet someday. I don't see how Margaret can cause a problem where Tessa is concerned."

Ewan shook his head. "Margaret can create problems where no one else could imagine. I think you've forgotten her wily ways. Laura may be right: Meeting with her is probably a mistake."

Panic took hold in the pit of Ainslee's stomach and surged with such force that it spread through her body like a crashing wave. She tightened her fingers around the armrests of her chair. This need to heal the rift in their families had taken hold, and she couldn't turn loose. If she was going to meet with even a degree of success, she needed to begin anew.

"You've both pointed to Margaret's past misdeeds, and I agree that the things she's done have been dreadful. Her actions have forever changed us, but she hasn't caused our ruination. We've become stronger in spite of her. That doesn't mean I excuse or disregard her behavior. In the past, both of you have talked with me about forgiveness. Particularly about my need to forgive Adaira."

Ewan held up his hand. "There's no comparison between Adaira's actions and—"

"Please let me finish, Ewan." Ainslee frowned at her brother. "Adaira's decision to elope and leave me in the lurch didn't affect the entire family, but if you consider what it did to me, I believe there are similarities. Adaira forever changed my life in order to seek her own happiness. I was forced to leave Grafton and fulfill what had been her dream. I also lost my twin sister and closest friend. For me, Adaira's betrayal cut even deeper than Margaret's deceit toward you because it was emotional rather than financial." She glanced back and forth between Ewan and Laura. "Both of you told me that I needed to forgive Adaira. Shouldn't you heed that advice as it pertains to Margaret?"

Ewan frowned, and he settled deeper into the cushioned divan, but Laura leaned toward Ainslee. "There is truth in what you've said, Ainslee. Without forgiveness, bitterness takes hold and affects everything we do, as well as our character. I want you to know that I forgave Margaret long ago. That doesn't mean that I've forgotten, or that I want her to become involved in our lives once again."

Ainslee scooted forward in her chair. "Can it hurt at least to talk to her? I promise I won't ask you to do anything more than go to the hotel and hear her out. See for yourselves if you believe she is repentant and worthy of a second chance."

Laura reached to her side and grasped Ewan's arm. "Ainslee is right. Meeting with Margaret doesn't commit us in any way. If she inquires about matters we don't wish to discuss, we aren't required to give her answers. What harm can it do?"

Ewan rubbed his temples. "Agreed. We'll see what she has to say. I'll see that a message is delivered to her. When would the two of you like to meet? I say the sooner the better, but I'll leave it to you to decide."

"She said she dislikes dining alone. Why not tomorrow for the noonday meal? If she doesn't want to remain another night, she can depart on the late-afternoon train." Ainslee shifted in her chair. "Is that agreeable with both of you?"

"Aye, 'tis fine with me. I can leave the pottery and bring the carriage for the two of you." Ewan looked at his wife. "Laura, shall I send a message to the hotel?"

"Yes, I think that's a good plan."

Ainslee exhaled a deep sigh. This hadn't been easy. She hoped Aunt Margaret wouldn't muddy the waters with any bad behavior.

Shortly before noon the following day, Ewan arrived as promised. After their initial greetings, the three of them rode to the hotel in silence. Ainslee laced her fingers together in a tight hold. She'd prayed after she'd gone upstairs for the night, she'd prayed until Ewan arrived, and she prayed on the buggy ride to the hotel. Perhaps today could be the beginning of restoration for the family as well as the brickyard.

Once they arrived at the hotel, Ewan escorted them into the dining room and requested a table for four. "I'll check at the desk to make sure Margaret didn't leave a message, and then I'll join you. We're a wee bit on the early side of noon." Moments later, he returned and sat down. "No message, so I'm thinkin' she'll be coming down anytime now." A waiter stepped to their table, and Ewan glanced at the two ladies. "Would you like to order coffee or a cup of tea while we wait?"

"Tea," they replied in unison and then smiled at each other.

Ewan looked up at the waiter. "And I'll have coffee. We're expecting another person, so we'll wait until she arrives to order our meal."

The waiter scurried off and later returned with their tea and coffee. The clock in the lobby chimed noon, and while other diners came and went, the three of them waited. The minutes continued to tick by and still there was no sign of Margaret.

Ainslee suffered a cramp in her neck after a half hour of

twisting to watch the hotel staircase. Where was Margaret? She dipped her head low for one final look and then turned to Ewan. "Do you think she checked out of the hotel and boarded the morning train?"

He withdrew his timepiece from his vest. "She's forty minutes late." He pushed away from the table. "I'll make certain she's still registered. If so, I'll go up to her room and knock on the door."

Tightness pulled at Ainslee's shoulders and held her spine as straight as a broomstick. "It seems Aunt Margaret wasn't nearly as intent upon this meeting as I was led to believe. I hope this isn't a sign that she can't be trusted."

Laura gave a slight shake of her head. "I don't think we should draw any conclusions just yet. Let's wait and see what Ewan discovers."

Once again, Ainslee offered a silent prayer that Margaret would keep her word and prove to be a changed woman.

Ewan returned moments later and shook his head. "There's no answer at the door. The clerk says she didn't check out and he didn't see her leave, but he was away from the desk for a short time so she may have decided to go into the main part of town and do a bit of shopping." He dropped to his chair and tapped his fingers atop the table.

"Why would she go shopping when she's expecting us to join her for the noonday meal? It doesn't seem logical." Ainslee doubted her brother was going to wait much longer. He'd shown little enthusiasm for this meeting, and his impatience was increasing by the minute. She lifted the napkin from her lap and stood. "I'm going to see if the clerk will give me a key so I can enter the room. Perhaps Margaret fell asleep."

"I would think Ewan's knock would have wakened her, but I suppose it's possible she didn't hear him. Traveling over the past few days and worry about the brickyard and meeting with family could have caused her to fall into a deep sleep. She's likely not able to hear as well either, what with her age." Laura leaned forward. "Perhaps you should accompany Ainslee, Ewan. But it might be wise if you wait outside the door until she can assure you that Margaret has dressed for the day."

Together, they secured a key from the front desk. Had he not known Ewan, Ainslee doubted whether the clerk would have handed over the key so willingly. Ainslee glanced over her shoulder. "If she isn't in her room, we can leave and I won't bother you with this any longer."

"If I weren't willing, I wouldn't be here, Ainslee. I'm still not making any promises about helping Margaret, but I'm truly willing to listen."

Ainslee knocked several times, then placed her ear against the cool wood of the door. Hearing no sound, she inserted the key and gave it a sharp turn. The lock released and she twisted the doorknob while Ewan positioned himself near the entrance.

Ainslee pushed open the door and shrieked. Margaret lay facedown in the thick pile of the Aubusson carpet, fully dressed and still clutching her reticule.

Her stomach churning and body trembling, Ainslee backed out of the room, barely aware of Ewan's hands on her shoulders. She turned to face him. "I think she's dead."

Her throat closed around the words as she slumped into Ewan's arms.

Chapter 24

Ainslee pushed a hand away from her face and shook her head. A terrible odor stung her nose and caused her to sputter and cough. She forced her eyes open and was met by piercing dark eyes bordered with wrinkled lines. Unfamiliar curtains hung at a window not far from the bed. Where was she? Fuzziness clouded her eyes and muddled her thoughts. Once again the dark eyes drew near. She pushed her head deep into the pillow and turned away from the weathered face of a strange man staring down at her and a horrid smell she longed to escape.

"She's back with us." The craggy-faced man leaned back and looked toward the other side of the bed.

Ainslee rolled her head to the left. "Ewan." Her voice was but a whisper. "Where am I? What happened?"

"You had a bit of a fright and fainted. The doctor brought you 'round with a whiff of ammonia."

Using her elbows to bolster herself, Ainslee attempted to push up. The doctor shook his head and wagged his finger. "Unless you want to take a chance on fainting again, don't sit up just yet." He lifted a white cloth and touched his nose. "You don't want to smell this again, do you?"

The doctor smiled when she dropped back onto the pillow. Ainslee gestured for him to move the cloth away from the bed. "How long have I been out?"

Ewan glanced toward a china clock on the bureau. "Not long. We're at the Grafton Hotel. Do you remember coming upstairs?"

A cold rush of fear washed over her. "Aunt Margaret?" She looked up at Ewan. "Is she . . . ?"

He nodded. "Aye."

Panic seized her. "What happened? She didn't . . . hurt herself, did she? Was she so desperate she took her own life?"

"Nay. The doctor believes it was a problem with her heart." Ewan looked to the doctor for confirmation.

"That's correct. It was time for her to meet the Maker and receive her eternal reward." The doctor returned several items into his black leather bag before he once again looked at Ainslee. "I want you to rest here for another half hour or so before your brother takes you home. I've got to take care of some other things right now." He stepped to Ewan's side. "I'll see that your directions are followed."

Ainslee frowned. "What directions?"

"Margaret will be buried alongside Hugh in Bartlett. Her body will need to be returned there."

The thought made her woozy, and she shrunk back into the bedcovers. "Did she . . . was she . . . already?"

"The doctor said she probably died an hour or two before we went to her room. There was an envelope on the writing desk addressed to you. Are you feeling up to having a look at it?"

"Yes. At least I think I am." She swiped her clammy palm down the bedsheet and was thankful for the cool breeze that whistled through the cracked window.

Ewan withdrew the envelope from his pocket and handed

it to her. "If ya begin to feel lightheaded, let me know. I don't want ya to faint again. Ya scared me, lass."

For a moment, she stared at the handwriting on the envelope, then lifted the seal and withdrew the letter. "This says she wasn't feeling well last night and that she had doubts she'd make it through the night." Ainslee looked at Ewan. "I wonder why she didn't send for a doctor last night." A gasp escaped her lips. "She says she has a will and testament back in Bartlett and that it's located at the bank. She changed the contents before coming to see me. This says she left the brickyard to you, Ewan."

Her brother's eyes widened, and he shook his head. "Nay, that canna be true."

"See for yourself." She handed Ewan the first page of the letter and continued reading. "Crothers Mansion is yours to live in, as well. She says if you don't want to live there, you should sell it and send the proceeds to Kathleen."

Ewan dropped to the chair beside the bed and raked his fingers through his hair. "I do na know what to say. The woman must have had a genuine change of heart." He stared at Ainslee. "You told me she was repentant, but I wasn't sure I believed it was true. Seems the problems at the brickyard caused her to take a long look at her life. I canna think she'd have softened her heart toward me or Kathleen without a strong nudge from the Lord." Ewan waited while she finished reading the letter. "Any other surprises in there?"

Ainslee smiled and shook her head. "Just a paragraph thanking me for attempting to help her. Even when Aunt Margaret and Uncle Hugh had lots of money, they weren't particularly happy, were they?"

"Nay, but you know 'tis not money that gives us true happiness while we're on this earth. I regret we didn't settle the differences between us before she died. I'd forgiven Margaret, but I now realize I continued to let an ember of spite burn in my heart. For that I'm truly sorry."

She wrapped her arms about her waist and shivered. "Strange how we all know death is just around the corner for each of us, yet we act as though we'll live forever. Her death can serve as a good reminder that it's foolish to think we can wait until tomorrow to heal our differences." Ainslee pushed to a sitting position. "I think I'm feeling well enough to go home. Is Laura downstairs?"

"No. I thought she should return home." He pushed up from the chair and extended his hand to her. "Stand beside the bed and make certain you're steady on your feet."

Ainslee did as he requested, then took a deep breath and nodded. "I'm fine."

She clutched Ewan's arm as they entered the hallway. The door to Margaret's room remained ajar, and though Ainslee didn't want to look, her gaze was pulled toward the room. The lid of Margaret's trunk remained open, and her hairbrush and comb sat atop a dressing table.

Ainslee stopped outside the door. "What about her belongings? We can't just leave them here."

Ewan reached around her and pulled the door closed. "I've already spoken to the hotel clerk. I'll come back later. Her belongings will be sent back to Bartlett on the train. Everything has been arranged. You need not worry."

They descended the hotel steps and Ewan hailed a carriage. He hadn't mentioned a wake or funeral, but she was certain Ewan would notify all the relatives. She wondered how many of them would attend. There was no denying Margaret had become an enemy to most of the relatives who'd come from Ireland to work for Uncle Hugh. And then there was her sister, Kathleen. Would she want to attend the funeral?

She glanced over her shoulder at Ewan as he helped her into the carriage. "Will we all attend the funeral in Bartlett? If you want me to remain in Grafton and look after Tessa, I'd be willing."

Ewan settled on the leather seat beside her. "We'll talk to Laura. Since her mother is living at Woodfield Manor, Laura may decide to have Tessa come with us. I'm going to telegraph Grandmother Woodfield after I take you back to the house." He sighed and massaged his forehead. "There's much that needs to be completed before I lay my head on a pillow tonight."

"This has been a day none of us will soon forget."

"Aye. And if the letter Margaret wrote to you is true, her death is going to bring about some big changes, as well. The problems at the brickyard will need to be resolved as soon as possible. I can't oversee the operation from Grafton, and from the bits and pieces Margaret shared with you, there's nobody to step in as an overseer."

"Do you think Laura would be willing to return to Bartlett?" She giggled. "I suppose I should ask if you want to return and take over the brickyard before I inquire about Laura's wishes."

Ewan chuckled. "You are a perceptive young woman. You know I wouldn't go back unless Laura was in agreement. A sound marriage is more important than the brickyard, yet that place is chiseled in my heart. When I was forced out of the business, I felt as though I'd lost a part of myself. Purchasing the pottery and overseeing the contracts and accounts has helped me to regain some of that loss, but it isn't the same. Just as I had deep ties to the brickyard, it's Rose and Rylan who have developed a strong attachment to the pottery. So, yes, I would like to help restore the brickyard to what it was before Margaret took over."

She smiled and nodded. "Then I think Laura will support your desire to return."

When they arrived at the McKay house, Laura hurried from the parlor. "How are you feeling, Ainslee? I didn't want to leave you at the hotel, but Ewan thought it best for me to return home to Tessa."

"I'm fine. Ewan and the doctor took good care of me." She removed her cape and hung it on the hall tree near the front door. "I've never before experienced a fainting spell."

Laura leaned sideways and wrapped Ainslee's shoulder in a hug. "You can be sure that if I had been the one who walked into that hotel room, I would have fainted, too. Seeing something so tragic and unexpected is enough to cause even the strongest among us to faint." She directed Ainslee toward the parlor. "Why don't we sit down in here for a moment?" When Ewan didn't immediately comply, she waved him forward. "I have a bit of news, so you may want to join us, Ewan."

He strode into the room and stood at the end of the divan. "If it's good news you're bearing, then pleased I am to join ya, my love. If not, I'd rather be on my way."

Laura nodded toward the empty space on the divan. "Please sit down."

While he took his place, she reached into the pocket of her blue-and-gold day dress. "A telegram arrived shortly before the two of you returned." She looked at Ainslee. "It's from Levi, but I didn't read it."

"Levi!" Fear took hold and the lightheadedness and clammy feeling she'd experienced earlier returned full force.

"Take a deep breath and relax, Ainslee. I'm sure he's fine." Laura retrieved a small bottle from the parlor table. "If you feel like you're going to faint, you need to tell me. I'll sprinkle a few drops of spirits of ammonia on my handkerchief and hold it near your nose."

Ainslee wasn't sure if it was the threat of ammonia or Laura's assurance that Levi was well that caused her to rally, but she straightened her shoulders and reached for the message Laura held in her hand.

Ewan leaned forward, obviously hoping to keep her in his sights in case she toppled to the floor.

Ainslee let the telegram drop to her lap. "It's Noah. Levi asks that I return to Weston immediately."

"Does he say what's happened to Noah?" Laura's brow creased with concern. "I do hope all the drawings haven't caused undue strain. I wouldn't like to think the tile project has worsened his condition in any way."

"He's gone missing from the asylum." The whispered response stuck in Ainslee's throat.

Ewan reached for the telegram. "He does na say when his brother went missing, but I'm sure Levi is filled with worry and grief. The lad needs you there to manage the tile works so he can give his full attention to locating his brother. There won't be a train to Weston until morning, but you must go to him, Ainslee. There's nothing more you can do for Margaret, and Levi needs you."

She nodded her head. The moment she'd read the telegram, she knew she must return, but Ewan's affirmation helped ease the guilt of leaving him with all that must be done. Had she not brought Margaret to Grafton, Ewan wouldn't be in this position. Yet they had at least talked the day before Margaret's death—and that was a good thing. Ainslee prayed Ewan owning the brickyard again would prove to be a good thing as well.

Ainslee bid her good-byes to Tessa and Laura at the house the following morning while Ewan brought the carriage around.

Ainslee had enjoyed only a little time with Tessa, but she promised to visit again once their lives returned to normal.

She leaned forward and waved from the carriage until Laura and Tessa were out of sight. "I hope that by the time I get home, Noah has returned to the asylum. Levi will never forgive himself if something terrible has happened to his brother."

Ewan slapped the reins and urged the horses to a trot. "Levi should not hold himself responsible. If his brother was able to leave the asylum without being seen, it's the people who care for him who are at fault."

"I know you're right, but Levi will still hold himself accountable. And with Noah creating all of the designs for the foyer and main hall, it makes this all the worse. I hope his recent sketches are still at the asylum. If not, we may have difficulty meeting Mr. Harrington's schedule."

"There's plenty of time before any of the tiles will be needed. They've just finished preparing the site and begun the foundation. Don't stack unnecessary worries on top of each other. First you must get back to the office and relieve Levi of the day-to-day duties. You need to make sure the orders for the standard tiles are completed and shipped on schedule. Once Noah has been found, Levi can return his attention to the mosaics."

"Yes, but . . ."

Ewan stayed her. "Please listen to what I'm telling you, Ainslee. If you return to Weston and you skitter about like a cat on hot bricks, you'll be no help to Levi or the business. You need to keep your wits about you and remain calm so he'll do the same."

She nodded her head. "I'll do my best."

The train hooted in the distance as they arrived at the station. Ewan helped her down from the buggy and had her trunk delivered inside. "I want ya to send word and let me know when ya locate Noah. And if there's any other problems brewin', send a telegram." He grasped Ainslee's elbow and directed her toward the platform.

"Where do I send the telegram? Bartlett or Grafton?"

He sighed. "Unless you hear from me saying we've returned to Grafton, send it to me in care of Woodfield Manor in Bartlett. Right now, I'm thinkin' we may be there for a good while. I'll be seeking the Lord's direction about the future for all of us." His lips curved in an encouraging smile. "You do the same."

"I will." She lifted to her toes, brushed a kiss on his cheek, and boarded the train. She settled in her seat and waved, though she could barely see Ewan through the coal-smudged window.

A young girl clung to her mother's skirt and giggled with excitement as they sat down opposite Ainslee. The child wriggled with delight when the train blasted a whistle and chugged out of the station. Ainslee stared across the narrow aisle and recalled the excitement of riding the train with Rose and Adaira when they'd arrived in America. It seemed so long ago that she and Adaira had run into Ewan's arms when they'd first arrived in Bartlett. She'd had not a worry or care in the world. How quickly all of that had changed.

Chapter 25

The journey to Weston had been fraught with worrisome thoughts of Noah and his unexpected disappearance. While the wheels squealed and clattered along the railroad tracks, Ainslee weighed and measured every word Levi had reported concerning Noah and the drawings. There had to be some explanation for his behavior, yet she could think of nothing. Noah had been elated when asked to create the sketches for the entry hall. From that day forward, he had eagerly set to work. As time passed, his passion had never waned. The doctor had enthusiastically reported a miraculous transformation in Noah's behavior since beginning the project. So why would he disappear? It made no sense.

Ainslee's head throbbed when she finally stepped down from the train three hours later. Though she hadn't sent word to Levi of her arrival plans, she'd half expected him to appear. Silly though it was, disappointment descended upon her like a thundercloud. She gestured to a porter and arranged for the delivery of her baggage to the boardinghouse before entering the station.

Shoulders sagging, Ainslee trudged toward the doors that

opened onto the front street. She grasped the door handle and was yanked forward as someone pulled from the opposite side.

"Levi!" She lost her footing and tumbled forward into his arms. Hat askew and hands trembling, she clutched his arms. "How did you know I'd be on this train?"

Still holding her close, he grinned down at her. "I didn't, but I knew you'd return once you received my telegram, so I decided to meet every train until you arrived."

A passenger cleared his throat and tapped Levi's shoulder. "Could the two of you step aside? I need to get into the station."

Levi apologized as the two of them stepped away from the doors and onto the wooden sidewalk outside the station. "Wait here. I'll arrange for your baggage."

She shook her head. "There's no need. I've already arranged for it to be delivered."

Grasping her elbow, he led her to a waiting buggy. "Do you want to stop at the boardinghouse or go to the tile works? Have you eaten? We can have lunch at the café near the tile works if you'd like."

"There's no need to stop at the boardinghouse. Mrs. Brighton will see that the trunks are taken upstairs to my room, but lunch sounds wonderful. I didn't eat much breakfast before I left Grafton, and now I'm famished. I'm eager to hear everything about Noah, and I have a great deal to tell you, as well."

"Why don't you tell me your news first? Then we can talk about Noah."

She'd been worrying and praying about Noah ever since she'd received word, but she'd honor Levi's wishes. Perhaps he needed to think about something other than Noah for a short time.

Ainslee sighed. "So much happened in such a short time that I'm not sure where to begin."

Levi chuckled. "Let me help you with a question. Did Mrs.

Crothers behave herself like a proper lady while you were in Grafton?" He didn't wait for a response. "Given what you told me about her past behaviors, I have to admit I thought she might prove difficult for you to manage. I hope Ewan wasn't angry you'd taken it upon yourself to arrive without giving him notice Mrs. Crothers would be with you."

Ainslee shook her head, thankful for his question. To simply blurt out the fact that Margaret was dead would have been cold and unfitting. "Ewan was more than a wee bit surprised to see Margaret in my company when I stepped off the train. However, he treated her civilly and agreed to consider a meeting. After I had a brief conversation with Laura and Ewan, they agreed to meet Margaret for lunch the following day."

He helped her down from the buggy and paid the driver. The weather was cool, but they were accustomed to walking the short distance from the café to the tile works or from the tile works back to the boardinghouse before and after work most days.

Levi held the door and then selected a quiet table in the far corner of the room. The café didn't boast linen tablecloths or fine china, but it was clean and they served good fare for a reasonable price.

The wooden chair scraped across the plank floor as he pulled it from beneath the table and seated Ainslee. He dropped into the chair opposite her. "Tell me, how did the meeting go? Is Ewan going to help her get the brickyard back in order?"

Ainslee didn't realize she'd been holding her breath until she exhaled. "There wasn't any meeting. Margaret passed away before it occurred. I found her in her hotel room."

"You?" Levi's brow creased with concern. "Are you all right?"

"It upset me at the time, but I'm fine now." She forced a smile. "Don't worry about me. You have enough concerns of your own. As for the brickyard, I'm not sure what's going to happen in the future. But since Margaret left the business to Ewan, I believe he and Laura will return to Bartlett and move back into Woodfield Manor with Laura's mother."

"Not into Margaret's fancy home?"

Ainslee shook her head. "I would be surprised if Laura wanted to live there. I think she'd rather the place be sold and the funds go to Kathleen. Of course, I'm only guessing. Right now, they're intent upon making the final arrangements for Margaret."

They both ordered the chicken and dumplings. Once their food had been delivered, Levi offered a blessing for their meal and asked God to help him find Noah. When he'd completed the prayer, Ainslee looked up at him. "So you haven't found Noah. Since you were asking questions about Margaret, I thought . . ."

He shook his head. "No, but now that I know what happened in Grafton, I regret having sent word for you to return. You need to be with your family, not here."

"No, I need to be here with you, Levi. Ewan insisted that I return. There's really nothing I could do in Grafton or Bartlett. Ewan is the one who must make the arrangements and see to Margaret's funeral and her estate.

"I want to hear everything about Noah and his disappearance. Tell me who discovered he was missing and exactly when they noticed his absence." She poured a splash of cream into her coffee and stirred. "Where have they looked and how many people have been searching?"

He placed his fork on his plate and grinned. "Which question should I answer first?"

"I'm sorry, but I was thinking about Noah's disappearance and praying the whole way home."

"They realized he was missing the day you left with Mrs. Crothers." He shook his head. "Can that only be three days ago? Anyway, he'd told one of the orderlies he wasn't feeling well earlier in the day. Said he didn't want any lunch and that he was going to lie down. When he didn't appear for supper, the orderly thought he was still not feeling well. He should have checked on him, but he didn't. When I went for my evening visit, Noah wasn't in his room."

"So that's when you realized he'd run off?"

"No. At first I thought he was somewhere else in the asylum. I began to look for him and asked several of the men who work in the men's wing, but none had seen him since morning. One of the doctors alerted the administrator, who ordered a search of the entire asylum, including the grounds." Levi spread butter and strawberry jam on his biscuit. "There was a hasty search of the area outside the fence, but since it was already dark, that search was soon called off until the following morning."

"Why would he flee the asylum? It seems he would have given you a hint that something was wrong and he wanted to be discharged."

Levi hiked a shoulder. "He may have believed I would object to such a suggestion, and I probably would have. He still needs medical treatment and care before we can assume he is stable enough to live outside the asylum. Running off like this will only make his release less likely."

Several workers from the local glass factory sat at a nearby table, and their laughter and loud voices made it difficult to hear Levi. Ainslee scooted her chair a bit closer. "Did you ask if Noah had experienced any problems with the staff or other patients during the days before he disappeared?"

Levi finished his biscuit and pushed his plate aside. "I did. They said there had been no reports of any problems. I've searched everywhere I can think he might hide." He sighed and folded his arms across his chest. "I've run out of ideas, and I can't continue to spend my days looking for him when there's work to be done. If we get too far behind on production, there will be no way to catch up."

She wanted to assure him they had plenty of time, but Levi had meticulously developed a schedule for each of the tiles that would be created for each room in the museum. He'd begun work on the drawings Noah had completed, with a plan to create the tiles that would be placed in the center room and represent the state of West Virginia before beginning work on the tiles for any of the other rooms.

"From what you've said, I'm guessing Noah didn't leave any of his latest sketches at the asylum when he disappeared."

Levi's mouth drooped. "No—which adds to my worry."

Ainslee longed to say something that would remove the frown from his face and ease the burden he was carrying in his heart. "Whenever any of us at home would begin to fret and worry, Grandmother Woodfield would pull out her Bible and point us to sixth chapter of Matthew. Do you know what it says about the birds of the air and God's care for all of us?"

He nodded. "I do, but it's hard to think God has time to worry about me and my problems with all the other people in the world."

Ainslee longed to ease his concern. "But the Bible says that we should remember that if God cares for the birds, He surely cares for us, too. He's looking after us. You need to remember that." She spoke the words with conviction, but couldn't bring herself to add that what he wanted might not be God's plan for Noah, or for him.

A jolt fired through her. Here she sat speaking of God's will to Levi, when her own faith had wavered when Adaira ran off to wed. She'd never spoken of her doubts to anyone. She hadn't believed God could be part of a plan to drop her in the middle of a town where she didn't know a soul and expect her to manage a business for which she held no enthusiasm. But look what He had done. And if He could see her through and change her life for the better over these past six months, surely He would protect and do what was best for Noah and Levi.

God planned for her to meet Levi and to discover the joy of managing a business. If she'd had her way, none of this would have happened. Gratitude filled her heart until it nearly burst. "God knows what is best for Noah."

"I try to remember God cares about Noah even more than I do, but when something like this disappearance happens, it becomes more difficult." He offered a sad smile. "There are times when I need to be reminded of God's love, and this is one of them. Having you here helps."

"I think we all need encouragement from time to time. I believe God understands that we need others to remind us that He cares about us when difficulties come our way." She hoped her words would encourage him. "If it helps to ease your concerns, Ewan doesn't believe progress on the museum will take place as quickly as originally scheduled. If you recall, progress was slow when we were waiting to hear about our contract. I don't think Mr. Harrington considered the time it would take to gather unanimous decisions from his other investors. The same will be true with the other bids they're seeking. They've broken ground and begun work on the foundation, but there is much to accomplish before they'll be ready to lay the tiles."

He nodded, but his sad look remained intact. "But we shouldn't depend upon delays in the construction of the building. We need to fulfill our obligation as outlined in the contract, so I believe we should hire more workers before we fall behind. There were a couple of fellows who came in looking for jobs while you were in Grafton. I didn't hire them, but I think they'd both make good apprentices. One of them worked in the tile business for a time so he at least knows how to work with clay. The other has some artistic talent and I thought I might be able to train him as a cutter for the mosaics. He was excited about learning."

"I trust your judgment. If you thought they would be good workers, you should have gone ahead and hired them. We need to have men trained to help you on the mosaics."

"Right. Trouble is, the time I spend training them slows me down, but I guess that's the only way we'll have skilled workers." He sighed. "If I'm going to complain about not having enough time to get things done, I suppose sitting here any longer makes no sense, either. Still, I hope you know there's no other place I'd truly like to be than with you."

Her cheeks warmed. "Thank you."

Once they'd paid for their meal and were on their way to the tile works, Ainslee asked how she could help in the search for Noah. Levi grimaced. "I wish I had something I could tell you, but I don't even know what else to do myself. We've searched the entire area. There's no sign of him anywhere."

"Did he have any money? Do you think he might have boarded a train and gone to another town—or rented a horse from the livery? Have you checked those possibilities?"

"I haven't looked into a train ticket or asked at the livery because he didn't have any cash or any way to obtain money."

Ainslee tugged on his arm, pulling him to a stop near the front door of the tile works. "But you didn't think he could get out of the asylum, either. Noah was lucid enough that he could have passed himself off as someone visiting a patient at the asylum. He could have requested a ride into town, and be anywhere by now. I don't mean to frighten you, but I think the search should go beyond the asylum area."

Levi turned toward her. "You're right, of course, but the asylum isn't going to use their staff to search the entire town. I talked to the sheriff, and he said he didn't want me saying too much in town about an escaped lunatic, or the whole town would be shooting at every stranger that came near, and the women would be afraid to have their husbands out of their sight for even a minute."

Once inside the office, Ainslee dropped her reticule on the desk and removed her brown felt hat trimmed with ecru velvet and pink roses. She despised the ornate hat. However, both fashion and Laura dictated she wear such frippery, especially when traveling. Levi hurried forward to take her matching brown velvet cape and hung it near the office door.

"Oh, *pshaw*! If they knew Noah was harmless, I doubt there would be any great concern with the townspeople. Something must be done to find him."

"I agree, but other than going against the sheriff's orders and knocking on doors, I don't know what it would be. I waver between walking around town looking for him and staying here to work on the tiles. Truth is, I can't seem to do either thing very well." He sat down opposite her and leaned forward. "I'm at a loss."

Ainslee thought for a moment. "First, we're going to pray, and then you're going to go out to the tile shop and set to work. I'm going to send word to those two men you spoke with and offer them jobs so you can begin their training. Then, I'm going to give some real thought to where Noah may be hiding. If I must go against the sheriff's orders, so be it." She sat down in the chair beside him. "Let's ask God to direct our work as well as our search for Noah—and to keep him safe until we locate him."

When they'd finished praying, Levi's lips curved in a warm

smile. “Thank you. Having you here means more than you can know.” He cupped her cheek. “I missed you so much.”

Ainslee covered his hand with her own and reveled in the warmth of his touch. “I missed you, too. We’re all going to be fine, Levi. I’m sure of it.”

She folded her arms across her waist and watched Levi cross the courtyard before turning back to her desk. A stack of time sheets sat beside the ledgers awaiting entry. Levi had offered his apologies for not entering them each day as promised. In truth, she didn’t know how he’d accomplished any work once he’d learned of Noah’s disappearance.

While she was entering the men’s hours into the ledger, her thoughts remained on Noah and what might have happened to cause his unexpected behavior. From all reports, he’d been content and happy since beginning work on the sketches, so why would he disappear? Perhaps she’d pay a visit to the asylum herself. There might be something more she could discover.

Chapter 26

Levi set to work tamping clay into a plaster mold that had been created from one of his brother's drawings. The beauty displayed in the details of Noah's pictures never failed to amaze Levi. There was no doubt his brother had been gifted with far greater artistic talent than his own. Receiving Noah's agreement to use his designs in the museum fulfilled one of his dreams for his brother. He longed to reveal the depth of Noah's gift to all who would one day walk into Mr. Harrington's museum. Now he wondered if the entire idea had been a mistake.

Had the deadlines and number of drawings needed for this project been too difficult for Noah? Had he broken under the strain of trying to meet goals rather than creating pictures he considered worthy of his talent? On more than one occasion, Noah had bemoaned the fact that his drawings didn't contain enough detail, yet Levi had brushed aside the comments. Instead, he'd encouraged Noah to continue working on the next batch of drawings. Although Levi had explained that not all the details could be included in the tiles, his reasoning hadn't seemed to appease Noah.

Levi's thoughts plagued him while he was scraping the excess clay from the mold. He had only himself to blame for Noah's disappearance. After removing the last of the surplus clay, he tossed the scraper onto a nearby table, then muttered under his breath when the tool clanged and then dropped to the floor.

"What's eating at ya, Levi?" Robert stooped down and retrieved the scraper. He placed it on the worktable beside the mold. "You still worrying over your brother?"

The sheriff didn't want word of Noah's disappearance spreading throughout the town, so Levi had told only Robert and Harold. He'd repeated the sheriff's warning and asked them to keep the matter to themselves. In truth, he probably shouldn't have told either of them, but he'd needed someone to talk to. Besides, they'd been good about keeping an eye out for strangers on their way to and from work. Levi had given them a description of Noah, but other than being a stranger in town, his brother didn't possess any distinguishing features that would set him apart from most other men.

Levi nodded. "Between worrying over him and worrying over the time limit to complete the tiles, I'm tied in knots most of the time."

Robert wiped the perspiration from his brow. "You got your problems and that's a fact. Don't envy ya any. Me and Harold are agreeable to help however ya see fit. If you want to teach us how to make the plaster molds or fill 'em with clay, we're willing, or if you want us to go snoop around in town when we're not busy, we can do that, too. You just say the word."

Levi was touched by their offer. Neither of them had been keen on the idea of the mosaics, and they hadn't held back with their opinions. Robert, in particular, disliked change. He saw no reason to expand the products offered by the tile works, and had no desire to make or sell anything else. Harold had immediately agreed with Robert, but after listening to Ainslee, he had begrudgingly accepted the idea. Now to have them offer to learn a part of the process was something Levi had never imagined would occur.

"Thank you both. I appreciate your willingness to help with the tiles, but I think we'll have a couple of new fellows starting as apprentices in the next few days. I don't want either of you to have to fall behind on your own orders. As far as going into town, I doubt Miss McKay would approve of you leaving the tile works during work, but if you continue keeping a watch if you go to the café at noontime or whenever you're in town, I'd be thankful."

"Now that you mention lunch, I been meaning to mention that some of the diggers and a few of the packers have been grumbling that food's been missing out of their lunch pails lately." Robert nodded toward the outside of the building, where the diggers and packers were hard at work. "Same thing happened to me and Harold a couple of times, too. I'm thinking we should find another place where we can keep 'em in sight instead of down in the pit. Ain't no need to put 'em down there now that the colder weather's set in. We can use one of the packing boxes and sit it out under the overhang. That way, both the diggers and packers will have a good view of 'em. One of the packers is sure it's one of the part-time diggers that's been stealing from all of us. If it is him, he's mighty careful, 'cause I ain't never seen him go down in the pit. Harold and me always lower the pails on the dumbwaiter in the morning, Malcolm takes 'em off, and we use the same method to bring 'em back up at noon."

Levi scratched his head. He couldn't say for sure if anything had been missing from his lunch pail or not. Mrs. Brighton packed his lunch most mornings, and he was never sure what he might find inside the metal container. However, now that he thought about it, there hadn't been as much food as usual in his pail.

"I think you have a good idea. Go ahead and tell the men to store their pails in a crate under the hanging eaves along this side of the wall. We'll see if that solves the problem."

Ainslee stopped at the boardinghouses that the two recent applicants had listed as their addresses. Neither was home, so she left word with the keepers to have them return to the tile works tomorrow morning if they were still interested in employment. Both women had promised to pass along the messages and appeared relieved that their respective boarders might soon be gainfully employed.

That task completed, she continued onward. The day was crisp and the bright sunshine provided more warmth than she'd anticipated. She now wished she'd foregone her heavy cloak. She was drawing near the Wilson Hardware and Mercantile when she heard someone call her name.

"Over here." Dr. Thorenson waved his hat in her direction.

Ainslee turned and spotted him standing beside a horse and buggy outside the local bank. She waved in return. "Good afternoon."

"When did you return to Weston?"

She stepped off the board walkway and approached the buggy. "Earlier today. I had some calls to make and then was going to the asylum."

"Then you must ride with me. How is Levi? I've been worried about him." The doctor assisted Ainslee into the buggy. "I know he's been terribly worried about Noah. I've assured him we are doing everything possible to locate him."

"Are you?" Ainslee settled in the seat beside him.

The doctor's brow furrowed. "Yes, of course. The entire staff feels a deep responsibility to find him."

She nodded. "As they should. I'm sure all of the families who entrust their loved ones into your care don't expect them to go missing for days on end." Ainslee peeked around the brim of her bonnet. "I don't mean to sound harsh, but Noah could be anywhere by now—he might even be injured or . . ." She couldn't bring herself to say what she was thinking.

"Now, now, it serves no purpose to think the worst. Noah was doing well. There's no reason to think he's come to any harm. You need to remain positive—for Levi's sake." He spoke to her as if she were a child—or one of his patients. "We're truly doing all we can to find Noah."

Ainslee gave him a sidelong glance. She didn't want to sound like a woman bordering on hysteria, yet from what Levi had told her, the asylum wasn't doing a great deal to locate his brother. "That's why I was coming to visit this afternoon."

He looked at her as if she'd spoken in a foreign tongue.

"I'd like to know all that's been done to find Noah, and I want to speak to the orderlies who had been caring for him before he disappeared."

The doctor wagged his head. "We've already spoken to them, and they told us Noah had been doing fine. Nothing out of the ordinary occurred."

"I thought he told one of the orderlies he wasn't feeling well, and he'd gone to his room without eating. Isn't that considered unusual?"

"Well, yes, but other than that, nothing happened."

Ainslee sighed as he helped her down from the buggy and escorted her down the walkway to the main entrance. "But that's when he went missing—while he was supposed to be in his room. If he complained of illness, why wasn't he checked by one of the doctors on duty that day?"

"Patients saying they have a stomachache or aren't hungry isn't considered a reason for medical care unless it continues for more than a day or two, Miss McKay." Side by side, they walked up the wide stairs to the front doors. "Please believe me, we give our patients the best of care. Unfortunately, because Noah was doing so well, the staff didn't keep him under the same watchful eye as they did back when he wasn't lucid." Once inside, they stopped in the foyer. "Do you want me to summon the orderlies who were on duty? If you talk to them, will that ease some of your concern?"

She nodded. "It won't ease my concern regarding Noah's current safety, but it will help me to understand more of what happened and might offer some clue as to where he might be."

He offered a somewhat patronizing smile. Did he think she was as irrational as some of his patients? "Would you like to wait in my office?"

"No, thank you. If you'd send them to the library, I'd be most appreciative. While I wait, I'll see how the ladies have been doing while I was gone. I suggested we merely catalog by author and title for the time being and the patients can sign books in and out on a sheet at the desk. I want to see if that's been working for them or if we need a better system."

"I haven't heard reports of any problems, but since you'd like to check, I'll see if those orderlies are on duty." He turned and rushed off as though he feared she'd ask another question about Noah's disappearance.

For a moment she stared after him, perplexed by his hurried and abrupt behavior. All of her encounters with Dr. Thorenson had been pleasant until now. She could only guess that the administration was more concerned over Noah's disappearance than he'd indicated. Did they fear Levi would seek legal counsel? Perhaps that was it, though she doubted the thought had entered Levi's mind—at least not yet.

She reached for the brass doorknob and pulled open the heavy library door. Several ladies were seated with books, and Zana Tromley was sitting at the desk with a stack of books near her elbow. She looked up and smiled when Ainslee stepped inside.

"Good to see you." Ainslee kept her voice low, but two of the other patients glanced in her direction and waved. She returned the gesture and stepped to the desk. "Has the library been busy the past few days?"

Zana pointed to the sheet and nodded. "Just look at all the books that have been signed out. The ladies are enjoying them a great deal. They've even been discussing the books they're reading."

The encouraging news created a welcome lightness in Ainslee's chest. "How wonderful. Perhaps we should gather periodically to discuss books. Do you think there are enough ladies who would be interested?"

Zana twisted in her chair and gestured toward the divan positioned near the windows. "The lady over there in the burgundy dress is Gertrude Sachs. Gertie's the one you should talk to about discussing books. She can read an entire book faster than anyone I ever saw, and then she recommends books to the other ladies—at least the ones she likes."

"Thank you, Zana. I'll do that right now." Ainslee crossed the room, and when the woman looked up, she introduced herself.

The woman placed a finger between the pages of her book. "Pleased to meet you, Miss Ainslee McKay. I'm Gertrude Sachs. You can call me Gertie, and I'll call you Ainslee."

Ainslee smiled. "I'm pleased to meet you, as well. I understand you're a voracious reader and you make book recommendations to the other ladies."

She leaned closer. "I do. Many of them simply can't make a decision. That's what comes of being married. They've become so accustomed to their husbands telling them what they should say and do that they can't even choose a book for themselves. 'Course, it's those same husbands who signed them into this place when most of them are as sane as you and me."

Ainslee chuckled. She didn't agree with Gertie's assessment of all husbands, but she'd learned that it wasn't good to be confrontational with patients. "Tell me, Gertie, since you're not married, who signed you into the asylum?"

Gertie removed a handkerchief from her pocket and used it as a bookmark before placing the book on a table beside the divan. She scooted back and folded her arms across her waist. "Truth is, it was my brother. He found out from the local banker that I had a tidy sum of money in an account, and he figured the easiest way to get it was to say I was a mental defective and bring me here. The law makes it easy as can be for men to keep putting us in places like this when they want to be rid of us. Once a judge says he can have the money in my bank account, he'll probably come and sign me out of here. At least he said he would, but he's not all that trustworthy."

"So it seems. I'm sorry you're here under such circumstances. Can the doctors do nothing at all to help?"

She snorted. "They follow whatever those judges tell them to do, but I'm content enough for now. This library is a blessing, for sure, and I like tending flowers when the weather's nice and my rheumatism isn't acting up."

Gertie greeted the idea of book discussions with enthusiasm and immediately agreed to take charge. The two of them had already exchanged several ideas when the library door opened and two orderlies entered—probably looking for her, and they didn't seem too happy about being summoned.

"Wonder what they're doing here. None of them like to read. Probably looking for another patient that escaped." She nudged Ainslee's arm. "They still haven't found the fella who took off the other day."

"That's why I'm here. I want to ask some questions about the man who disappeared. He's the brother of a close friend."

"Ask that tall, dark-haired orderly about the argument he had with that artist fella the day he ran off. I think that has something to do with why he disappeared." She lowered her voice as the men approached. "I'll talk to you more when they aren't around."

Before the men reached the divan, Ainslee stood. "Why don't we sit at that table over there? It will be quiet and we can talk without interruption."

The men didn't answer, but they followed her to the table and sat down on opposite sides of her and introduced themselves. Because she wasn't a relative or close friend of Noah's, Ainslee had never been given a pass to visit on the men's wing, so she didn't know either of the men. When she began to question them, they crossed their arms and leaned back in their chairs as if to distance themselves.

"We've already answered all of these questions before." The shorter man's lower lip protruded like that of a pouting child.

The taller one agreed. "We've got work to do. Why don't you read the report instead of forcing us to come in here and talk to you? I thought Noah's only relative was his brother." He curled his lip, and suspicion glistened in his dark eyes.

She turned her full attention upon him. "I have both the doctor's permission and Levi Judson's permission to be here.

What I'd like for you to tell me is not the same things you've been repeating to others. Instead, I'd like you to elaborate upon the argument you had here in the library with Noah the day he disappeared." Ainslee forced herself not to blink as she pinned him with a hard stare.

"Well, I . . . I'm . . . Who told you we argued?" Perspiration dotted the taller orderly's upper lip.

"Who told me doesn't matter, but telling the truth does. Either tell me what happened, or I'm going to call Dr. Thorenson in here right now."

"Promise you won't get me fired. I need this job. I have a family to feed." Fear quickly replaced his earlier look of suspicion.

Ainslee tapped her fingers atop the table. "You're not in a position to bargain with me, but I guarantee you'll feel like a weight's been lifted off your chest if you tell the truth."

The shorter man nudged the dark-haired orderly. "Go ahead and tell her. She already knows you had an argument. Better to fess up now and not get in any deeper trouble."

Ainslee nodded. "Your friend is giving you good advice. You should listen to him."

He raked his hands through his dark hair until it formed peaks that looked like tall clumps of grass. "I found him here in the library and told him he had to come down to the dining room for the noon meal, but he wanted to finish drawing his picture. He said something about the light being perfect to finish the drawing and he didn't want to eat." He sucked in a deep breath. "We argued back and forth until he said he wasn't feeling good and was going to his room."

"So did you leave him here in the library or take him to his room?" Ainslee studied the man's worried eyes. "I'll do whatever I can to keep you from being discharged, but I need the truth."

"I left him here, but he promised he'd go to his room in

fifteen minutes." The orderly fidgeted with the buttons on his jacket. "Can I go now?"

"Yes, although Noah's brother may have further questions for you after I pass along this information."

Ainslee turned and watched the two men depart. She'd not yet digested all the orderly had told her when Gertie strode to her side. "Noah was still in the library when everyone else left for the dining rooms, so you know what that means, don't you?"

Ainslee looked up at the older woman. "Not entirely. What do you think it means?"

Gertie dropped into the chair where the orderly had been sitting only moments before. "It means there wouldn't have been much of anyone in the hallways at that time. Instead of going off to the west-wing dining room, he could have exited through the front doors and out the gate just like he was a visitor. And we all know he's as normal as you and me." Her lips drooped into a frown. "Why *is* he in here?"

Ainslee stiffened and leaned back in her chair. "Noah isn't always lucid, Gertie." Though it somehow seemed improper to discuss his condition with a woman whom she barely knew—and a patient, at that—Ainslee nonetheless sought to defend Levi. She wanted Gertie to understand that Levi's decision was made out of love and concern, not because he wanted to rid himself of Noah, as her brother had done to her.

Gertie's lips curved in a gentle smile. "You don't need to be defensive, my dear. I believe my question was quite valid, given the fact that Noah is such a talented young man who was always in control of his behavior in my presence." Gertie pushed up from her chair. "If you'll excuse me, I want to give further thought to the book we're going to discuss." Her brow furrowed. "You do want me to continue with the idea, don't you?"

"What?" With all the talk of Noah, Ainslee had momentarily

forgotten her earlier request. "Yes, of course. Please go ahead and choose a book, and I'll be in touch with you." Ainslee had no desire to argue with the woman. In truth, she simply wanted some time to digest what she'd learned from the two orderlies. While it didn't give her as much as she'd hoped for, at least she could tell Levi there appeared to be a sound reason why Noah had disappeared. Above all else, he wanted to draw. But where? That was the question. Since Levi was in Weston, she didn't think Noah would leave. Besides, how far could he go without money? Yet how was Noah sustaining himself—and where was he hiding?

Chapter 27

Levi strode across the courtyard and into the mixing room of the tile works. Harold waved him forward and held out a sketching pencil. "Found this down in the drying pit and figured it must be yours." He grinned at Levi. "You going down there to do your drawings nowadays?"

Levi turned the pencil between his fingers and shook his head. "This isn't mine. It's from a set of drawing pencils I gave Noah when he began working on his sketches." His thoughts jumbled together like a cat with a basket of yarn. Had Noah discovered a way to enter the tile works at night, and had he been sleeping in the drying pit, where he would be warm and hidden from anyone who might return later in the evening? While it was possible, Levi was sure the doors were locked every night to prevent such a happenstance.

A short time later, he returned to the office while still pondering just how the pencil had gotten into the drying pit. He'd barely cleared the door when Ainslee rushed toward him. "I just returned from the asylum and I have news."

Levi dropped the pencil onto the desk. "They've found Noah?"

She shook her head. "No, I wish I could tell you they had, but I did discover the orderlies didn't tell the whole truth."

They sat down in the chairs near the desk, and Ainslee detailed all she'd learned during her time at the asylum. "While we still don't know Noah's whereabouts, I think this may indicate that he left the asylum because he wanted to continue drawing and they wanted him to participate in other activities. I don't think he'd had a relapse of any sort. Rather, I believe he was quite lucid and wanted to make his own decisions about what he could do. That's encouraging, don't you think?"

The excitement in her voice warmed him to the depths of his very soul. Even though she must be weary from her journey to Weston and concerned about arrangements for Mrs. Crothers's funeral, as well as the problems at the brickyard, Ainslee had taken time to go to the asylum and make inquiries regarding his brother. Only a woman with a caring and generous heart would do such a thing.

"I agree that it's encouraging, and I think this might be, too." Levi picked up the pencil Harold had discovered in the drying pit and extended it toward her.

"Your drawing pencil?"

Her blank expression caused him to chuckle. "That's just it—this isn't my drawing pencil. It's one I gave to Noah, and Harold discovered it in the drying pit earlier today."

While they continued their discussion, the bell clanged to announce the end of the workday. The men soon filtered into the courtyard and then disappeared up the path leading toward their homes.

Ainslee peered across the expanse and focused upon the doors leading into the mixing room. "I'm sure Harold locks those doors every night, but there could be a broken window that might have allowed him access." She stood and gestured to Levi. "Let's go and look before we return to our boardinghouses."

Their inspection of the premises didn't reveal any broken

windows, and the door leading into the mixing room was tightly locked. Levi shrugged. "Maybe he's sneaking in before the doors are locked for the night. He could be in there right now. Should I go and get the keys from the office and go in?"

Ainslee nodded. "Yes, we may be a little late for supper, but after we explain, I'm sure we'll be forgiven."

Levi glanced back at the door to the mixing room as they hurried toward the office. "If he's sleeping in here during the night, I wonder where he goes during the daytime."

"He could hide most anywhere," Ainslee pointed out. "I imagine he keeps moving about in the woods."

Levi slapped his forehead when they neared the office door. "The lunch pails!"

Eyes wide, Ainslee stared at him. "Whose lunch pails and what about them?"

"Harold and Robert said some of the diggers and packers had mentioned food had been missing from the lunch pails recently. Nobody could figure out how it could go missing because they lowered the pails into the pit in the morning and brought them back up at noon. Only Robert and Harold went down there, and neither of them was taking food. I told them that since the weather was colder now, they could store the lunches in one of the packing crates under the eaves by the digging area, where someone would be sure to see anyone trying to sneak food from the lunches."

"You think Noah . . ."

"Yes. He must have stayed down there until after they lowered the lunches, but I don't know how they wouldn't have seen him." He shook his head. "I wonder if he's been able to locate any food since the men switched the storage space." His stomach tightened. "I may have taken food from my own brother's mouth."

"Don't think that way, Levi. It's not as if you knew he was

staying down there and you intentionally took food away from him. The truth is, you still don't know that he's been down there or that he's the one who was taking food out of the lunch pails. Neither of us should jump to conclusions."

He chuckled. "You mean *I* shouldn't jump to conclusions." She nodded and he pulled her close. "I don't think you know how much you mean to me. If I didn't have you by my side, I don't know if I could make it through all of this."

"You'd make it through with God's help, but I hope having me around makes it more pleasant." She smiled and tugged on his hand. "We'd better hurry. I don't want Mrs. Brighton drawing any wrong conclusions when she discovers both of us are late."

He chuckled again. "I think she already suspects. The other day she said something about love taking bloom in the boardinghouses."

"And what did you say?" Ainslee arched her brows as she awaited his reply.

"I did what most men would do—I ignored her." They entered the office, and he picked up the keys to the workrooms before he turned and grinned at her. "But I'd be happy to tell her that love has taken bloom in my heart and that I'm hopeful it has done the same in yours."

Her cheeks flamed bright pink. And while he regretted causing her embarrassment, he was pleased for the unexpected opportunity to affirm his feelings for her.

She flashed him a shy smile. "I think you must know by now that I have deep feelings for you, as well." She glanced toward the adjacent building and let out a slight gasp.

"What's wrong?"

"I thought I saw a figure moving through the outer hallway." She hesitated. "Perhaps it was merely a shadow. It's hard to tell at this time of day."

Levi stooped down and looked out the window, then shook his head. "I don't see anything, but let's get over there."

Ainslee locked the office door, and the two of them hurried across the open expanse and unlocked the door leading into the main hallway. Careful to keep as quiet as possible, they continued a short distance down the hall to the room where Levi cast the plaster molds. They remained silent as church mice on a Sunday morning. Ainslee tensed and listened, but the only thing she could hear was the pounding of her heart.

After waiting for what seemed an eternally long time, they heard the shuffle of feet in the adjacent room. Ainslee reached for Levi's arm and squeezed tight. He nodded and signaled for her to remain in place. He had no idea how Noah might react when confronted, if the culprit indeed was Noah. In that case, he certainly didn't want Ainslee's presence known.

Once the shuffling ceased, they waited a short time. Thankful for the bit of daylight that still filtered through the window, Levi quietly stepped to the door. In one swift motion, he yanked it open and then rushed through the mixing room and to the ladder-like steps leading down to the pit.

His mouth was as dry as a wad of cotton. "I know you're down there, so you better come on up here. I don't want to see anyone come to harm." His heart pounded like a thousand hammers beating on a piece of cold iron. "Come on now. No harm will come to you, if you do as I ask." The tinny words stuck in his throat. The only sound was the incessant thrumming in his ears. "Come on or I'm coming down after you."

The shuffle of feet and then a low whisper sounded. "Levi? Is that you, Levi?"

"Noah! Yes, it's me. Come on up here. I've been worried sick about you."

"Are you angry with me?" He sounded like a little boy who feared the wrath of an irate father.

"No, I'm happy to know you're safe. Come on up here and let me see you."

Noah slowly climbed the narrow steps and stepped out of the drying pit and into his brother's arms. "I'm sorry I worried you, but I needed to work on my drawings and they wouldn't give me enough time at the asylum. I had all these ideas, and I wanted to get them on paper in case my problems returned. Wait until you see the drawings I've made for the room that's going to have events from the Bible."

Levi looked deeper into his brother's eyes. Maybe he wasn't as lucid as Levi had thought. "You aren't supposed to be sketching scenes from the Bible. You've completed your drawings."

Noah gestured toward the pit. "I wanted to do more. Now that I've begun to draw, I don't want to quit. I have a lantern I take down in the pit with me. That way I can work if I can't sleep. Wait until you see them."

Levi lightly grasped his brother's elbow to propel him toward the other side of the room. "Before I see any drawings, we need to talk. Come with me. Ainslee is in the other room. We can get her and then go over to the office, where it's more comfortable. You can tell me what has happened since you left the asylum."

Noah shook off Levi's hold and took a backward step. "I'm not going anywhere without the drawings. Let me get them, and then I'll go with you to the office."

Fierce determination shone in his brother's eyes, and Levi understood it would be better to relent on this point. While his brother wasn't suffering from a terrible relapse, he still wasn't completely lucid. Levi patiently waited until his brother returned with a bulging roll of drawings tucked beneath his arm. From the size of the cylinder, his brother had indeed been busy.

Noah willingly accompanied Levi into the adjacent room where Ainslee awaited. Levi stepped to Ainslee's side and gently pulled her closer. "Noah, this is Ainslee McKay, the lady I've told you about."

Noah offered a sheepish grin and lowered his gaze. Rather than a young man of eighteen, he looked like a schoolboy. "Pleased to meet you, Miss McKay. Any friend of Levi's is a friend of mine."

"Thank you, Noah. I'm pleased to meet you as well. Your artistic talent is truly amazing."

Her words appeared to embarrass Noah, and Levi nodded toward the door. "Let's go over to the office."

Once inside, Noah placed the roll of drawings on the desk, but before he could untie the string, Levi stayed him. "We're going to talk before we look at your drawings. I want you to tell me everything, Noah. How and why you left the asylum and everything that followed until this exact moment. Can you do that?"

"I think I can."

He leaned back in the chair and told them of his argument with the orderlies in the library. "I tried to tell them that being allowed to draw was the only thing that helped me feel normal, but they wouldn't listen. They wanted me to stop." He exhaled a long breath. "After they left me alone to finish my drawing, I took my art supplies and hurried through the doors leading to the main hall into the administration area."

Ainslee frowned. "But that door is kept locked."

"Either they keep it open for the staff while meals are being served or someone forgot to lock it." Noah shrugged. "There was a coat hanging on a hall tree near the front doors. I don't know who it belonged to, but I took it." He glanced at Levi. "I know that's stealing, but earlier in the day I heard one of the orderlies say it had turned cold outside. I figured I was going to need it. I suppose we should return it."

Levi nodded. "I think that would be a good idea." He leaned toward his brother. "Where did you go once you left the asylum?"

"I stopped at a store in town and asked for directions to the tile works. I watched from the hillside so I could study the routine of the men coming and going and slipped down there late in the afternoon, when there weren't any workers in the courtyard. I was able to walk inside, and I went down the hallway into a small, empty room and waited. That's when I was the most scared, 'cause I didn't know if someone would walk in on me."

Levi leaned forward and rested his arms across his thighs. "Tell me about the pit."

Noah nodded and continued. "I went through the entire area that night, looking for where I might be able to hide and still have enough light to draw. When I found the pit, I decided it would be a good place to sleep. It was warmer down there, and it felt kind of snug with those racks of drying tiles around me. Hiding from the men in the early morning until they dropped down the lunch pails was easy. They didn't expect to see anyone, so when the fella came down and removed the lunch pails from the dumbwaiter, I hid back in the corner behind the racks."

Ainslee arched her brows. "Did you stay down there all day?"

"No. I could hear everything those fellas said, so I knew when they were going outside to fetch more clay or get water. They usually went together so they could smoke their pipes. I'd sneak back down the hallway to that little room. Most days I could find a time when no one was in the courtyard and sneak off through the trees. I never used the main path. Then I'd sneak back in late in the afternoon."

He looked up at Ainslee. "It was easy enough, but I did have to sleep outside one night. I got so busy with my drawing that

I didn't notice the sun setting. By the time I got back, the place was locked up. I thought about breaking a window but decided against it." He scooted forward on his chair and leaned toward the desk. "Can I show you the drawings now?"

Levi had additional questions, but they could wait. It was more important to let his brother reveal what he'd created during his absence from the asylum.

"First I did all the drawings for the West Virginia room. There's sketches of the flowers, trees, animals, coal miners, farmers, and everything else I could think of that would symbolize the state. If the museum fellow has any other ideas he wants, I'd be glad to draw them, too."

Levi examined each of the pictures and then gave each one to Ainslee for her review. They were flawless. Levi didn't know how anyone could find fault with them, and he said so. Noah beamed at the praise.

"You really like them?" He looked back and forth between Levi and Ainslee.

"I think they are gorgeous, and I am sure Mr. Harrington will agree. Don't you, Levi?" Ainslee touched his arm.

"I do." His voice was thick with emotion. "I think you have drawn more than we need. We may have to choose our favorites, and it will be difficult."

Noah grinned and pushed the remaining pile of sketches in front of his brother. "These are the ones that have some scenes from the Bible. I finished this one last night. It's the city of Jerusalem. I'm not sure that's exactly how it looked, but I tried to remember what I'd read in the Bible and did my best."

Levi ran a reverent finger over the drawing. "You did your best in every one of these, Noah. I'm truly amazed."

"I'm glad you like them." He pushed up from his chair. "I guess it's time to go back to the asylum."

Levi's heart cinched in a knot. There had to be another way to help Noah. Maybe if he, the doctors, and Ainslee put their heads together, they could come up with a plan. But would Ainslee's feelings for him change if he suggested Noah come live with them once they were married?

Good grief. What was he thinking? He hadn't even asked for her hand.

Chapter 28

Almost a month had passed since Aunt Margaret's death, and though Ainslee had received several telegrams from Ewan telling her that the funeral and burial had been completed and there had been a reading of her final will and testament, she longed for further details. Ewan had insisted Ainslee's presence in Weston was more urgent than her attendance at Margaret's funeral. Though she'd agreed with his conclusion, the decision to remain in Weston had been difficult. Today, Ewan would arrive to inspect the progress they'd made on the tiles. Mr. Harrington was going to be returning at the end of the week, and Ewan wanted to be assured they were ready to answer any of his questions.

Ewan had asked her to meet the train and to lunch with him at the hotel before going to the tile works. She looked forward to this time alone with him. While Levi wasn't present, she needed to explain Noah's presence at the tile works. If Ewan had any objections, she wanted to immediately resolve them.

The moment Ewan stepped off the train, Ainslee rushed to meet him. He enveloped her in a tight embrace and then took a backward step. "You look wonderful. I thought maybe the pressure of meeting with Mr. Harrington at the end of the week, the incident with Margaret, and Noah's disappearance might have had an ill effect upon you. If it has, you're hiding it well."

She shook her head. "I must admit that a lot has happened in the last month. Although there's always concern about meeting with someone as important as Mr. Harrington, I believe he'll be impressed with our progress. I know that I am."

"That's excellent news. Let me get my bags and we'll go directly to the hotel. I don't know about you, but I'm famished." Ewan patted his stomach. "I hope you won't make me wait until noon."

"We can eat whenever you'd like."

She waited on the platform while he secured his bags, and soon they headed off to the hotel.

Once Ewan had registered, they entered the hotel dining room. There were few patrons and Ewan requested a table near a window. The waiter arrived with a pitcher of water and filled their glasses before securing their orders.

When the waiter departed, Ainslee placed her napkin across her lap. "I'm eager to hear everything about the funeral and what's happened since. Did any of the family attend her wake?"

"Aye, but only a few. Fia and Melva were there. They told me Margaret had changed a great deal in the past year and had finally treated them as though they were relatives rather than merely hired help."

"I'm pleased to hear that. I was always surprised they continued to work as Margaret's servants after Uncle Hugh died. I feared she would treat them worse once he was no longer around to remind her they were related to him."

Ewan chuckled. "I think Uncle Hugh tended to forget they were his kin from time to time, too."

"And what of Beatrice? Was she there?" Ainslee was curious

if the distant relative who had worked as Tessa's nanny and moved with them to Grafton had continued her wily ways. Thoughts of Beatrice and how she'd caused strife within the family stirred so many bad memories.

"Aye. Beatrice and the rest of her family attended both the funeral and the reading of the will. From Beatrice's behavior, I'm guessing she expected Margaret to leave her something. When the lawyer finished the reading, she jumped to her feet and stomped out of the house. Fia tells me she married a coal miner, but she's not happy with her lot in life."

Her brother's accounting of Beatrice's behavior didn't come as much of a surprise. "Unless Beatrice changes her ways, I doubt she'll ever be happy. We need to continue praying for her."

"Aye. For sure, she's a sad creature who needs much prayer." Ewan signaled the waiter for more coffee. "Laura and I have been talking a great deal about the future and what we should do with the brickyard."

"Have you come to any decisions?" Ainslee leaned forward, eager to know what they had been thinking.

"We have. After a lot of prayer, we've decided to return to Bartlett, and I'll take over the brickworks again. It's going to take time to get it reestablished and regain its old reputation, but I believe it can be done. I talked to a few of the workers the last time I was in Bartlett, and they're willing to return if I come back. The business is important to both Laura and me, so we're going to move back to Woodfield Manor."

"What about Crothers Mansion?"

Ewan shook his head. "Kathleen has written to Laura stating that she has no desire to return to Bartlett. She asked that the house be placed for sale. I'm not sure how quickly a buyer will be located, but you never know—there may be someone who has the money to purchase it. For Kathleen's sake, I hope it will sell. She wrote that if there are sufficient funds from the proceeds, she'd like to purchase a small home in New York."

"That would be nice. Kathleen deserves some happiness in her life. Is she continuing to work for the milliner?"

"Aye. She likes the work. Laura suggested she might want to purchase a shop of her own, but she says she's content working for someone else. I don't think she wants the extra worry and responsibility of owning her own business."

Kathleen's life had been difficult from the time she'd arrived in Bartlett. If she was now happy working in a millinery shop and desired nothing more than a small home of her own, Ainslee was pleased to know that some of Margaret's money would one day provide a bit of stability for Kathleen.

"What do Rose and Rylan think about your decision to leave them in Grafton to run the pottery on their own?"

Ewan's lips tipped in a smile. "We both know that Rose has always considered that pottery to be her venture into the business world—and so have I. In truth, I haven't been needed to help manage the pottery since the day she married Rylan, but they've let me believe I was necessary."

Ainslee leaned back as the waiter arrived and placed a steaming plate of pork chops in front of her. "I think your role in the pottery was much more important than you'll admit, but I'm pleased that Rose and Rylan aren't going to object to your decision. That would make it all the more difficult."

Ewan carved into his pork, took a bite, and murmured with delight. "For sure, my stomach is thankful for some good, warm food." He tapped the edge of his plate with the tines of his fork. "What this hotel lacks in style, it makes up for with its fine restaurant."

"The food is good, but no better than what Mrs. Brighton serves at the boardinghouse."

"Aye, Mrs. Brighton. How is she doing? Still requiring notice if you aren't going to be present for the evening meal?"

Ainslee giggled. "Indeed, she is, but she's proved a caring woman. Levi and I recently asked her to go a bit beyond her normal routine for us and she's been most helpful."

"How so?"

"You'll recall that I sent a telegram when we located Noah and told you he was lucid and doing well."

Ewan bobbed his head. "Aye. You said he'd continued with his drawings. Has he had a setback?"

"From time to time he's experienced some problems, but Dr. Thorenson says that's to be expected. If Levi is able to hold Noah's attention and redirect him, he comes around, so we have not sent him back to the asylum. Levi and I both fear returning might cause him to decline. Dr. Thorenson had us meet with a group of doctors. Some of them agree with our plan, others don't, but we haven't been swayed by those who don't agree."

Ewan's brow creased. "'Tis good to listen to the advice of doctors. They have studied and know more about such ailments than we do."

"I know, but Dr. Thorenson agreed with our plan, and Mrs. Brighton has helped us carry it out. So far it has been working surprisingly well."

"So what is this plan?"

Ainslee smiled and then detailed their decision to have Noah live with Levi at the boardinghouse and work at the tile works during the day. "Levi rented a larger room so the two of them could share. Noah takes his evening meal with the rest of the men, and Mrs. Brighton packs his lunch each day, just as she does for her other boarders. Levi supervises Noah here at the business, and he has been doing excellent work. He's even learning how to make the plaster molds."

"I am pleased to hear he is doing well, but what if he begins to have difficulty? Do you have a plan if that should happen?"

She nodded. "He goes to see Dr. Thorenson once a week. If he begins to have problems and needs to return to the asylum, we're right here in town and they will readmit him."

Ewan lifted the bowl of applesauce and dipped another spoonful onto his plate. "You are an amazing young lady, Ainslee."

"Levi's the amazing one. He's so loving and kind. Once we made our decision, he talked to the other workers and explained Noah's problems. He asked that they treat Noah with kindness, but if there were any problems, they should immediately come and tell him. So far there have been no complaints. I'm pleased to say that the men seem quite fond of him. They have seen his drawings, and he's proved to be a good worker. The men admire his talent and willingness to help where needed."

"Then it sounds as though your decision was a good one. And if the two of you marry?"

"Ewan!"

"Don't tell me you haven't considered the possibility. What would happen to Noah then?"

"*If* that were to happen, he'd be part of our family, just as I was part of yours."

"Good." Ewan grinned and wiped his mouth with the linen napkin. "I'm eager to see how much you and Levi have been able to complete."

She lifted her napkin from her lap and placed it on the table. "It's really Levi, Noah, and the other workers who have been hard at work. I've merely been keeping the workers informed as to how much must be completed to keep us on schedule with the mosaics and making certain we meet the contracts for our regular tiles." She smiled. "And, of course, maintaining the books. We've been requested to bid on two contracts for our quarry tiles, but I wanted to talk to you and see whether you think it is wise to send out new bids right now."

Ewan pushed away from the table. "I'll be pleased to take a look at how things have been progressing in both areas of the business. You must remember that we don't want to let the mosaics take over to such an extent that the regular tile business falls off too much. We can't predict how much business will come to us for mosaics in the future, but we do know there will be ongoing demand for the other tiles."

Ainslee knew he was right. While she and Levi were tempted to devote all of their time to the beautiful mosaics, they needed to be wise in their decisions. On the short buggy ride to the tile works, Ainslee mentioned her recent letter from Adaira.

"She seems to love being in Paris. In her letter she said she'd been helping Chester with some of his purchases for the store. I think she must enjoy being able to pick out beautiful items and order them without the worry of paying. Adaira said she and Chester are treated like royalty when they are on their shopping excursions."

Ewan nodded. "Her letters to us haven't been frequent, but she does sound happy. I'm glad the two of you have mended your differences. I know that while you're separated, it's impossible to regain what was lost by her actions, but I'm thankful you've both made that first step. When she returns home, I hope the two of you can draw close again."

"So do I, Ewan." Ainslee hadn't had time to give much thought to Adaira recently, but she did miss her sister and wished her only happiness.

Ainslee inhaled the scent of fallen leaves as they descended the road to the tile works. Winter would soon be on their doorstep. She'd need to determine how much more clay they needed to dig before the ground became too hard. The clay for next year's tiles would need to weather throughout the winter months, and she didn't want to run short next year.

How odd to feel so excited about a future at the tile works. God truly worked in unusual ways.

Levi peered out the office windows as the buggy approached the front of the tile works. While he greatly admired Ewan and welcomed his advice, today's visit was different. Today wasn't entirely about business. If Ewan objected to Noah's employment, Levi would need to rethink his own future. Before she'd departed to meet the train, Ainslee had assured him his worries were unfounded.

Ewan had admired Noah's artwork and agreed to have his drawings made into tiles, but accepting Noah's daily presence in the tile works was another matter and could easily meet with Ewan's objection. Levi remained still as a stone until Ainslee and Ewan entered the building. His breath caught as Ainslee closed the distance between them. Her beauty and assurance never failed to captivate him. Her eyes glimmered and her lips curved in a generous smile that helped ease his uncertainties.

She stepped close and whispered in his ear. "No need to worry. Everything is fine."

Relief washed over him as he helped her remove her coat, and then greeted Ewan with a hearty handshake before taking a seat. "I'm glad you were able to arrive before the meeting with Mr. Harrington. I'm eager to show you our progress."

Ewan nodded. "I trust Noah is going to join us since he's become an important member of this project."

"I'll go and get him." Levi jumped to his feet. The jarring motion sent his chair toppling to the floor, and he scrambled to set it aright. "Sorry, my enthusiasm got the best of me." He grasped the back of the chair in a tight hold. How clumsy of him. Heat climbed up his neck.

Ainslee reached across the short distance that separated them and placed her hand atop his. "Why don't you stay here with Ewan and arrange the drawings? I'll go fetch Noah."

Levi glanced at Ewan, whose gaze was fastened upon his sister's hand. Levi's discomfort mounted, and he immediately slipped his hand from beneath her grasp.

Ewan folded his arms across his chest. "Aye. Let Ainslee go and fetch your brother. I'd like a wee bit of time to visit alone with you."

Apparently Ainslee hadn't noticed her brother's stiff posture and tight voice, for she merely offered him a bright smile before donning her coat. As soon as Ainslee had cleared the doorway, Levi stepped toward the desk, but Ewan gestured to the chair.

"Sit down, Levi."

The moment Levi sat, the older man scooted his chair forward until they were almost knee to knee. Ewan's piercing blue eyes shone like two fiery arrows. "From what I saw a moment ago, it appears there's more than a friendship going on between you and my sister." Levi opened his mouth, but Ewan shook his head. "I'll do the talking. You listen. When I finish, you can say your piece."

Levi clamped his lips into a thin line. He hadn't expected to have this conversation today. He had planned to speak to Ewan about his love for Ainslee, but their meeting today was supposed to be about the tiles. Though they didn't need Ewan's approval of the remainder of the drawings that he and Noah had completed thus far, his opinion would likely be similar to that of Mr. Harrington.

"I am guessin' ya know that coming to Weston was difficult

for Ainslee. This tile works wasn't her dream. I told her I would seek a buyer, but things have changed and she has developed an excitement about the business. And from what I just saw, I'm guessin' she's also developed an affection for you." His brows dipped low. "I will not tolerate a man who toys with my sister's affections or does not treat her like a lady. Are we clear?"

"Yes, we're clear." Levi nodded.

"That's good." Ewan dropped back in his chair.

"May I speak now?"

Ewan grinned. "Aye. Say your piece."

"I know that I should have asked your permission to court Ainslee, but I didn't think a telegram was a good way to ask." He glanced at the floor. "We've become extremely close while working together, and my love for her has increased day by day. I hope she will agree to marry me once we complete the museum tiles. I love her so much that I'd like to marry her tomorrow, but I think such a big change in our lives would make it difficult to concentrate on the project."

"Aye, 'tis wise to wait. Arranging a wedding and beginning a new life together while working on the museum job would be too difficult. So are ya asking me if you can continue to court my sister, or are ya asking if I'm willing to have ya marry her?"

"Both. I haven't yet asked her to marry me, but when the moment is right, I'd like to know you have no objection." He held his breath. What if Ewan was worried about Noah's disability and voiced the same objections Ann's parents had given Levi when he asked for permission to marry her? In spite of the coolness inside the office, a rush of heat washed over him. He swiped his sweaty palms down the front of his pant legs.

"Though I haven't had much time to become well acquainted with you, I'm impressed with what I've seen thus far. Is there anything you feel I ought to know?"

Levi swallowed hard. He didn't want to elaborate upon Noah's problems, but he didn't want Ewan later to regret they hadn't discussed the matter. "So you have no concerns about . . . about possible mental deficiencies if we should have a child. I mean . . . you don't think that's a reason to object to our marriage?"

"Nay. 'Tis not my job to consider such an issue. My wife worried about the matter of children before we married, but her worries were for naught. The good Lord sent a wonderful little daughter into our lives. I'm sure the Lord will handle the matter of children for you and Ainslee, as well."

A whoosh of air escaped Levi's lips. He reached forward and shook Ewan's hand as the door clicked open and Ainslee and Noah entered the room.

Ainslee stepped toward them, a question glistening in her blue eyes. "Did the two of you reach some sort of agreement while I was gone?"

Levi grinned and nodded. "We did, but it's not one we can talk about right now."

Chapter 29

A few days later, anticipation ran high among every employee in the tile works as they waited for Mr. Harrington to arrive for his inspection of the completed tiles. Although their contract for the tiles was binding, a negative response from Mr. Harrington would create complications. The men had worked with Levi to create a system to produce the tiles. It was a method they weren't keen to change at this point. Each man had his assigned task, had learned it well, and had trained at least one other worker to perform the job in his absence.

The men had initially thought it a waste of time when Levi insisted upon having at least two employees who could perform each task, but it had soon proved beneficial when one of the piece workers became ill and another man had to step into his position and re-create the mosaic picture from the final glazed pieces. If another worker hadn't already learned the process, Levi would have been required to step in and take over.

At the sight of an arriving carriage, Levi ceased his preparation and one final time thumbed through the stacks of drawings to make certain each one was in proper order.

Ewan stepped to Levi's side. "You have gone through those stacks at least five times since I arrived this morning. No one has touched them. You need to take a deep breath and calm yourself. Mr. Harrington is going to be pleased with what you've accomplished." Ewan glanced over his shoulder. "And you, too, Noah."

Noah fiddled with the collar of his shirt. "I would rather go out to the tile shop. You don't need me to be here for this meeting."

Levi spun around and shook his head. "You do need to be here. Many of these drawings are yours, and if Mr. Harrington has questions or wants any changes, I want you to be here. You're an important part of this project."

Noah beamed, though he slowly took several backward steps. By the time Mr. Harrington entered the tile works, Noah was plastered against the rear wall, once again fidgeting with his collar. Perhaps he shouldn't have insisted Noah remain at the meeting. His brother wasn't accustomed to meeting with strangers, and being forced into an uncomfortable situation might cause him to go into a downward spiral, but it was too late to send him back to the tile shop now.

Levi leaned close to Ewan's ear. "Who is that with him? I didn't know he was bringing anyone else along. Did he tell you?"

"Nay, but I'm guessing it's one of the men helping finance the museum. No need for worry." Ewan turned and gently propelled Levi toward the visitors. "Go and greet them."

"Good morning, gentlemen." Levi extended his right hand to Mr. Harrington. "We're glad you could come and review our progress." Levi glanced toward the other man and then looked back at Mr. Harrington.

Mr. Harrington turned toward his companion. "I'd like to introduce all of you to my friend and a fellow contributor to the museum, Malcolm Withers. Malcolm is most interested in your work, Levi. Not only the mosaics, but your brocade tiles, as well."

"I'm happy to hear of your interest." Levi nodded and then introduced him to Ainslee, Ewan, and Noah.

While he was always pleased to visit with potential customers, Levi hadn't scheduled time for such a meeting today, and Levi was a man who liked a schedule. Mr. Withers' arrival was going to interfere with his detailed plans for the day.

Ainslee stepped close and offered Mr. Withers a bright smile. "If you would like a tour of the tile shop while Mr. Harrington reviews the drawings, I'd be pleased to accompany you. I don't make the tiles, but I believe I could answer most of your questions."

The balding man hesitated, then glanced at Josiah Harrington. "I don't think you were looking for my opinion on the drawings, were you, Josiah?"

Mr. Harrington chuckled. "No, I plan to choose what I believe is best. If I give you an opportunity to express your judgment, the other contributors will think they should do the same. We'd never get anything accomplished. You go ahead with Miss McKay. She knows everything there is to know about this tile works. She and Levi are quite a team."

Mr. Withers tipped his head. "Then lead the way, Miss McKay. I'd like to see the entire operation."

The tension in Levi's shoulders eased. How had Ainslee known what to do without him saying a word? It was as if she could read his thoughts. He strode to the long wooden table near the windows and gestured to Noah, Ewan, and Mr. Harrington. "Shall we begin?"

After Mr. Harrington had reviewed each of the drawings there were only a few that he vetoed. Not because he disliked the ideas but because Levi had pointed out that they needed to pare down their numbers for three of the rooms in order to place the tiles in the patterns specified in their original layouts.

Mr. Harrington leaned back in his chair and cupped his chin between his thumb and index finger. "Don't discard those drawings that we won't be using in the museum. I may want to use them elsewhere. If necessary, I'll pay you for them now so you hold them in my name."

Levi shook his head. "That's not necessary. It's the least we can do for you. This project is going to permit thousands of people to see the work we can produce here in Weston."

Mr. Harrington turned in his chair and shifted his attention to Noah. "You and your brother are very talented. I'm particularly pleased with the drawings that symbolize our great state of West Virginia."

Noah didn't move away from the back wall, but he did offer Mr. Harrington a slight smile. "Thank you. I enjoyed creating them for you."

The older man shifted in his chair and removed a pipe from his breast pocket. "Unless you've already hired additional workers, I think you'll soon need to expand. You have a building large enough to accommodate many more workers. The tiles will be one of the last things we install in the museum, which will give you ample time if you can produce the mosaics more rapidly." He filled the bowl of his pipe with tobacco. "Of course, I don't want you to rush so much that you sacrifice quality." He chuckled and pushed up from his chair while puffing on his pipe. "I don't suppose you need me telling you how to operate your business, do you?"

Levi followed the older man's lead and stood. "I'm always open to hearing the opinions of others, Mr. Harrington. We have already hired a few new workers, and it will be an ongoing process as we continue to increase production of the tiles."

"Speaking of the tiles, I'd like to take a look at what you've completed. I'm eager to see how some of those first drawings have come to life."

As they prepared to leave, Mr. Harrington clapped Ewan on the shoulder. "How's the pottery business in Grafton going for you, Ewan? I've heard some good reports about the fine pieces your family has been creating. My wife recently purchased a hand-decorated urn that she tells me was created in your pottery. I believe it was signed by one of your sisters."

Ewan nodded. "Yes, that would be Rose. She's quite the artist. Her husband, Rylan, has been overseeing the day-to-day business at the pottery, and she spends a great deal of her time in the decorating shop."

Mr. Harrington chuckled. "I envy you. It sounds as though you have a good deal of leisure time to enjoy yourself."

"Not for long. My wife and I, along with our young daughter, will soon be moving back to Bartlett." Ewan detailed the circumstances surrounding the impending move as they stepped inside the tile shop.

Mr. Harrington shook his head. "A pity we've already closed the bids for the museum bricks."

Ewan nodded. "My aunt had hoped to bid on the bricks before her death, but I'm glad she realized the folly of that idea. I won't have the yard ready to produce quality bricks until next spring. I've got diggers working long hours to get the clay dug so that it can weather throughout the winter, and then we'll begin production on a small scale. I want to make certain we'll be offering the same high-quality bricks C&M produced and sold years ago."

"Then I'll be sure to keep you in mind for any future projects." He tapped the bowl of his pipe on the doorframe. Once the ashes fell to the ground, he tucked the pipe into his pocket.

They proceeded down the hallway and into a room lined with long wooden tables, where they were joined by Ainslee and Mr. Withers. Levi lifted the mosaic of a coal miner wearing an oil-wick cap lamp and carrying a metal lunch pail, with the open shaft of the coal mine reflected in the distance. "We began with the tiles that represent West Virginia. Now that the men are trained, we're moving at a swifter pace. This is one of my favorites."

Mr. Harrington's eyes glistened as he examined tiles bearing replicas of a short-eared owl, cardinal, hummingbird, rhododendron, and mountain laurel—all symbols of the state. "These are beyond my expectations. You are a true artisan, young man. After seeing your tiles, I fear I'm going to be anxious when the first visitors walk on these beautiful pieces of artwork. If one should crack or break, it will be most distressing."

Ainslee drew near Levi and Mr. Harrington. "I don't think you need to worry about these tiles any more than you would regular tiles. We don't expect any breaks, but please remember that we can replace any piece that might be damaged in the future."

Mr. Harrington turned and grasped Levi's shoulder. "If you're as smart as I think you are, you'll make certain you don't let anyone take this young lady away from you."

Levi grinned and looked at Ainslee. Her cheeks flamed with color. How he longed to pull her into his arms, but he dare not do anything so bold in front of all these men. Instead, he could only hope she would hear the conviction in his voice and see the love in his eyes. "Believe me, I don't intend to."

Two days later, after all the visitors had departed, Levi assisted Ainslee into the waiting buggy. She had promised to give a reading at the asylum library, and she didn't want to disappoint the ladies. Her thoughts, however, weren't on the library. Rather she'd been scouring her memory in an attempt to recall any reason why Ewan and Levi would have shook hands on another business agreement—and why they would keep it from her. She could think of nothing, and it was as though all remembrance of the conversation between the two men had flown from Levi's mind.

Levi covered her hand with his own and gently squeezed her fingers. "You seem lost in your thoughts. Are you deciding upon a reading for today, or perhaps not feeling well?"

"I feel fine, and there was no difficulty deciding upon what I would read today." She tapped her leather bag. "I'll be presenting the ladies with a special treat. Nettie's story that will be published in *Godey's Lady's Book*. She asked that I not tell the ladies in advance."

"I'd wager she's as excited about having her story published as we've been about the tiles. It seems she may have a promising career with her writing, but unlike Noah, she has no one to lend her a helping hand."

Ainslee smiled. "Oh, but she does. I wrote to Grandmother Woodfield about Nettie and her plight and received word from her a couple days ago. If the doctors declare Nettie mentally stable, Grandmother has agreed to have Nettie live at Woodfield Manor. It will be a good arrangement for both of them. Nettie will provide companionship to Grandmother, and Grandmother will provide Nettie with ample encouragement to continue her writing career."

Levi's eyes widened. "That's wonderful news. I'm surprised you didn't tell me."

She pinned him with an unnerving stare. "Frankly, my thoughts have been focused on the conversation between you and Ewan earlier this week." When his brow furrowed, she sighed. "You said the two of you had reached an agreement of some sort. I was going to wait until you mentioned it, but my curiosity has gotten the best of me. What was it the two of you agreed upon the other day?"

He grinned. "Oh, *that* conversation." He gently tightened his hold on her hand.

"Yes, that conversation." She arched her brows. "Are you going to tell me?"

"Ewan gave me his consent to court you."

She tipped her head back and laughed. "Did he? I fear he's a wee bit late with his consent and you're a wee bit late asking. Did you mention we've been seen together all over town for some time now?"

"I told him, but he'd already surmised as much. I was thankful he wasn't angry that I hadn't written and asked before courting you."

Ainslee peeked from beneath the fur that trimmed her hooded cloak. "What did you plan to do if he said he didn't approve?"

"I didn't have a plan. I prayed he wouldn't disapprove, and my prayers were answered." Levi pulled back on the reins, and the buggy came to a halt near the asylum gates. Instead of jumping down to assist her from the wagon, he turned to face her. "While we were talking, I asked him something else, as well."

She waited, and when he didn't continue, she nudged his arm. "Well, are you going to tell me what it was, or must I continue begging for each morsel of information?"

He shook his head. "No, you need not beg. I asked Ewan for permission to ask for your hand in marriage." She could feel him trembling. "Since I now have your brother's approval, I'm asking you to marry me."

Her heart skipped a beat as his words took hold. "Oh, Levi! Nothing would please me more."

He cupped her cheek in his palm, leaned forward, and tenderly kissed her. "I love you and promise to do everything in my power to make you happy."

A burst of excitement rushed through her. "I love you, Levi, and I'm certain we will be amazingly happy." She hesitated a moment. "We'll need to be careful that Noah doesn't feel left out. If we purchase a home and he doesn't want to live with us, perhaps we could find a place with a carriage house where he could live."

He wagged his finger. "We don't need to worry about houses or Noah just yet. There's another part of my agreement that I haven't yet told you."

Her heart fluttered an uncertain beat. "What is it?"

"I promised Ewan we wouldn't wed until after the museum project is complete." When she opened her mouth to reply, he touched his finger to her lips. "Let me finish. Waiting will give us far more opportunity to enjoy planning for the wedding and time to look for a proper house. We both need to concentrate on the mosaics. Our future with the business depends upon our making a good impression. If we don't complete the project on time and to Mr. Harrington's satisfaction, it won't bode well for the tile works. Back when we were negotiating with Mr. Harrington, I believe you warned me that we wouldn't want to breach the contract in any way."

"You're right. There wouldn't be time to plan a proper wedding while working on the tiles, but I can't say it pleases me to wait so long."

Levi leaned toward her and captured her lips in a lingering kiss full of promise. When he pulled away, he traced his fingers along her cheek. "Remind me again why I agreed to wait to marry you?"

She giggled. "The mosaics."

"Oh, yes, those." He raised her hand to his lips and kissed her fingertips. "I guess this will be a wonderful incentive to get the order filled as quickly as possible."

"I couldn't agree more." Ainslee's heart swelled. "I intend to make certain there's no slacking."

"Yes, ma'am." He gave her a mock salute, his eyes alight with joy.

Oh, how she loved this man! She'd do everything in her power to move the mosaic project along quickly so they could begin their life together.

She blinked and drew in a breath. This must be how Adaira had felt when she eloped.

Chapter 30

Fall 1877

Ainslee turned to Levi and adjusted his cravat. "Are you ready to see your work displayed to all those who enter the West Virginia Museum of Art and History?"

"Our work." Levi smiled at her, then turned to Noah, who stood beside him. "All of us had a hand in this."

Ainslee glanced at Ewan, Laura, and Tessa, who had come to join them for the grand opening of the museum. Even Rose and Rylan had arrived on the morning train. The day would have been perfect if Adaira could have returned in time for the festivities, but she had promised to be back in time for Ainslee's wedding. Their long letters over the past months had helped the twins regain their intimacy, and Ainslee was delighted her sister would be her attendant when she and Levi married in two months' time.

When Mr. Harrington stepped to the wide red ribbon strung across the front of the museum, the crowd fell silent. "Ladies and gentlemen, thank you all for joining me today as my lifelong dream comes true. I'd like to thank the other benefactors in this project." He motioned toward the men on his left. "And my thanks to those who were instrumental in the building of this fine structure. They gave of their enormous talents to make this museum a work of art." This time he turned toward those on his right.

The crowd applauded, and Mr. Harrington held up his hand. "Without further ado, let me permit you entry to the West Virginia Museum of Art and History." Using a pair of long scissors, he cut the ribbon with a flourish.

Ainslee and her family followed the others through the front doors into the giant foyer where Noah's tiles were featured. Was it possible for the mosaics to be even more beautiful now that they'd been laid?

With the doctor's permission, Noah had accompanied Levi to Wheeling, where the two of them had assisted with and overseen the laying of the tiles. Ainslee had missed Levi terribly during his absence, but knowing their marriage would take place only two months after completion of the project had made their time apart easier to bear.

"Look at this, Noah." Levi touched the plaque on the wall. "What do you think?"

Noah ran his fingers over the engraved letters. "I can't believe my name is listed below the name of the tile works. This makes me believe I should continue with my artwork."

"And you should." Ainslee bobbed her head. "Everyone who comes in here will know that some of these tiles are your works of art."

Mr. Harrington approached them. "Well, Miss McKay, what do you think?"

"It's lovely. All of it." She glanced around the room, taking in the many exhibits that portrayed the state and its history. "I can't wait to see the rest of the rooms."

The older man nodded. "I think you'll find each room exciting and unique. Levi's work will prove to all who visit this museum that he and Noah are true artisans." He reached forward and patted Levi on the shoulder. "And if you hadn't been here to supervise the setting of the tiles, I shudder to think what would have happened."

"Everything beautiful needs a good foundation." Levi flashed a grin at Ainslee.

"That's very true." Mr. Harrington gave a slight nod. "So do you have another project planned after this, Levi?"

He chuckled. "I certainly do." Levi reached for Ainslee's hand. "This young lady is going to become the artisan's wife."

Dear Readers,

Writing the REFINED BY LOVE series has been a pure delight for me. I have enjoyed the opportunity to portray the beauty of West Virginia, reveal a few of the historic towns, and depict some unique working environments throughout this series. As it draws to an end, I wanted to share a few of the real and fictional people and places included in the series.

With the exception of known political figures, all of the characters in these books are fictional. I did draw upon my personal culture and heritage when I chose the settings. My father's ancestors arrived in Pennsylvania from Ireland and were of Scotch-Irish descent. They later moved to West Virginia, where they settled in the areas where I've set these books.

In *The Brickmaker's Bride*, the town of Bartlett is fictional, but my thoughts centered upon Philippi, West Virginia, while writing the book. I gathered a great deal of information and visited Adaland (a mansion situated outside of Philippi) while researching. The construction of Crothers Mansion is loosely based upon Adaland. As stated in the book, the capitol of West Virginia was located in the Linsly Institute Building in Wheeling during the time period of *The Brickmaker's Bride*, but history reveals the capital moved back and forth several times before finally remaining in Charleston.

C&M Brickyard was based upon a brickmaking operation once located in Colfax, West Virginia. After visiting with historians at a library in Fairmont, West Virginia, I made a visit to the town in an attempt to locate any remnants of the business, but to no avail. The brickworks has long since disappeared, although the post office is constructed of bricks that were made in that facility many years ago. The brickmaking process described in *The Brickmaker's Bride* is authentic to the time period.

In *The Potter's Lady*, the Philadelphia School of Design that Rose attended is authentic. The town of Grafton is a small community located in north central West Virginia. The Grafton train depot and hotel are authentic. The pottery is fictional, although there were a number of potteries located in the area where I situated the McKay Pottery. Lead poisoning in potteries and the lack of sanitary conditions had already come to light during this time period, although few potteries addressed the issue. The Franklin Hotel in Pittsburgh is fictional, but the funicular railway (now referred to as The Incline) is authentic. You can still ride up the hillside to Coal Hill, now known as Mt. Washington, and look down on the city of Pittsburgh where the Monongahela and Allegheny Rivers come together to form the Ohio River.

In *The Artisan's Wife*, the town of Weston and the asylum are both real, although the tile works is fictional. I based the tile works upon the Moravian Tile Works located outside of Philadelphia, Pennsylvania. The process for making the mosaic tiles, as well as the mission-type structure that housed the industry, was created by Henry Mercer and the building is still in existence and open to the public for visits. The curator, Charles Yeske, aided me immensely in my research.

The West Virginia Museum of Art and History is fictional. The idea of creating unique tiles for the floor of the museum was based upon the fact that Henry Mercer was commissioned to create decorative tiles for the floors of the Pennsylvania capitol building in Harrisburg.

A few additional comments about the Weston Lunatic Asylum: While mental institutions generally evolved into horrible places where the mentally ill were warehoused and mistreated, the early institutions were a great improvement over the practice of locking the mentally ill into large jail cells. The list of reasons a person could be institutionalized ranged from "asthma" to "death of a son in war" or "desertion by husband." In many cases, the institutions were used as a method for a husband to rid himself of a spouse.

The Weston Asylum was constructed under Thomas Kirkbride's theory of creating a curative environment. His design provided proper lighting, ventilation, and access to a rural environment with grounds that were "tastefully ornamented" and buildings arranged to resemble a shallow V if viewed from above. This design allowed for long, rambling wings that provided therapeutic sunlight and air to comfortable living quarters so that the building itself promoted a curative effect, or as Kirkbride put it, "a special apparatus for lunacy." These facilities were designed to be entirely self-sufficient, providing the patients with a variety of outlets for stimulating mental and physical activities. Unfortunately, a facility that was originally constructed for two hundred and fifty patients soon housed far more, and the care and conditions eventually returned to the pre-asylum era.

Thank you for taking this journey into the past with me and permitting me to share my love of history and the joy of Christ's love.

Blessings,
Judy

Special thanks to . . .

. . . My editor, Karen Schurrer, for her sharp eye and gracious spirit.

. . . The entire staff of Bethany House Publishers, for their devotion to publishing the best product possible. It is a privilege to work with all of you.

. . . Charles Yeske and the staff of the Moravian Tile Works, for the private tour and for answering my innumerable questions.

. . . Mary Greb-Hall, for her ongoing encouragement, expertise, and sharp eye.

. . . Lorna Seilstad, for her honest critiques and steadfast friendship.

. . . Mary Kay Woodford, my sister, my prayer warrior, my friend.

. . . Justin, Jenna, and Jessa, for their support and the joy they bring to me during the writing process and throughout my life.

Above all, thanks and praise to our Lord Jesus Christ, for the opportunity to live my dream and share the wonder of His love through story.

Judith Miller is an award-winning author whose avid research and love for history are reflected in her bestselling novels. Judy makes her home in Topeka, Kansas.

If you enjoyed this novel, you may also like . . .

Ewan McKay came to West Virginia to help his uncle Hugh start a brickmaking operation. But when Hugh makes an ill-advised deal, the foundation Ewan has built begins to crumble. Can the former owner's daughter help Ewan save the brickworks—and his future?

The Brickmaker's Bride by Judith Miller
REFINED BY LOVE, judithmccoymiller.com

Rose McKay has plenty of ideas on how to make her family's newly acquired pottery business a success—too many ideas, in longtime employee Rylan Campbell's opinion. But can these two put aside their differences and work together to win an important design contest?

The Potter's Lady by Judith Miller
REFINED BY LOVE, judithmccoymiller.com

Still reeling from her father's death, Lucinda Pennyworth arrives in New York seeking a fresh start. As she begins to establish a new life for herself, she dares to hope that a handsome West Point cadet may have a role in her future.

Flirtation Walk by Siri Mitchell
sirimitchell.com

More Historical Fiction

Shipwrecked and stranded, Emma Chambers is in need of a home. Could the widowed local lighthouse keeper and his young son be an answer to her prayer?

Love Unexpected by Jody Hedlund
BEACONS OF HOPE #1
jodyhedlund.com

At Irish Meadows horse farm, two sisters struggle to reconcile their dreams with their father's demanding marriage expectations. Brianna longs to attend college, while Colleen is happy to marry, as long as the man meets *her* standards. Will they find the courage to follow their hearts?

Irish Meadows by Susan Anne Mason
COURAGE TO DREAM #1
susanannemason.com

Stella West has quit the art world and moved to Boston to solve the mysterious death of her sister, but she is in need of a well-connected ally. Fortunately, magazine owner Romulus White has been trying to hire her for years. Sparks fly when Stella and Romulus join forces, but will their investigation cost them everything?

From This Moment by Elizabeth Camden
elizabethcamden.com

BETHANYHOUSE